ALSO BY JOSEPH P. DESARIO:

LIMBO

SANCTUARY

SANCTUARY

JOSEPH P. DESARIO

DOUBLEDAY

NEW YORK   LONDON   TORONTO   SYDNEY   AUCKLAND

PUBLISHED BY DOUBLEDAY
a division of Bantam Doubleday Dell Publishing Group, Inc.
666 Fifth Avenue, New York, New York 10103

DOUBLEDAY and the portrayal of an anchor with a dolphin
are trademarks of Doubleday, a division of
Bantam Doubleday Dell Publishing Group, Inc.

This novel is a work of fiction. Names, characters, places, and
incidents are either the product of the author's imagination or
are used fictitiously. Any resemblance to actual persons, living or
dead, events, or locales is entirely coincidental.

"Grass" from *Cornhuskers* by Carl Sandburg, copyright 1918 by
Holt, Rinehart and Winston, Inc. and renewed 1946 by Carl
Sandburg, reprinted by permission of Harcourt Brace
Jovanovich, Inc.

Library of Congress Cataloging-in-Publication Data

DeSario, Joseph P., 1950–
    Sanctuary: a novel of terror and suspense / Joseph P. Desario.
— 1st ed.
        p.   cm.
    ISBN 0-385-24487-8
    I. Title.
PS3554.E8353S26   1989
813'.54—dc19   89-1090
                                                        CIP

Printed in the United States of America
July 1989
FIRST EDITION

To *los desaparecidos*

SANCTUARY

1

3 MANIK   5 CUMKU

AT THE COMPLETION OF
12 BAKTUNS
18 KATUNS
8 TUNS
14 UINALS
7 KINS

"I'm here about the two-headed shar-pei."

Given the full scope of his experience, it was something Matt Teller could say without even a trace of self-consciousness. He was not uncomprehending of the oddness of his opening statement, but oddness was quantitative. It had value, dimension, intensity. If there had been alligator clips to attach and a spectrum analyzer to take a reading, the meter would barely have registered a *mildly curious*. He had begun other encounters with "I'm here about the

lizard-man" and "I've come to see your petrified feces collection."
Such things were relative.

The face on the other side of the screen door did not change
expression. It was a young face—bloated and dumb. The mesh of
the loose screen gave it a whiskerless five o'clock shadow. The eyes
blinked and the mouth gnawed mechanically on an undercooked
chicken leg.

Matt had seen his share of weirdness. He had witnessed au-
topsies of the Lodi cattle mutilations, documented the court-for-
bidden copulation of two Thalidomide victims, measured, photographed and verified innumerable curiosities including the world's
largest human wart, but the sight of raw chicken being eaten still
made him queasy.

Matt looked away, down at his own shadow which rose like a
thin, crooked stairway along the shingled wall of the tiny house.
The sun was almost down and the shadow was in its death throes.
A steady hush of hot air was rising up from the desert, crossing an
awareness threshold where it was perceptible as a sound if not yet
a force. The shadow wavered and Matt sensed the incredible isolation of the place. Not all that far from the congested, insane
turmoil of Los Angeles, but still no-man's-land.

Turning back toward the chicken-eater, Matt pulled the tabloid out of his back pocket. In the past, it had worked better than
his business card. *"Here and There* weekly," he said, nodding toward the masthead. "You called us."

The face behind the screen answered with two randomly
spaced eyelid contractions and the continued methodical cleaning
of the chicken bone knuckle. A watery stream of poultry blood
dribbled down the chin. From deeper inside the house came the
opening strains of the "Gilligan's Island" theme. Someone turned
up the volume.

"I'm a reporter with *Here and There* weekly," Matt explained using a remedial intonation. "You called our office. . . . Someone called and said you had a two-headed shar-pei. My publisher assigned me and I drove out from L.A. to take the pictures and write the story." Matt pointed to a picture on the front page and smiled.

Another face joined the one behind the screen. It was younger but potentially more intelligent. There was a dim flicker of recognition, a hint of cognizance in the way it panned to one side, regarded Matt peripherally, then cranked toward him as if about to respond. But the only words came from the Skipper calling for Gilligan somewhere in the darkness behind the door.

If experience had desensitized Matt to life's various and sundry oddities, it had not inured him to anger. "Fucking lobotomy brothers," he mumbled under his breath, thinking of Barnie Schiff, his publisher, and wishing him every possible unscratchable itch. He'd been in Barnie's doghouse for weeks, goaded in front of the entire staff, put on every bullshit, late-hour, backwater animal story that popped up. Inferior writers had been given the choice stories: the celebrity scandals, the latest diets, the newest exercise fads. Matt got two-headed shar-peis.

"Look, I got lost because the directions sucked," he tried again, enunciating each word as if speaking to a four-year-old. "Now the sun's gone so I'll have to use the flash and the pictures won't be worth shit." Matt unzipped the Adidas gym bag which hung from a strap off his shoulder. In it was a Nikon 35-millimeter camera, lenses of various size, boxes of film, a Sony cassette recorder, tapes, any number of pencils, pens and markers, numerous maps, some note pads from K mart, the last third or so of a roll of paper towels, a half-empty bag of Fritos and a super-jumbo bottle of Excedrin. He pointed to the camera and said very slowly, "I want to take the doggie's picture. So I suggest we get the pooch out here *toot sweet.*"

The second face, the *smarter* one, drifted back toward "Gilligan's Island." The first completed its stripping of the chicken bone.

"Do you or do you not have a two-headed shar-pei?" Matt demanded.

"What we got is a two-headed Browning, mister."

The voice came from behind Matt. There was no mistaking the threat of violence in it. Matt turned slowly, forcing his most disarming smile and facing the speaker, a tall, overweight man in his late twenties dressed in greasy jeans and a torn T-shirt. A double-barreled twelve-gauge shotgun was held casually in one hand, the butt braced against his thigh. The man was sitting on the edge of a doorless old refrigerator that lay on its back in the front yard like a porcelain casket. Behind him and all round, stacked, toppled and just sitting there, were dozens of other appliances: washers, dryers, freezers and more refrigerators; some dismantled; some barely recognizable; all of it old. This is where the Kenmores and Whirlpools come to die, Matt thought. He recalled hearing about a place out in another desert where hundreds of B-52's had been retired—all those heavy bombers sitting out in the sand like a grounded flock of fossilized pterodactyls. There was always something stranger, a better story just beyond the next turn in the road. *This* he thought, even as he noticed the pillar of washing machine impellers which supported one corner of the salt-box roof sloping off the house.

"We ain't got what you're lookin' for," the man with the gun announced.

"No, that's for sure," Matt quickly agreed as he zipped up the Adidas bag. "Just a big mistake. Sorry to have taken up your time."

"What's that?" the man asked.

The dual muzzles were pointed directly at the newspaper in

Matt's hand. He knew it was a dangerous question. *Here and There* often provoked violent reactions. "Controversial" was the least venomous adjective ever assigned to the paper. "Scandal sheet" and "dirty rag" were infinitely more popular descriptions. It had been widely labeled as pornography, filth and smut even though its T&A content was probably less than in the conventional press. Those with extreme political leanings called it communist or fascist depending on their own particular brand of paranoia. Religious fanatics—and there were more of those every day —saw it either as an apocalyptic herald or as the devil's own work. Lawyers loved it for the libel suits it copiously provided, celebrities hated its invasion of their privacy, but grocery shoppers bought it.

"It's just a job, pal," Matt hedged. "I'm a writer. . . . I just write for these guys. Take some pictures. It pays the bills. You know how it is."

"We do appliance removal and salvage," the man offered. "Ya buy a new washer, we take out the old one. Strip it for parts and sell 'em to the fix-it shops."

Matt stepped away from the door sensing that a crisis point had been passed, that in the reciprocity of exchanged résumés there had been established some narrow strip of common ground where the confrontation could continue at least a few more seconds without the involvement of firearms. Matt noted the location of his car some fifty yards beyond the shotgun. Beyond the car was the road, a miserable, goes-nowhere, shitty little two-lane county road winding its way through the great emptiness of Imperial County. Of course, there was nobody on the road, nobody going nowhere through nothing, nobody to help. Just a lot of sand and rocks and scrub all around, for miles on back through the desert.

"Must be interesting work. Bet it keeps you busy."

"Did for a while. Now the chains started doin' it themselves.

We built a good trade and they push us out." The statement, punctuated as it was by a well-aimed honker wetly pinging in the nearest dispossessed washer tub, conveyed utter disgust, the pain of betrayal, a loss of faith in "human nature." The gun barrel lowered a bit, as if its bearer had suddenly grown weary.

"Well, you've got quite a stockpile here," Matt offered, not quite knowing what else to say.

"That's another problem. Just last week I caught a dirt biker up from San Diego rifling the ice maker out of a Frigidaire. Said he just thought it was there for the taking."

"Can't be too careful these days," Matt commented sympathetically.

He pictured the ill-fated trespasser from San Diego, his bones out there somewhere, bleaching on the roadbed, mutely attesting to the danger like the skull of a longhorn steer at a bad water hole. *Beware Ice Cubes in the Desert:* The thought could have been amusing were it not for the close presence of the Browning.

He started cautiously toward the car, trying to keep some of the larger appliances between the gun and himself.

"What paper you with?" the man asked again, his tone turning dark.

Matt was caught between a Norge front-loader and a GE side-by-side. To his back was a steep hill of heavy parts—a veritable organ bank of motors, transmissions, timers, condensers and the like. There was no clear escape route save the one directly past the gun.

"It's just a job," Matt answered plaintively.

Matt heard the screen door open behind him. There was the slow scuffle of feet moving out of the house.

"He's with the *Here and There,* Dale."

It was the first face who fingered him. The second stood

mutely at his side, nodding in agreement. Matt tensed, waiting for the tight pattern of buckshot to open in his chest.

"No shit, Merle," said Dale, the man with the Browning twelve-gauge.

"That's what he said," Merle confirmed, tossing his chicken bone into the open top of the nearest washer.

"Yeah, he did," chimed in the other one.

"That so?" Dale demanded.

"It's all really just a mistake," Matt explained. "Someone called and said he had a two-headed shar-pei. We've had two-headed cows, two-headed goats, sheep, collies, snakes, frogs, even people. Never had a two-headed sharpie. And that's the hot breed these days. Must have got the wrong address. . . . Really sorry . . . Just doing my—"

"Sharp who?"

"Shar-pei . . . Little Chinese dog . . . Ugly as sin . . . People pay thousands for them. Looks like a rug that's been all balled up, wrinkled, folded over itself. Stick eyes in the middle and you've got a shar-pei."

"And they got two heads?"

"Not normally."

"Just the one you're lookin' for?"

"That's right."

Dale mulled over these last bits of information. Matt watched nervously as Dale's forehead creased and a fingernail raked slowly through his thin but long mustache, combing out small particles of unknown origin to flutter down into the sand at his feet. It was obvious to Matt that the man was in deep concentration, that he was harnessing all of his mental resources, limited as they might be, in order to decide his fate.

"You do the story on Earl and Elmo Beldine?" Dale finally asked. His eyes had contracted to two suspicious slits.

Matt sensed it was a loaded question. "Hard to remember all the stories," he stalled. "We get so—"

"Sure you remember. The big act with the Mongrel Show . . . Died up in Bakersfield."

"Look, if he's related or something, I—"

"Hell, no, we ain't related to no tent-show freak . . . though I mean no disrespect."

"Did you know him?"

"No, but you did, didn't you? Damn! You wrote it, didn't you?" Dale moved closer. The gun came with him, lifted back up to his hip where it looked far more ready to be used.

"Yeah . . . sure," Matt stammered, his eyes glued to the twin black holes at the end of the muzzle. "It was an assignment. I had to."

Dale shook his head in amazement. "Merle, Roy!" he called out toward the shack. "This guy here wrote that story I told you about. Best damn piece of investigative journalism I've ever seen. Real provocative. Damn! I'm glad to meet ya."

A blast from the twelve-gauge would not have surprised Matt. A beating or cursing out could also have been anticipated. But to hear the word "provocative" pass through Dale's lips—let alone in reference to his own work, the very piece which had landed him in Schiff's doghouse—was beyond the realm of human prediction. He stood there, mutely, having his hand pumped and imagining that his own expression could not now look one IQ point more perceptive than Merle's. He did notice, through the fog of his surprise, but with all due appreciation, that the shotgun had been set down in the horizontal refrigerator.

"That damn story had me laying awake at night for weeks," Dale continued. "Tried to get my brothers to read it, but you can't get the young ones off the TV long enough to read the back of a cereal carton."

"Print is dead, so they say."

"That so?"

"Dead but not buried," Matt elaborated, testing for further signs of latent intelligence.

"Don't know about that."

"Nothing to worry about."

"Tell me, you do all the two-headed stories?" Dale inquired earnestly.

"No."

"Well you should."

"Thanks."

" 'Murder or suicide,' " Dale quoted from memory, adopting a stentorian tone, " 'victim or killer, both or neither—only Earl and Elmo know for sure.' "

" '*Knows* for sure,' " Matt corrected. "I used the singular form. But that's pretty close."

"I liked the stuff about his souls. I ain't big for religion but that really had me thinking. You think he had two?"

"No. Just one. Two heads, one soul. It's what killed him."

"Damn!"

"If you believe in souls and such."

Matt extricated his hand and started once more for the car.

"Wanna stay to supper?" Dale asked.

"Maybe some other time."

"I doubt it. We're headin' back to Oklahoma next week."

"Sorry to see you go."

"You wouldn't know where we could get our hands on an accumulator for a '76 Hotpoint, would you?"

"Afraid not."

"So how 'bout some eats?"

"No . . . really."

"It's now or never. Whad'ya say? We got more than enough chicken."

"Love to, but just can't," Matt responded, quickening his pace. "Deadlines, you know."

"Well, keep it up. Someone's got to tell it straight."

"True enough."

Matt reached the car just as the last dim light of the sun faded out. It happened quickly, desert-fast. It had the feeling of a movie dissolve, the "fade to black" just before the credits roll. He got in the old Mazda and turned the ignition. As he switched on the headlights, he looked back toward the house. The beams were pointed down the road and didn't illuminate his view. There was nothing to be seen of the shabby house, the three brothers and their collection of appliance carcasses. Then he saw a dim, blue flickering light, which he realized came from the TV. He could make out a window and a silhouetted shape in the front yard which was either Dale or a stack of washing machine tubs.

"Take her easy."

The voice didn't seem to have come from the silhouette. But the wind had picked up and it was hard to be sure.

"This the quickest way back to the interstate?" Matt shouted through the open window.

"Down to the crossroads, then north. Picks it up at Indio."

"Thanks."

"Got gas?"

"Half a tank."

"Water?"

"Think so."

"Happy trails."

Matt heard the screen door slam shut. Before pulling out onto the road, he reached into the gym bag for the cassette recorder. He depressed the red RECORD button and held the device close to his mouth.

"No bicephalous yuppie puppies between Palm Springs and the Salton Sea. No report. Another bum tip."

Matt ejected the cassette, which was labeled *H&T,* and replaced it with another entitled *GAN Notes #114.* Once more he held the recorder to his mouth.

"I have met my first fan. The emotion is depression. Henceforth, I must include suicide as a possibility."

Matt put the recorder back on the seat and put the car in gear. Before it moved, he hit the brake and took up the recorder again.

"The suicide bit is hyperbolic—I think."

With that, he jammed the accelerator and fishtailed onto the road.

Matt was not a desert person. He had never found it particularly beautiful or peaceful or majestic or any of those other qualities which its devotees so rapturously attributed to it. To Matt, it was a big, hot, ugly place you went around if you possibly could. There were those who got off on the flora and fauna, the myriad examples of evolution under pressure, those extreme manifestations of nature's runaway imagination. Matt saw sand. In the sand grew ugly creosote bushes. Next to the creosote bushes were rocks, and under the rocks, no doubt, were snakes, Gila monsters, tarantulas and other undesirable things. So his trip through the wasteland, at night with the wind raising a gritty effluence of mica over the twisting, ill-paved county road, after his close encounter with the Browning twelve-gauge, was less than a pleasant experience. The car radio had stopped working two years ago, so there was no relief from the tedium to be found there. And the music cassettes which he usually played in the Sony had been stolen three days ago at Redondo Beach. There was simply nothing to keep his mind from confronting the uncomfortable fact that Dale, the desert mogul of appliance removal and salvage, elder sibling of the lobotomy brothers, had called his work "real provocative."

Into the recorder, Matt said, "It cannot be denied that the universe has an utterly perverse sense of irony."

Immediately after arriving at this conclusion, as Matt piloted the Mazda at seventy-eight miles per hour through a mildly descending turn, like so many that had passed before, the headlights caught sight of an obstruction in the middle of the road where it crossed over a narrow dry wash. Hard braking at the end of the turn put the Mazda into a sidelong skid, which ended only when Matt released the pedal. After the car straightened, he tapped the brake once more and came to rest well short of what he at first thought was a bed. Within seconds he more precisely identified it as a cot, a metal army cot. He saw, in the sand-washed beams of the headlamps, a naked body on the cot, and even at that distance, he knew it was a corpse.

He fumbled for the recorder, at the same time grabbing the Nikon and flash attachment from the bag. "Coincidence is the first casualty of fiction," he announced to the *GAN Notes #114* tape. "Thank the gods that reality has no such prejudice." He scooped up the *H&T* cassette and dropped it into his shirt pocket. Then he was out of the car.

As he approached the corpse, he snapped the flash unit into the camera's hot shoe. He was still about fifty feet away when he began clicking off shots, walking a slow zigzag pattern, changing angles, stopping almost imperceptibly with each triggering of the shutter. At fifteen feet, he stopped, squatted down and knocked off five fast frames from a low angle. He especially liked the look of these, the feeling that this thing had swooped down like a rocket sled just moments before, its exhaust fumes—the billowing sands suspended in the headlight beams—still rolling away in the background. He wondered if the effect would be lost to the flash and so he removed it, opened up the aperture, slowed down the shutter speed and took three more shots.

Standing, he slung the carrying strap of the camera around his neck and once more swapped cassettes in his recorder. With the *H&T* tape locked in the transport mechanism, he pushed the red button and began his description:

"It's on County Double-G about fifteen miles shy of the crossroads. There's a sign at the side of a dry creek cutting under the road. Says 'Coombe's Ditch.' In the middle of the road, dead center and perpendicular, is a metal cot. Just the frame. No mattress. On the bare wires is a naked body. Male, I think."

Matt moved closer, reminding himself that he had seen a lot of weird shit. Still, he was starting to feel sick.

"It *was* male," he continued. "This guy's package is just about gone. Hacked . . . ripped . . . something."

He took a deep breath, fighting the urge to upchuck. *You've seen worse*, he told himself. He drifted along the line of an arc that took him to a point still no closer than fifteen feet away but now opposite the foot of the cot and aligned with its longest dimension. He looked across the blankness of the desert. There was a rock formation just ahead, in perfect orientation with the linear axis of the cot like a compass point, its jagged silhouette backlit by the full moon which stood balanced on the leftmost of its two highest outcroppings. Between the two promontories was a deep notch. A blue star twinkled coldly, nestled at the base of the juncture. Matt did not record these observations; they were not details likely to interest the readers of *Here and There*. He simply took them in, an exercise in perception dimly registered. He was regrouping, focusing on the skyline mandala, letting it calm him.

Finally, he was able to look back down at the corpse.

"The wrists and feet are tied down. He's stretched out like he's on the rack. The middle toe on the left foot is missing."

He started moving again, continuing his slow orbit around the body.

"There's a long gash running from one armpit, down the side, under the ribs and back up to the other armpit. It doesn't seem to be deep. The right eye has been torn out. It's just hanging loose from the socket. The right ear looks black. Maybe burned . . ."

Matt was even with the dead man's head. In the dim light, at his previous distance, he had thought the man was wearing a sort of skull cap which glistened in the moonlight. Now he saw how wrong he had been.

"Jesus! This guy's been scalped. It's just been peeled right off. And there's something written on what's left of his forehead. I can't quite make it out."

If Matt stepped but a few paces closer, chances were he'd be able to read the word scrawled in blood. But he remained, for the time being, at what felt like a "safe distance."

"The thumbs have been sliced off. Christ, this guy died slow. Real slow . . ."

Matt released the RECORD button. Fearful thoughts were floating down, winding out of those last unfinished observations, unraveling, encompassing. A moment before there had been the singular phenomenon of a story on the road. Now there was a victim, a man who had undergone incredible pain for reasons unknown. That *the victim* was also *the story* did not lessen Matt's feeling that a splitting had taken place, that some terrible viral nucleus had divided. More threatening still was the realization that the process was ongoing, incubating perceptions which sired doubts which in turn became fears.

The man hadn't *died* slow; he'd been *killed* slow. Others

were involved. There was a *they,* he reasoned; no one person had done this. Here was the kind of cruelness that was the engorged sum of many efforts. This had required cooperation, approval, encouragement, a mounting of hatreds. To be tortured to death was the worst possible fate imaginable to Matt, and there was damn feeble solace in the thin hope that the man had somehow resisted his inquisitors. After all, he was dead—naked and dead— strapped to a bed frame in the middle of County Double-G. If this was the legacy of some act of heroism, then bravery meant failure, integrity was a hollow dream, and futility stood at the right hand of every human equation. But such grim conclusions rested on the shaky premise that some noble reason had brought the man to this end—a cause, a secret, something to have incited such focused violence, something so desperately needed by others it had led them to abandon their own humanity. It was hard for Matt to consider the unlikely possibility of facing such persecution, but he knew that at the mere threat of pain there was no one he would not sell out, no secret he would not divulge, no cause he would not disown. It was not a pleasant thought, but neither did it spark any great self-condemnation. There simply wasn't anything in his life—or even the illusion of anything—worth such agony.

Matt felt the nuclei splitting once more, multiplying, differentiating, complicating.

What if there had been no reason for this other than the desire to cause pain? No secret to guard; no loyalty to embrace. Just pain to be endured, pain followed by death. It was too terrible to grasp. Matt began to tremble. In the cascade of horrible thoughts that followed, he felt it significant that he had suddenly remembered that snakes crawl up on the road at night for warmth.

Matt fought the urge to run. *You've seen it all,* he reminded himself, although it seemed increasingly irrelevant with each passing moment. *Get busy. Get back to work.* He pushed the RECORD button.

"This has got to be some ritual deal here . . . a cult or something. The word on the forehead makes me think of 'Helter Skelter.' "

He switched the Sony off and rewound over the last two sentences. Schiff wanted the facts. Not so much the traditional investigative *who, what, why, where, how,* as much as their sensory counterparts, *the sight, the smell, the sound, the feel.* Schiff wanted the word on the man's head and Matt was still too far away to read it. He needed to get closer, but when his feet started moving they continued on in the elliptical track around the body, still respecting the self-imposed force-field which kept five yards of concrete between him and the mutilated corpse. The circumnavigation ended where it began, with Matt opposite the midpoint of the cot, the car behind him. He stood there a moment as the wind kicked up and the sand rasped against his face, making it feel all the more as if he was not meant to take a closer look. Clouds were moving across the moon, pushing the whole scene in and out of focus. He wiped his eyes, but they filled with grit. The light from the headlamps had dimmed, the swirling sand blunting its glow and diffusing the weakened beams over the shoulder of the road. Matt thought he saw something move in the rocks at the edge of the shallow wash, a shadow moving among others that didn't. Matt reattached the flash unit to the Nikon and sent a burst of light out toward Coombe's Ditch, but there was nothing to be seen.

Just then the car engine coughed and died. "Fuck this," he hissed. But instead of returning to the Mazda, he moved quickly forward. Hovering over the body, he stared down at the letters on the man's forehead: NOSAL. Matt lifted the Nikon and triggered a short burst of tight shots. He kept the camera tight to his eye. Through its lens, he saw the mouth was open, grotesquely open, so wide it seemed to want to swallow the world. Matt could see the man had been screaming at the very moment of his death. Even now, as the wind billowed up in random gusts, a thin, hollow resonance could be heard coming from that mouth. Like an angry seashell, Matt thought. But then the wind changed direction, caught the opening at a different angle, and a nightmare bassoon moaned tremulously from the orifice.

Matt's fascination with the man's mouth and the voice it still possessed had kept his attention from another sound, a soft but persistent pulse ticking away at the periphery of his awareness. As the wind-sound diminished, the other sound did not. Matt detected its presence, tuned to it and scanned for its origin, still looking through the Nikon. Finally, he zoomed in on his own right shoe. Blood was dripping onto it from the slit in the corpse's side.

Matt had covered enough homicide stories to know that corpses don't bleed—at least not for very long. Once the heart stops there's no pressure to cause blood flow. Open wounds leak for a short time and then seal off. There were but two explanations for the drops of blood which splattered with metronome regularity on his gray Reebok: Either the man was still alive or he had expired but moments prior to Matt's arrival. Matt lowered the camera and faced the man, unshielded and newly terrified. It *was* a corpse that lay in the middle of County Double-G. He wished it wasn't so, but it was. Undeniably a corpse. He touched the man's chest with the back of his hand. *A warm corpse, just dead, just killed.*

The killers were close at hand. They were watching him now. He felt them in the desert, all around, enjoying his reaction, his fear. He would not look past the edge of the road. It would mean acknowledging his fear to those who watched. It would be like pouring blood into a shark tank. His only chance—he was certain —was to brazen his way back to the car, feign ignorance of their presence. He took the first few steps. They were wobbly, telltale. He considered stopping, but knew he'd never get going again. There always seemed to be movement now, just beyond the scope of his side vision, up in the rocks, beside a low dune. And sounds too, not quite recognizable but perhaps shoes crunching on gravel or guns cocking. He quickened the pace, sucking in gulps of air with every stride, never turning toward the sights and sounds which threatened from the shadows. He was closing in, marching off those last few paces, feeling that the road had pitched upward, that each step now was progressively more dangerous, closer to the trigger point. He was sure they were waiting for him to reach the door handle, to think he had made it. Then and only then, guns would fire, traps would spring. At three paces away, the Sony slipped from his hand. His adrenaline-enhanced reactions enabled him to reach down instantly with his other hand before it had fallen more than ten inches. He wasn't able to catch it but he did tip it back upward, so that he came staggering forward to the precise spot where he expected calamity to strike, fumbling the recorder like a clumsy wide receiver at the goal line and finally deflecting it through the car's open window.

As he sped away in the Mazda, barreling into the cot and sending it spinning into Coombe's Ditch, he attributed his escape to the unexpected, random quirkiness of those last few stumbling, juggling moves caused by the dropped recorder. When sufficient distance had elapsed, he once more exchanged the cassettes, pushed the red button and said, "Dumb luck is the ultimate inspiration. Chance is the choreographer supreme. Sony is my savior. . . . That or the distinct possibility there was nobody there to begin with."

•

The geographic algebra of professional baseball did not include Guatemala in the prime subset of its talent colonies. The game was played there, but it had not reached fruition in the mega-star likes of a Clemente, an Aparicio or a Valenzuela. Such gleaming facets had been chipped from the diamonds of other countries in the region, and those who toiled in the Latin American scouting operations of the various franchises tended to spend their time in those more productive environs. Mexico, Venezuela and the Dominican Republic were currently considered to be the best sources of talent. Cuba, before Castro, had spawned its share of big-leaguers; Nicaragua had just begun to look promising before the Sandinistas. But Guatemala was one third-world country with a reputation for growing decidedly second-rate players. There were few scouts who'd spend time there. There were fewer still who'd wander out past the city limits of the capital even in pursuit of a bona fide lead. There was but one who'd risk the bus trip through the insanely knotted traffic of Guatemala City to Lake Amatitlán, past the volcano Agua, across the sweaty coastal plain all the way to the dreary town of Escuintla just to check out a crazy rumor overheard in a hotel bar.

The bus was legendary. *Chipi chipi,* the persistent drizzle, leaked in through the roof of the old International so steadily that the riders routinely held open umbrellas to keep themselves dry; the smell was reminiscent of a minor-league locker room, but rendered even more pungent by the added elements of diesel and guano; chickens going to and from market were allowed in the passenger compartment and it was inevitable that one or two would have the predictable gastrointestinal response to the swaying, lurching, bumping motion of the vehicle; it was also inevitable that at least one member of the poultry contingent would, before journey's end, make a break for freedom, hopping toward one of the broken windows in an explosion of feathers and scratching feet, cackling insanely and otherwise adding to the general chaos of the ride. If one possessed the questionable inclination to sojourn to Escuintla under such conditions, one had but to hand over the pittance of a fare, throw caution to the wind and trust that the rosary hanging from the rear-view mirror would ward off the seemingly narcoleptic tendencies of the aged driver.

Bill Buchanon made the trip. By the grace of God—or NoDoze—he was deposited, shaky but more or less intact, at the bus stop in Escuintla. That portion of his expense account earmarked for car rental had been depleted in the worthy cause of downing innumerable daiquiris and other such indigenous libations in the bars of Guatemala City, and so the bus ride hadn't been so much a matter of choice as necessity. With some regret, he took inventory of the toll it had exacted.

His new white linen suit, bought specifically for the occasion, was drenched. The seat of his pants had been perforated on an exposed seat spring. His shoes were splattered with chicken shit. But the worst calamity had befallen his pocket flask. It had been jarred from his hand by a particularly merciless pothole and its contents had drained out on the floor. Thus deprived of the dog that bit him the night before—dark rum—the morning's routine hangover had, during the tumultuous bus ride, steadily escalated to become the evening's four-alarm skull-burner.

His boss had told him not to go to Escuintla which was, of course, enough to insure that he would. "Guatemala's a zero. The whole fucking place." With such blunt, unequivocal reasoning had Ed Kandler, the Director of Player Personnel, written off Buchanon's chances. It was indicative of Kandler's world view—his "management style," some called it—that all things were reduced to such simple terms: a presence of worth or an absence of worth, a yes or a no, a do or a don't. Like the computer on his desk which organized and structured the ever-changing machinations of his trades, drafts and waiver deals, he had begun to think in binary. Yes-things were ones; no-things were zeroes. Guatemala was a zero.

But Ed Kandler hadn't been in the bar at the Holiday Inn in Mexico City the night a cross-eyed Dutchman came in raving about an Indian kid who at thirty yards could hit and break a stalk of sugar cane with a thrown rock. Furthermore, the Dutchman had bragged, the kid could do things with a baseball that simultaneously caused Abner Doubleday and Isaac Newton to spin in their graves. Ed Kandler hadn't pulled the Dutchman aside and pestered him for details, even though all the other scouts in attendance had laughed in disbelief. Nor had he lain awake nights ever since thinking about this Indian phenom, thinking that this was the big find, the one that would resurrect him from the purgatory of south-of-the-border scouting.

Ever since that night in Mexico City, Bill Buchanon had been consumed by his fascination with the Dutchman's story. He had pursued every related lead, grossly neglecting his other duties. When Kandler had prohibited his going to Guatemala, Buchanon had gone over his head to the G.M. Rebuffed at that level as well, he had petitioned the owner. On the basis of wildly exaggerated reports, he had been granted permission to make the trip. He had bet his career on the word of a cross-eyed Dutchman.

Somehow, despite the firefight raging in his cranium, Buchanon found his way to the stadium. He made his way out to right field and lent halfhearted attention to the game preparations occurring around him: Young players in ill-fitting uniforms played catch and took batting practice, pausing occasionally to flirt with the girls who sat along the fence; a trio of groundskeepers idly scattered sand over the puddles in the infield left over from the afternoon's rainfall; a brown-and-black dog wandered in from the bullpen, sniffed second base, then continued on across the field; beyond the outfield fence, kids climbed up into trees to watch the game.

Swatting at mosquitoes with tortillas bought from a vendor, Buchanon pondered how the great American pastime had migrated to such a place. What unfathomable chain of events had brought the game of games down the isthmus to this strange land where pyramids stood abandoned in the jungle, dragging him along, compelling him to put everything on the line for a seventeen-year-old pitcher he'd never even seen?

He was lost to these reflections and to the frustrating, cul-de-sac meanderings of hangover-blunted introspection. The sun went down and the field lights came on. At length Buchanon realized that the players had gone to their dugouts and that he alone remained on the field. It appeared all concerned—players, managers, umpires, fans—were waiting for something to happen that once having occurred would allow the game to begin. It was not difficult to deduce, even in his impaired condition, that the *something* involved his leaving the field of play.

The few hundred people in the wooden stands behind home plate and along the foul lines watched him with an interest equally divided between amusement and awe. They sensed he was some important *gringo* and the rumor had quickly spread that the big *Yanqui* was also a Yankee. But for a man of such distinction, he also looked somewhat ridiculous, all 6'4", 230 pounds of him, standing out there like a cockeyed tombstone, hanging up the game and waving tortillas like Japanese fans. They saw in his bloodshot eyes the dull look of a *borracho*. In contrast were the hard, square lines of his face: tough, confident, carving an expression which was more like a warning flag. "Don't tread on me," it seemed to say. Or more precisely: "Don't tread on me *again*." Notice was served—in the rock-hard jaw, in the oft-broken nose, in the scar that crossed over his left eyebrow—to make way, to steer clear.

As Buchanon finally moved from his spot, walking directly across the infield, his thick, short hair seemed to blow in every direction at once. But in the narrow ring where a baseball cap had been screwed down for so many years, the sandy hair was matted flat to his head. This did not escape the notice of at least one spectator who was inspired to dub him *Santo Yankee* in reference to this hairy halo. But most of the crowd was more interested in the ragged hole in the seat of the big man's trousers.

Buchanon completed his parade across the infield, in keeping with time-honored baseball superstition making sure not to step on the foul line. Having thus at least recognized the possibility of bad luck, he then settled into one of the "good" seats behind home plate, bought two bottles of cold Gallo beer to hold against his throbbing temples and watched eight innings of the most amazing baseball he had ever seen.

His prospect, Santiago Akabal, was pitching for the visiting team, the Universidad Hidrocálidos. Akabal's fastball was getting by most of the batters on the Tropicales of Escuintla, but that alone wasn't enough to impress him. There wasn't one pimply-faced pitcher in the Florida Instructional League who couldn't have mown down the Tropicales without breaking a serious sweat. When you went deep into the Latin American bush to sign a hotshot thrower, and had gone over the boss's head right to the owner making all kinds of wild promises, the kid better at least be ready for Double-A. He better have one hell of a nasty curve and an aspirin-pill fastball that zapped the radar gun into the nineties. Akabal could definitely start up in Double-A *and* he had the two basic pitches—plus a nifty change-up and a purely evil screwball. But what really caught Bill Buchanon's critical eye was his control. Not only was Akabal pitching a no-hitter, but through eight innings he had not thrown one pitch unintentionally out of the strike zone. Not one. He had never seen anything like it.

Buchanon had maintained the respectable rate of one beer per inning, first holding it against his head before downing it so as to get the full service of its numbing properties from both without and within. By the middle of the fourth inning, his hangover was under control. By the sixth inning, he had actually begun to feel almost human. By the bottom of the eighth, he was ready for anything. He had won. He had discovered next year's big find. He had shot craps with the assholes in New York and he had rolled a come-out seven. They'd have to give him a coaching job for this. They wouldn't be able to put him off anymore. No one else in the organization had ever come back with an arm like Akabal's.

Buchanon stood up and bit the end off a Maconudo Prince Philip he had saved for the moment of victory. He lit it with a match from the Mexico City Holiday Inn, took a few puffs, inhaled deeply and let the smoke slowly leak out of the corners of his mouth. He stood there during the between-innings pause, puffing contentedly, savoring each drag of the big cigar like a proud new papa. Those few fans unfortunate enough to be seated directly behind him found themselves deprived of their view of the field. They didn't say anything at first, expecting him to retake his seat when play resumed. But when he continued to stand there, the curses began to fly. Somebody threw an orange which bounced off the screen and fell into the lap of an old man seated to Buchanon's left. As the ninth inning got under way, the unrest grew. A bottle broke high up on the screen, the pieces of glass rattling down through the chain-link mesh. One of the voices behind him, emboldened by liquor, began shouting insults—most of them dealing with Buchanon's parentage and acts performed with barnyard animals. Although only a few fans were affected by

Buchanon's eclipse, a groundswell of solidarity drew most of the spectators into the clamor.

Buchanon heard it all but didn't care. His only concern was the game. The capper for this incredible day would be Akabal getting the no-hitter. Unfortunately the pitcher for the home-team Tropicales, playing up to the competition, had himself only given up three hits. The score was tied at goose-eggs with Akabal's team at bat in the top of the ninth. Buchanon had no doubt that if the Hidrocálidos could score even one run in their half of the inning, Akabal would hold on in the bottom of the ninth.

When the first batter singled sharply up the middle, Buchanon shouted encouragement and excitedly waved the huge Maconudo over his head. This renewed the fans' anger. Not only was the gringo rude, but he was openly rooting for the wrong team. Indignation mounted, rising quickly toward a flashpoint. Still, Buchanon remained on his feet yelling encouragement to the visiting team.

Suddenly, the angry crescendo sputtered to silence. Moments later, the second batter popped what was supposed to be a sacrifice bunt directly into the glove of the second baseman, who then tossed over to first completing an easy double play. Strangely, there was no roar of approval from the home-town fans. Buchanon slumped back down onto the bench, threw the Maconudo down and stomped it out in disgust.

"Such waste," a man behind him said. The accent was barely noticeable. "Piteous."

"Pitiful fuckin' right," Buchanon murmured, noticing that the old man seated beside him and others in the front row had begun heading for the exits. "Hey, *amigos,* it ain't over till the fat lady sings!" he called after them. "It's friggin' tied in the ninth inning!"

"You agree then, *señor.* It is a bad strategy."

Buchanon realized the man was talking to him. He answered without turning. "Worst fucking goddamn play in the book." He heard more people moving on the wooden stands behind him. He didn't detect any pause in the exodus when the next batter hit a long triple into the gap in right-center. "There it is. Could have scored the lead run."

"Precisely," the man agreed as he stepped over the lower bench and sat next to Buchanon.

A manicured hand was extended. Buchanon shook it perfunctorily. He noticed the red stone in the man's cuff link and wondered if it was a ruby. He let his eyes travel from the darkly glowing gem up the immaculate sleeve of the man's pleated silk shirt. He was wearing a bow tie and a cummerbund. A dinner jacket, folded inside-out, lay neatly on his lap. His hair was black going to gray at the temples, closely cropped and curly. His eyebrows and mustache were also tinged with gray, hinting at an age more advanced than would otherwise be guessed. He had half-eye reading glasses balanced on the tip of his nose and Buchanon surmised he had been studying a newspaper that was rolled up in his other hand. Dark eyes flashed greetings over the glasses, reinforced by a tight, controlled smile. It was the same smile Buchanon had once seen on a reticulated python in the Bronx Zoo.

"The sacrifice—it requires a certain finesse, I think. Not just willingness," the man observed. "These boys . . . well, they are lacking, no?"

"They ain't gonna make anyone forget Rod Carew," Buchanon replied tersely, hoping the reply would discourage further dialogue. He kept his attention on the game, watching the batter pop out weakly to the shortstop, retiring the side.

"What would you do in that situation?" the man asked persistently.

Buchanon considered ignoring the question, but knew that

his inquisitive companion would pester him until his curiosity was satisfied. "Dig in and swing from the heels," he answered.

"But the coach—he's giving you the order to do this sacrifice?"

"The *sign?*" Buchanon asked in exasperation. "The coach is giving me the bunt sign?"

"*Sí.*"

"The game is on the line, ninth inning, tie score, man on first and no outs and he gives me the sign to lay one down."

"Yes, exactly," the man confirmed, his face all eagerness and expectation. "What do you do?"

"I miss the sign."

The man nodded, smiling as if the answer had been anticipated. He removed his reading glasses and slipped one of the templates between the middle two studs of his pocketless shirt. Buchanon couldn't help but notice the drastic effect this had on the man's already imposing appearance. He had seemed all questions moments before, all curiosity and inquiry, a student of the game. Now he had the resolute look of one who had reached some sought-after bottom line, some important conclusion from which revelations sprung.

"Because you are a home-run hitter," the man pronounced, emphasizing grandly with his hands as if he were conducting the *1812 Overture.* "An all-star, Number 12, Billy the Buster. You know the thing to do. No one else tells you."

"They sure as hell tried," Buchanon answered wearily. "I led the league in fines for five years running."

"But you have the satisfaction."

"Yeah, I get the satisfaction of being on the outside looking in."

"Ah, Mr. Buchanon, what a disappointment."

Buchanon wasn't sure whether he had heard sympathy or

scorn in that last remark. "I don't get recognized in Yankee Stadium anymore," he shot back, focusing his best chill-out stare, "and I was a goddamn fixture there for the better part of a decade. Down here sittin' on the back side of nowhere you know my name. Do I know you?"

"Possibly. But I know you. That's more to the point," the man answered smugly but without losing the tight, reptilian smile.

The old chill-out wasn't working. Buchanon had never known it to fail. Even when it didn't send its recipient running off for cover, it usually inspired knocking of knees or trembling of hands or, on some rare occasions, wetting of pants. Buchanon considered the possibility that alterations might be required to make it work on suave-looking south-of-the-border types.

"You are a celebrity," the man offered by way of explanation.

"Shit! I'm a fucking has-been."

"Well, at the risk of sounding impertinent, I suggest that those qualities are not incompatible."

Buchanon tensed. Old instincts had him rearing up in his seat, half twisting toward his nemesis, cocking his arm back. He turned the empty beer bottle in his hand so that it was now held like a weapon.

"I apologize," the man quickly interjected.

It sounded sincere and Buchanon loosened his grip on the bottle. In doing so, he felt something elusive slip away, a shifting in the balance. He regretted not having bashed the guy when the moment demanded. Life seldom granted him second chances.

"I fear I have insulted you, and you are a guest in my country."

"I'm no guest, pal," Buchanon clarified gruffly. "Everywhere I go, I pay my way."

"Again, not incompatible. You are here because we have said you could be here. It is only by our permission. So you have some obligations, like a guest—a guest who may be allowed to stay or who may be asked to go. Do you see my point?"

Buchanon didn't see the point at all. He was about to tell the smug bastard where to jam his point when a ball ricocheted off the top of the screen. After eight innings of pinpoint control, Akabal's first pitch in the bottom of the ninth had sailed twenty feet over the batter's head to crash high on the chain-link backstop. Buchanon focused on his prospect, who had also noticed the arrival of the silk-shirted man. Akabal walked a jittery, tight circle over the mound, kicking the rubber and fidgeting with the rosin bag. Something was wrong.

"You *are* my guest, Señor Buchanon," the man continued. "I am the *patrón*. I'm sure you will not offend my hospitality."

The statement had the ring of absolute authority. That in itself was normally enough to light Buchanon's fuse. But his attention was rooted on Akabal. The stadium had grown so quiet since the fans had mysteriously left that he could hear the young Indian panting on the mound, his breath coming in nervous gasps. Akabal gazed toward his infielders. They, in turn, looked down, suddenly interested in the condition of the playing surface. They tended meticulously to every stone and divot. Buchanon put the beer bottle to his lips, but it was empty.

"Why did you take that miserable bus to get here, Mr. Buchanon?" the man asked. It was not so much a question as it was a demand for information. "Surely a man of your prestige could hire a car."

Buchanon ignored him. His total concern was with the seventeen-year-old boy who stood alone at the center of the infield. Akabal threw ball two. The catcher returned the ball. Akabal made the sign of the cross and fired ball three high and wide.

"Perhaps you felt it was more inconspicuous," the man persisted. "But then you stand out in the outfield for all of Escuintla to see. It's quite curious, I think."

The man flicked his fingernail twice against the empty beer bottle in Buchanon's hand. He did it as one might tinkle a dinner bell to summon a servant. It made a similar sound. The big scout turned toward him slowly, mechanically, like the turret of a tank panning for a target. From the corner of his eye he saw the catcher diving for ball four and the batter ambling down to first base.

"Look, Chico," Buchanon responded, "just what the fuck is it you want? My autograph? Money? You want me to meet your *seester? What?*"

"Why did you come secretly on the bus, Mr. Buchanon?" the man asked.

"Secretly?"

"I'd like to know."

"Well the truth is, patronski, I'm traveling incognito. I'm the advance man for the commissioner's task force. We're lookin' to expand, you know. Play your cards right and you could wind up with a franchise down here."

"You are amusing," the man replied, totally unruffled. "This invention of yours interests me. Lies often reveal more than the truth. The lie creates an illusion, but it always leaves fingerprints on the truth it has altered. I find this most useful. But of course, the truth often turns out to be the biggest illusion of them all."

Buchanon was not used to being spoken to in such a manner. The man was too smart and too unafraid. It was an unsettling combination. Buchanon wished he hadn't drunk quite so many beers. He knew the booze was undermining his ability to cope, to come up with that one zinger to shut the guy up. He was missing something fundamental which everyone else—the fans, the players, his prospect—already knew. *Fucking booze,* he cursed to himself, even as he craved another beer. He stared out onto the field, taking in the game situation, focusing on those things he did understand, hoping they would clear his mind: no outs, man on first, 3–0 on the batter. *How the hell did he get behind 3–0 so quick?* Ball four came bouncing in.

"Mr. Buchanon, what is your interest in Akabal?"

"Baseball!" Buchanon said it as if the word were a declaration of war. He was surprised, himself, to hear so much anger concentrated in the one word.

"That is all?"

"What else?"

"I think he's not so good to be a Yankee."

"He's got a good live arm. The rest we can teach him."

"And you will sign this mediocrity and take him to America?"

"Yeah!"

"It is a great mistake."

"I've made 'em before."

"Not such as this."

"What's *your* interest in him?" Buchanon asked.

"I think you know that already, Mr. Buchanon."

A horrible thought suddenly occurred to Buchanon. "You're a goddamn bird dog for the Mets!" he accused.

The man laughed. "Then again, perhaps you are exactly what you appear to be."

"Anyone but the Mets," Buchanon groaned.

"You will sign him tonight after the game?"

"You bet!"

"You are not concerned that he is a loser?"

"He's a winner."

"He will lose this game. He will walk in the winning run."

Buchanon glanced toward the field. The third batter had just walked on four pitches. The bases were loaded. "It's possible," he replied.

"But you are not concerned?"

"I like his arm," Buchanon reasserted.

"That's all?"

"That's my interest. The arm."

With the bases loaded, Akabal looked plaintively toward the dugout, obviously wanting to be pulled. Buchanon saw the manager turn his back, and in witnessing that simple, gutless act, he relived every disappointment, every humiliation that the lords of the game had ever heaped on him. The son-of-a-bitch manager was going to let the kid twist in the wind. He was a fucking spineless bastard just like the rest of them. They all knew when to turn their backs.

Akabal blew on his fingers, trying to dry the perspiration. Buchanon saw the kid's hand was shaking, the wonderful gifted hand that an inning ago could impart such wizardry to a simple baseball, endowing it with just the right mixture of velocity, trajectory and rotation. What had gone wrong? Whose fault was it this time? Staring at the manager who had positioned himself in the far corner of the dugout, his back to the field, Buchanon threw the empty beer bottle down, jumped to his feet, grabbed the backstop with both hands and shook it violently.

"Fuck you!" he screamed.

The words were directed in the general direction of the dugout, but Buchanon's rage was far more encompassing. The man with the dinner jacket assumed the expletive was meant for him. Certainly he was included in the army of antagonists, past and present, here, there and everywhere whom Buchanon blamed for all that had gone wrong in his tumultuous life.

"Fuck you!" Buchanon repeated, this time not as loudly, but

with a violent shake of his head as the words were spit out like bitter pills.

"Bravo! American eloquence at its best," said the man in the silk shirt. He rose from the bench, carefully draping the dinner jacket over one arm and then applauding with slow, delicate, mocking claps. "Finally we have hostility. This should have been your first response. Or better yet to take a swing at me. That would be almost convincing. Always go with your strong suit, Mr. Buchanon. In your case, the short temper, the forced confrontation, the 'swing from the heels.' You hit an umpire, Mr. Buchanon. You broke his jaw. They threw you out of baseball. This is the root of your celebrity. Violence I could have trusted."

Buchanon released the backstop. Whenever Buchanon got really excited he'd thrust his face square up against his antagonist's. It was a habit left over from countless arguments with umpires. The rules said you couldn't touch them, but you could get in their face and give them a good whiff of yesterday's meat loaf. It was purely a reflex action when Bill suddenly found himself nose-to-nose with the man who still held onto the controlled, self-satisfied smile.

"But you've mellowed with age," the man continued. "Yes, time is a burden to be carried. Did you know this is a Maya concept? Think of time as weight, Mr. Buchanon. Such ideas were born here. As was the idea of zero. Long before the Hindus thought of it. Something we take as a given, this concept of zero. But without it where would we be?

"Do you think your burden of time has grown too heavy, Mr. Buchanon? Is that why you have no heart for violence anymore? The Buster has been lost, I think. Yes, we have lost the Buster and we have found the . . . the *borracho*."

Buchanon's fists were clenched but they remained at his

sides. He looked down at them as if to question their lack of action.

"No. You are no longer the Buster, are you?" the man chided.

"Beats the piss out of me," Buchanon replied quietly, wondering if the son-of-a-bitch was right.

"An option that is still available," the man replied glumly as he stepped back two paces and slipped into the dinner jacket. He sighed as if the words had caused him some pain. The smile was finally gone. Then he turned away and walked quickly out of the stadium.

Bill Buchanon never saw the last pitch of the game, a curve out of the strike zone which forced in the winning run for the Tropicales. He stood there, looking down at the empty beer bottles that lay discarded at his feet. He remained there, staring at them as if they had a tale to tell. He pushed them gently with the tip of his shoe and watched them roll into each other, changing the configuration of the unfathomable hieroglyphic. He pinned one of the bottles under his foot and rolled it over a roach that had been investigating the malty foam which clung to the debris on the floor. The roach was unharmed and crawled out from under the bottle. Buchanon was amazed the insect had survived. He mounted a new assault and again the roach crawled away unhurt. Suddenly the field lights went out.

Eventually, Buchanon made his way to the dugout where the visiting team was packing up their equipment.

"Santiago Akabal?" he asked. *"Dónde Akabal?"*

There was no reply.

Buchanon approached the nearest player and made a pitching motion. "Akabal," he repeated. The young player placed his bat in a long canvas equipment bag, picked up the bag and walked away.

All the players now hastened to finish their packing as Buchanon went among them, peering under the bills of their caps and asking about his prospect. One by one they walked off in silence and climbed onto the old bus parked behind the stadium. Buchanon followed the last one out and watched helplessly as the bus pulled away.

"Where's Akabal?" he called out. "Where's my arm?"

•

The "house that trash built," as it was called by the old-timers at *Here and There*, was no house at all. It was a steel-and-glass, six-story residential condo with a baronial view of Marina del Rey. Barnie Schiff had funneled 2.8 million dollars of *H&T* profits into developing the property. Unfortunately, he had done so in his wife's name. At the time, the move had been perfectly in keeping with the overall tax-shelter mentality of the investment. But when Francine Schiff divorced her husband a few years later, she walked away with controlling interest of the real-estate holding company he had formed. What Barnie had kept from Uncle Sam was a pittance compared to the bonanza the holding company had reaped. That all that money had gone to Francine, who had then jet-setted off to Monaco, was irrefutable proof to Barnie that woman was a creature with infinite capacity for causing pain. Francine's final insult was to leave Barnie with the penthouse unit they had purchased at an inflated price from what was technically her company. On the first of every month she took particular delight in imagining Barnie as he wrote out the gargantuan mortgage check.

Matt stood in the lobby with his finger pushed against the button that caused what he knew to be a very loud buzzer to sound in Barnie Schiff's apartment. The building security guard watched him with mounting irritation through a video monitor on his console situated at the far end of the lobby. He was annoyed that the visitor continued to lean on the button. At such a late hour, a considerate caller would no more than tap and release, lest the resulting buzzer awaken the unsuspecting resident with all the nerve-shattering insistence of a submarine's dive-alarm. The security guard considered confronting the rude young man, but doing so would mean losing his place in the magazine that was spread over the console, standing up and walking thirty feet to the other end of the lobby. These were all exertions he'd rather avoid. The primary advantage of the graveyard shift was its lack of physical demands: The monitors on the console told the story; cameras could be controlled with a flick of a switch; doors were locked and unlocked electrically; a bank of color-coded telephones gave him instant and varied communications capability. If the security of the building depended on him, then his own sense of well-being rested on his proximity to the control console. Behind the desk, in tune with its various electronic perceptions, he was omniscient, he was comfortable, he was protector and protected. Sedentary in that place, he had a weightiness, a critical mass, a heaviness rooted in inertia which he understood as importance. Away from the monitors and the phones and the switches, he was no more—and no less—than a retired pipe-fitter trying to supplement a meager pension. He decided to wait another thirty seconds before taking the risk of going ambulatory.

Schiff's voice came booming over the intercom speaker: "Who the fuck is it?"

The security guard smiled. Patience had its rewards after all. He turned his attention back to the magazine.

"Let me up," Matt answered.

"You're fired!" Schiff bellowed.

"Front-page stuff, Barnie," Matt said into the intercom.

Instantly, the electronic door clicked open.

Matt rode the elevator to the top floor. A synthesized

"Windmills of Your Mind" droned vacuously from an overhead speaker. When the doors parted, Schiff was standing there to greet him. He was naked except for the gold chain around his neck and the towel wrapped around his waist.

"I thought you were on pet stories," Schiff said, grabbing the large manila envelope out from under Matt's arm, fumbling to undo the clasp with his stubby fingers and starting down the hall toward his apartment.

"Not anymore."

"Who says?"

"You," Matt answered. "In about ten seconds."

As Schiff passed through the apartment door he succeeded in opening the envelope. He yanked out the first of four eight-by-ten black-and-white photographs. "Goddamn!" he said, falling into a coughing fit which he addressed by lighting up a Camel plucked with a diamond-studded lighter from the étagère.

Matt followed him in and closed the door.

"Double-fucking goddamn," Schiff wheezed, dropping into the corner unit of the sectional sofa. He shuffled quickly through the other photos, then spread them out on the glass coffee table.

"No more pet stories," Matt said. "All right?"

Matt pulled an ottoman up to the coffee table and sat down directly opposite his boss. He studied Schiff's face. It was a relatively new face, a post-Francine face. It had been tightened surgically. The nose had been shortened and deveined. It was not the best job Matt had seen, but it was a substantial improvement over the vegetal-looking thing nature had provided. Schiff's skin was permanently bronze thanks to long hours spent in the casket-like tanning beds. His capped teeth tended toward light ocher, but they were perfection in their straightness and alignment. The bonded hairpiece, in the right light, could pass for natural.

It was as good a face as Barnie Schiff could have. At fifty-

seven years old, it was the best face money could buy. It was a
better face by far than Francine had ever seen on him, and it had
given him great satisfaction to send a framed glossy of his new
mug to her. The carefully chosen photo caught him in the thankful embrace of Miss Nude Zuma Beach, whose title and sash he
had just bestowed. He had predicted to *H&T*'s editorial staff that
the photo would send Francine scurrying off to the nearest li-
posuction clinic, and for months afterward, in the halls and
around the water cooler, staffers referred to their boss as the "Save
the Whales Poster Boy," for there would surely be no more need
of blubber once Francine had her ample bottom and flanks
vacuumed of their bountiful lard. Secretly, however, Schiff feared
that some day soon a large envelope would arrive with a Moné-
gasque postmark. In it he would find a photo of a face-lifted, tits-
raised, ass-tightened Francine—and next to her would be some
young European stud with a pecker the size of a fence post.

Schiff was sucking hard on the Camel. Both feet were nervously tapping on the parquet floor. It was the same pulse, Matt
thought, as produced by a dog's tail under the dinner table, waiting for the scraps to fall.

"This week's cover, Barnie," Matt pronounced. "That's why
I rousted Bonnie out of bed and made her open up the lab. It
couldn't wait. It's this week's cover." He said it softly but persua-
sively, as if the conclusion were so obvious it had no need of
further emphasis.

"We're already at the printer's," Schiff answered, shaking his
head, but sounding as if it wasn't the final word.

Matt knew the photos had tugged sentimental cords. In their
goriness they more closely resembled the raunchy material of
H&T's early days than the tame celebrity shots which more regu-
larly graced the front page now that the tabloid had gone after a
wider audience. It was the kind of stuff Schiff had brought in back

when he was doing most of the writing and photography himself. Matt knew the shots appealed to Schiff beyond their composition, exposure and newsworthiness. There was nothing less than the magic of nostalgia reaching out to Schiff from the glass plane of the coffee table.

Schiff finished off the Camel with one last concentrated drag. As he ground out the butt in an ashtray, he steeled himself against the temptation. "It's good, kid, but something like this . . . The *Times* will have it tomorrow and we're not out until the day after. Unless you got an angle they don't . . ."

"It's exclusive, Barnie."

"How can this shit be exclusive? You kill him?"

Matt smiled. "I drove into it out in the desert . . . on some godforsaken road . . . nobody else around."

"Jesus! You got some luck. But somebody's found it by now."

"I don't think so, Barnie. I got spooked. When I drove off, I knocked the cot into a ditch. I don't think anyone is going to find it tonight. Tomorrow maybe. Someone will see buzzards and call the cops. The *Times* might make a late edition, but they ain't gonna get this. If they somehow get there before the cops, they get a stiff that's been out in the sun all day, all chewed up by the birds. They won't print that. They'll do some safe, half-ass story. As usual, they'll leave everyone hanging. Next morning, bang! We got the picture they missed: the fresh kill, coast to coast."

"And we catch them asleep at the switch."

"Beautiful, isn't it?"

"Scooped by a weekly."

"On *hard* news, Barnie."

"It would be sweet to beat 'em in their own backyard," Schiff added wistfully.

Schiff leaned back and let his head drop back against the sofa. He was savoring the prospect of upstaging "the high-and-fucking-mighty"—as he was prone to say—Los Angeles *Times*. Matt knew Schiff would not be able to resist such an opportunity. At any moment, his boss's head would snap forward, out of its reverie, all smiles, eyes bright, perhaps a tiny residue of drool clinging to the corner of his leer, and then he would rush off to the phone to reenact the classic "stop the presses" scene.

But when Schiff's head did rise off the sofa, the expression on his face was anything but happy. The publisher's face was tight, constricted, a compressed knot of flesh. In the scant moments before Schiff spoke, Matt prepared himself for the unexpected, wiped his own expression blank, hardened himself for some patently bizarre "Schiffism." He saw in Schiff's knitted brow not the menace of a trigger ready to be pulled, but the contraction of a constipation about to be relieved.

"How much does your goddamn girlfriend know about this?" Schiff demanded.

"She's not my girlfriend," Matt retorted, mad at himself for letting it sound defensive and for not anticipating Schiff's concern, predictable, even logical, as it was.

"I don't care if you're fucking her. I just don't want you talking to her."

"Neither one, Barnie." Matt felt his throat tighten.

"Well I hope you did get to fuck her, because she sure as hell screwed you."

Matt wanted to add something more about Kelly Wode, an insult, a curse, anything to assuage his boss for what she had done.

"I could have fired you," Schiff continued.

"The pet desk is worse. Take my word."

Schiff felt a smile of satisfaction trying to be born. He aborted it with another Camel quickly jammed in and lit. He let the smoke cloud around his face, further hiding the joy Matt's last words had given him. His wisdom had once more been made manifest. By keeping Matt when he could have sacked him, by punishing him instead of cutting him loose, he had made possible the very moment which was about to happen. His instincts had come through—again.

"You go home and call the cops, whoever has jurisdiction." Schiff pointed to one of the photos.

"Imperial County Sheriff's Office."

"Perfect. Those guys are not exactly rocket scientists. You call them. Now there's a record with the phone company. Nobody can say you're obstructing justice or failed to report a felony or any of that other horseshit. You babble some hysterical crap about a murder. You're very distraught, very confused. You're so upset you accidentally hang up before you give them your name."

"Don't they record those calls?"

"Shit! How long have you been in this business? You find some administrative number to call, not the emergency number. And you get the name of who you're talking to. Once you make the call it's his problem. He'll either shitcan it if you sound loony enough or he'll pass it along to Sergeant Thumb-Up-His-Ass who'll give it to Lieutenant Shit-For-Brains and so on. Either way you've done your civic duty and we buy a little more time."

"Got it," Matt asserted, impressed with Schiff's grasp of the situation.

"Then you do your story. Three hundred words. Straight, but our way straight. Stick their noses in it. But no speculation. Whodunnit ain't the point here. Don't fuck it up, Matthew, or you'll be back on the fantastic Goat Patrol. Understand?"

Matt understood: He was off the pet desk.

"Get me the fucking telephone!" Schiff ordered.

Matt sprang up and retrieved the cordless from the étagère. As he carried it back to Schiff, he dialed the printer's number.

The call was ringing through by the time he handed the phone to his boss.

"You know what it takes to change a press run?"

"A hundred grand?" Matt ventured.

Schiff shook his head, but was then distracted by what Matt discerned was someone answering at the other end. "Tommy!" Schiff barked into the mouthpiece. "I got a new front page for you." The publisher looked quickly back to Matt. With his free hand he reached down toward his crotch, cupped it through the towel and gave it a firm shake. Then his attention went back to the telephone: "I don't give a fuck how many you already printed."

Matt laughed. Yes, he thought, that's precisely what it took: balls. Schiff had them, the brass-plated variety. And the old man wasn't shy about putting them on the block when circumstances demanded. Whatever else could be said about Barnie Schiff, he had gonads.

Matt wandered off toward the library. The room had been converted into a card parlor. A hexagonal, felt-covered poker table stood in the center of the room. A well-stocked wet bar had been installed along the near wall.

Matt poured himself two fingers' worth of Jack Daniels in a tall glass, raised it, made a silent toast to Schiff's balls and took a sip. The first taste always caused a slight shudder. He had come to understand these mild tremors as the duty-bound, if unheeded, protests of his body, his insides trying to tell him something the good folks in Lynchburg, Tennessee, didn't want him to know.

He finished his drink, set the glass down on the bar and considered leaving. But Schiff had not yet officially dismissed him. He decided to wait until his boss finished the phone call. Apparently, there were some problems. Matt overheard Schiff saying in exasperation, "For crissakes, Tommy, let's not invent a new art form here. I just want to change the goddamn front page." Matt strained to hear more, but Schiff was pacing back and forth in the living room, moving in and out of earshot. And there was another sound, which although barely audible, was competing for Matt's attention. As Schiff walked further away it became more distinct, just as when he approached closer, it became harder to hear. At first it was just an annoyance, a thin veil thrown over his ability to eavesdrop, a subtle part of the apartment's ambience, no more or less obtrusive than the quiet hiss of the ventilating system or the barely perceptible drone of the refrigerator. Matt lingered at the bar, tuning into this other voice—he had, by now, decided the sound was human—as it oscillated with Schiff's. When his boss reached the furthest recess of the living room, Matt zeroed in on the origin of the sound: It was coming from behind a closed door at the end of the hallway.

He headed for the door, slowly, stopping occasionally, then listening closely to that other voice—a female voice, he was now certain—which seemed to be calling him without words. Finally, he stood at the door and saw it was slightly ajar. With the back of his hand, he gave it a gentle push. As it swung an inch away from the jamb, the sound poured out.

A woman was moaning, long, exquisite sighs which were either the result of intense pleasure or pain. Which, he couldn't be certain. It was a tempting, seductive sound, hypnotic, primal but tainted. Listening to it uncorked a rush of feelings, all of them blood-strong. Sometime later that night, after he had thought about it, after he had rendered those feelings into an idea and the idea into words, he would confess to the Sony, "I either felt like fucking my way through a squad of cheerleaders or filleting a cat with a chain saw. I wasn't quite sure just which I'd like to do—or do first."

He could have listened all night, but from what little he

could see through the crack of the door, he knew he stood at the threshold of Barnie Schiff's bedroom. Whatever was going on inside, no matter how intriguing, was best left undisturbed. Matt was about to retreat when he saw the rectangular pattern of light in the corner of the immense bedroom—the cold, phosphorescent glow of a console television.

Matt opened the door and walked directly to it, mad at himself for having been seduced by the lousy boob tube. His psyche had been debauched by nothing more real than a soundtrack. On the TV was a VCR. Beside it was the empty sleeve to a VHS tape, the white, cardboard, generic type. On its side, written in grease pencil, was simply *S&M 6*. Matt watched the girl on the screen as she resisted three hooded persecutors. The tape was low-quality, but the performance was flawless. Repulsive in its brutality—although Matt could not look away—there was no hint of fakery. Matt could not understand how they were able to make it look so realistic without actually injuring the girl. Indeed, just when it looked as if the girl could take no more, the tape cut to a different scene with a different, seemingly terrified, young woman. Then, totally out of context, there was a close-up shot of yet another woman's face. The expression on her face was identical to the one on the corpse at Coombe's Ditch on County GG. Matt finally looked away as the next scene began.

Suddenly, everything felt very wrong. Matt relied on his sense of detachment to cope with the tawdry, tacky world of *Here and There*. He stood aloof, took his photos, wrote his copy and moved on. He wasn't *of* that world; he was just passing *through* it, recording impressions, cataloging experiences, perceptive but immune, on his way to becoming a *real* writer. Now, standing in Schiff's posh bedroom, the memory of Coombe's Ditch fresh in his mind, *S&M 6* playing just below, he felt contaminated, the dirt of *H&T*'s world on his hands, its mud caked to his shoes. The night had taken its toll.

Matt examined himself in the mirror which ran the length of the wall except for the area directly behind the TV. He was twenty-eight but he saw thirty—maybe thirty-five—years looking back from the mirror. He saw the coarse wildness of his hair, but not its rich brown color. He saw the missing inch that kept him from being a six-footer and the five extra pounds no one else would ever notice. He saw the slight twist in the line of an otherwise perfect nose where it had collided with a steering wheel, the only casualty of a teenage driving accident. There was the chin which wasn't weak, but which wasn't really strong either. Another eighth of an inch of jawbone and his face would have had character. That, and eyes slightly wider set, a tad more open, and any other color than the dull hazel which always made them appear less than piercing.

Matt sucked in his gut and thrust out his chin. He opened his eyes wide and brushed the hair off his forehead. He squared his shoulders, locked his hands at the waist and flexed his biceps. He turned slightly, looking for a more favorable angle, a more reassuring view. Then, in the mirror, he saw the woman on the bed behind him. They studied each other's reflection—he, in mute, fascinated horror; she, without any indication of shock or surprise. She had been watching him the whole time, he gathered. His arms dropped to his sides, his shoulders sagged, total embarrassment shone in a pink flush on his cheeks. He stared back at her image in the glass, hoping he could derive from her own vulnerable circumstances a lessening of his humiliation. She was spread-eagled and trussed to the bed posts with short lengths of rope. He saw she could easily free herself if she was so inclined, but she didn't seem to be. A sheet had been hastily thrown over her torso. In one of her bound hands she held the remote control for the

TV. If she was embarrassed, it didn't show in her eyes, glassy and rooted blankly on his reflection in the glass. Matt detected the movement of a leg, a bare knee flexing, rising as far as the rope around her ankle would permit, the sheet sliding down her thigh.

Suddenly, Schiff was at his side. Matt, Schiff and the woman all studied each other in the mirror. Matt diverted his eyes, wondering if there was a way out. Schiff's arm looped over his shoulder.

"You did good, kid," he said, patting Matt on the back. "Tell you what, you want her, she's yours."

Matt saw his own jaw drop just before he turned away from the glass to confront Schiff. Before he could respond, the publisher reached down to the VCR and ejected the tape. He thrust it into Matt's hands and then lit up another Camel, laughing, choking and coughing all at once.

•

Buchanon was dimly aware of the stout, middle-aged woman sitting on his lap. He had lost track of time and his left hand. The former was not to be accounted for, but the latter was eventually tracked down. It had traveled—with some coaxing, he assumed—under the woman's dress. She had it firmly clamped between her thighs, immobilized and starting to go numb. The woman was also doing something annoying to his hair, swirling her fingers through it, playing with his ear. He didn't like it and he reached for her arm with his free hand. His elbow brushed one of the empty beer bottles on the table. It clanged against others, fell over and rolled off the edge to break on the floor. He pushed the woman's hand away from his ear, but she persisted and began to laugh, revealing a huge gold incisor. Buchanon touched the big shiny tooth with the tip of his index finger and the woman laughed harder. He tickled it and she laughed harder still.

Buchanon's head fell back over the edge of his chair. The

ceiling was painted lavender. Vaguely he remembered that the door to the *cantina* was painted that same sickly, faded, incongruous color—a pussy color. He recalled seeing a metal sign over the door, hanging crookedly from a wooden standard and all but rusted through. There was no name legible on it, but the faint outline of a beer bottle could be seen through the corrosion. It was more than enough, however: Buchanon had sniffed out better hidden taverns than this one; where booze was concerned, he was a bloodhound nonpareil.

Buchanon's eyes drifted to the bar. It was standing parallel to the right wall and had obviously been lengthened at various times as the cantina had been expanded. Each addition had evidently been accomplished with whatever building provisions had been available at the time: Mahogany led to plywood, plywood to fiberglass, fiberglass to pine, and on back through the progression of time and drunkenness, on past the floating damask of cigarette smoke which hid the back of the place and made it seem bigger than it probably was. A black hole could have stood behind the opaque curtain of smoke. If there was a wall somewhere beyond the nicotine cloud, it was not a boundary; rather, it was a teasing thing, an apparition, a thing that swallowed you up like the right-field fence at Fenway Park or the center-field wall at Comiskey. Buchanon knew better than to test those limits: He stayed on the near side of the smoke.

The serious drinkers were perched on the stools along the bar. At the tables were those who still found some distraction in conversation and companionship. Buchanon would have wound up at the bar had a stool been available. Instead, he had been forced to settle in at an oval table exactly like one that had occupied a corner of the kitchen in his boyhood apartment back in the Bronx—except that this one had been lengthened with a leaf that didn't match. There were no two tables alike in the whole place.

It was as if a renegade caravan of kitchen furniture had sought refuge there, a lost generation of fifties and sixties formica, fugitives from Goodwill, hiding out from the Salvation Army in the niches and alcoves along the left-hand wall.

"Bumper cars," Buchanon said to a moth hovering over his face. The moth apparently understood, for it immediately winged up toward the ceiling to spread the word among others of its kind fluttering about a dim light bulb. All those mismatched tables in random clusters on the yellowed linoleum, no rhyme or reason to their placement on the floor—it had bothered Buchanon ever since he had walked into the place hours before. "Bumper cars," he repeated to the moth who had been so quick to comprehend, although it was now indistinguishable from the rest of its brethren on the ceiling. And indeed the scattered tables were reminiscent of amusement park bumper cars that had come to rest askew at the flip of a switch. Buchanon polished off another beer, draining the bottle in one continuous gulp, immensely satisfied to have solved the riddle of the tables. "Bumper cars, bumper cars," he whispered over and over, concentrating on picking his own voice out of the laughter, the squeaks of bar stools against the linoleum, the tinkling of bottles and glasses, the throbbing bass of a juke box hidden behind the cigarette smoke and the interminable, maddening, indecipherable babble of Spanish voices—

". . . and they just disappear," someone said.

Buchanon had the sudden urge to kiss the woman. He reached but she wasn't there. The jukebox had stopped playing and there seemed to be less people in the place. A young man in a brown sleeveless T-shirt was seated across the table. A red kerchief was tied cowboy-style around his neck. "It happens all the time," he said to Buchanon, and then looked furtively over his shoulder as he sensed the approach of the boy who had been acting as Buchanon's waiter all night. Buchanon shoved his last American ten-dollar bill into the boy's hand and motioned toward the empty beer bottles on the table. The boy ambled off toward the bar as Buchanon tried to recall if the kid had ever given him change back from his previous purchases.

After the boy returned with the beers, the young man with the red kerchief pulled his chair closer to Buchanon's, once more cast a glance over his shoulder and then took hold of Buchanon's arm.

"You don't know, do you?" the man asked urgently, tightening his grip on the scout's arm.

Buchanon looked at the brown fingers tightening on his sleeve and tried to understand. He concluded, somewhat disappointedly, that he was not being threatened. That would have been easier: He was good at confrontations. But it seemed the man had grabbed his arm to effect a sort of intimacy, just as one might do before delivering some bad news or whispering a secret. Buchanon focused as best he could on the man's face.

"You *don't* know," the man said, this time not as a question but as a pronouncement as fact. "Coronel Efraín César Alvarado Guzman," he said solemnly, as if the words had some lethal power. Then he released Buchanon's arm and sat back in his chair.

"Glad to meet you, Colonel," Buchanon replied decorously, waving a salute with a beer bottle. "I eat your chicken all the time."

The young man was not amused. *"My* name is Héctor," he snarled, once more leaning back over the table. "The man you met at the ballpark is Coronel Alvarado."

"My arm!" Buchanon groaned. He slammed the beer bottle down on the table top. Suddenly he hated the young man with the red kerchief for causing him to remember what he had so diligently struggled over the last many hours to forget.

"He is a high *comandante* in the G-2, the intelligence section of the army. He has an elite platoon of *Kaibiles* under him, counterinsurgency special forces. He has total power. He does not even answer to Guatemala City. He has the support of the big landowners so he does as he pleases and no one can stop him. Whoever tries, disappears. That is why they call him Mago. It means magician."

"Voodoo," Buchanon knowingly replied, nodding slowly. *"Voodoo-black-fuckin'-magic!"*

Héctor stared at the big American as one might watch a trapeze artist who has fallen to the net for the third and final time.

"The last year I played," Buchanon went on, "between May 25 and June 18 I batted .067. I couldn't get me so much as a loud foul."

"You do not understand," the young man protested.

"I didn't, but I figured it out. I looked it up. It's all in the fucking ball. They go through thirty to fifty balls every game. Forty, fifty thousand a year. That's the common denominator. Different pitchers, different managers, different parks, different time zones, temperatures, barometric pressures, wind currents, lights, backgrounds, reflections, different goddamn umpires. But one thing stays the same, that little round bastard. Forty, fifty thousand a year and each one is exactly eight and three quarters inches in circumference. Each one weighs exactly four and one eighth ounces. Each one's got exactly one hundred and eight stitches. And you know where each and every one of those fuckers is made? You don't have the slightest idea, do you?"

Héctor looked blankly at Buchanon. He shook his head because he truly pitied what he beheld. The scout took it as the answer to his question.

"See," Buchanon continued, "you're the one who don't understand. And I'm not talking about the cork they get from Portugal and the rubber they get from somewhere in fucking Asia that goes into the pill. But you didn't know that either, did you?"

"Just as you do not know how your beloved game came to this part of the world!" Héctor retorted belligerently.

"It's no game, friend."

"Oh, I do agree."

"You just forget the game bullshit. Would they take something you play a game with and shoot it out of a cannon at eighty-five miles an hour against a wall eight feet away just to see if it can keep its precious shape and bounce back at precisely the right speed?"

"Why not?" Héctor ventured. "They brought baseball with their cannons to Nicaragua in 1927. Your marines. For five years they chased Sandino and when they weren't chasing him they played baseball."

"Well, *semper* fuckin' *fidelis.*" Buchanon chugged down a beer.

"Sandino's dead over sixty years, but we still *play ball.* Hey, Señor Buchanon?"

"I never *played ball,* kid," Buchanon remarked sourly. "Never did."

"Neither did I," Héctor replied.

Buchanon believed him. He saw the familiar curse of stubbornness in the young man's face. It was in his eyes and the hard line of his mouth.

"You know how they always call it horsehide?" Buchanon went on wearily. "Well it ain't. That's another little lie. It's *cowhide* . . . from Tullahoma, Tennessee—not that it means a spit's worth of difference."

Buchanon fished the Red Man tin out of his breast pocket. He opened it but didn't find enough for a good plug. He sprinkled the tobacco slowly on the floor. A bereaved widow scattering the ashes of her dearly departed spouse would not have done it with more ceremony. When he was done he closed the tin carefully and placed it in the center of the table, in the midst of the beer bottles standing as honor guard.

"They take the cowhide from Tennessee and the cork from Portugal and the rubber from Gooksville and miles of wool yarn and thread from God-knows-where and send it to fucking Haiti. Of all the broken-down, busted-ass countries in this sad fucking world, they got to put sonovabitchin' baseballs together in Haiti. You know what they got in Haiti besides goddamn Haitians? They got voodoo. It's the frigging voodoo capital of the universe. Some bitch down in Port-au-Prince makin' three cents a week is sittin' there sewing baseballs. It's classic. We go to voodoo-land and pay somebody to stick needles into baseballs. You can't make shit up that crazy. And I'm standing there on a goddamn Sunday afternoon in June wondering why I can't touch the ball off some puss-arm who couldn't break plate glass. *Shit!*"

Buchanon saw the pity on the young man's face. Nothing so enraged him as another man's pity. Clumsily, he lunged across the table, sending a dozen "dead soldiers" to the floor. Héctor held his ground even as Buchanon grabbed hold of the kerchief. His hand clamped onto Buchanon's wrist.

"Where's my arm?" Buchanon demanded.

"Akabal is no more," he answered solemnly. "He joins the *desaparecidos.*"

"Who are they, some beaner team?"

"No. They are the ones who have disappeared and are no more. They are the ones for which there is only tears."

"Disappeared?" Buchanon asked, wobbly and confused, holding onto the kerchief like a subway strap.

"Mago," replied the young man, as if that one word said it

all. "Did you not see the stadium empty when he arrived? The people fear him more than the devil himself. He is the one who comes in the middle of the night. He is the one who brings nothing but pain and desolation."

Buchanon didn't understand. "Why?" he asked dully.

Héctor suddenly had a knife in his free hand. Before Buchanon could react, he cut the kerchief from his neck. The scout fell facedown on the table, the sliced kerchief drooping limply over his fist like the petals of a dead poinsettia. The young man jumped to his feet and glared down at the prostrate American.

"So that gringos can sleep safe and sound in their beds and not have nightmares," Héctor snarled. "That is *why!*"

"I just want my arm," Buchanon mumbled, not bothering to lift his head.

The big man lay there for a few minutes, watching the comings and goings at the bar sideways and through the empty bottles. It was a perspective with which he was not altogether unfamiliar. He was aware that Héctor had not left. The young man seemed to be hovering above and behind him, calling him a *chingado* and saying he wasn't worth helping. The moth returned to light on the empty tobacco tin. Buchanon gently extended a crooked finger as if he expected it to perch like a trained parakeet. When it fluttered away, Buchanon pushed himself up off the table.

The sudden movement dizzied Buchanon, but it also shook him to a slightly higher level of alertness. He was instantly aware that some drastic change had occurred within his surroundings. He caught a last glimpse of Héctor fading out back toward the smoke and heard him whisper, "Mago's *pintos.* Beware!" Buchanon wheeled around, but Héctor was already gone, as were most of the other drinkers who—he felt almost certain—had been there but moments before. Those who were left had gone suddenly quiet, motionless, staring downward, absorbed in their drinks.

"Horses?" Buchanon muttered to himself in total mystification as he turned back to the table. *"Mago's pintos?"*

Buchanon saw the front door open. A man entered, looked around, then motioned for others to follow. Six men came through the door, and as they walked into the light, Buchanon saw they were dressed in spotted military camouflage uniforms.

"Pintos!" he bellowed triumphantly, breaking the silence like a shotgun blast in a mausoleum and pointing at the closest of the spotted figures.

The six men gravitated toward Buchanon's table, surrounding it. Five of them wore red berets and carried Galil assault rifles. The sixth man approached closer than the others. He was hatless and carried no weapon. His beret was tucked neatly under an epaulet on his right shoulder. The three bars and one star of the *capitán primero* rank glimmered on his collar. His hair had receded well back from the crest of his forehead to an incongruous spot in the middle of his skull where a fastidious black pompadour began. In the dim light of the cantina, the man's face looked alien, the large bulbous forehead tapering down to an all but nonexistent chin. The face had a dull waxen sheen, a smoothness which could have been formed from marzipan or clay and which seemed incapable of sprouting whiskers or ripening to a blush. As the man prepared to speak, his thin, colorless lips drew back revealing long, yellow teeth which seemed to want to remain tightly clamped shut so as to resist any effort at communication.

Finally, the teeth parted and the man said, "You may enjoy yourself, Señor Boccanno? You may drink so much, yes-no?"

Buchanon put both hands on the table and forced himself upright and out of the chair. He teetered for a second, but found a semblance of equilibrium, enough to allow him to look down on the man as he said, "What the fuck are you supposed to be?"

"I am Capitán Reyes," the man answered without a trace of emotion, his voice never wavering in volume or pitch, a slight gurgle warbling with each word from the back of his throat.

"You work for this Mago guy?"

"You speak Coronel Alvarado. Better, yes-no?"

"The asshole in the tux."

Reyes did not respond. His face betrayed no sign of comprehension.

"*Tux-eee-do.* The cocksucker at the ball game in the white monkey suit. You his errand boy?"

"Coronel Alvarado wants you may happy. *No problema.* Jez go home."

"*No problema,* my sweet ass! There's gonna be plenty of fucking *problemas.* You tell your boss man I ain't leaving without my arm. You tell him that. I ain't goin' nowhere empty-handed. Comprendo?"

Reyes turned to go without giving the slightest indication he understood. It was a completely mechanical reflex which ignored any responsibility to acknowledge Buchanon's words: A message had been delivered; a reply had been procured; mission accomplished; time to go. Buchanon did not consider the snub intentional. All he knew was that he was looking at the man's back. He pushed the table aside and took three quick but wobbly steps toward the departing captain. He lurched forward, meaning to grab Reyes by an epaulet and jerk him back like a piece of wayward luggage on an airport conveyer—

Something detonated at the back of Buchanon's head and he slumped to his knees. A dark, green, mottled shape walked slowly into view and separated into triplicate images. Three Captain Reyes's continued out through three lavender doors without so much as casting a glance to note what had occurred. A small army followed as three identical pintos wiped blood in unison from the stocks of Galils. The scout saw the floor rise up and wrap around him as he sagged and rolled under the table.

Then there was only blackness and the sound of an umpire's deep baritone calling out from some hidden closet at the back of his brain: *"Yer out!"*

•

Matt opened his apartment door and was greeted by the unmistakable stench of old tuna. Apparently, Rosa, the cleaning woman, had not made her scheduled weekly visit. Unlike some of her predecessors, Rosa was scrupulously reliable. Matt concluded she was either sick or had fallen into the hands of the Immigration and Naturalization Service. No sooner did he find a good cleaning lady, than the *migra*—as the INS was called by the chicanos—would deport her. He dreaded to imagine how many duplicates of his apartment key were rattling around in the pockets of aprons and housedresses in Tijuana, Mexicali and Nogales.

He slammed the door and marched into the kitchen where a tower of garbage had been crookedly erected in the corner, bag upon greasy bag, gutted potato chip bag upon empty milk bottle, flattened six-pack upon soggy pizza carton, and topping it all, a capstone of three Chicken of the Sea tins. There was a brief moment when he actually considered attending to the debris himself, picking it up piece by slimy piece, carrying it down the stairs and throwing it in the dumpster, but fatigue overruled cleanliness in his immediate consideration of priorities. He just stood there, shaking his head as if witnessing the aftermath of some unalterable and calamitous act of God while waiting for the governor to fly over in his helicopter and declare it an official disaster area. At length he turned his back on the mess and walked away, muttering, "There's never a wetback around when you really need one."

Matt trudged off across the living room and into the bedroom. He dropped the Adidas bag on his desk and collapsed into the highback, "tiltomatic" swivel chair he had pilfered from *H&T* a couple of years ago when Barnie had redone his office in art deco. He extracted the Sony from the bag, checked to see that the *GAN Notes* cassette was still in the transport and deposited his feet on the top of the monstrous double pedestal desk he had also appropriated from his employer.

"Three days of garbage is Bohemia," he recorded. "Days four through six are more like Buffalo. The seventh day is Bangladesh. Every week I require enforced hygiene. I can endure days five and six only because I know a Spic and Span colonic is scheduled for day seven. I think this is related to my rigor of weekly deadlines over the last many years, but I leave further analysis along such lines to those more qualified—psychotherapists, Roto-Rooter men and medical technicians experienced in the administration of lower GI's all come to mind. That I have become predictable in this routine has no doubt come to the attention of our public servants at the INS. They have systematically conspired to deny me my inalienable right to affordable maid service. The criteria for making Immigration's most wanted list would seem to be twofold: Does she do windows and do the windows that she does belong to Matthew Thomas Teller?"

Matt ejected the *GAN Notes* tape and replaced it with the *H&T* cassette. He rewound and then played the observations recorded at Coombe's Ditch. When it finished, he rewound once more, sat up in his chair and dug the photographs out of the bag. He spread them out on the desk and replayed the tape, looking at each of the photos synchronously with his commentary. From the lower desk drawer he extracted a blank sheet of bond and fed it into his big green Royal manual.

Ten minutes later, the paper was still blank and Matt reluctantly dipped into the gym bag once more. He fished out Schiff's *S&M 6*, ripped it out of its sleeve and jammed it into the VCR, which sat on a console TV beside the desk. "Thank you very much, Mr. Schiff," he said as the picture came up on the old television. After only a few minutes, he began to type:

EXCLUSIVE
   Bloodcurdling moans coming from a horribly mangled corpse turned out to be no more than gusts of wind echoing in the man's open mouth. But other mysteries remain about the unidentified naked man found tortured to death on County Road GG at Coombe's Ditch in Imperial County, California.
   The victim had been tied to a bed frame and left in the middle of the isolated desert road. When the body was discovered by an *H&T* investigative reporter, it was still warm and oozing blood from its many grisly wounds.
   It appeared that the man had been diabolically tortured for a long period of time prior to expiring.
   He had been castrated, and fire may have been used. The acrid stench of scorched flesh was still pungent when the body was found.
   It also appeared as if the man's right eye had been slowly disgorged with a sharp knife. The eyeball, barely attached to shreds of muscle and nerve, was hanging loose and out of its socket.
   The middle toe of the left foot and both thumbs had been cut off, obviously with something sharp enough to hack right through the bone. The victim's right ear had been mangled beyond recognition.
   Reminiscent of some wild-west lore were the wounds to the man's head. It appeared that he had been scalped, the

top layers of skin and hair having been excruciatingly peeled back off his skull.

A U-shaped, shallow slit cut across the victim's abdomen and up his sides. The incision, although not deep, was almost medically exact and seemed to follow a preconceived design as might be found in ritual sacrifice.

Matt paused to change the paper. Quickly, he scanned what he had written, carefully considering whether his allusion to "ritual sacrifice" had violated Schiff's caution against speculation. Schiff had prohibited specific conjecture as to "whodunnit." Broad reference to "ritual sacrifice" was not like saying the Manson Family was alive and well in Imperial County—even if readers might come to such a conclusion, or something else equally as bizarre. Matt decided to let it pass.

Schiff's instructions were always subject to interpretation. It was never enough to do what Schiff *said* to do. The requirement was always to do what Schiff *meant* to be done. Since the latter was definable only after the fact, only after Schiff had the benefit of twenty-twenty hindsight, the proper implementation of a Schiff command demanded considerable competence as a fortune-teller. Schiff could only be counted on to react as his readers reacted. If they liked something, he liked it too. It was impossible for a reporter to be right all the time, to always predict what the readers would like—or more precisely, *would buy*. Survival at *H&T* didn't depend so much on the writer's percentage of correctness as it did on the writer's ability to suffer Schiff's wrath on those many, inevitable occasions when he was wrong.

Matt started page two:

The word NOSAL was written in blood on the victim's forehead. It is not known at this time if the word has any occult significance, such as in cases where pentagrams have been carved into the bodies of satanic sacrifice victims. Another possibility is that the word is the "signature" of the perpetrator(s) of the gruesome murder.

The *H&T* reporter whose investigation led to the discovery of the body is cooperating with the Imperial County Sheriff's Office. The police have no leads at this time, nor have they made a statement pertaining to the case. However, residents of the area, as well as travelers, are cautioned to exert extreme caution until it can be determined if those responsible are involved with a cult and whether or not they are still operating in the vicinity.

Matt pulled the sheet out of the typewriter. His eyes drifted to the television. The tape had ended and the TV was crackling with static. Somewhere, in one of the shoeboxes piled up on top of a file cabinet in the living room, was a *GAN Note* tape—#58, Matt thought—which contained his observations on untuned televisions. Something about how they revealed the intrinsic hostility of electronic media, he recalled: *video killer bees swarming the screen . . . the fiery buzz scratching to get through the speaker.* What crap, he thought, just like most of his old stuff.

Matt began rewinding the videotape, stopped at a random point and pushed the PLAY button. The scene was different from those he had viewed earlier. Instead of one woman suffering at the hands of a few brutal males, there was now a couple on the screen, a man and a woman, both seemingly willing, each taking a polite turn at visiting some humiliation on the other.

That such a scene would make him think of Kelly Wode was logical enough, but he was surprised that it provoked him to throw a copy of her book, which had been lying on the corner of his desk, peacefully and unobtrusively enough, across the room and through the door. It landed with a thud and skidded into a wall somewhere in the living room. When he retrieved it a few moments later, he knew it could no longer be allowed to reside within the walls of his home. He took it into the kitchen and stood with it before the pillar of garbage. Its title, *The Yellow Pages*, was printed in a greatly magnified, ragged-looking courier pica on the bright canary jacket. He lingered, then placed it delicately atop the tuna cans.

There was a tiny bit of satisfaction in having disposed of the book prior to its making the best-seller list, which it was sure to do. Nonetheless, he recognized the pettiness of the act and the hollowness of its symbolism. He couldn't dispose of her so easily. He had not seen her in months, but still he felt as if the relationship had not really ended. It was typical of them to survive long "dormant" periods—even when survival was the last thing either of them wanted, even when both of them did their best to chop at the very roots of whatever it was that so painfully insisted on drawing them back together. God, how he hoped it wasn't love, how he feared it might be. Like gravity—just as subtle, just as implacable, just as useless to resist. No, he could not throw her away. Not yet. He could only throw away the thing that was both her achievement and her most unforgivable sin, the thing that stood as the object of his envy and his scorn, the thing that had really caused Schiff to relegate him to the mutant pet desk. Schiff had blamed the two-headed Beldine murder/suicide story, which had coincidentally been published the same day. But everyone knew the real reason for Matt's demotion: *The Yellow Pages: Inside the Tabloid Press*. Schiff's pride had prevented him from admitting that a journalist from the hated *L.A. Times* could possibly cause him grief—a woman, the girlfriend of his favorite reporter. But grief she had caused. It was her forte.

Matt turned away and stormed back into the bedroom. Kelly

Wode was the last thing he wanted to be thinking about. There was the call to the police yet to make. There were photos to select and captions to write. Someone would be calling any second for the copy and the negatives. And there was a strange picture taking shape in the back of his mind. It had been unfolding ever since he had first stood at the threshold of Schiff's bedroom door, emerging out of murkiness like one of his negatives in a tank of developer.

Cheerleaders . . . Chain saws . . .

He reached for *GAN Notes #114.*

•

Buchanon awoke under the formica table in the film of dirt and beer on the cantina floor. Grabbing hold of one of the chrome legs he pulled himself into a sitting position. Instantly, he had his bearings. The blow to the head had—as so many had threatened—knocked some sense into him. The alcohol in his blood stream seemed to have evaporated, as if his body could not take the dual assault of concussion and intoxication. He had only to deal with the pressure balloon expanding and contracting ever so slightly inside his brain pan, a dull, even, nauseating respiration of pain. Still, he knew where he was, how he got there, and why his head hurt so bad. Looking around he quickly ascertained he was alone in the tavern. He even had the presence of mind to remember exactly what it was that had called him to Escuintla, what he still needed to get, what it was they were waiting for back in New York: his arm. In a desperate sort of way, as he wiped the caked blood from his neck and the back of his head, prospects appeared pretty simple: Find Akabal. That was all there was: Get the arm back to New York. It didn't really matter that he hadn't a clue as to how this might be accomplished. At that moment it was enough to know what to do, if not how to get it done. Purpose is a blessed thing when you're sitting in the malty residue of a thousand spilled beers watching a large yellow Guatemalan spider do its arpeggio parade over your pant leg. Purpose begets clarity, and clarity was something Buchanon was ready to embrace.

Eventually, he made it to his feet. A squadron of angry flies was buzzing overhead, making spastic sorties down toward a base-ball equipment bag that was lying on the table. Some were crawl-ing on it, on patrol along the zipper line, scouting for a way inside. Buchanon looked around, once and for all confirming he was alone.

The bag had been left for him. If there was any question about that, it was answered by the number 12 crudely stenciled on its side.

Buchanon approached with the caution of a minesweeper. He fingered the zipper delicately, flipping it back and forth like a switch, half expecting to trigger an explosion. A fly lit on his wrist. Another buzzed menacingly at his ear.

He ripped the zipper down the full length of the bag and spread it open.

Buchanon could not remember the last time he had cried. Not even when his mother died had he shed a tear. It was not his way. But now he sobbed, he trembled, he clawed at his hair and wailed like an old Italian woman at the funeral of a favorite niece. He stumbled back from the table, pushed by the horror through the godawful lavender door into the street. He threw up, he kicked clouds of dust into the night, he pounded his fists against the stucco walls. "God almighty, God almighty!" he cried with each blow until his voice grew hoarse and his knuckles bloodied. Then he ran out into the middle of the street and screamed, "Mago!" No one who heard that evil word echoing through the lanes and alleys of Escuintla could mistake that it carried a threat of death, and many crossed themselves because they knew the one who had voiced the threat was the one more likely to die.

At length Buchanon was able to calm himself. He forced himself back through the lavender door, meaning to do some "right thing," something appropriately respectful, reverent—although he had no idea what that might be. But the bag was already gone. The bag that contained his arm, cleanly severed at the shoulder, still in the sleeve of its pin-striped uniform, fingers still tightly curled around a baseball.

2

4 LAMAT   6 CUMKU

AT THE COMPLETION OF
12 BAKTUNS
18 KATUNS
8 TUNS
14 UINALS
8 KINS

the next day . . .

The blackness of the night was just beginning to weaken in the predawn skies over the small Guatemalan town of San Pedro Carchá. On a mountain slope east of the village, the young Quiché Indian standing at the mouth of a small cave noticed the slight dilution of the firmament from pitch to charcoal. Soon, he thought, the Great Abyss would show itself in the coming light: the canyons, the gorges, the treacherous descent of the high country—his ancestral home—to the hostile lowlands leading out to the sea. Like his distant Maya ancestors, Juan Guarcas Tol was short in stature, just a little over five feet tall. His nose was flat and broad, his lips full and sensuous—features which mirrored the ancient stone likenesses at Palenque and the murals at Bonampak. He had stood there all night in the thick bushes, motionless, even though he was dizzy from the sweet smell of the White Nun orchids that covered the hillside. His arms were outstretched as if crucified. A dark woven blanket stretched from hand to hand behind his back, forming a shield which blocked any light coming from within the cave. Below him, the mountain fell off steeply to a brief plateau which had been staked and subdivided by nylon lines into neat square plots. A narrow trench ran through the first three sections. As the sky lightened to deep slate, Juan saw the hand tools that lay scattered on the ground like dead men's weapons on a battlefield: picks, shovels, hammers, chisels, brushes of many shapes and sizes, sifters, small tweezers and probes, and many items he neither recognized nor could imagine a use for. He looked up to the ridge where the new guardians of Nim Xol, the Great Abyss, were stationed. The three pintos were grouped at the foot of a jack pine. Two were sitting, leaning against the truck —probably asleep, thought Juan. The third was groggily running through a manual of arms with his Galil in an effort to stave off fatigue. He hadn't noticed the creeping advance of the dawn. Juan reckoned there was still a bit of time left before the sun would reveal him.

Inside the cave, Manuel Xom Calel and his younger brother Luis were on their knees, side by side at the far end. Each held a flickering candle in one hand and dug into the hard earthen floor with the other, pressing into the clay with steady pressure, moving slowly back and forth, pushing in deeper with every pass. It was painstakingly slow, arduous work. They had been at it all night, making their way almost to the end of the forty-foot-long cleft. Behind them the ground had been meticulously churned and searched down to a depth of about fourteen inches. Their excavation was being conducted according to the old daykeeper's precise instructions, and as they dug they murmured homage to Jaguar Quitze, Jaguar Night and Mahucutah, the progenitors of the Quiché people, the lineages of the Cauec, Greathouse, Lord Quiché, Tam and Iloc.

Manuel's hand was beginning to encounter the rock wall that dished under the earthen floor at the back of the tiny cave. It occurred to him that perhaps the old daykeeper was wrong, that his vision had been false and that the object of their search would not be found. The palm of his hand scraped against something sharp. More rock, he thought—the end of their hunt. His buried hand stung; he knew it was bleeding. Undaunted, he continued his tilling. Again, as his hand probed over the same spot, it rasped against something jagged. The pain was more intense this time. It felt as if the sharpened nail of a subterranean finger had raked a furrow of flesh from his palm. Despite his efforts to ignore the pain, he winced. Luis noticed and stopped digging. His candle had guttered out. He crouched beside his older brother and put his hand on his shoulder.

"Manuel," he whispered, "the earth is empty."

"I thought so, too," Manuel answered, "but it takes my blood. That is a good sign."

"We are too close to Cobán—only eight kilometers. It has always been a place of evil for the Quiché people . . . where the lands drop off to the great eastern sea. The old ones call the river which runs through this region *Puhia.*"

"Pus water. I have heard them. But Puhia is also the name of the river that crosses the road to *Xibalba.*"

"The underworld. It is another bad omen."

They heard the muffled chirp of a ground squirrel followed quickly by the call of a *zopilote.* It was the prearranged signal from Juan. Luis blew out Manuel's candle. A moment later, Juan entered, the blanket wrapped around his aching shoulders. The pale gray light of dawn came in with him.

"We must leave immediately," Juan whispered. "Sneaking by the pintos at night was child's play, but getting by them in daylight will not be easy."

"Practicing *la costumbre* is always dangerous," Manuel teased, winking at his brother.

"Yes, and I would like to continue to *live* dangerously," Juan answered, hoping Manuel's penchant for taking foolish risks would not doom them.

Manuel nodded. Juan was good with words and he was right. Practicing *la costumbre*, the old ways, *was* dangerous. But the idea was to keep the old ways alive—and themselves. Nonetheless, Manuel kept digging.

"We must go now," Juan insisted.

Manuel looked up at him. His arm was buried up to the elbow. "There is something down there!" he said triumphantly, his eyes glowing with expectation.

"It is the rock, brother," chided Luis, "and your hope in old men's dreams."

"We must go," prodded Juan, looking nervously toward the mouth of the cave. The sunlight was brightening as the early dawn clouds began to burn off. The pintos could be heard stirring up on the ridge. "Manuel!"

Luis grabbed his brother and tried to pull him from his task, but the older, larger boy easily resisted his efforts.

"I have it!" Manuel announced.

Juan and Luis looked at him with disbelief. Each one knew there would be no way to convince him to leave until whatever he found was dug up. They crouched beside him and frantically clawed at the ground with their hands. As they burrowed down, a shaft of sunlight poked at them from a fissure in the cave ceiling. One of the pintos could be heard coughing outside, and there was the unmistakable sound of a man pissing on the leaf-matted ground.

"You see, it is just the rock!" Luis whispered angrily, the beam of light slicing a line of whiteness across his face.

The rough face of a small agate stone collected Manuel's blood in its many cracks and pits. Manuel strained to pull it from the hard clay in which it was embedded. Juan and Luis exchanged looks of exasperation and fear. Knowing there was no other way to get their comrade to leave, they once more began scraping away at the clay.

Finally, the stone came free from its resting place of a thousand years, making the *thup* sound of broken suction. Manuel turned it over in his bleeding hand. It was about the size of a playing card and the shape of a human heart. The side which was now revealed to the three Quiché boys was flat and engraved with the glyphs of the ancients. It was the object of their quest, the thing both foretold and foretelling. They stared at it with awe.

The pintos were very close now. The three teenagers could hear them joking. They were on the narrow trail that wound down from the ridge, over the roof of the cave and then cut back across its mouth. The beam of sunlight coming from the fissure flickered as the soldiers walked by up above. Within moments they would be on top of them.

Manuel felt his younger brother's hand clamp over his mouth. *How stupid does he think I am?* Manuel thought, angry at his brother's impertinence. *Does he really think I'd betray us by speaking?* He turned and scowled at Luis. The younger boy looked back with such an incomprehensible expression upon his face that Manuel instantly forgot his anger. There was the resolute look of age in his dark eyes, the look Manuel had seen in the eyes of the old ones, the look that comes with having seen unavoidable destiny. But there was also the unbounded wonder of youth in Luis's eyes, as if he were seeing things for the very first time. Manuel realized what was about to happen. He felt as if he had been buried alive, rendered helpless, suffocated. Horror, sadness and anger churned in the pit of his stomach. He shuddered, knowing that, indeed, Luis was trying to keep him quiet. But it was not some inadvertent utterance that Luis feared. Rather it was the inevitable protest already forming in Manuel's throat which Luis sought to stifle. Manuel saw the tears slowly pool in Luis's eyes and felt the press of a farewell in the warm hand which cupped his jaw.

As Luis pulled away, Manuel did try to protest, but Juan's muffling hand quickly replaced his brother's upon his mouth. Manuel reached out to stop Luis. Juan pinned him against the side of the cave, preventing him from interfering. Manuel saw his brother disappear through the opening.

There was a brief moment of stillness, those few ticking seconds of calm which are but the lit-fuse precursor to disaster. Then the false serenity was shattered as the first pinto saw Luis running down the slope toward the plateau. Manuel heard the burst of warning shots, then the ignored commands to halt followed by shouted curses and threats. He saw three dark shapes run past the mouth of the cave on their way after Luis. Immediately, Juan pushed him toward the opening. They burst into the daylight and quickly made their way undetected up the path which the pintos had just descended.

At the top of the ridge, Manuel pressed the heart-shaped stone to his chest as he looked back down the slope to see his brother for the last time. He saw Luis hurdling across the nylon ropes, stopping suddenly to pick up an abandoned shovel, making it look as if the tools were all he was after.

The pintos soon tired of the chase. All three fired at once. Three lines of stitched earth converged at Luis's feet. Sparks flew from the head of the shovel. There was the pinging sound of shells ricocheting off metal as the shovel sailed out of his hand. Luis collapsed and rolled onto his back. After a few moments he sat up. Manuel saw him looking at himself, checking to see where the bullets had entered, staring dully at the red blood-flowers which were slowly blooming on his linen clothes. Two of the pintos approached slowly as the other one tended to the ankle he had twisted on his dash down the slope.

Juan pulled Manuel from the crest of the ridge and into the cover of the forest. "Pray your brother is dead, Manuel!" he whispered through his own sobs.

Manuel clutched the ancient stone with one hand and the crucifix which hung from his neck with the other. The stone felt very heavy, as if its mass was directly related to its age or its power or the terrible price they had paid for it. The crucifix was light but sharp. So hard did he squeeze the metal Christ upon the ebony cross that his already injured hand began to bleed anew. He thought of the university student who came to his village many years ago and said that the Spaniards brought Christ to America in order to crucify the Indian. He remembered how the old ones had nodded and how surprised he had been when at the next ritual reading of the council book, the Daykeeper, as he had done in the past and continued to do presently, crossed himself and said an "Our Father" beforehand. And he was equally surprised—as well as a bit ashamed and angered—that he, himself, now chose to pray to the God of Christendom: "Let him be dead. By the *Santa Cruz* let him be dead."

The two Quiché boys turned east and clumsily plowed through the thick underbrush, hardly able to see through the tears in their eyes. After they had gone about a half a kilometer they heard a short report of gunfire echoing up from behind the ridge.

"Thank you," whispered Manuel.

•

It was a most unusual way for Barnie Schiff to start the editorial staff meeting. The others gathered around the large oak conference table eyed each other suspiciously. All present shared a seasoned wariness of anything other than the usual preface of insults and ridicule. But this morning he had said nothing. The silence was unnerving. A quiet Schiff was dangerous. It meant something was up. He was stalking. When he pounced, there would be no time to escape.

Savoring a Camel, Schiff leaned back in his chair and plunked his Guccis up on the table. As soon as he attained a position of sufficient recline, he fell into a coughing fit and had to spring forward to reach for a glass of water. Having doused the tobacco arson in his throat, he turned his attention to the newspapers spread out before him. It was the second time he had gone through them, page by page, evidently not finding whatever it was he was looking for and keeping everyone else on the edge of their seats.

Grace Collero, the photo editor, nervously fingered the huge red bauble dangling from her right ear. Matt watched her twist and turn the large crimson hoop, working off her anxieties and looking as if she were trying to fine-tune her auditory faculties, no doubt to hear the inevitable falling of the other shoe. Grace was a crusty old warhorse, going back almost to the beginning days of *H&T*. Lately she had become a favorite target of Schiff's criticism. Her health was failing and she was constantly going in for various surgeries. Parts were being removed at an alarming rate. She had undergone a hysterectomy, an appendectomy and a gall bladder operation all within the last two years. During the same period, the sheer poundage of costume jewelry she wore had increased almost in direct proportion to the amount of organ tissue she had lost to the surgeons. Matt could easily imagine two good-sized Amazonian parrots perched comfortably on the gargantuan hoops which were now suspended from her ears.

Izzy Greene, the managing editor, was the biggest five-foot-nine man Matt had ever encountered. He was almost entirely bald. His few remaining strands of jet-black hair were plastered across the full contour of his liver-spotted dome. His jowls were porcine in dimension and his full lips had the look of two rancid breakfast sausages. Universally despised by the entire staff, his obesity had earned him the nickname Jaba the Hut. Small frogs would mysteriously appear in his desk from time to time, a phenomenon which he never quite understood. Izzy was also the quintessential brown-nose. It was speculated that his proboscis was so far up Schiff's ass that if Izzy ever sneezed, the sheer force would rid Schiff of his troublesome hemorrhoids. When Izzy was nervous—as he was right now—he had a tendency to pick his nose. He had a certain covert approach to these excavations which was meant to disguise the deed. He'd lean back in his chair and loop his chubby right arm chimpanzee-fashion over his head so his hand drooped down about even with his left ear. When he was sure no one was watching, his little finger would sneak its way into his left nostril, meticulously clean the rim and then poke its way in past the first knuckle for some serious reaming. Matt glanced at him and caught him in the act. Izzy immediately extracted his finger but gave no sign of embarrassment. He had reached such a plateau of grossness that embarrassment had become a redundant concept.

Matt shifted his attention to Marlene Browne. More precisely, he shifted his attention to the considerable cleavage spilling out of her all but unbuttoned linen shirt. Like Matt, Marlene was a senior staff reporter. Unlike Matt, she wasn't very good at her job. Many of her stories were kept in a gray banker's box on top of a file cabinet in the editorial department. They were there to serve as illustrative aides when Schiff felt the need to challenge anyone's writing ability. Schiff liked to reach in, pull a page out at random and mercilessly dissect it for the benefit of some young rookie who feared his own work might some day be so ridiculed. Marlene gave very little indication these episodes caused her any grief. All in all, she was considered a pretty good sport, and what she lacked in grammar and syntax she more than made up for in dedication. She worked long hours and never complained about an assignment. She seemed to understand she was kept around strictly because of her looks, which were nothing short of sensational. For male staffers, ogling Marlene was one of the few fringe benefits of laboring at *H&T*. She never disappointed. Painted-on jeans and thin cotton tank-tops were her usual apparel on routine days, but for special occasions or important assignments, she'd switch to tight skirts which invariably were slit, as Matt once commented, to well above the Mason-Dixon line. Matt's fondness for Marlene went beyond his appreciation of what Schiff often called "the best legs in the business." Matt understood that Marlene dressed the way she did out of some cockeyed sense of reciprocity, as if it was a requirement of employment. Ironically, given her lack of writing talent, it probably was. Nonetheless, she was no pushover. It was generally known she had refused many "command performance" invitations to Schiff's condo. Matt respected her for that. His only misgiving about Marlene was her hysterical vulnerability to Schiff's personal jibes. While she was completely immune to Schiff's mockery of her writing, a slight to her coiffure, her makeup or her wardrobe devastated her. These were her assets, her contribution. While other reporters checked and rechecked their copy prior to deadline, she checked and rechecked her mascara. Matt watched as she slipped the compact from her briefcase. He had seen her go through the entire makeup routine just prior to the staff meeting: the pads, the pencils, the brushes and the rest of the paraphernalia. But Schiff's strange behavior had unsettled her. She was searching in the tiny mirror for flaws.

Matt scanned across the rest of the nervous group gathered around the table: Larry Cruthers, the other senior staff writer, was fidgeting with his glasses, adjusting the templates, blowing on the lenses, wiping them endlessly with a handkerchief that looked as if it had been used to clean a dipstick; Nadine Sills, Schiff's secretary, nibbled hamster-like on the eraser end of a Faber Castell #2; Beverly O'Malley from layout was popping Tic-Tacs nonstop; Cal Horton, the copy editor, whittled away at the point on his blue editing pencil, letting the shavings fall into an ashtray. All of them flinched when Schiff broke the tense silence.

"Last night I was forced to change the press run," Schiff announced solemnly. The comment sired a new round of seat-squirming and brow-blotting. "This is not something I do casually. Usually, I only undertake such radical action when one of you has fucked up so bad that my attorneys—may they all get the clap —tell me we have committed some heinous libel which is absolutely, positively, no-doubt-about-it going to cost me major dollars. It is an expensive enterprise. It tends to piss off the printer who is not a cheerful man to begin with. It is something that is done when there is nothing else to be done. It is the last resort."

Beverly O'Malley, positive she was the guilty party, choked on a handful of Tic-Tacs. Schiff had criticized the color she recommended for the border on the new "Randall's Remedies" feature, a compendium of non-conventional medical news briefs: megavitamin cancer cures, miracle hair restorers and the like. The color was a dark, nondescript blue-gray—a good, "serious" color, Beverly had thought. "What the fuck color is this?" Schiff had demanded. "Pantone 534," she responded. "Ten parts green to six parts rubine red," she added for clarity. "It's ten parts blah and six parts your ass if you don't get me a color I can recognize on sight!" Schiff retorted. "This color is not found in nature, Beverly. Lose it!" And Beverly had, but only to the extent that she changed the shade to #532, which through the addition of another four parts of black, appeared ever so slightly darker, and thus, she thought, more obviously recognizable as gray. Schiff had not been available to approve the change before deadline. She feared #532 had doomed the press run—and her career.

Matt, who was sitting next to Beverly, patted her on the back. After a moment, the Tic-Tacs in her windpipe dissolved and she was able to catch her breath. She whispered, "I'm sorry," and stared down at her lap.

Schiff continued, not hiding his impatience at having to wait for Beverly's trachea to clear. "Last night, at tremendous expense, I completely re-did the front page."

Beverly sighed in relief; the front page contained no #532. Larry Cruthers almost snapped the template off his tinted aviator glasses. He had done the lead story on the first page.

"Mr. Teller over there took a definite career risk in order to bring to my attention a story he had quite literally stumbled upon —which is only to say that he is as dumb as he looks."

All eyes went to Matt. Respiration returned to normal. Postures relaxed around the table. Izzy Greene, who had no love for Matt, grinned from ear to pudgy ear.

"The prodigal returneth. Today we welcome back shunned Matthew to the ranks of the living," Schiff said dramatically as Izzy's smile sagged and sunk in the folds of his face. "He was lost and now he is found. He was dead and now he is alive. He was fucked and now he's unfucked. From this moment he is repatriated from his exile on the Goat Patrol. Those unique responsibilities will revert back to the previous keeper of the fauna flame."

Matt shrugged and looked sympathetically across the table toward Marlene. Having been the prior occupant of the Amazing Pet Stories desk, she had just been handed a demotion of sorts. She smiled vacantly at Matt. Apparently she didn't mind.

"I am one happy camper," chuckled Schiff as he raised the proof copy of the new first page. Then he passed it around for all to admire. Everyone made appropriately complimentary comments.

"But this is not the essence of the moment, boys and girls. I have here before me the *El Centro Valley Imperial Press,* the *Brawley News,* the *Indio News,* the *Palm Springs Desert Sun* and the *San Diego Union.* And not one of these fine and proper practitioners of the fourth estate has a single line of coverage on our desert stiff. Not a blurb, not a picture, not a death notice, not an obituary, not a police call report, not a fucking nothing."

He threw the hefty pile of newspapers onto the center of the table.

"And here in my hands I have the goddamn high-and-fucking-mighty Los Angeles *Times.* And you know what? They ain't got the story either. Do you know what that means, children? It means one of two things. Either our friend Matthew has faked the whole mess or our humble little weekly is about to scoop those bastards on a real, actual, authentic chunk of hard news. The former I rule out because the concerned party doesn't have the testicles to pull off such a thing. The latter . . . the latter doesn't really mean much, I suppose. Most would say it's a trite and petty thing to gloat over. But since it is to the trite and the petty that I owe my fortune, indeed shall I gloat. I shall smoke a large Cuban panatela. I shall partake of beluga caviar. I shall sip bubbly from the vineyards of Dom Pérignon. I shall fuck vestal virgins in my dreams and whatever I can get between my sheets. I shall be unbounded in my joy and I shall give thanks to reporter Matthew, who has gone where no *Times* fucker has gone before."

Schiff stood up.

"I salute you, young Matt."

"Don't you think it's strange that no one picked it up?" Matt asked, skeptical at their good fortune.

"Do not piss on my parade, young Matt. Let's not forget it was you who first speculated this could happen."

"The *Times*. I could see the *Times* missing it. But I thought one of the locals would get it."

"Well they didn't," Schiff replied, starting to get irritated.

"Then the *Times* would pick it up tomorrow," Matt reasoned. "We're out tomorrow with better coverage, so we still look good, because we're not supposed to have it in the first place."

"What the fuck is wrong with you?" Schiff bellowed, walking toward the door. "Nobody's got it but us. You come fuckus interruptus to my house in the middle of the night and convince me to print this and now you're having kittens. Can't you take success, goddamn it? You want back with the fleas and ticks? When I first got in this business I did a story on a heifer that had a spot the shape of Abraham Lincoln's profile on its ass. You want that?"

Schiff ripped the door open and screamed for Pete Nolan, the sales manager. Nolan answered the summons within seconds.

"I want tomorrow's edition in every store within a square mile of the *Times* building," Schiff commanded. "At least a gross in every store. Understand?"

"Sure Barnie, but—"

"Who's our rep over there?"

"Ted Van Der Hode."

"Ted? Shit! He couldn't sell pussy on a troop train. Put someone over there who's at least breathing hard."

"Jeez Barnie, I don't know if we can open that many new accounts so fast."

"Then give the fuckers away. Even numbnuts Van Der Hode should be able to handle that."

"Why around the *Times?*"

It was a stupid question. Nolan regretted having asked it. There wasn't a person in the room who didn't know the answer. As Schiff stormed out of the room, pushing Nolan out of the doorway, the publisher said what everyone already knew: "Because I am the most vindictive son-of-a-bitch who ever sucked air."

•

Deputy Jess Chamberlain was not having a good day.

His wife was still pissed at him from the prior Saturday when he had hugged and kissed Dottie Montalbano after their team had won the Imperial County Police Association's bowling tournament. All attempts to explain the incident as nothing more than a spontaneous victory celebration had fallen on deaf ears. She hadn't talked to him since. Nor had she cooked, cleaned or slept in the same bed with him. As a result, he arrived at work hungry, horny and in a dirty, wrinkled uniform.

His first assignment of the day was to transport three teenaged drunk-and-disorderly's from the sub-station at Calipatria to the courthouse at Brawley. One of the D&D's puked all over the backseat of his patrol car. Chamberlain spent the better part of the morning cleaning up the punk's mess. The temperature was 102° and the smell was enough to make a rhinoceros faint.

Chamberlain's second assignment appeared to be no improvement. His sergeant ordered him to escort a reporter out to a desolate spot called Coombe's Ditch way the hell out on Double-G in the middle of the goddamn desert. On the evolutionary scale, Chamberlain ranked reporters, in general, somewhat lower than toadstools and only a tad higher than common bread mold.

But definitely somewhere within the family of fungi. A reporter from Los Angeles, no less than one from such a trashy piece of crap as *Here and There,* represented a subspecies which he classified lower still, even under such malignant life forms as defense attorneys and New York liberals. There was very little else humanoid which he would place lower—faggots, maybe; feminists, for sure.

Jess Chamberlain was having a rotten day.

Matt was not exactly thrilled with the way his day was going either. An argument with Schiff had followed the staff meeting. Only after lengthy debate had the publisher allowed him to return to the scene of the crime. It had taken him three hours to get there, only to find no trace of the body. Then he had made the long drive to the sheriff's office in Brawley. His inquiries were met first with indifference and then with outright skepticism. No one knew anything about a mutilated corpse out at Coombe's Ditch. After many spins around the bureaucratic merry-go-round, Matt was finally able to persuade the ranking cop to send out a deputy with him. Then, there was the long ride in a very bad-smelling police car with a Neanderthal type in a wrinkled shirt who ignored his questions and munched constantly on large Jonathan apples plucked from a brown bag on the front seat.

When they reached Coombe's Ditch, Matt got out of the car and walked to the spot where the cot had been.

"This is where the body was," he told Deputy Chamberlain.

"What body?" the peace officer asked between bites of his fifth Jonathan.

"The body I've been telling you about for the last half hour, which is the same body I told your sergeant about for a half hour before that, which is the same body I called in to your office last night. That body," Matt answered pointedly.

"Well I don't see it."

Matt caught himself and did not say the first thing which came to mind. It was not wise to call a six-foot-two-inch man with limited capacity for humor a stupid son-of-a-bitch. It was even less wise if the man was a cop and had a large Smith & Wesson strapped to his leg. "Don't you think that's odd?" Matt asked instead.

"What?"

"That a fucking dead body just up and disappears."

"Not if it wasn't there in the first place."

"Are you saying I'm lying?" Matt asked, imbuing the question with the most plaintive, incredulous quality he could muster.

"I'm saying you guys would do just about anything to sell newspapers." Chamberlain leaned back against the front fender of the car. He had the Jonathan down to a slender core, but he kept at it, taking small bites, turning it in his hand to get at every tiny morsel.

"Then tell me how I did this," Matt demanded.

He ripped the photos out of a manila envelope and handed them to Chamberlain. The deputy looked at them casually, as one might browse through a neighbor's vacation snapshots. Even the one that showed the Coombe's Ditch signpost clearly in the background did not draw a response. He handed them back to Matt and shrugged.

"Nobody reported a body out here?" Matt inquired.

"I thought you said you did," Chamberlain replied acidly.

"Besides me," Matt snapped.

"Not that I'm aware of."

Matt took out a pen and a small notebook from his back pocket. Answers tended to improve when one realized they were being recorded for future reference.

"How about missing person reports?"

"Sure. Get 'em everyday."

"Something that matches this guy?" Matt held up one of the pictures.

"We got nothin' that matches that mess."

"How about before it was a mess. Look at the face—what's left of it."

Chamberlain sighed and took the pictures back into his hand. He gave the first one a closer inspection than he had before.

"Look, we got lots of active missing person cases," the deputy said tiredly, "but this don't jump out at me. Most of our cases are juveniles. Or wives running out on husbands or the other way around. We get reports from migrants too. Lots of farms in the valley. By the time we run down a lead, the person who filed the report is gone. A missing person who's gone over forty-eight hours has about a zero chance of being found. That's just the way it is."

"Can we compare whatever you've got in descriptions against these pictures?"

"No."

"Why not?"

"There's nothing to compare. There's no case. There's no body."

Matt snatched the photo out of Chamberlain's hand and stuffed it back into the envelope with the others. He walked out to the edge of the road where it overlooked the wash. For a moment he stared at the notched rock formation in the distance.

"What's that called?" he asked.

"They're called rocks," answered Chamberlain gruffly.

"Thank you. Does it have a name?"

"No. Not that I've heard."

The formation looked different than it had last night. A third finger of granite now filled the cleft between the first two peaks. Matt remembered how the cot had aligned perfectly with the star that he had seen clearly at the base of the notch. From his present location he would not have been able to see the star; it would have been blocked from view. Matt drifted slowly to his right and the third promontory slid behind the right peak. He moved further and it reappeared on the right side of the formation. Slowly he backtracked to the precise spot that duplicated the view he remembered. He checked the location of the signpost, the only other orienting landmark. Then he spun back toward Chamberlain and pointed to the center of the road.

"There *was* a body," he insisted. "Right there."

"Yeah."

"There's got to be blood, tissue, hair, something left," Matt speculated.

Chamberlain laughed. "You don't know the desert, do you?" he asked, moving away from the car toward Matt. He gestured with the apple core. "Looks like there's nothing around here, right? Just rocks and scrub. It's so damn hot out here in the basin all that'll grow is creosote and burro-weed. Cactus can't even cut it out here. But if I toss this core out on the road, there won't be a trace left within an hour after we leave. Something will eat it. Nothing gets wasted out here. The birds will come if nothing else. And they won't leave a trace behind. Not a scrap. Not a seed. Nothing."

Matt considered the information. It was Chamberlain's turf, after all. Then he pictured in his mind the gruesome scene he had encountered less than twenty-four hours ago.

"The birds didn't eat that cot," Matt said after some deliberation.

"Fine. Good. You want to file a report?" Chamberlain was thoroughly exasperated. He threw the apple core into the rocks and headed back toward the car.

"I want to look around. This guy had a lot of parts gone. Maybe the birdies weren't all that hungry this morning. Okay?"

"Knock yourself out. I'll be in the car."

Matt started down the incline into the wash. "Watch out for rattlers," Chamberlain called out over his shoulder. "Fuck you," Matt answered under his breath.

There was nothing to be seen in Coombe's Ditch but rocks and sand. Things unseen were a different matter, and Matt feared Chamberlain's caution might come to life at any moment. Nonetheless, Matt forced himself to climb down to the spot where he estimated the cot had landed after he hit it with the Mazda. The small shelf of boulders sat below the roadbed but just above the depression of the wash. He tried to walk across the tops of the largest rocks but he slipped off, creating a small avalanche of fist-sized stones which slid into the wash. A cloud of dust rose up, hiding from view any slithering live things that might be lurking about his feet. He scampered back up onto the nearest large boulder and contemplated his next move.

The intense heat reflecting off the desert floor seemed to be focused directly on him. It was hard to breathe, as if all the oxygen had been burned out of the air. He couldn't focus his eyes. It was like looking through isinglass. Everything was shimmering brightness, flat wavy planes superimposing without resolution. The relative distance of an object was incalculable. There was no horizon.

Matt could not imagine a more hostile place. When he heard the police car's ignition engage he feared Chamberlain was intending to abandon him. He struggled back up the incline and saw that the deputy was still there, slouched in the front seat, his hat shaded down over his eyes, evidently quite comfortable in the air conditioning.

Matt turned back toward the wash. Out of the corner of his eye he thought he saw something narrow and thin slide into a nearby crevice. Maybe Schiff *was* right, he thought—leave well enough alone. He decided he had seen enough and headed for the car.

•

Braxton Wells was a community only in the sense that it's three hundred or so scattered residents shared the same zip code. It existed, unincorporated, without so much as a signpost, in a pie-shaped valley nestled in the San Bernardino foothills between Banning and Cobazon just north of Interstate 10. It was a place not easily found. There was not even much cause to pass through on the way elsewhere. Only one road, Lomax Lane, led to the place. Occasional strangers who wandered through by virtue of having made the wrong turn for either the Indian Bingo Parlor or the Pit Family Date Market (both of which were located further east along the interstate) usually passed entirely through the community without noticing it. They'd follow the narrow winding road through terrain that gradually progressed from low desert to grassy chaparral until it dead-ended at the south border of the Morongo Indian Reservation. There they'd turn around at the end of the road, at the top of the highest hill, in the crushed stone driveway of the Church of the Word.

The church building itself looked very little like a house of worship and very much like a VFW hall, which is precisely what it previously had been. When the Veterans of Foreign Wars abandoned the premises for a bigger, more accessible facility in Palm Springs, residents of the area had figured the structure would remain empty. They had been surprised when a young couple from Michigan had bought the place. They had been even more surprised to learn that the young man was a preacher and that he intended to convert the building, which had housed its share of smokers and poker games, into a church. The story went around that a denomination back east had financed the acquisition and renovation in hopes of converting the local Indian population. But the Morongos already had a Catholic and a Moravian church within the confines of the reservation, and it was considered unlikely they'd be interested in a third theology. Neither was it thought the young preacher would draw many souls into his flock from the valley—not that anyone had yet noticed him trying. The inhabitants of Braxton Wells—or at least those inclined toward regular Sunday worship—were affiliated with various churches in nearby Banning. None of them felt a spiritual yearning strong enough to venture up the hill to the new church.

Six days out of seven, the sounds of pounding hammers and buzzing power saws could be heard drifting down through the pinyon pines and juniper from the new church. Today the hilltop had been quiet. The calm should have alerted those down in the valley that something was afoot at the end of the road, but it didn't. Curiosity and acceptance tended to blend smoothly in Braxton Wells. If there was a keen eye for the new, there was also a tolerance for it. There was scant opportunity for gossip over backyard fences—which tended to be barbed wire; or on street corners—which didn't exist. The residents of Braxton Wells, for the most part, lived in small houses or trailers far removed from each other. They were a community of loners; privacy was held almost sacred. They had taken note of the preacher and his wife. In their own way, unmet, without greetings or handshakes or so much as a "Hello," they had accepted them as neighbors. If on this one afternoon the new couple had uncharacteristically decided to put down their hammers and saws, it was their business. The interlude was noted, but not noteworthy.

Rebecca Miles carried a chiffon cake up what she and her husband had been calling "the cellar stairs." The lower floor of the church building was not really a cellar. Basements did not exist in that part of California; the sandy soil did not permit them. The structure had been built on the hillside, and a lower level had been incorporated under the back half of the church, where the grade sloped down sharply. But to Rebecca and her husband, Nathan, both raised in the Midwest, the lower level was a cellar, even though none of it was actually below ground level. The idea was further reinforced by the high placement of the windows in the "cellar" and the absence of an exterior door. The only way in and out was via the stairs that led to the side vestibule.

At the top of the wooden stairs, Rebecca balanced the cake with one hand and opened the door which blocked her way. There was no landing and the door opened inward. She had a precarious moment as she leaned back, juggled the cake and swung the door toward her. She wished Nathan had reversed the hinges, making the door open the other way, but there just hadn't been time. She went through, entered the tiny vestibule, made a quick right-angle turn and then pushed her way through the second door which led out to the small parking lot. Their blue-and-white Ford pickup was parked about twenty feet away. Next to it, partially in the shade that it afforded, was a card table on which she had placed a bowl of fruit, a pitcher of lemonade, some dishes, a stack of paper cups and a pyramid of knives and forks, each pair of utensils neatly wrapped in a napkin. She carried the cake over to the table and set it down.

Nathan was up on the road, his hand shaded over his eyes as he peered down the hillside with the intensity of a setter at point. Rebecca watched him, sensing his excitement and wishing she could share it. He looked so tall, she thought, up there at the top of the hill with just the limitless blue of the sky behind him. That he *was* tall, so very tall and skinny that his old friends back in Flint called him Stick, did not temper her observation that with the help of the hill and sky he *appeared* tall. She saw his hands go to his hips, assuming a posture of impatience. Then he paced back and forth across the road with that funny step he had when he was bursting with anticipation, like a man on stilts. It was the step she imagined he'd employ in the waiting room when she gave birth to their first child, who was planned but not yet conceived.

Rebecca twisted the side mirror of the pickup and looked at herself. There was no makeup to check or fancy hairstyle to adjust, only a few reassuring moments of staring without any apparent purpose. It was something she found herself doing more and more lately, these stolen little peaks in the glass. At first it had caused her some guilt, the act seeming so vain. But now the forays into the mirror had become almost routine and she had ceased to judge; every now and then she treated herself to a quick look, a check, a glance at that distant creature with the long, straight blond hair and blue eyes, the high cheeked-boned, oval face so much tanner now than it had ever been, the pronounced lower lip, the dimpled smile—when it would come.

"They're here!" Nathan called out. Rebecca readjusted the mirror and turned toward the road. Nathan was trotting down the drive toward her. The short run and the heat had him panting by the time he reached the table. He took both of Rebecca's hands into his own and asked, "Are you ready?"

"I don't know," she answered nervously. "I think so."

"I want to know what you feel in your heart," he said urgently, taking a quick glance over his shoulder back toward the road. "If you feel it so, you'll be so."

"Nathan," she said sternly. She didn't like it when he quoted lines from old sermons to her. "Not now."

"It's important," he insisted, his voice laced with urgency. "What do you feel? Good beginnings are the key. A good start makes for the right finish."

"Oh Nathan, please."

"I'm sorry, Rebecca. I miss preaching so much." He gave her hands a squeeze.

"I know."

"But it's important. I've dragged you out here and the good Lord knows you've never complained. You've worked like a mule and done everything I've asked and more. But if your heart is not in this, all our good work will be in vain. I must know how you feel."

Rebecca sighed and looked away from him.

"Please," he pleaded, gently shaking her hands.

"I feel we're not ready," she answered reluctantly. "I feel we should have fixed the cellar door. I feel we should have completed the partitions in the—"

"No, no, no!" he cried, breaking away. He walked around the table with his hands pressed against his temples. "That's what you're *thinking*. I'm not interested in that."

"I know," Rebecca heard herself saying.

"That's not important. I want the voice of your heart. I want . . ."

His voice trailed off as he turned his attention to the red U-Haul truck which was rising into view, straining to gain the crest of the hill. The truck went slightly past their drive, stopped, and then, after grinding into a reluctant gear, began to back in.

"They're here, Rebecca!" he said excitedly, watching the approach of the truck. "This is what we've worked for! What is in your heart?"

"Fear," she answered softly, her eyes downcast.

He spun toward her. "We do His work. There is nothing to fear."

"We do His work. There is everything to fear," she clarified, letting her eyes meet his.

They heard the sharp squeal of brakes as the U-Haul came to a stop. Rebecca took a deep, fortifying breath, picked up the bowl of fruit and cradled it with one arm. "We have guests," she told her husband as she walked toward the truck.

Nathan stood there a moment, deeply disturbed by his wife's words. "Dear Father," he whispered, "grant Rebecca that which she needs through your Son, our Lord Jesus Christ. Amen." Then he followed her, jogging to catch up.

Two men had climbed down from the cab. The passenger had circled around the front of the vehicle to join the driver at his door. They said a few words to each other before approaching Nathan and Rebecca. The driver extended his hand and said, "You must be Nathan. We've spoken on the phone. I'm Gregory."

"Glad to meet you at last," Nathan said cordially as he shook the man's hand. The grip was firm and the skin felt rough. A worker's hand, thought Nathan. Another laborer in God's vineyard. "Rebecca, this is Father Townes. I've told you so much about him," Nathan said to his wife.

"We welcome you to our home, Father Townes," she said. She didn't offer her hand. She wanted to and knew that etiquette allowed her the initiative, but felt uncomfortable about being so forward with a man, even if this one was a priest—not that he looked it, young and handsome as he was, deeply tanned and dressed in a polo shirt and khaki shorts. She didn't quite know what to do when he reached out and gave her a hug. Her arm tightened about the fruit bowl. Nonetheless, a peach spilled out onto the drive.

"Us Maryknolls aren't too formal," said Townes. "Out in the bush, the first thing we lose is our titles. Then our last names go. Please call me Gregory." He bent down to retrieve the peach. He wiped it against his shirt and took a bite. "This is Pastor Vail," he continued, introducing his passenger.

Vail nodded to them and mumbled a "hello." He fumbled

with a package of LifeSavers, spilled a couple, popped a few more into his mouth, and then, almost as an afterthought, offered some to the others. Everyone politely declined. It appeared all were waiting for something substantial to be said, when Vail's eyes fell upon the pitcher of lemonade on the table. "Could I have some of that?" he asked.

"I'll pour you some," Nathan offered.

Townes grabbed Nathan by the arm before he could tend to the lemonade. "Patrick doesn't mind helping himself," the priest said.

"Not at all," Vail agreed. He headed for the table, seemingly anxious to get away, at least for the moment.

Rebecca still felt the obligation of hospitality. "I'll get it," she said taking a step toward the table.

Townes looped his free arm around her shoulder, corralling her as well. The half-eaten peach was still in his hand. It dripped on her sleeve as he led them back toward the truck. At his prodding they all took a seat on the rear bumper.

"Have you done any missionary work?" he asked.

"No," Nathan answered after some hesitation, wondering where the priest was headed with his inquiry.

After a few moments of silence Rebecca realized Townes was waiting for her to answer as well.

"We sort of consider this to be field work," she replied.

"Yes, I can see that, Rebecca," Townes agreed. "The work is similar, but the place is still home."

"Rebecca doesn't mean to compare our effort here to your work in the foreign missions, Father," Nathan clarified.

"Oh I think she does, Nathan, and the point is well taken. I merely specify that there is there and . . . well . . . here is here. But I suppose that's obvious."

"That is obvious, Gregory," Rebecca said quickly, before Nathan could respond. "But what you're trying to say is not."

Townes nodded. "What I am trying to say," he went on, "is that when you are in a strange place and you have lost your titles and your family name, your home, your past and everything else that you have ever cherished, the next thing that will go is manners."

Townes pushed himself off the bumper and knocked twice on the tailgate door. The priest smiled at Rebecca and motioned for her and Nathan to get off the bumper. Then he knocked once more. Immediately, the overhead door began to roll upward. Nathan took Rebecca's hand. They drifted back toward the table, where Vail was holding an empty cup and staring apprehensively into the black maw of the truck.

A young couple stepped out on to the motorized lift-gate, squinting into the bright sunlight. A young child, whom Rebecca judged to be no more than one year old, was in the woman's arms. The man held a large white laundry sack over his shoulder. When they were situated, Townes pushed the lever that caused the lift-gate to descend. As it lurched into motion, the baby, who had been sleeping, began to cry.

"How's your Spanish coming?" Townes asked over the whine of the lift-gate motor.

"Poco a poco," Nathan answered.

"There hasn't been much time to study," Rebecca added.

"Well, you'll find nobody really wants to talk that much anyway," Townes remarked as the lift clunked onto the stone surface of the drive. The priest motioned for the couple to approach Nathan and Rebecca. They did so hesitantly.

Rebecca held out the bowl of fruit, but the man and the woman bashfully declined, their eyes downcast. The woman rocked the baby in her arms as the man hummed and dangled a scrap of red cloth in front of the child's eyes in an effort to comfort him. Man, woman and child—together they presented such a model picture of familial bliss that Rebecca felt warmed in their company, refreshed, renewed in the human spirit. She felt better about what they were trying to accomplish. She found herself looking into her husband's eyes, smiling at him and hoping he was imagining, as she was, how they might look when a child blessed their union.

"We call them Sergio and Yolanda," Townes said as he reversed the lever, making the lift go back up. "They have very little English. The boy is Sebastian.

"Sergio's wife disappeared one night after she left her history class at the university. Word is they raped her for six months before they got tired of her. Yolanda's husband died in a fire. They say he was a rebel. She says he was a union steward. Nobody knows the boy's story. Just found him in an alley. They make a nice family, don't they? I've been meaning to marry them up. Maybe you could do the honors."

"Certainly . . . of course," Nathan stammered.

Rebecca felt the bowl slipping from her grip. She wrapped her other arm around it, hugging it tight against her belly. There was a terrible, hollow feeling in the pit of her stomach, a spasm of emptiness, a longing for something that had been brutally ripped away. Her throat was tight; breathing was an effort. She struggled not to let the shock rise up onto her face. She choked it back, forced it down, swallowed it whole. She focused on Townes, trying to fathom why he chose to be so cavalier. From the corner of her eye, she saw Sergio and Yolanda walking toward the side door, as if they already knew the way.

The lift-gate had not completed its ascent when a man leapt down from the truck. A laundry sack came tumbling to the ground behind him, evidently kicked out by someone still inside.

The man ignored it. He was short and wiry. A crooked part divided his hair into two greasy wings which flopped down on either side of his head. The blood vessels of his arms protruded to such an extent they looked external to his flesh. To Rebecca they appeared to be a mesh of blue cords binding him together.

"Soto. You are always so impatient," Townes remarked. "Haven't you heard that all comes to he who waits?"

"Fuck you, *chingado* priest," Soto cursed. Then he spit in the general direction of Townes.

"Yes. Our friend Soto here has managed to pick up the essentials of the English language," Townes commented, completely unflustered. "I would imagine communication will not prove too difficult at all."

Soto took in his surroundings with quick, birdlike jerks of his head. When his eyes fell upon Rebecca, an evil smile took root, growing weedlike into an obscene leer. He started toward her.

"Soto has had some disagreements with the law enforcement establishment in his homeland," Townes added. "But he assures us he is fully rehabilitated."

Rebecca stood grounded in place as Soto approached. She had not yet come to grips with the tragic stories of the first three visitors, and already that concern was being forced from her mind. She struggled to find the strength to confront this new menace, this vile creature who approached. *A child of God,* she reminded herself, but it did little to calm her fears. She looked to Townes for help but he was busy tending to the lift, which had jammed. Soto was only two paces away.

Suddenly, Nathan stepped into the breech between them and said, "I bid you peace, brother." The words brought Soto to a standstill. He stared at Nathan as if the young preacher were some never-before-encountered circus amusement. Rebecca sucked in air, thankful for the momentary reprieve and amazed it had come at her husband's hand. Townes stopped monkeying with the lift and watched the confrontation with an interest balanced between outright fascination and professional curiosity. Pastor Vail quietly returned the knife—which he didn't remember picking up—to its place beside the cake plate on the table. A thin melody of cynical laughter echoed from the cavern of the truck, quick and cutting like a raven's song in a dark canyon.

Nathan was not sure just how to press his advantage. The man seemed totally immobilized and Nathan felt it his responsibility to once more put back into motion—hopefully now on a benign course—that which he had stopped. He made a grand gesture with his arm back toward Rebecca and said, *"Fruta."*

The word brought back the leer to Soto's face. He closed the gap between Nathan and Rebecca and fell to his knees at her feet. His hands rose from the ground like the heads of two charmed cobras, tracing in the air the outline of her legs and hips but without actually touching her. They slithered up on each side of the fruit bowl and took hold. For the first time Rebecca noticed the man had no thumbs.

"¡Basta!" Townes shouted.

Soto rose, took the bowl and walked away with it toward the vestibule door.

"I told you about manners," Townes remarked, turning his attention back to the lift which, with the help of a kick, once more began its upward movement.

"Thank you, Nathan," Rebecca said softly.

He didn't seem to hear. He had the look of a man who, having attained his lifelong dream, realizes it a nightmare.

Four more people rode down on the lift. An immense, middle-aged man stood at the left side. His tattooed arms were crossed over his chest. The white line of a scar cut across his forehead, disappeared under an eye patch, reappeared on his cheek and sliced all the way back to his ear. A woman stood next to him. Her black hair was pulled back tight to her head. Wrap-around sunglasses all but covered her entire face. A younger man —twentyish and quite handsome, thought Rebecca—stood at the right side, supporting a frail old man in a large straw hat. Four bundled laundry sacks descended with them.

"This is Coh," Townes said, nodding toward the big man with the patch. "It's a name of his own choosing. It's an Indian word. Right, Flynn?"

"My name is Pablo," the younger man replied bitterly. "Do not call me Flynn."

"But you look so much like a young Errol Flynn. Oh well, humor me. Coh *is* an Indian word, is it not?"

"It's Quiché for puma," Pablo answered reluctantly.

"Yes. Appropriate. Even if Coh is not Quiché."

Just before the lift touched down, Coh hopped off. He reached back to take the four laundry sacks, but the woman grabbed hold of one. Coh did not contest the issue and walked off toward the vestibule with three sacks slung over his meaty shoulders. He did not bother to pick up Soto's, which still lay in the stones.

"You'll find that Cristina is quite independent," Townes remarked as the woman stepped off the lift, dragging the heavy sack behind her. "I suspect she understands more English than she lets on. Same goes for Coh."

The old man stood trembling on the lift. He was reluctant to step off.

"On the other hand," the priest continued, "dear old Abraham here does not speak a word of English, and young Pablo, our scholar who insists on keeping his real name, speaks it perhaps better than any of us."

Rebecca went over to help with Abraham. He appeared so

frail and afraid. When he saw her, his eyes brightened and he took a wobbly step toward her.

"*¿Nieta!*" he said. "*¿Dónde estabas?*"

"*Ella no es su nieta,*" Townes said.

"*María,*" Abraham called out in a shaky voice.

"*Muerta,*" the priest replied. "*María está muerta.*"

"*Rosa Estela,*" the old man cried out plaintively, reaching a hand toward Rebecca's face.

"*Muerta,*" Townes repeated.

"*Florentina.*"

"*Muerta.*"

"*Isabela.*"

"*Muerta.*"

"*Magdalena.*"

"*Muerta. Todas muerta.*"

Abraham shook his head, as if what he had heard were not possible. His hand caressed Rebecca's face, gently squeezing, almost as if he were trying to mold it into a different form.

"*Abuelito,*" Rebecca said softly, holding his hand still against her cheek. Her own grandfathers had died when she was a young child. She barely remembered them. She didn't think they'd mind that she called this poor, confused old man "Grandpa."

Abraham smiled, gazed affectionately into her eyes and began to nod. But then his face clouded over, shadowed in a brief, passing squall of lucidity. "*No, no,*" he murmured. He patted Rebecca thankfully on the shoulder and then let Pablo lead him away.

Townes closed up the truck.

"We must try to do more for the *campesinos,*" he said. "We tend to focus our efforts on the townsfolk when there are so many, many more out in the country like poor old Abraham."

"He's lost so much," Rebecca offered sympathetically.

"They all have," Townes said.

"We were expecting twelve," Nathan interjected.

"Change in plans," Townes replied curtly. "The rest won't be coming."

The priest headed for the card table.

"Does that door lead to the lower level?" he asked, nodding toward Pablo and Abraham who had just entered the vestibule.

"That's the side entrance to the church," Nathan answered. "From the entry there you can either go straight into the church or through a door on the left which leads down to the cellar."

"Does the cellar door have a lock?" the priest inquired as he cut himself a piece of cake.

"Yes."

"Does it lock from the outside?"

"Yes. From the vestibule."

"And once locked can it be opened from the other side?"

"No," Nathan replied, somewhat confused by the line of questioning. "It's a keyed deadbolt. We've been meaning to change that but we just haven't had the time. Obviously, for safety reasons—God forbid, a fire or something—we weren't planning on even closing that door. We'll just lock the outer door. That one can still be opened from the inside in case of an emergency."

"Is there another way out of the cellar?" Townes asked as he poured himself a cup of lemonade.

"No. That's it."

"Do you have the key for the cellar door on you, Nathan?"

"Why yes, of course."

Nathan extracted a ring bristling with keys from his pocket.

"Please give the key to Pastor Vail."

Nathan did not understand the request. He looked for guidance to Rebecca, but she was also mystified. She walked up beside her husband and asked Townes, "Why does Pastor Vail need the key?"

"Rebecca, you have both agreed to cooperate," Townes said firmly. "There is an element of trust in all this. Give the key to Pastor Vail."

Nathan and Rebecca stared at each other, mired in indecision, each one hoping the other would know what to do. Finally, Nathan brought the key ring over to Vail and pointed out the one in question.

"Lock the cellar door, Pastor," Townes commanded.

Vail started for the vestibule.

"Now just a minute!" Nathan protested. "This is outrageous, Father Townes."

"How do you know I'm Townes?" the priest asked. He gulped down the lemonade and motioned to Vail, who had hesitated at Nathan's outburst, to continue on. "How do you know?"

"I've talked to you on the phone how many times? . . ."

"You recognize my voice then. Most people cannot make positive identification by voice recognition alone. Are you trained in this?"

"You are the man I've talked to on the phone," Nathan said emphatically.

"And how do you know that man, that voice on the phone, is Father Townes? How was that proved to you?"

"He told me. . . . *You* told me."

"And you believed."

"I thought there is an element of trust in all this," Rebecca said pointedly.

"Yes indeed. To the extent where our movement has been infiltrated by the INS, the FBI, the Justice Department, perhaps even by the very governments these people are fleeing. Father Montez and Father Hansen in Albuquerque have just been convicted and sentenced to ten years in federal prison. We have about trusted our way into oblivion. Reverend Cole in Tucson, Sister Gabriella in Phoenix, Reverend Bell in Brownsville, Mike Templeton and his whole group in San Diego—all either under indictment or in prison. Last week forty-seven refugees were deported back to Honduras because we trusted the wrong person. What kind of reception do you suppose they received?"

"What does that have to do with locking those poor souls in our cellar?" Nathan demanded.

"It's for their protection."

"They come here for freedom and we lock them up," Rebecca said caustically.

"They come here for sanctuary," Townes clarified. "That's all we can offer. We are a way station, a rest stop. We shuttle them up to Canada, that's all. There they can look for freedom, citizenship, a new life, whatever. We are not the destination. We are a conveyance, and if we can offer a soft bed and warm food along the way, so much the better."

"And what of God's peace?" Nathan asked.

"Nathan, I've been to the Sumpul. I lost a dear friend at Panzós. I've seen countless bodies without names, talked to countless mothers who will never know what happened to their sons. There is very much more of God's peace behind a locked cellar door than will be found where these people came from."

"Where is that?" Rebecca asked.

"These are all from Guatemala—which is telling you more than you should really know."

"We are a long way from Guatemala, Father Townes," Nathan said sharply. "Whatever problems they have there are behind them. I see no reason to lock these people up. They seek sanctuary in my church and I have granted it. They are free to come and go as they please."

"Go where? To what? With what? These people are in your care. You are their salvation, Nathan Miles. You are responsible for them until I can get them to the next sanctuary up the road. You'll do whatever is required to insure their safekeeping and to preserve whatever little integrity is left to our network."

"You weren't honest with us!" Nathan accused. "You didn't tell us we were to be jailers."

"I asked if you were prepared to do what was necessary. You said you were. If I left out some of the details, I apologize."

"This is not what I was expecting."

"You were expecting something harmless like a canned food drive, a little weekend altruism for the less fortunate? You thought our poor little Latin brothers and sisters were going to come here hat in hand, singing folk songs, *muchas gracias, muchas gracias.*"

Townes balled up the empty paper cup and threw it into the pickup truck.

"I knew you weren't ready," the priest continued. "I knew you'd have second thoughts. But I don't have anybody else. The whole movement is undermined. There isn't another church within three hundred miles I could safely send them to. God knows there are many who'd take them willingly, but I have to act as if the entire old network is known to our enemies. You're new to sanctuary. Your first contact was through the mail. Nobody saw that letter but me. No records were kept. Since then, every time we've talked I've called you, always from a different pay phone. I've been very careful with you. I took great care that we were not followed today. You are in the middle of nowhere. The chance of somebody stumbling onto you out here is almost nonexistent. Right now, here, today, for these people, you *are* the sanctuary movement."

Townes approached them with his hands outstretched.

"We need you, Nathan and Rebecca. I need time to rebuild

the network, to find others like you, willing to break the laws of rich men to help the poor, willing to provide homes for the homeless, willing to give to those who can give nothing in return, willing to go to jail if that is what it comes to. Are you still willing to help?"

Nathan felt cornered. He gazed over at his church. Vail was standing outside the door, staring off into the trees, obviously not anxious to rejoin them. No answer would come to Nathan's lips. He looked to Rebecca.

"What must we do?" she asked Townes.

"Keep them locked in the cellar at all times. Tell no one of your involvement, not friends, not parents, not fellow clergy. I've instructed you not to tell your superiors back in Ohio."

"Michigan," Nathan corrected. "I've not told them."

"And when are they coming to dedicate the church?"

"Two weeks."

"Tell them it won't be ready."

"You want me to continue to deceive my church leaders?"

"I want you to lie, goddamn it!" Townes said furiously. "I want you to bury them in bullshit. I want you to con them right out of their collars. Can you handle that? Can you lie to keep eight people alive?"

"Yes . . . I think so."

"Your only contact is me. Nothing happens unless I say so. I'm the only one who can move those people up the road. I'm the only one who knows where they are."

"What about Pastor Vail?" Nathan asked.

"That was unavoidable. But I trust him implicitly. He's an old hand. This is sort of his last job. He insisted on coming along. I would bet my life that he would not compromise you, no matter what might happen."

"Just what *might* happen?" Rebecca asked apprehensively.

Townes deliberated before replying. "Usually what is least expected," was all he could honestly say.

Nathan put his arm around Rebecca. He squared his shoulders, straightened his back. He made sure he was looking Townes straight in the eye.

"We are not afraid," he said.

"You should be," Townes replied. "Fear is only logical."

•

The ride back to the sheriff's office in Brawley was not pleasant. Chamberlain made a point of hitting every pothole on his side of the yellow line. He took every turn at maximum-g and bottomed out at every dip. Even though Matt's stomach churned and threatened to return his luncheon taco, he refused to let on that the ride was causing him any discomfort. When Chamberlain barreled into the office parking lot, he slightly overshot the driveway. The right front tire hit the curb full force and Matt's cranium was propelled up into the headliner. He recoiled just as Chamberlain stomped the brake pedal. By the time Matt peeled himself off the dashboard, Chamberlain was already out of the car. The driver's door slammed shut with such force that the vehicle, whose springs and shocks were still coping with the complicated physics of such an abrupt interruption of its forward motion, shuttered with a new sideward wobble—not unlike a skiff pitching on a choppy lake. After a number of nauseating gyrations, it finally came to equilibrium. Matt's stomach did not make the adjustment quite as fast. He watched Chamberlain storm through the office door and felt the skeleton of a word rattling around in his gut, rendered, stripped to the bone in the bubbling acid. It rumbled out of him, rising on the fumes of a vile-tasting belch: *"Asshole!"*

Matt dragged himself into the office and collapsed on a wooden bench situated under a gallery of sun-bleached Wanted posters. A uniformed matron, seated behind a large desk on the other side of the room, did her best to ignore him.

"Where's Chamberlain?" Matt asked gruffly, not looking up from the checkerboard pattern of white-and-black asphalt floor tiles.

"He's busy with Sergeant Anderson," the matron answered coldly, not breaking the machine-like rhythm of OFFICIAL POLICE FILE imprints she was stamping onto a pile of documents.

"He's supposed to be doing a report with me," Matt said tiredly.

"He said you could wait. As soon as he's done with the sergeant, he'll take your statement. Unless you'd like to come back tomorrow."

"I'll wait."

"It could be quite a while."

"I'll wait."

"Suit yourself."

Matt hunched over and began to row with imaginary oars, each stroke in time with the pulse of the ink stamp. Matt imagined the tempo was roughly equal to the ramming speed of an ancient Phoenician galley. The matron never looked up to see his pantomime.

"I'll wait," he repeated. "It's only a mutilation-murder."

The comment drew no response.

Matt knew from his earlier visit that the only way into the inner sanctum of the sheriff's office was through a door controlled by a button on the matron's desk. He sighed, quit "rowing" and stretched out on the bench, using his equipment bag as a pillow.

"No laying down on county property," the matron pronounced officiously.

"Would that be a misdemeanor or an out-and-out felony?" Matt asked as he pulled himself up to a sitting position.

"Just common decency," she droned. Her tone implied a patronizing understanding that "common decency" was a concept beyond the pale of present company. The assessment was unequivocal, as if there were something missing in Matt's very genes which prevented him from sharing in the comprehension of such things. "You don't put your shoes up on furniture," she explained.

Matt jerked the zipper open on the bag and snatched out the Nikon. He focused on the matron and clicked off a frame. She ignored him; the steady beat of the rubber stamp did not waver. Matt eased off the bench and stalked closer to the desk. A quick focus, a shot, the fast ratchet of the auto-winder, a step closer, another shot, but still no break in the matron's rhythm. Matt approached closer still, inching around the side of the desk. He crouched low, slowly rotated the camera 90° and adjusted the lens. Three fast clicks. A step closer and two more. The matron's head twitched, she missed the pad on one re-inking stroke, her left hand went from the papers to the hem of her skirt, she gave it a tug: The rhythm was broken.

Matt ran to the front of the desk and burned the rest of the roll of film, snapping off frames from every conceivable angle. The matron tried earnestly to recover her punch press efficiency with the stamp, but it just wouldn't come. Finally, she slammed it down on the desk, buzzed open the connecting door and marched back into the hidden domain of her fellow officers. Matt smiled at the thought of the tirade she was undoubtedly venting on Chamberlain for having left her to cope with such a disgusting sort as himself. He removed the exposed roll of film and dropped it in her empty coffee cup. Then he walked back over to the bench, got another roll out of the bag and reloaded.

Chamberlain charged through the door, nightstick in hand. The matron followed closely on his heels. Matt realized, with a large degree of panic, that he had underestimated the deputy's inclination for overreaction.

"Just what is your problem?" Chamberlain bellowed.

Matt brought the camera to his eye. It was a gesture of self-defense.

"He isn't worth it, Jess," the matron warned. "Not his kind."

Chamberlain stopped suddenly as if someone had switched off the source of his locomotion. He slapped the baton once against his open palm and glared at the reporter.

Matt held the camera tight to his eye but didn't add the provocation of pressing the shutter. Through the viewfinder, Matt watched Chamberlain and the matron. Neither one moved. It was as if they were already frozen on the exposure. He sincerely hoped Chamberlain had found some truth in the matron's sage advice, namely that Matt's "kind" was not worth beating the shit out of. Matt realized the logic was a bit cracked, seeming to imply that if he had been of another "kind"—which by all possible reasoning could only be an improvement since it was obvious they placed "his kind" somewhere to the left of and behind the Antichrist— he might then be worth pounding into the dust. Nonetheless, the matron's words appeared to make sense to Chamberlain, at least to the extent that his inaction indicated some deliberation of the issue she had posited.

"She's right, Jess. I'm not worth it," Matt said from behind the camera.

"You've scraped better off your shoes," the matron remarked.

"Listen to her, Jess," Matt advised. "This woman knows shoes."

"I'm gonna dent your helmet, smart-ass," Chamberlain snarled.

"That's big-time trouble, Jess. *I am just not worth it.* No way."

The deputy didn't appear convinced. He looked at his baton wistfully, as if contemplating the bodily harm it could induce. Matt doubted they could all coexist in such a suspended state of grace longer than a few more seconds. He was overjoyed to hear the rumble of vehicles pulling up outside. "Company's coming," he announced sarcastically. Car doors slammed and voices rose up on the other side of the wall. As the scuffling of many footsteps approached, Chamberlain reluctantly put the nightstick back on his belt.

A bevy of cops barged in through the front door. They dragged, pushed, half-carried and otherwise conveyed three twisting, squirming, handcuffed prisoners into the room. Instantaneously, the place was transformed into a bedlam of activity: Other cops entered from the back room, demanding to know what had happened; one of them threw a blanket over the first of the near-naked prisoners; once covered, the prisoner fainted, knocking the pile of documents off the matron's desk as he tumbled to the floor; one of the cops revived him with smelling salts only to have him faint again; the matron scrambled frantically to retrieve her papers from the floor. Matt took a few pictures—just for the hell of it.

A deputy was trying to communicate in Spanish, but the captives didn't seem to understand. They appeared to be delirious —possibly the result of sunstroke—and prattled on in a strange language no one could decipher. Matt decided it was not a language he had ever encountered, although from time to time a word would surface that was undeniably Spanish in origin.

"Whatcha got, Kirby?" Chamberlain asked.

A portly deputy detached himself from the knot of activity and walked over toward Chamberlain. He took off his hat and wiped the perspiration off his forehead with his handkerchief. "The traffic plane spots these three monkeys wandering in circles out by Devil's Plate," Kirby answered as he drew himself a cup of water from the cooler next to the bench. He eyed Matt suspiciously before proceeding. He didn't notice the reporter reaching into the gym bag to push the RECORD button on the Sony. "Hobey and Tate take the call and track 'em down near the old Swede's place up on 78. Hobey sees these guys are sun-nuts or something. He goes up with a canteen and the short one over there—"

"They're all short," Chamberlain interrupted.

"That one by the desk," Kirby continued. "He ain't no taller than my wife. Well, hell if he don't take a swack at Hobey with this-here."

Kirby pulled a small knife from his breast pocket and handed it to Chamberlain.

"It's a goddamn steak knife!" Chamberlain announced with a laugh.

"That's a Ginsu goddamn steak knife."

Kirby pointed to the trade name that was etched on the stainless steel blade just above the handle. Matt muffled a chuckle of his own. He snapped on the telephoto lens and took a shot of the knife in Chamberlain's hand.

"They sell this on TV, right?" Chamberlain asked in amazement, although it wasn't the first time in his career he had encountered an assault with a kitchen utensil. "Wonder if it really does cut through a beer can."

"Sure ripped the shit out of Hobey's arm. Laid it open down to the bone. He's gettin' stitched up over at the hospital."

Chamberlain's mood went sour once again. "That little wetback piece of shit cut Hobey with this?" Chamberlain held the knife between his thumb and index finger, accentuating its delicateness and the irony of such a slight instrument inflicting damage to a fellow lawman.

"Wetback, sure, but I don't think they're no Mexicans. Ramirez over there's been yackin' at 'em ever since we picked 'em up. They get a word here and there, but that's about it."

"Any papers?"

"Shit! Papers my ass. They ain't even got shoes."

At the word "shoes" Matt broke up. Chamberlain glared at him with renewed rage. "Get the fuck out of here!" he screamed at Matt. Kirby looked on uncomprehendingly.

The prisoner who had fainted suddenly regained consciousness and wriggled free from the group at the front desk. Kirby made a grab for him as he ran by, but missed. Chamberlain dove at him, clumsily tackling the man against the water cooler. The ten-gallon bottle toppled off and crashed on the floor. The deputy and his prisoner grappled on the slick tile, rolling over and over.

"Ride him, cowboy!" said one of the cops over by the desk. The others laughed, as did Matt.

"Kirby, you son-of-a-bitch, help me out!" Chamberlain screamed.

Kirby walked over, gingerly stepping across the puddles and the pieces of glass. When he was in position, he knelt on the prisoner's chest. The extra two hundred pounds situated on the man's diaphragm seemed to take the fight out of him, although he continued to try to bite Chamberlain's arm, which was wrapped around his throat.

The scene was odd enough to warrant a few more shots: Chamberlain lying on the wet floor; the prisoner lying on top of him, teeth bared like a rabid mastiff; fat Kirby kneeling atop them both, looking as if he was about to say a bedtime prayer. Matt brought the camera into position, forgetting that the telephoto lens was still screwed on. He found the viewfinder filled by the prisoner's bare feet.

Matt didn't bother to change the lens. Instead, he zoomed in tighter until he had just the man's left foot in the frame. Then he snapped off six shots of the foot, which like the left foot of the corpse at Coombe's Ditch, was missing its middle toe.

•

It took Juan Guarcas Tol and Manuel Xom Calel over seventeen hours to get from Nim Xol to the refugee camp called La Salvación in Chiapas, Mexico. They followed the dirt road that ran east from Cobán to Chelac, where they boarded a bus headed up to Sebol. At Pajal, where the road turned north, the bus was stopped and searched by a squad of pintos looking for saboteurs who had dynamited a coffee works in Lanquín. Being *Indigenas*— no less than Quichés in a Kekchí area, seemingly without cause— Juan and Manuel immediately qualified as prime suspects. They would have been taken into custody were it not for the intervention of a feisty old priest who was also traveling on the bus. The priest convinced the sergeant in charge that the two young men, who had boarded west of their current position, could not possibly have participated in the destruction, which had occurred a short time ago and thirteen kilometers to the east. Reluctantly, the sergeant allowed them to continue on. Worried they might encounter another roadblock, Juan and Manuel, with the blessings of the priest, got off the bus three kilometers south of Sebol and followed an obscure horse trail up to Rubelquiché. North of the town, they recovered the tiny dugout they had hidden previously and portaged down a steep hillside to the Río de la Pasión. They floated downstream, joining a small flotilla of cargo canoes transporting supplies to Sayaxché, hoping to look inconspicuous in the company of the other boats. The river took them into the mosquito-infested rain forests of El Petén, through the tall stands of mahogany, cedar, rubber and balsam and past the silent, brooding ruins at Cancún, Seibal and La Amelia. None of the other boats ventured past the jungle outpost of Sayaxché. The last miles were the most dangerous, as they approached the junction of the Río de la Pasión and the Río Chixoy. There the two rivers joined to form the Río Usumacinta, which marked the border with Mexico. Alone, under cover of night and the heavy tree canopy, they hugged the shore, hiding from the searchlights of the border patrol helicopters. They slipped onto the Usumacinta at Altar de Sacrificios and crossed over to the Mexican side just downriver of Santa Rosita. Having ditched the canoe, they headed down a well-marked trail, wider than the road from Cobán, trampled and worn by the bare feet of thousands of refugees. Two kilometers later they stumbled, exhausted, into the camp at La Salvación.

In tent number 47 on the far side of the sprawling camp, the Daykeeper waited for them. For the past two nights he and his wife had let blood in accordance with the oldest accounts of the Vision Quest. A knotted cord of thorns had been pulled through a hole in her tongue. With invocations to Perforator God, stingray spines had been inserted into his ear lobes. Their blood had been collected on fig bark paper and then thrown with copal incense onto the fire. The blood, transformed to smoke, was the sustenance of the gods, their tariff for creation.

Each night the Daykeeper had seen the Vision Serpent rise from the flaming brazier, writhing upward, undulating, its long feathers trailing behind, its flint tail thrashing against the floor. Each night Monkey Scribe had crawled up the Serpent's back. It had been followed by Girded Tapir. Each night the Serpent's bearded mouth had opened to spit forth the same face.

The face was recognizable, familiar to him although incongruous, unfathomable in the context of his quest, a conundrum in blood and smoke. It was an impossible face, a jest of the gods, a taunt for an old man not ready to understand. *How could it be?*

Tonight, the Daykeeper decided to let his blood in the most ancient way of kings, the way most pure, most painful, the way preferred by the gods. He cut three slashes into his penis with a black obsidian blade. As the virile blood dripped onto the scrolls of fig bark paper, he visualized the inscription on the stela found at Nim Xol, the place the ancients had called the Great Abyss of Carchah. From memory he recited the puzzling prophecy from the Stone of Nim Xol:

> " 'These are the times
> When there is destruction,
> When there is annihilation,
> Usurpers of the mat,
> Usurpers of the royal seat:
> Before 11 Lamat, the Yearbringer,
> Before the last katun,
> In the ways of Xbalanque,
> In the ways of Hunahpu,
> Through the deeds of two come
> Sky-Sword Bringer
> Calabash
> The True Lord of the Mat
> Begetter of the New Age
> Preparer in the Last Katun,
> His name is . . .' "

All the Daykeeper could see was a heart-shaped blackness etched on the canvas side of the tent, the shape of the missing piece of the stela found at Nim Xol, the piece which carried the name glyph of the Begetter of the New Age, the Preparer in the last 7,200-day Katun of the Great Cycle of Man, the only one who could prevent the days of annihilation.

"Show me his face. Give me his name," the Daykeeper prayed.

So much had to be accomplished. There was so little time

left, only fourteen days until the end of the twenty-day month of Cumku. Then would come the ill-fated five-day period of Uayeb which closed the *haab* year. Even though the date on the stela equated to the first day of the new year—11 Lamat 1 Pop—it was not wise to expect anything but misfortune to occur during Uayeb.

"Show me his face. Give me his name."

As the blood flowed, a chemical reaction took place in the Daykeeper's brain. Endorphins were produced, substances which acted on the central nervous system to induce hallucinations. The Daykeeper was unaware of the physiological changes taking place in his body. He knew only that the gods had created the middle-world of men and they required blood in return. Of maize and water had humankind been fashioned, transformed into flesh and blood. When he gave his blood back to the gods, they consumed it and allowed him to walk in their world ever so briefly, to see those things only gods see.

The Vision Serpent coiled out of the flames, mightier, stronger this time, born of the blood of his very manhood. It curled around him, as thick as a tree trunk, its skin smooth and shiny between flayed segments. It kept circling around, coil upon coil, higher and higher, driving through the tent and up into the heavens, building a hollow pillar in which the Daykeeper was encased. The slender, flint-edged tail slithered up between his legs and curled around his member. The bearded head looked down on him from high above, from the North Star where the serpent column had stopped.

" 'By the Maker, Modeler, named Bearer, Begetter,' " the Daykeeper prayed, quoting from the sacred *Popol Vuh:*

> " 'Hunahpu Possum, Hunahpu Coyote,
> Great White Peccary, Tapir,

Sovereign Plumed Serpent,
Heart of the Lake, Heart of the Sea,
Maker of the Blue-Green Plate,
Maker of the Blue-Green Bowl,'
Let me see his face;
Let me know his name."

The head of Vision Serpent twisted further down into the vertical tunnel of its own coiled body. It looked upon the Daykeeper with the haughty indifference of a true god. No answer was granted. The Daykeeper cut again with the obsidian knife. Another blood-drenched scroll was thrown on the fire. The Vision Serpent could not resist the offering. Its head roared down the spiraled column as its body corkscrewed upward. Its mouth opened. A thunderous cataract of visions poured out and spilled over the Daykeeper, a cacophonous tangle of past and future events, of linkages between history and destiny, of possibilities mounted upon each other into the infinity of chaos, of places unknown, of things not understood, all leading to or stemming from a single point in time, the 1,860,788th day of the Cycle of Men, the date carved into the Stone of Nim Xol, the date which had the face he'd seen before, the face he could not accept.

"Why can I not know his name?" he groaned weakly, falling to the dirt floor from his stool. He was on the verge of passing out. The fire had burned down; the Vision Serpent had vanished. Others gathered around to render aid. They brought him to a mat and laid him down.

The Daykeeper felt as if he were floating, seeing all around him from a place suspended in space and time. Everyone in the tent was an actor in a rigidly scripted play. No one could deviate from the ordained word. No one could alter the outcome.

He watched as two young men were admitted to the tent.

They were exhausted, dehydrated, dirty. They were brought before him and only at length did he recognize them as Juan Guarcas Tol and Manuel Xom Calel.

Manuel presented the flat, heart-shaped stone he had unearthed at Nim Xol. The Daykeeper motioned for his wife to bring the lantern closer so he could look upon the glyph.

How foolish it was to question the gods. Three nights running he had distrusted their word, doubted their vision. But here in Manuel's hand was the name of the face he had already seen, the name he already knew, the name which had been chiseled in stone over a thousand years ago. How cruel were the gods to give him this name, this face, now that the man was gone, beyond his reach.

The Daykeeper saw himself reciting the glyph to the others. He saw how the young ones repeated it in awe to each other, how it became a battle cry in the night, renewing their hope, rallying them to slip across the river and attack the garrison at Santa Rosita. He saw them shouting the name, painting it on the Quonset hut barracks. He saw how it brought ruin upon them, how it destroyed their last slim chance.

He would have to keep it to himself, bear the secret alone.

But it was too late: He could still see ahead, but he could not alter what was to be.

Crying, he read the glyph aloud: "The name is . . . 'He Who Walks in Old Words.'"

3

5 MULUC   7 CUMKU

AT THE COMPLETION OF

12 BAKTUNS

18 KATUNS

8 TUNS

14 UINALS

9 KINS

the next day . . .

A stringer for *The World-Sun* was the first one to hear of the tryst in Malibu. He was tipped off by the kid who'd delivered the pepperoni pizza the day before. The kid had not received an adequate gratuity from the very famous personages who placed the order. In fact, the celebrated starlet (sans blouse) and the eminent congressman (sans toupee) were so drunk or high or otherwise parted from reality that it took more than fifteen minutes of wheedling, haggling and begging just to get them to cough up the food tab of sixteen dollars and eighty-five cents. The kid called the stringer (who also sold mozzarella cheese at wholesale to the pizzeria) and gave him the address on the promise of a double sawbuck (which he never got). The stringer made the mistake of telling his girlfriend who worked at a nail boutique in Venice. She told numerous customers, one of whom was married to an unemployed photographer. The woman and her husband argued vociferously over the merits of easy money versus the integrity of keeping one's art pure. The photographer, seeing he was losing the debate, repaired to the nearest bar and ingested seven Long Island Iced Teas in less than thirty-nine minutes. His voice was loud, his discourse detailed, his complaints many. He lamented the death of Art and sang the exact address of the tryst site repeatedly to the tune of "Amazing Grace." Many of those present in the bar were heard to remark that the photographer's voice was reminiscent of a young Tom Jones. Others were seen writing frantically on napkins, match books and whatever else was easily available. By nine o'clock on the following morning, a small army of tabloid journalists, photographers, paparazzi, stringers and assorted gawkers had assembled on the embankment overlooking the Malibu love-nest. Among them were an irate stringer for the *World Sun,* a hungover photographer and Matt Teller.

By noon, doubt had set in. A rumor went around placing the starlet at the commissary on the Paramount lot and the congressman at a subcommittee briefing room in D.C. The story was actually concocted by one of the old hands on the scene. Predictably enough, many of his greener counterparts, as well as those easily discouraged and others just plain gullible, began to depart the embankment at about 1:15 P.M.—not coincidentally, exactly when the mercury was peaking at 97°. By two o'clock, the contingent on watch was down to less than a dozen hardcore veterans. Most of them knew each other. A few actually even liked each other.

One of the more affable characters remaining at the site was Armand Soltz, an independent stringer (of mysterious origin) who had enough money socked away (from sources equally mysterious) to retire if he was ever so inclined. Unlike the others on the Malibu hillside, he chased photos and gossip strictly for the fun of it—"to catz zee big fish," he would say. He was strictly a feeder: He never wrote final copy; he never even developed his own pictures.

Armand lumbered up the hill like the big train who couldn't, smoke pouring back from the ever-present Garcia y Vega. Wheezing, he headed over to where Matt was leaning against a telephone pole. He fanned himself with the latest issue of *Here and There*, which had hit the street that morning. Matt's photos and story blanketed the front page.

"You gotz zee big tuna, hey Matz?" he said.

It was the third compliment Matt had received from his peers over the course of the morning and afternoon. The praise only made him feel less like waiting in the hot sun for a nympho cinema queen and her politician boyfriend to make their appearance. Ironically, such assignments were considered choice. Schiff had sent him out with a pat on the back and a "You earned it." Then the publisher had sauntered back into his office, patrician-like, satisfied with the quiet easiness of his "generosity." The bone had been tossed; Matt was supposed to be grateful. But Matt wanted to go back to Imperial County. Instead, he had to wait for the two famous lovers to make a break for the silver Lamborghini parked fifty feet away from the front door in the carport.

"Just tripped on it, Armand," Matt replied humbly enough.

"So? Vahts deefrentz?" Armand asked shrugging. "You trips, you lukes, you verks like zee donkeez, you sleep all daze lazy like my vife—no matter nahting. Important ting eez *you find. You find gude*, hey Matz boy?"

"I find really good, Armand."

"So who eez he, dis guy dey make cold cutz out of?"

"Don't know."

"Matz, Matz, you pulling my ting here. You know who dis guy eez."

"I really don't, Armand. Don't know who he is. Don't know who killed him. Don't know why."

"Oh Matz, maybe heez some big shotz guy. Mob guy or someting."

"No. I don't think so. Way too messy for a hit."

"Are you kiddink? Messy! I show you messy. Remember my pitchoorz of zee Gozanolli hit. Some mess dis vaz."

"The Giovanelli hit was a mercy killing compared to this. This is world-class slice-and-dice, Armand."

"Like zee slasher ting last year, hey?"

"No . . . different . . . More purposeful . . . More . . . I dunno. Just different."

"Well, gude catz, Matz boy. Congrazulashinz."

"And it ain't in the *Times*. It's two days old and it ain't in the *Times*."

"About dis you care?"

"Schiff cares."

Armand laughed. Cigar smoke billowed about his head, wafting through the thick tangles of his beard.

"Of corz. He never forgetz, dat one. Dis eez eemportent to Barnie boy."

"Very."

"You big star for Barnie boy now. Maybe he fire that fat hippomazumus Izzy and make you editor."

"That's a good idea." The voice came from behind them. Matt and Armand wheeled around. Don "Koz" Koslowski from *The National Eye* had circled around the back of the hill and sneaked up behind them. His normal posture somewhat resembled a dwarf olive tree, all twists and bends, stunted and crooked. He was a corkscrew of a man, in a dirty brown polyester suit. As usual, he looked agitated. "You'd be perfect for the job," he continued, his face reddening with every word, making him look like the "Before" ad for a hypertension remedy. "You're qualified, Teller. You know exactly which stories are worth stealing."

Matt sighed and shook his head in disgust. "Did you hear something, Armand? Something insignificant, yet annoying? Like if athlete's foot had a sound."

Armand, who tried to get along with everyone, struggled not to laugh. "Hallo, Koz," he said guardedly.

"You just fell into this, huh?" Koz asked sarcastically, waving an issue of *H&T* in Matt's face.

Matt swatted the paper out of Koz's hand.

"What wrong, Koz? Acid flashbacks, PMS, what?"

"You couldn't find a story like this on your own if you did it yourself."

"Actually I did do it myself. I was practicing up. Wanna head out to the desert tonight? We'll get some cheap wine, sit on a dune, watch the sidewinders by moonlight. Then I'll show you some tricks with my Swiss army knife."

"Maybe I'll show you some tricks of my own."

"Always the master of repartee."

"It's not your story, asshole. You just think its yours."

"I found it. I wrote it. We printed it. How could I ever think it was my story?"

"It's *not* your story," Koz repeated. "You don't have the nose for it. You don't have the instinct."

"What I got is the front page."

"Of a piece of shit."

"Yes, well the *Eye* gets all the good stories. I especially liked your piece on the nun with the plastic surgery. What page was that on? Six, seven? Very snappy: 'Novena Nets Nun New Nose.' Glad to see the Alliteration Police haven't confiscated your typewriter."

"At least it's my story."

"And this is mine." Matt picked up the copy of *H&T*. He pointed to his name on the byline.

"It ain't!" Koz countered. Then he stomped off down the hill.

"Jesus! That's weird even for him," Matt commented to Armand.

"Vize he geeve you such hard a time?"

"Remember that two-headed murder-suicide story I did a few months back? He says I stole it from him."

"So dit you?"

Matt chuckled. "Yeah."

"Oh, you terrible, Matz boy."

"He got it first. I got it right."

"Dat's not stealing. He should know better."

"Well . . . his notes did sort of disappear."

"Oh, Matz. Vaht do I do vit you."

There was a subtle change in the activity at the bottom of the hill. A free-lance photographer who had been watching the house through an 800-millimeter zoom lens suddenly unscrewed the unipod from the base of his camera, switched to a shorter telephoto and walked quickly from his vantage point opposite the front picture window to one more in line with the path between the front door and the carport. Matt and Armand had been around long enough to know it wasn't necessary to watch the house. It was far easier to watch the guy with the longest lens who, in effect, watched the house for you.

Without another word between them, Matt and Armand

bolted down the hill and took positions among the others who had also deduced something was about to happen. There was a bit of jostling, but no overt pushing or shoving. Matt checked his f-stop and readied himself.

The front door flew open and the lovers charged out at full sprint. A clear field of focus would only exist for five to ten seconds before they reached the Lamborghini. Matt dropped to one knee and tightened the zoom. Just as he depressed the shutter, someone moved in front of him, blocking the shot. "Shit!" he cursed, leaning clear of the obstruction. But the person in front moved with him, and then back again as Matt jockeyed for an unimpeded shot. By that time the lovers were speeding away, shielded from view by the black privacy glass of the sports car.

"What the fuck is wrong with you?" Matt fumed, jumping to his feet.

Koz turned, all smiles. "Got some great shots. She gave us a lot of leg when she jumped over that flower bed, didn't she? How'd you do, Teller?"

"Son-of-a-bitch!"

"Tough break," Koz smirked. Then he headed for his car.

Armand patted Matt's shoulder consolingly. "I geeve you nize negateeve gude cheap on dis one," he said with all the sympathetic decorum of a funeral director quoting casket prices. "You tell Barnie boy."

Just *how* to tell "Barnie boy" was the tortured preoccupation of Matt's cogitation on the drive back to the office. He'd blown his first assignment since being pardoned from the pet desk. Schiff was not known for his tolerance of fuck-ups. Matt considered blaming it on an equipment failure. It was not an absolving excuse, but it stood an outside chance of at least deflecting some of Schiff's rage.

Matt slunk into the office, being careful not to walk past

Schiff's door. He sat at his desk, cupped his head in his hands, and stared down at a copy of *H&T*. *Nice work* was written in Marlene's flowery scroll along the border next to his headline: DEATH IN THE DESERT.

The day had started off so well, he thought—

A hand dropped onto the page. Not the hand of someone pointing or pounding or grabbing or slapping—just a hand, partially decomposed, black and bloated, dismembered above the wrist and missing its thumb.

Matt lurched back from the desk. Standing just on the other side were Dale and his brothers Merle and Roy. All of them had the same glutted, self-satisfied look of accomplishment, as if they had just found the Holy Grail itself—or a working accumulator for a '76 Hotpoint refrigerator.

•

"We found the cot back there," Dale explained, pointing to a rocky slope behind his shack.

Matt anxiously followed the three brothers around the side of the house and into the still twilight of the desert, his expectations rising with each step.

The sun was almost down. It simmered on the horizon, a cherry half submerged in a lumpy soup of low cumulus. It had taken most of the afternoon to get back out to the deep desert. Matt had tailed behind the brothers' pickup and so had been forced to make the journey at the exasperating *mañana* pace they set. He hadn't said a word to Schiff before leaving the office. Matt imagined he had reached full meltdown by now, stomping around editorial, ordering the maintenance man to throw his desk out into the alley and threatening various acts of violence. It was a big risk, but if Matt came back with installment two of "Death in the Desert" all would be forgiven.

Dale pointed to a clump of bushes. "It was right there, layin' on its side in the mesquite."

"With the body still on it?" Matt asked.

"No. Nothin' on it. Not even a mattress. If it had a mattress we most likely would've kept it."

Matt felt the wind going out of his sails. In his mind was a picture of Schiff pouring lighter fluid over his personnel folder.

"You *would* have kept it?" Matt asked tenuously, knowing he was leading with his chin.

"Yep. Think so."

"So you didn't keep it?"

"Nope."

"Where exactly is it?" Matt inquired, trying desperately to keep tight rein on his anger.

Dale and his brothers exchanged inquisitive looks. Roy shook his head. Merle shrugged and said, "West Texas, I'd bet."

Dale nodded. "Sounds about right."

Matt rubbed his eyes and gazed out over the desert. Each scraggly snarl of creosote reached out over the barrenness with its own Medusa shadow, groping blindly along the dead floor of the basin. Matt knew from a previous story that creosote was among the oldest continuously living entities on earth. In New Mexico or Arizona—he didn't quite remember which—there was a specimen reputed to be over ten thousand years old. Ten millennia had come and gone, but the creosote remained. Matt's cot had come and gone, too—less than a minor ripple in history, an event obscure in its passing, a thing done and over, but witnessed nonetheless by the gnarled, ugly bushes all around. He wondered if he'd do better interviewing the creosote.

"The cot—*my cot*—is in West Texas," Matt said slowly, hoping that having heard those inscrutable words uttered by another, the brothers might either recant or offer an explanation.

"I think Merle's right," Dale said. "When we traded it to the Mexicans, they said they were headed for the grapefruit harvest. That'd be east Texas. But they said they had people back outside of Presidio. So allowing for about fifty miles an hour average and a few stops along the way, I'd say it's safe to ascertain they made it at least that far by now. Unless they broke down. That old Dodge—"

"When did you find the cot, Dale?" Matt asked brusquely.

"Yesterday morning."

"The morning after I was out here?"

"Yep. Did you ever find that two-headed dog you were looking—"

"What did you do after you found it?"

"Ate breakfast."

"After that?"

"We threw the cot in the truck and took it up to Indio."

"Why was that, Dale?"

"We took it to the swap meet."

"And you traded it. Is that it?"

"We got a crock pot for it. A nice one, too. All it needed was a new plug and it works just fine. We've had a stew goin' all day. You sure are welcome to join us."

"You traded my cot to some grapefruit pickers for a crock pot."

"Four-and-a-half-quart capacity," Dale boasted, winking slyly.

"That is a consolation," Matt remarked acidly. "Look. I almost hate to ask, but where did you find the hand?"

"When we got back from Indio, it must've been 120° out here," Dale recalled.

"You could fry yourself a Spam-burger on a flat rock," Merle added.

"The first thing we seen when we got back was all the buzzards. They were thick as flies, up in the air, on the ground out there by the refrigerators." He pointed to the area. "You could tell they were on to something, patient-like, just sort of gettin' ready, waitin' to get at it. I figured it was a wounded coyote or a sick badger, something like that, maybe even a big jackrabbit, probably burrowed up in one of the fridges. So I got my Browning thinkin' to put it out of its misery." Dale started back toward the place he had indicated. "C'mon. I'll show you."

When they were about twenty feet away from one of the groups of appliances, he stopped and took Matt by the arm.

"We were right here," Dale continued, "give or take a few feet, and all of a sudden, it just exploded."

"What exploded?" Matt asked.

"You see that Kelvinator fridge lying on its back?"

"The green one?"

"Yep. You see how the door is hangin' open like that?"

"Yeah."

"Well, it was closed and it just blew open."

"Like it burped," Roy interjected. Merle laughed, drawing a harsh look from Dale.

"It popped open, exploded," Dale went on. "But it didn't sound like a bomb. It just sounded like a . . . a . . . *boof.* It made a boof sound and flew open and blood and guts and gunk is spraying out all over the place."

Matt could not keep the grimace of incredulity from his face. Dale nodded assuringly.

"The buzzards went full-blown nuts," Dale continued. "They were peckin' and clawin' and scrapin', chewin', squakin', rippin'. They went pure bird-crazy. Feathers were flyin' right and left. I tell you, we didn't know whether to crap or call home. We were all flat on our bellies on the deck back here not knowin' if it was the sweet-Jesus end of the world itself. No lyin', we were spooked good."

There was a round of head-bobbing from the three brothers. It seemed to reinforce their recollection.

"And?" Matt pressed.

"When we finally got the nerve to go on over, there wasn't a heck of a lot left. Those birds had it pretty much down to the bone."

"The body's in the Kelvinator?" Matt asked, brightening with anticipation and hurrying over to it.

"We scraped up what was left and threw it in the lime-pit out back."

Matt stared dejectedly into the empty porcelain interior of the prone refrigerator. A black, crusted residue coated the back of it. Splatters blotched the side and lid.

"Why didn't you call the police?" Matt asked despondently.

"We don't like to get the police into our things," Dale answered nervously. "Hard truth is, Mr. Teller, we've had a problem or two in the past. Anyway, this poor fool was as dead as dead gets."

"In pieces dead," Merle added.

"There was nothin' the police could do 'cept cause us grief. We took care of the body as best we could," Dale explained.

"Even said a prayer out by the lime-pit," Merle said.

"It was a poem, not no prayer," Roy clarified.

"Well, it was all we had," Dale explained. He extracted his wallet from his back pocket and fished out a folded, yellowed newspaper clipping. He handed it to Matt.

Matt read it aloud:

" 'Pile the bodies high at Austerlitz and Waterloo.
 Shovel them under and let me work—

I am the grass; I cover all.

And pile them high at Gettysburg
And pile them high at Ypres and Verdun.
Shovel them under and let me work.
Two years, ten years, and passengers ask the conductor:
What place is this?
Where are we now?

I am the grass.
Let me work.' "

Matt folded the clipping into its original one-inch square.

"I figured you for a plasticized photo of Mom," Matt re-marked, handing the clipping to Dale. "Or an old blood-donor card. Maybe a Trojan or two. But Sandburg in your wallet . . . I would not have guessed. You are full of surprises, Dale."

Dale unfolded it once more and showed Matt the other side. There was a small picture of a helmeted high school football hero and an article recounting some long-past big game in an obscure little Oklahoma town. At first Matt didn't understand. Finally he realized the gridiron star and Dale were one and the same.

"The poem just sort of came along with it, you know," Dale said sheepishly.

"Well, you never know when one's gonna come in handy."

"Do you think it was appropriate to the situation? As a writer, I mean."

"Yes. Absolutely. Carl would be proud."

"I took the liberty of changing all those names to places around here we know."

"I don't think it's a problem."

"And wherever it said 'grass' I said 'lime.' "

"Perfecto."

"Thanks. It means a lot coming from you."

"What about the hand, Dale? How come the hand isn't in the lime?"

"We didn't find it till today. We'd been into town this morning and picked up today's *Here and There*. It didn't take us long to figure this was connected to your story. We ain't never been in anything like this before. So we got out here hopin' there was something left to show you. Damn if we weren't down on our hands and knees. Sure enough, Roy found it in that crevice right under that G.E. Must've got blown there and the birds couldn't get at it. It was kind of raunchy from the heat so we put it on ice and headed in to see you. Think you're gonna write us up, Mr. Teller? Roy and Merle never been in the paper and me but the one time."

"It's all up to my editor, Dale," Matt hedged, although it wasn't really a lie. "And what about the police? Aren't you worried they'll come snooping out here? I wouldn't want to get you in trouble."

"Let 'em. We're gone come tomorrow. Oklahoma-bound," Dale explained. "We'll pick up next week's paper there."

"Right. I forgot."

"Think we'll be in it?"

"All depends, Dale. I need more details. All I got here is a crock pot and a gamy hand."

"Without a thumb," Dale clarified.

"Yeah. That's good. But it's still mighty thin. Do you have anything else for me?"

"I don't believe so."

"Do you have any idea how the refrigerator popped open like that?"

"Nope."

"Are there any chemicals in there that would cause that to happen? Freon maybe?"

"No. That couldn't do it."

"How about machinery? Power tools?"

"No."

"Shotgun shells? M80's?"

"No."

"Any idea how the body got here?"

"Nope."

"Who might have left it?"

"No."

Matt sighed, shrugged. "The Mexicans who traded for the cot, did you get their license plate number?" he asked.

Dale shook his head, somberly indicating they hadn't noted the license number. Looks of dejection passed between the brothers as they saw their chance for notoriety slipping away.

Merle's head was the first to snap up, sparked by the dawning light of realization. As his eyes met Roy's the awareness communicated. Their faces cracked into yellow grins simultaneously. Dale was the last to catch on, the symbiosis of his younger siblings taking place at a lower level than where his own perceptions normally operated. Once tuned in, his head began to pump affirmatively.

"Did you get the truck's number?" Matt asked again, now with renewed hope.

"No," Dale answered, cocky and self-assured. He paused for effect, building Matt up and letting him know there was more: "We got the number of the cot."

Matt groaned and reached into the Adidas bag. He groped for the jumbo bottle of Excedrin.

•

Pastor Patrick Vail and Father Gregory Townes sat across the aisle from each other in the last pew of the Cob City Lutheran Church. Only one light was on, a dim, milk-glass ball hanging over the pulpit at the front of the small church. The dark, hunched figures were barely visible in the shadows—two sluggish silhouettes, scarcely animate, all but absorbed in the surrounding gloom. Occasionally, one of the windows rattled under the steady force of the desert wind. The doors were locked. No one else was in the building.

"I cannot carry the weight," Vail said, his voice weak and tremulous. "I have prayed and prayed. I've searched for reasons. I've looked for solace, for affirmation. Gregory, I would settle even for some semblance of righteousness."

"You'd like to feel that God is on your side."

"It would be comforting."

"Every villain has God on his side," Townes observed cynically. "You're no villain, Patrick. Leave it for the generals and the TV preachers. We go it alone, like all honest men. We do what we do without name-dropping."

"I pray and I find only doubt—despair. We've set something in motion, something terrible. I feel helpless and guilty as sin."

"We have nothing to feel guilty about."

"Gregory, we are culpable. You can't deny it."

"I do deny it!" Townes stated emphatically, banging the pew with his fist. "My conscience is not a problem. The guilt lies elsewhere."

"I can't pass the blame so easily."

"We are the solution, Patrick. Not the problem."

"We are *not* the solution. You said as much yesterday to Miles and his wife."

"Yes, yes, I know. But we are part of it. We are a link."

"A link in touch with both points it connects. One point is

corruption, pain, suffering. The corrosion creeps down along the chain."

"With such reasoning how could we ever extend a hand to the poor, the filthy, the diseased?"

"Such reasoning never plagued me before, Gregory. It's new to me and it sickens me, I admit. I'm mortified at what I've become. I fear the eternal flames of damnation. For the first time in my life I dread Judgment Day."

"If you burn, Patrick, I burn with you."

"That is scant consolation, my friend."

Both men laughed, but it was a false humor, a whistling past the graveyard. Soon it sputtered to silence.

"How do you stay so clear of it?" Vail asked earnestly.

"I believe in our work. You should too."

"I believe in God. About all else I have my doubts."

"Oh, Patrick," Townes sighed. "How well we are matched, you and I."

"I never thought so," Vail muttered defensively. Not only did he disagree, but he had detected a patronizing tone. "I see very little in common between us."

"Exactly. I did not say we are alike—only that we are well matched. Hand and glove, tongue and groove, positive and negative. You doubt the world and believe in God. I trust the world and . . ."

"You've lost your faith?" Vail asked in astonishment.

"I've lost God."

"He is there, Gregory," the pastor replied with as much certainty as he could muster. "Deep down you must know that."

"He may be *there*, all right. My faith is not so impotent that I deny His being. Only His proximity, Patrick. I have not bumped into Him lately."

" 'Inasmuch as you do it to the least of these my brethren,

you are doing it unto me,' " Vail quoted from memory. "Yesterday you bumped into Him eight times. You locked Him in the cellar."

"I did what was necessary."

"What is necessary is not always His way."

"Nor is it His way that more of them die."

"And how many wrongs to finally make a right, Gregory?"

"Little wrongs. *Small* wrongs."

"How many?" Vail demanded, jumping out of his seat. He rushed across the aisle and stood at the opening to Townes's pew, looming over the priest. "There is no end to it, is there? Our movement has become more important than those it moves. We've institutionalized it, Gregory. It has a life now, a will to survive. That is what you protect. We erect fences around fences."

"And still it is not enough."

"How can it be enough? Every fence is a fear, every fear a reason good and proper for doing what is *necessary.* Fear mounted upon fear, necessity mounted upon necessity. No wonder you have lost God."

"What would you have me do, Patrick? You've been involved since the beginning. You're no less committed than I. You founded this church out here among the scorpions for but one purpose. The wasteland flock isn't exactly beating a path to your door. . . ."

"The desert has been good for me. I don't deny that. I don't deny I enjoy the solitude, that I was running away. Perhaps that's why I was so willing to help others run away."

"We all have our reasons."

"Mine are not served by lying, by deceiving poor, trusting, well-meaning souls like Miles and his wife, by imprisoning people who come to us for help. And they are certainly not served by . . . by what has happened. . . ."

"We are not at fault, Patrick," Townes insisted, rising to his feet.

"Who is? We set the stage. We allowed—"

"We allowed a lapse in security. We have taken steps to prevent it from recurring."

"You're beginning to sound like a bureaucrat, Gregory."

Townes groaned and slumped back down into the pew. "That is the lowest of blows."

Vail turned away, unable to face the priest and still say what was in his heart. "When I first met you, you had the words of an evangelist. You could have been the Baptist himself. Your words had fire. They were alive with the Spirit."

"And now?"

"No. I have no right."

"You have every right. You've done everything I've ever asked. I've put you in harm's way more than once."

"I was willing."

"No matter. Tell me. Once I was John crying out in the wilderness and now I am what? A cynic? A skeptic? I would accept that."

"It goes beyond that."

"So what have I become, Patrick?"

"A clerk. You have the words of a clerk: 'a lapse in security,' 'steps to prevent it from recurring,' 'preserve the integrity of the network.' My God, Gregory, you talk *around* things. You build fences even with your words. I'm sorry if it offends you, but that's how I feel."

Townes had no reply, no refutation. He struggled to find a response but everything that came to mind rang hollow, seeming defensive at best, dishonest at worst. He sat there in the dark, speechless, motionless, his hands folded prayer-like over the bridge of his nose, crushed under the weight of his friend's assessment.

Vail walked up the aisle, allowing the priest his moment of reflection.

"The ride is swift and dizzying," Townes said at last.

Vail walked back to him and placed his hand on Townes's shoulder.

"Maybe we *are* damned," Townes mused solemnly. "Maybe we are."

Three loud knocks on the door interrupted them, sharp, metallic thuds which rumbled through the entire building. Vail trembled at each of the jolts. His fingers dug into the priest's shoulder. He stared into his friend's eyes but found only mirrors of his own dread. Townes nodded hesitantly, signaling his readiness, however reluctant, to answer the call.

"No," Vail whispered. "It's my door."

The pastor walked slowly to the door. He hesitated, took a deep breath and slid back the heavy bolt. He pulled it open.

There was only the black of night; wind like hot breath; concrete; sand; rocks; a slight, sour smell of jimsonweed; the moon low and orange in the west; a Union 76 sign turning at the top of its mast a half mile away; a DC-10 cutting across Ursa Major on its way to L.A.; pulley ropes pinging against an idle flagpole; somewhere a dog barking; somewhere else a car engine gunning, backfiring, dying. The weather vane on the roof of the hardware store across the road squeaked as it throttled between northeast and north-northeast. The store was dark, having closed hours before. The old house next to the store was also dark. There were no cars parked along the road.

Something fluttered beside Vail's ear. Startled, he wheeled around and saw the newspaper nailed to the church door. A stirring of the wind caused the pages to ruffle. It was a copy of the new issue of *Here and There*.

Vail tried to pull the nail from the door, but the heavy spike had been driven well into the wood. He ripped the paper down and slammed the door shut, quickly resetting the bolt. He ran up the aisle, motioning frantically for Townes to follow. Under the globe light at the front of the church, he spread the tabloid out on the pulpit. The two men examined it in shocked silence. Townes steadied himself by holding onto the pulpit. Vail hung onto the priest's sleeve.

"What have we done?" Vail gasped.

The pounding on the door began again. The thuds were echoed on each of the side doors—a synchronous, heavy, malevolent pulse.

Townes dropped to his knees and crossed himself. Vail looked on numbly.

"Make your peace," Townes said urgently.

Vail shook his head. He folded the tabloid and hid it under a hymnal on a lower shelf of the pulpit. Then he ran to the center aisle, paused, and looked about as if contemplating which door to answer. As he turned from one to the other, he compulsively wound his wristwatch.

A window at the back of the church shattered. Vail heard something drop onto one of the pews, roll along the seat and then fall to the floor. It was only a matter of seconds now, he realized. His sudden calm, the lucidity of his thinking, amazed him. He was joyful, almost childlike, as he ran down the aisle.

"Ready or not here I come!" he screamed.

•

Matt drove east on County-GG. As was his habit, he kept the speedo at a steady ten miles per hour over the limit. The sun had gone down and his headlights barely cut through the wasteland night. He triggered the windshield washer, but there was only enough fluid in the reservoir to produce four dribbling spits on the glass. The wipers dragged the damp sand and the dead bugs back and forth across the windshield, smearing it and making visibility worse. After a few passes, the wipers began to screech. Matt shut them off and was left only with the monotonous drone of the Mazda's Wankel engine and an intermittent, worrisome ping which Matt desperately hoped was not the harbinger of some mechanical calamity about to befall his vehicle.

Next to him, on the seat, was a meatkeeper from a '71 Frigidaire. In it was the hand, neatly wrapped in saran and sitting in a slush of rapidly melting ice. The Adidas bag, as usual, was on the floor. Matt reached into it for the Sony. He flicked on the dome light just long enough to make sure it was the *H&T* tape that resided in the servo.

"The cot is number six," he recorded. "I'm not sure what that means, but Dale is positive this is of utmost significance. He claims that on the underside of the frame, where a crosspiece joins the two rails, the numeral 6 was stenciled in green paint. Now it's just a matter of contacting the Department of Sleepware Registration and running a routine computer search. No problem."

He fingered EJECT and expelled the tape. Keeping one hand on the wheel, he deftly exchanged it for a fresh *GAN Notes* cassette, *#115.*

"Uncle Pete was in the Pacific during World War II," he began. "He used to tell war stories. I think I was the only one who used to really listen. I remember he was in the combat engineers. He saw a lot of action—Kiska, the Solomons, Truk, Eniwetok, Kwajalein, places that sounded like they needed a war to put them on the map. His unit had to clean up after the Marines went in. They'd torch the pillboxes, secure the landing site for heavy equipment and, after all the shit was over, they had to get rid of the dead Japs.

"They *were* Japs back then, as they are becoming once more. I'm sure they're *Japs* once again in Detroit, Allentown, Pittsburgh and Peoria. The events which I cite, after all, occurred just post-Pearl. That they were briefly *Japanese* during the roughly forty years they were fucking us back for dropping the big one on them is irrelevant to this particular story, a mere bell-top in the parabola of international relations. Therefore, without apology, the reference will be to *Japs* throughout this episode."

Matt took his eyes off the road for a moment to glance warily at the Sony, as if he had suddenly realized it possessed some latent, malevolent power. The capstan continued its relentless, efficient rotation as the tape continued to feed through the recording head, an all but imperceptible hiss marking its passage. The Mazda's engine pinged ominously as it coped with a slight upward deviation in the grade of the road.

"On second thought," Matt continued, "in the spirit of world harmony, I will overlook the ill-feeling of that period and the present. Henceforth, they shall be called 'Japanese'—at least until I reach the first outpost of civilization.

"Anyway, old Uncle Pete said that on one of the islands—I don't remember just which one—they were ordered not to remove the dead *Japanese* soldiers from the beach. It was toward the end of the war. The Japanese had thrown kamikazes at them at Okinawa and their commanding officer had heard about the Snake Alley bit in Taipei and some of the other trick stuff. Two of the bodies on this particular beach had been booby-trapped. One engineer had been killed and another one lost a leg. So it was decided to just let them rot where they lay. Uncle Pete said that after a few days in the sun, besides smelling like nine kinds of hell, the bodies started to swell up. Then, one by one, they started to pop."

Matt hit the STOP button as he approached Coombe's Ditch. He slowed down, turned on the brights and reached across to lock the passenger door. He looked back toward the rocks. The star was a little higher in the sky. The moon was nowhere near the notch. He didn't stop.

"I suppose it's fermentation or some similar process," he continued, one eye trained on the rear-view mirror until sufficient distance had been put between himself and Coombe's Ditch. "The skin must trap all the gas from the decomposing sugars in the gut and such. Pressure probably builds until something gives. I guess the body in the refrigerator underwent more or less the same process. It's got to be hotter here and the closed refrigerator would act like an oven. The whole deal would be speeded up and the . . . 'boof' . . . might be strong enough to blow that door open."

He was coming up on the crossroads. A right turn would take him south to the sheriff's office in Brawley. The textbook play would be to bring the hand to the cops, and he considered doing just that, but he doubted, given his earlier experience, they would open an investigation even once confronted with such dramatic evidence. They'd probably just arrest him for grave-robbing, he figured.

When he spotted flames licking away at the pall of the sky up to the north, his mind was made up for him.

"As all dogs must chase their tails," he commented into the recorder, "all reporters must chase fires. It's in our Credo."

He made a left turn and buried the gas pedal. As he approached Cob City he began to hear the sirens riding out on the wind, coming and going like drunken wraiths, randomly starting and stopping at the mercy of the wayward breezes that deprived the sound of its continuity, fragmented it and reassembled the familiar wail into a thousand little screams crying out in the night. Beams of light rising up from a still distant point of concentrated frenzy—white, yellow, blue and red—slashed up against the gloom and were swallowed by it. A tangle of uprooted sage blew across the hood and caught on the radio antenna where it remained, fluttering like a hellish pompom.

Matt urged the Mazda to "go, go, go, go go," but the car was already moving as fast as it could. The disturbing ping had turned into a constant machine gun-like clatter. It reminded him of the pseudo-motorcycle sound he had produced as a kid by clothespinning a bubble-gum card in the path of his bicycle spokes. But whereas that noise had provided him with greater impact on his surroundings, the present racket made him feel powerless and reminded him he was at the mercy of a rather quirky, aged, abused and foreign machine. He slowed to the low eighties, feeling each mile grind by like the ones in the damnable recurring dream that never bring you closer to home. The fire was diminishing, almost in direct proportion to his approach. By the time he reached Cob City, it was out. Only the beacons and the sirens remained to mark the spot where the blaze had occurred. Matt homed in on them, his anxiety rising as he was forced to downshift into the thirties by the sight of two police cruisers parked under a billboard that read COB CITY—YOUR GATEWAY TO THE SALTON SEA.

Reporters, like detectives, spent 90 percent of their time piecing together events already passed; there was nothing more satisfying than covering a story as it was happening and fires often provided such an opportunity. Conversely, there was nothing quite as frustrating as busting your ass only to arrive as the last ember fizzled out. Matt tried to prepare himself for such a disappointment as he turned onto a dismal street most inappropriately named Grand Avenue. He drove past Adler's Serpentarium, a 7-11 and the local Chamber of Commerce, which was housed in an Airstream travel trailer. Adrenaline-saturated, the gallop of his heartbeat refused to heed the warnings of his brain and raced faster as he closed in on the scene. A last turn just before the

Union 76 station brought him onto Cholla Drive. He parked in front of Mason's Hardware Store, grabbed the Adidas bag and headed across the street.

The sign outside the burnt-out building read COB CITY LU-THERAN CHURCH AND COMMUNITY CENTER. It was a U-shaped, single-story structure with two wings jutting out toward the street at right angles from a shorter connecting section. The fire seemed to have started in the right wing—which appeared to be the church—then spread through the other sections, which were progressively less damaged. The church was totally demolished: The roof had caved in; the walls had collapsed; twisted, half-melted lengths of electrical conduit snaked up out of a waist-high mound of charred debris; what little was left of the steeple cross lay on the front walk, still glowing red-hot. Police, firemen and paramedics were clearing away the rubble. A man wearing a yellow-and-black Caterpillar cap was manipulating the levers of a sputtering backhoe, causing it to claw away at the fallen roof timbers. A man on a stepladder trained a spotlight on the scene. Others standing close by shouted directions and cautions over the racket of the earthmover.

Matt took a few wide shots with the Nikon, knowing they wouldn't turn out well: It was too dark; things were too confused; there was nothing special, nothing personal or odd. Just a gutted building smoldering in the night.

Walking up closer, Matt zigzagged through the knot of police cruisers and emergency vehicles, stepping gingerly between closely parked bumpers and fenders, always ready to marvel at how cops and other civil servant types, given half an excuse, parked helter-skelter at the site of a disaster, if at all possible blocking traffic—cars up on curbs if any were available, trucks pointing every which way as if to underscore the urgency of their arrival. And of course, adding to the chaos, any light that could flash was flashing, all beacons were turning and every radio loud-speaker was blaring. The only thing missing, he thought, was the usual spaghetti tangle of fire hoses. He puzzled over it briefly, then concluded that the blaze had been allowed to burn itself out. Perhaps in the desert, he reasoned, water was more precious than property. He scanned for hydrants. There weren't any. He made a mental note to check it out later.

As Matt passed through a meager assembly of spectators and onto the front walk, a boyish-looking deputy holding an extin-guisher hurried over. "Please stand back, sir," he said firmly, but politely enough.

Matt produced a press tag, holding it out for inspection. "It's okay," Matt said confidently, still moving forward.

The deputy backpedaled, not sure whether or not to let Matt pass. "Reporter, huh?" he stammered.

"Yeah," Matt answered. He paused to snap the deputy's pic-ture.

"Down from Palm Springs?"

"L.A."

"Jeez, you must've flew."

"Grabbed the company Lear."

Matt smiled and tried to step past the deputy. The young man held his ground.

"I'm sorry, sir. You're not allowed any closer. It's not safe."

"It's okay, really," Matt reassured him.

"Sir, I have my orders."

"I've got permission. Why else would I be here?" Matt snapped, for the first time sounding impatient.

"Well . . . I guess I could check with Deputy Chamber-lain."

The young officer started toward the backhoe. Matt noticed

his nemesis for the first time. He was on the other side of the shovel, barking orders and looking as nasty as ever.

"Maybe you're right," Matt said quickly, grabbing the young deputy by the sleeve. "It does look a bit dangerous. What the hell are they trying to do anyway?"

"There's a body they're trying to get out."

"Dead?"

"Yes sir."

Matt took out his notebook. The deputy's eyes brightened. Matt guessed it was the first time he'd been interviewed.

"Any other casualties?"

"They took a body out of the back of the church . . . or the front. I mean it's the back if you're inside, but the front if you're outside. That's the funny thing about churches."

"Identification?"

"They're pretty sure it was the pastor." He pointed to a body bag lying on a gurney. "Vail was his name, Patrick Vail. Somebody recognized his ring. It was the only way you could tell."

"Your basic crispy critter, huh?"

"Pardon."

"The second body. Any idea who that could be?"

"No. They're going to have trouble with that one if it's half as burned up as Vail."

"Must have spread pretty fast to catch them inside like that," Matt speculated.

"Doors were barred from the outside. Two-by-fours were nailed right across. Least that's what Farley said. He was the first one here. By the time we got here the doors had burned through."

"That's weird," Matt commented, perking up.

"Yeah . . . but . . . meaning no disrespect or anything, Mr. Farley isn't the most reliable person we've got around here."

The deputy nodded back toward an old man in a red plaid

shirt taking long swigs from a pint of Wild Turkey. Matt took him to be Farley.

"I see," Matt remarked with a wink.

"Ever since his wife passed on," the deputy explained.

"Too bad."

"Yeah."

"Still, doors barred or not, this thing really burned," Matt observed.

"A few in town here say they heard an explosion."

"Gas?"

"Just got electric out this way."

"Those walls are what? Adobe?" Matt asked, pointing to the part of the building still more or less intact.

"Stucco over concrete block."

"And this part here was the same stuff?"

"Yeah, but you got your roof and all those pews. Wooden floor maybe. Plenty to burn."

"Sure, but look at that mess. The joint's totaled. I could buy an explosion. Could be a firebomb. Klan does it all the time down south. You got the Klan out here?"

"Don't think so," the deputy answered after some deliberation.

"Was Vail black?"

"He sure as hell is now," someone answered. "Black as the ace of spades. Coal-black."

It was Farley. He had wandered up behind the deputy and stood with his feet planted wide, straddling the beam of the fallen cross. He peered stuporously at the liquor bottle. It fell from his hand and shattered on the walk. He stared at his hand, seemingly befuddled by the absence of the pint.

"C'mon, Mr. Farley. You're gonna hurt yourself," the deputy warned, catching the old man as he teetered forward.

"I just might," Farley muttered.

The deputy led him away.

Matt looked around. No one seemed to be watching him. He headed quickly over toward the left wing of the building and made his way inside through a breech in the wall.

It was almost impossible to see. Vaguely, through the lingering smoke, Matt was able to discern he was in a kitchen. There was a charred refrigerator, a separate freezer, a six-burner stove, a counter, cabinets and a sink. Dishes and silverware were piled in the basin. A fine mist of water was spraying from one of the valves, mixing with the smoke into a steamy cloud. Matt groped across the room, his hand outstretched like a blind beggar's. He bumped into a long, narrow table, easily big enough, he thought, to accommodate the Last Supper. He felt his way along its edge, barking his shins on chairs and finally getting to the far side of the room where he found a door which opened onto a larger chamber.

Three windows directly aligned with the vehicles outside admitted the agitated light from their beacons. The flickering shafts pierced in, the colors rippling through the smoke and making it seem as if the place were still ablaze. Matt was stunned to see two rows of cots set up barracks-style along the walls. He inspected the nearest one, finding it similar to the one he'd encountered at Coombe's Ditch. He grabbed it under the rail, cursed—the metal was still warm—and flipped it over. What was left of the mattress tumbled onto the floor. He looked for a number in the spot Dale had mentioned but couldn't see in the shadows. Excitedly, he dragged the cot into the closest beam of light. 1 was clearly visible, stenciled neatly in green.

"Dale, you Dick-fucking-Tracy you!" he whispered, his heart quickening.

Matt counted the cots in the room. There were nineteen in all, nine along the closest wall, ten along the farthest.

An odd number.

"Nobody has *nineteen* cots," he finished the thought out loud. "Twenty, however . . . An even score . . ."

Matt started tossing each one over, moving quickly from one to the next: number 2, number 3, number 4. Just as he was about to reach for the fifth cot, a large chunk of masonry crashed down from the ceiling, missing his head by inches. Another piece caved in just behind him, the heavy slab of sheet rock impaling itself on the legs of overturned cot number 4. A cloud of gypsum dust wafted up from the floor, blinding Matt momentarily and making him cough. The roof joists creaked ominously; stalactites of crumbling plaster spilled down from overhead; a window frame bowed, making a sound like a yawning lion; the glass panes wrenched, then imploded, sending a shower of jagged shards into the room. Matt heard them whistle by like poison darts from a Pygmy's blowgun, tinkle onto the floor like so many dropped Christmas tree ornaments.

Then the place went eerily quiet, almost silent, just the hourglass streams of gypsum dust hissing down. Matt knew he had to hurry.

Frantically, he dragged the fifth cot over into the light and turned it over. It was completely scorched. He rubbed the scabrous, black crust with his handkerchief, but still couldn't make out a stencil. A hurried inspection of the Adidas bag didn't produce anything of sufficient sharpness to scrape off the char. "Shit!" he cursed, then remembered he'd seen a knife in the kitchen sink.

He ran back to the door and propped it open to let in the light before crossing over quickly to the sink. For the first time he saw the crumpled body of a dead dog over in the corner. It looked to be a hound of some kind—long-eared and droopy-skinned, a slab of tongue lolling out of its smoke-choked throat, the wide-open, lifeless eyes following him like those on a Jesus picture in a downtown novelty store. Matt found it curious he felt more remorse for the dead mongrel than for either of the human fatalities. Too much time on the pet desk, he figured, then turned his attention to the sink basin where the plastic handle of the knife had melted onto a plate. He snapped off the blade and ran back into the other room.

Carefully, he pulled the blade across the metal rail of the cot, shaving away the black crust. A speck of green began to show. He etched more away. Bit by bit, as he hoped it would, the number 5 appeared.

There was an empty space where the sixth cot should have stood. Matt felt all he had to do was find a 7 on the next cot in line. It would be proof enough. He had based stories on far less. Schiff would be proud. The Malibu botch would be forgiven.

A rumbling started in the walls, gradually spreading into the ceiling, encompassing Matt and making him feel he was in the gut of some underworld beast experiencing a bout of indigestion. Nails began tearing out of wood, little screams from deep within the walls. Matt grabbed the Adidas bag, unconsciously cradling it to his chest like a sleeping baby. Apprehensively, he gazed up toward the ceiling. Cracks were opening everywhere, zippering across each other. He took a scared step toward the cot he knew was number 7. A ceiling joist crashed down, driving through its frame. A squall of feathers from the punctured mattress went crazy in the light.

There was no time left. The place was breaking apart.

A sound like a bowling ball rolling down a flight of oaken stairs got Matt moving toward the shattered window. Roof timbers were giving way, one by one, breaking loose from the ridge plate, dropping through the ceiling and slamming to the floor. Matt felt a woosh of hot air as one swung down behind him like a blunt pendulum. At a full, panicked run, without breaking pace, he jumped onto a nearby cot, sprung off it like it was a trampoline, and flew through the window in a loose cannonball.

The rest of the Cob City Lutheran Church and Community Center fell in upon itself. The resulting dust cloud was so thick, nothing could be seen even of the mad, spinning lights of the police cruisers. Matt stumbled away, crawling at first, then running, falling, dragging the bag behind him, blindly crashing into something, cutting himself on it—an agave tree, maybe—picking himself up, running again, hoping he was headed in the right direction, away from the collapse.

Matt emerged from the cloud in the middle of Cholla Drive. He staggered toward the Mazda, leaving ghostly-white powdered footprints on the pavement. Exhausted more by the fear he had experienced than the effort he had expended, he fell across the front seat. At length he was able to catch his breath and calm himself. Slowly he took inventory: He was covered from head to toe by masonry dust; glossy patches on his arms marked various cuts and scrapes, none of which seemed serious; his left knee felt tight, swollen; the Adidas bag seemed to have survived. . . .

Something was in his hand.

The knife.

He sat up, switched on the dome light, wiped the powder off the blade and read the delicate engraving.

Ginsu.

4

6 OC   8 CUMKU

AT THE COMPLETION OF
12 BAKTUNS
18 KATUNS
8 TUNS
14 UINALS
10 KINS

the next day . . .

Rebecca Miles went into her secret place and locked herself in.

It was dirty, hot and cramped in the tiny storeroom behind the pulpit of the Church of the Word but Rebecca didn't notice. The space, small as it was, belonged to her, and so, there was no sense of confinement. The air was musty, but she drank it in as if it were ambrosia wafting over a mountain glen. It was her air; no one else breathed it: It was good.

She shared her meager cellar kitchen and table with eight

strangers; she slept behind a heavy silver curtain that had once hung in a local theater, in a room that one day would be a church; a problem with the hot-water heater forced strict apportionment of time spent in the one bathroom that yet functioned: The storeroom was a blessed retreat, her little aerie above the bedlam of the cellar. It was a liberating place whose four walls and bolted door did not shut her in. They locked others out.

Between teetering stacks of cartons, Rebecca came down the narrow, crooked aisle, as she had many times before, and sat on the trunk against the far wall in the weak light that fell from a small octagonal window up near the peak of the gable.

Most of what was left of their possessions was still packed away in the boxes which filled the room. She had already forgotten what her wedding china and silver pattern looked like, her Sunday dresses, her mother's collection of Hummels. She could only recall Michigan with great force of concentration, always picturing the view from the back porch of the old house, a winter scene with icicles tonguing down off the gutters and the barren cherry tree branches etching lines into the pewter sky like age cracks on an Etruscan fresco. Those things she remembered best were the things they had sold to finance their westward mission: the old Mason Hamlin baby grand, the massive breakfront tooled in Chinese lacquer with doors of crown glass, the Italian ceramic lamps, the Persian rug with the orange Kool-Aid stain, the goofy-looking bust of Mozart in Carrara marble, the mock-Chippendale dining room set, even the hideous Parisian street scene which hung in its gold-leaf frame over the sofa and which she hated, all the varied and wonderful things her parents had accumulated over a lifetime and left to her, none of it matching, none of it bought to decorate or to blend in, all of it special, one of a kind, with a story attached. And all gone; converted to cash. Most of her inheritance had been spent on the Braxton Wells real estate. Plywood, nails, tools, insulation, two-by-fours, shingles, plumbing supplies, circuit-breakers and a thousand other needs had quickly swallowed up the rest.

It was not productive to dwell on things past and gone—*material* things, no matter how sentimental. They were best forgotten. Nathan's work was what mattered, *his* church, *his* sanctuary. Across from her was a carton labeled TOWELS. She was tempted to open it, just to see the word HERS on something. She listened for a moment to the uneven rhythm of Nathan hammering up on the roof. It was the sound of the new life they were building—according to *his* plan.

She opened the brown paper bag she had carried in with her and pulled out a magazine. She had snatched a handful off the rack in the grocery store in Banning and plunked them on the cashier's counter without even looking. It was more fun that way, although she had repeated the ritual enough times to guess by the size or weight, the feel of the paper or an unintended peripheral glance, just which publications her "blind faith" had selected.

The little one, as she thought, was a *TV Guide*. They had sold their television along with the rest of their Michigan things. They were no longer to be watchers, Nathan had said; they were to be doers. It was essential to "the plan." Nonetheless, Rebecca went through it from cover to cover, amazed by how many of the programs had changed since she last had been a "watcher." The programs themselves, she speculated, were probably not that different from what she remembered, but at least the names had changed.

The next magazine was a *McCall's*. There were some wonderful recipes she wanted to try. One for roast leg of lamb looked especially delicious. And there were exercises for reducing flabby thighs and tips for "dressing to win." But she was most interested in the results of a poll entitled "What Women Really Want from Their Men."

The third periodical was *People*. She enjoyed thumbing through it, but couldn't help but wonder how it came to pass that some humans found their way onto such glossy pages while others wound up down below in her cellar. What was the blessing—or curse—that so violently separated destinies, that put some on the high road and others on the low? Nathan was comfortable with "God's will," but Nathan didn't read *People*.

The last publication to be pulled out of the bag was *Here and There*. She stared at the pictures on the front page for a time that only seemed long, like her first walk to the end of the high-dive at the municipal pool or her first slow dance at the tenth-grade homecoming. It was a time that cut itself into separate moments, each tick a chop of the guillotine, each instant a new fear or an old one brought closer, falling in a stream against each other like dominoes. She started to read the article by someone named Matthew Teller, but interrupted herself to glance back at the door, making sure the bolt was in place. Then she forced herself to read it straight through, fighting off the urge to look away, even to catch her breath. This horrible thing, which had happened so close by, came to her in jumbled fragments, dreamlike, a fever vision carried on words without reasons.

Nathan's hammering had stopped. Sometime while she had been reading, she suspected, the pounding had stopped. She became aware of the quiet. Its arms were around her. It had crept up and boxed her in. The only sounds came from herself—her breathing, fast and shallow, the creaking of the trunk beneath her as she shifted her weight, the agitation in her gut, the beating of her heart.

At that moment she wanted to fold herself up and pack herself away in one of the cartons, snuggle in and wait for the storm to pass. Instead, she rose, walked over to the center of the room and pulled down some boxes, setting them aside. Before long she was able to get to an old bassinet, an antique they had picked up near Battle Creek just before the move. Someday it would hold their child; now it held eighteen dusty old volumes of the *Encyclopaedia Britannica*, A through R. She pulled it into the aisle, leaving inky fingerprints on the white enamel.

A pole of light shot up through the oaken floor. She got down on her knees, put her eye to the knothole she had discovered the day before, and watched.

•

Matt was not surprised to see a gunmetal-gray, round metal trash can, well dented from numerous encounters with Schiff's Guccis, standing where his desk had once been. Nor was he alarmed that his fellow workers at *H&T* did their best to ignore his presence. He knew that even so much as a "hello" to one so prominently catalogued on Schiff's legendary shit list would be grounds for summary dismissal. He knew, too, they'd be watching closely from the well-practiced corners of their eyes for any subtle change in the direction of Schiff's ill-wind. But until the situation was clear, they would avoid all forms of contact, a circumstance which had at least two advantages: Izzy could be effectively avoided (if it was possible to entirely avoid someone roughly the size of a Toyota) and Marlene could be stared at for indefinite periods of time without fear of the ever-debilitating "just what do you think you're looking at" counter-stare. Unfortunately, he had no time to exploit either opportunity.

Matt marched straight through editorial and barged into Schiff's office without knocking. The trick was to act as if nothing were wrong. "I've got the front page for next week," he announced, trying to sound upbeat and confident.

Schiff looked up from his paperwork, put down his Cross pen

and scanned the office from corner to corner through the smoke which streamed from an ashtray filled with the remains of the morning's numerous Camels. Then, as if he had seen nothing, least of all another human being standing but five feet away, he picked up the pen and continued with his work.

"I got a firebombing in a church," Matt continued.

Schiff yawned.

"I got some weird native type with a cut-off toe."

The publisher stretched, arching his back to work out the kinks.

"I got burnt-up clergy," Matt persisted.

Schiff sifted through the mail in his in-basket, extracted a large green envelope and dumped the contents on the desk.

"And I got everything tied into the stiff at Coombe's Ditch."

Schiff finished off his Camel, sucking hard, squinty-eyed and looking as if he would inhale until it completely disappeared. When it was down to a tiny nub and threatened to singe his yellowed fingertips, he gave it up and whistled the smoke out through his teeth like steam expelled from a reducing valve. "Said stiff, by the way," Schiff replied acidly, finally breaking his silence, but without looking up from his work, "has yet to surface in any other publication save ours."

"That's good."

"That's odd!" The publisher ground the butt into the ashtray.

" 'Odd feeds the bulldog,' someone once said."

"Me. I said it," Schiff retorted, pounding his chest, getting ink on his shirt and popping out of his chair.

"You want odd, you get odd," Matt countered.

"I want a bimbo with big titties on my front page!" Schiff bellowed. He bounded around the desk in a clumsy, loping move that left him eyeball to eyeball with Matt. "I want her boyfriend looking guilty as hell but with a smile on his face. I want pictures. I want copy. I want an angle. Did they do it? Didn't they do it? Did they do it lying down, standing up or inside out? Is that too much to ask?"

"It's too little to ask, Barnie. That's the whole problem."

Matt wished he hadn't said it. He expected Schiff to turn crimson, invent at least three new expletives and give him the boot. Instead, the publisher walked slowly back behind his desk and retook his seat. He sat there not saying anything for at least a minute, staring holes through Matt who acted appropriately unnerved by the scrutiny.

"That *is* always the issue," Schiff said at last. "What you ask. What you want. What you take." The publisher looked down at the ink mark on his shirt and dabbed at it with a moistened finger. "You're smart, Matthew. Too damn smart to be working here. We both know that. We just don't know the why of it." Schiff sighed. He had managed to turn the one thin line of ink into a blue smudge the size of a quarter. "You take advantage of me and I take advantage of you. I indulge you and you indulge me. The only fundamental difference is that I write the checks you live on." He dug a fresh pack of Camels out of his pocket. "So. If I ask for more, what will I get?"

"Death in the Desert, Part Two," Matt answered.

"Part One ain't exactly turning the world upside down."

"What's wrong with it?"

"It's not selling. It's not clicking the way I thought. Retail is off four percent from last week."

"That's not exactly a disaster."

"I don't change a press run for *off four points.* By my definition it ranks right up there with famine, pestilence and drought."

"Ten years ago, I bet you couldn't have printed enough of these, Barnie."

"Blood still sells. The same market that bought blood ten years ago, buys it today. But the game is bigger. You got to go with the numbers." Schiff lit up another Camel. "Mama's embarrassed to cart home Coombe's Ditch with the butter and eggs. She wants celebrities and scandals. Who's fucking who at the zoo. It's safer." The publisher shrugged and made a circular motion with the cigarette, an indication Matt should tell his story. The mannerism carried a tone of disinterest, of "let's get it over with."

"These three strange-looking guys get picked up in the vicinity of the murder the day after," Matt began, settling into the chair opposite the desk and still feeling, despite Schiff's "indulgence," that he was on very thin ice. "They speak a language no one's heard before. Nobody knows where they came from. One of them is missing his middle toe."

"So?"

"So the stiff at Coombe's Ditch was missing a middle toe."

"The stiff at Coombe's Ditch was missing so much that the stiff himself is missing."

Matt ignored the sarcasm and went on with his story: "The three weird guys get hauled into the local pokey for attacking a cop with a Ginsu steak knife."

"I like that." Schiff smiled for the first time.

"I thought you would."

"So we got three guys in the slammer, some mumbo-jumbo and the blade with the lifetime warranty," Schiff recapped.

"They're not in jail," Matt clarified. "The sheriff turned them over to INS and by now you couldn't find them with a bloodhound and a herd of Mounties. Deported or sent to a detention center or transferred to a processing facility . . . I got a headache just talking with those guys on the phone."

"So we got three guys who aren't in the slammer and a stiff who ain't at Coombe's Ditch. This is sort of an un-story."

"Remember the cot?" Matt inquired, starting a new tact.

"Fondly."

"There's these three guys—"

"Without toes who aren't in the slammer."

"Different three guys. These three guys found the cot . . . also in the vicinity."

"And you've examined this cot and you are satisfied it's *the* cot?"

"The cot is not available to me."

"You are consistent, Matthew."

"It's the cot. There was a body, too."

"*Was?*"

"It blew up."

"Of course."

"And was eaten by birds."

"Novel."

"Scout's honor." Matt raised three fingers.

"And of course no trace, no shred could be found. Not an eyelash, a hairy knuckle or a belly button was spared, I bet. Not even a fingernail, let alone a fingerprint."

"A hand. A right hand."

"Really?" Schiff asked with genuine surprise.

"Yeah," Matt answered quite casually, as if it were no big deal.

"With fingerprints?" the publisher asked in a tone that said he was expecting a catch.

Matt opened the folder that was lying on his lap. It was empty.

"What the—"

Matt fumbled through the other files he had carried in with him. Schiff frowned, cupped his hands behind his head and rocked back in his chair.

"Jesus, Barnie, I've got them on a sheet of acetate. I must have grabbed the wrong folder. . . . I got in late. Everything's screwed up. I spent half the morning looking for a tape. Never did find it. . . . This Coombe's Ditch thing has got me all turned around. . . . Here it is!"

He removed a sheet of clear acetate from a folder labeled BACKGROUND.

"Must have put it in here by accident."

He handed it across the desk to Schiff, who peered at the fingerprint smudges Matt had recorded.

"Will your buddy in homicide track them down?" Matt inquired.

"It'll take a while. It always does. He's got to back-door it. Slip it into some other investigation."

"I know how it works."

"We're not going to tell him where we got these."

"Okay."

"These better not turn up belonging to the Archbishop of Canterbury or some bullshit like that."

"More likely they won't turn up at all."

"Either way we're not going to know shit by deadline. You better have more than this."

"The church in Cob City burns up last night," Matt continued. "Firebombed. Two guys get toasted. One's a John Doe. The other is the pastor, a guy named Patrick Vail."

"Old news. Film at eleven. *Last* night."

"I'm on the phone all morning getting bio on this Vail. I found out he spent ten years in the Amazon doing missionary work. They got lots of weird shit in the Amazon, Barnie."

Schiff shrugged. "They got their share."

"Remember the guy without the toe. Maybe he's talking

some jungle jive, some obscure tribal dialect. Maybe he belongs to some kinked-out cult that's into mutilation and human sacrifice."

"Maybe he's just some poor slob who got too close to the lawn mower."

"I think this Vail imported some of his old bush buddies and the natives got restless."

"Where's it connect to the stiff at Coombe's Ditch?"

"In the annex of the church I find nineteen cots just like the one at Coombe's Ditch. *Nineteen*, Barnie. That's a one-short number if I ever heard one. Nobody's got nineteen of anything. That's an accident number."

"Very thin, Matthew."

"The cot at Coombe's Ditch had a number. Number six."

"I don't remember that little detail from your story."

"The three guys who found the cot gave me the number."

"The three wise men who found the manger."

"More like the Three Stooges . . . Dogpatch-style."

"Just once, sometime before I croak, we're going to catch a break and get an eyewitness whose name ain't Lemuel or Silas."

"The cots in the church were numbered. And there's no number six."

"You checked all nineteen?"

"No. The roof caved in."

"Convenient."

"I found this at the church, too."

Matt removed the Ginsu knife blade from his pocket and handed it to Schiff. The publisher shrugged again and dropped it on the desk.

"There's ten billion of these things floating around. Everyone who has a TV set and credit card owns at least a dozen. And you don't even have it tied to the stiff."

"I got it tied to Mr. Mumbo-Jumbo without the toe."

"Who ain't tied to the stiff either."

"Something cut that guy up," Matt argued. "Just like one of these sliced that cop."

"And that's the only story you got here!" Schiff concluded, pounding the desk like a judge gaveling a decision into the record. " 'Ginsu Attack, Policeman Injured by Television Steak Knife.' I'll give you three columns on page seven. Make it funny."

Matt started to protest. "Barnie—"

"That's all I see here . . . for now at least."

•

Rebecca lay in her bed wondering what had become of her husband.

Since late morning, ever since the hammering on the roof stopped, there had been no trace of him. After prying herself away from the knothole, she searched everywhere, but Nathan was not to be found on the roof or in the cellar or anyplace in between. At first, she thought he'd gone into town for supplies, but the pickup truck hadn't been moved from its parking place. Her fears grew as the day progressed, germinating easily in the fecund ground of her earlier discovery. Only her stalwart act in front of the refugees, the cooking and cleaning and tending to baby Sebastian as if nothing were amiss, saved her. In the middle of it all, as she was changing Sebastian's diaper, the strengthening thought came: *Act as if you have faith and faith will be given you.* "Thank you, Paul," she said to herself, appreciating that there was a letter to Rebecca—or at least enough to fill a telegram—among all that voluminous correspondence to the Galatians, the Thessalonians, the Corinthians and the others.

But now there was no more acting to do. There was just waiting and worrying and being alone. It was the time of "doubt-bringers and faith-killers," as Nathan would say. Rebecca felt the claws scraping away at her resolve. Alone, in bed, with no one but herself to be strong for, she became weak.

Did she still love him? What a thought to come at such a time! Not a new thought, either. *Doubt-bringers and faith-killers indeed!*

She pulled the quilt up tight to her chin but it couldn't shut out the chill breath of fear.

The bed stood in the center of the Church of the Word. Lined up beside it like inventory in a resale shop were a maple dresser, a matching semainier, a deacon's bench, an antique armoire with one broken door and a china cabinet which had proved too large to pass through the cellar stairwell. The furniture —those few pieces they had brought with them—formed a partition of sorts, a barricade on one flank against the cavernous, threatening emptiness of the room. On the opposite side, the heavy silver curtain which had once draped the screen of the now defunct Banning Bijou hung from a cable rigged between two concrete stanchions. It, too, helped cut the room down to size, but Rebecca still felt as if she were sleeping in the middle of a railroad station. She even had dreams to that effect and others in which she "awoke" repeatedly to find the church full of people, crowded in pews all around her, singing hymns, bearing witness, their eyes cast up toward Nathan and delicately trying to ignore her.

She hated sleeping in that room. It was not a place meant for rest, for giving way to the night, for the closing of eyes and the balm of sweet dreams. The room always had the feeling of others passing by, of footsteps, of people watching, of things happening all around or about to happen. It was not a place for just two people.

It was certainly not a place for intimacy.

She felt ashamed. It was not what she wanted to be thinking about, but the thought, the question, kept returning.

How many times had they made love since coming west? Twice? Three times maybe? Two or three hurried couplings in the dark—each squeak of the springs echoing repeatedly, mocking them from the far corners like flocks of noisy crows, the covers pulled so tight around them it almost seemed as if they were fully clothed—two or three bigger disappointments on top of many smaller ones. She kept waiting for something which never quite happened, something scary and mysterious, fluid and irresistible— not just the shallow, quick orgasms she'd been lucky enough to experience from time to time—something she knew only by its absence, by its teasing, tempting unreachableness, something which Nathan seemed unable or unwilling to provide. They'd both been virgins on their wedding night, but inexperience no longer seemed a suitable excuse.

It troubled her that such longings could consume her so. It seemed so wanton, so selfish. But the more she struggled to deny her feelings, the more she felt as if she were being erased in tiny bits, morsels just rubbed out at random and lost forever. She'd come through a door or around a corner and suddenly feel that one more piece had been wiped out.

Nathan, even preoccupied as he was, had sensed that something was wrong. He'd blamed it on the newness of the surroundings. They would get used to it in time, he'd promised. They'd get a cozy trailer to live in; there they'd "make babies": That was part of "the plan." Nathan had planned everything—

A woman screamed.

Rebecca heard a timid, choked sound come from the back of her throat. It felt as if a brick had been dropped on her Adam's apple. She saw the goose bumps rise on her arms, the peach-fuzz hair curling up like insect feelers.

The scream continued, cutting through from the back of the church, sawing up from beneath the floor. She had heard it before, on each of the two previous nights since the refugees arrived, never to be acknowledged the following morning, let alone explained. Just as on the other nights, it stopped as abruptly as it started, leaving a morsel of charged silence in the brief interlude before baby Sebastian began to cry.

Rebecca stared at the key ring held tight in her fist. She had locked all the doors earlier. It was not the first time she had followed Townes's instructions, but it was the first time she had understood the reason for them. She tried to think of a prayer, but nothing particularly relevant came to mind.

The side door shook, the knob rattled, keys jingled, scraped, pushed into the lock. The old hinges growled as the door opened. It was Nathan. She knew from the footsteps. There was a pattern to everything he did and she knew each one. But when he appeared a few moments later, there was nothing familiar about him. It was a stranger who pushed his way through the silver curtain. Her husband, but a stranger.

"I was so worried!" she gasped, both hands now clutching the key ring.

"I was wrong, Rebecca," he said, panting and pacing back and forth in front of the curtain. The lamp on the floor next to the bed threw his shadow up into the pleats where it billowed like a trailing storm cloud.

"Thank God you're all right," she said fervently, meaning it, and happy that for once her emotions seemed to be the proper ones.

"I'm not all right! Nothing's all right!" Nathan snapped.

"Where were you?"

"In the desert. I went out. Way past the arroyo." He rushed over to the bed. "As far as I dared." He bent down and put his hands over hers. Looking into her eyes, he asked, "Do you know what's out there, Rebecca?"

"What?"

Nathan straightened up, smiled and shook his head. "Nothing," he whispered, as if it were a secret. "Nothing at all."

"I don't understand."

"There's no Burning Bush, Rebecca."

"Nathan, what's wrong?"

"We put the building first."

"That was part of your plan."

"Vanity deludes, ego destroys, intellect deceives!" he raved, pacing back toward the curtain, throwing his arms up in despair. "What an ingenious plan! How tremendously clever!" He noticed his monstrous silhouette and addressed his next woeful line to it: "Behold the sinner. Behold the fool."

"Behold the man."

"Said Pilate to the mob."

"I meant only that you are human, Nathan."

"Humanity is not an excuse, Rebecca."

"Sometimes it has to be."

"And often is. But I am not allowed that wonderful loophole. Never have been. I've always known better."

Rebecca had never seen her husband like this. He *had* always known better. He always seemed to possess some special map, drawn just for him, telling him just which turns to take, showing him the secret way around each of life's many obstacles.

"It was wrong to start with the building," he continued. "I knew better. Everybody knows better. You always start with the church. People, prayer, worship. We could have bought a small house closer to town, had meetings in our living room, done it by the book, built a congregation family by family, person by person.

The Catholics can start with a building. They seem to get away with it. They've been at it longer, I suppose. . . ."

His voice trailed off. He was standing in front of the curtain, staring blankly at his own silhouette. Rebecca sat up in the bed and watched her own shadow meet her husband's.

"You had a vision," she said consolingly. "You can't fault yourself for trying to do something more."

"How clever it was," he reasoned to his shadow. "A building first. A real buy, a *steal*. A building big enough to be a home for those who have no home. And with that purpose, upon that example, our church would be built. The people would come."

"And they will," Rebecca insisted.

"They can't!" he shouted. He swung around and marched back to the bed. "It's forbidden by Father Townes. Don't you remember?"

"Temporarily."

"But Townes is dead, Rebecca, and nobody else knows about our little jail in the desert."

Rebecca shuddered at the idea of Townes being dead. She crossed her arms across her breasts and gave herself a quick, reassuring hug. But Nathan was mistaken. Had to be. The man in the newspaper had died before Townes even brought the refugees. No wonder Nathan was so upset. She would explain, and since Nathan already knew about the murder she'd be spared the embarrassment of explaining how she had come to read a publication such as *Here and There*.

"No," she began, "it couldn't be Father Townes."

"Did you hear it, too?" Nathan cut in. "I was on the roof, finishing the work on the flashing. I had the Christian music station from Los Angeles on the radio. I couldn't believe it at first. The hammer dropped out of my hand. It's a good thing you weren't walking underneath."

"It can't be him, Nathan."

"I pray you're right. But something tells me it *was* him. Who else would be with Pastor Vail so late at night?"

"Pastor Vail?" Rebecca asked timidly, suddenly remembering Townes telling her to expect the unexpected.

"Poor soul. Burned to death in his own church."

"Oh my God!" she gasped, her hands coming together instinctively in the posture of prayer.

"I hope they won't identify the other body as Townes, but somehow I just know it's him."

Rebecca couldn't speak. She couldn't find a way to tell Nathan about the other death, the anonymous corpse on the front page of the tawdry newspaper she had no business reading. She couldn't recount the terrible mutilations, the disgorged eye like Coh's, the missing thumbs like Soto's, those plaguing coincidences that had so arrested her earlier. It would only make matters worse, and she was not prepared to endure the inevitable questions he would ask. There was no possible way she could justify why she felt it absolutely necessary to lock herself up in the storeroom from time to time and browse through magazines blindly plucked from the grocer's shelf, how she found something in those pages that kept her going, reconnecting her to a life *he* had forsaken but which *they both* had left behind. It would sound trivial, *grotesquely* trivial. And she didn't feel like lying.

"Nathan, what's happening?" she asked fearfully.

Nathan considered the question carefully. Rebecca watched as he turned it over in his mind, and for a moment, hoping against hope, she thought he might reply with some suitable analysis, some simple, satisfying, calming exegesis.

"Evil!" he answered.

It was not the explanation Rebecca sought, although it was one she had heard before, rendered, when no others were available, for various calamities. It meant he had given up. He would wait. He would dig in and pray.

"What can we do?" she asked.

"Nothing."

"No," she protested.

"Nothing. There is no right thing to do."

"Nathan, we can't pray our way out of this. We have to *do* something."

"I've been over it and over it a thousand times. . . ."

"We can't just sit here and wait."

"If Townes is true to his word, then no one else knows about us."

"I believe him."

"So do I."

"No one will be coming for them."

"Yes, Rebecca, that's the thought that had me stumbling through the desert. No one will come for them. We must keep them locked up in the cellar. And we can't tell them what has happened."

"They have a right to know. What will they think when nobody comes, day after day?"

"They'll think something has gone wrong. They'll become suspicious and turn on us."

It was a dismal prospect, but then Rebecca thought of something far, far worse.

"Nathan, what if somebody *does* come?"

5

8 EB   IO CUMKU

AT THE COMPLETION OF
12 BAKTUNS
18 KATUNS
8 TUNS
14 UINALS
12 KINS

two days later . . .

Buchanon awoke.

At least he thought he was awake. His eyes were lost behind warm globs of putty, air horns echoed in his ears, his limbs could not move—so there was no way to know for sure. But there were smells, earthy smells: sweat, dirt, urine, something cooking. It was his nose that led him back to consciousness.

The scout locked onto a pungent aroma, a smoky, oily, fried-thing smell that was completely alien and not at all appetizing. He picked out the strange scent from all the others as it drifted by, decided it was the one to follow out of limbo, took it in carefully through nostrils that seemed disembodied, felt it curl up behind useless eyes and sponged it up with the landfill that was his brain. Cell by cell, like a vial of salts taken into every dark nook and cranny of his protoplasm, the smell woke him up.

His eyes bored through. The putty opened. The optic nerve plugged back in. The pupils glistened, stung and began to focus.

The first thing he saw was a face, recognizable but unplaceable, someone he had seen before—years earlier or was it days?—alarm in the dark eyes, the brow creased with concern, the index finger held up to pursed lips, furtive glances to the right, then back to him.

The air horns were fading, drifting further and further back into the far grandstand, lingering faintly in the cheap seats, all but silenced. For a brief moment he saw the outfield flags, pennant after pennant, all in a row. The wind was blowing in, gently—

Again the face. Again the index finger to the lips. Overhead, laundry hanging from a line, mildly rippling in a breeze.

It was Héctor.

Recalling Héctor's name was an accomplishment. It told Buchanon he was among the living: His brain seemed to be functioning; he was remembering things. There was a fleeting moment of euphoria, quickly stomped out by the further recollection that the name was connected with that awful, sickly, purple dive where the unthinkable had occurred.

The familiar headache began. Buchanon groaned.

Héctor pounced on him, covering his mouth with his hand. The scout struggled to throw him off. Another man, much older but surprisingly strong, his face a dark shadow under the brim of an enormous straw hat, pinned his shoulders.

"Do not make a sound!" Héctor whispered. "These good people risk everything to have you in their house."

Buchanon did not understand. He bit into Héctor's palm. The younger man winced in pain but did not remove his hand. *"Mago!"* he hissed.

Buchanon's jaw went slack.

After he was sure the scout would remain silent, Héctor removed his bleeding hand and sucked on the wound. The other man continued to hold Buchanon down but there was really no need. That one evil word had rendered the big American motionless.

"Are you sober finally?" Héctor asked contemptuously.

Buchanon grunted.

"You have been drunk for many days. You have said dangerous things. Stupid things, threats you cannot even begin to fulfill."

"I'll kill him."

Héctor shook his head. *"El bolo dice que va a matar al Mago,"* he said to the older man. The man did not laugh, but Buchanon saw the bemused smile even in the darkness under the brim of his big straw hat. Buchanon looked around, for the first time realizing he was lying on the dirt floor of a tiny one-room house. Héctor and the other man were kneeling beside him. An old woman was cooking something over in the corner. She was mumbling to herself, half laughing, half coughing. A younger woman was taking clothes off the line that zigzagged back and forth across the room. She laughed boisterously, unable to contain herself even when cautioned to keep quiet, sounding as one does when one laughs at a child for making some outlandish, impossible statement. A teenaged boy stood at the door. He had it open a crack and was intently peering outside. His back was turned, but Buchanon could tell by the shudder that went through his body that he was snickering as well. Only the three children who were playing with a kitten on a woven rug in the center of the room seemed oblivious to the mockery. Two boys teased the cat with a cloth mouse which they held just out of its reach. The youngest child, a little doe-eyed girl, didn't like their game. She picked up the kitten and held it to her cheek.

"You are pathetic," Héctor said to Buchanon.

"He's a dead man," Buchanon vowed.

"No, Señor Buchanon, you are the dead man. Less than dead. You are no more. You are disappeared. Gone. Vanished."

The dull throbbing in the back of Buchanon's head spread forward into his eyes and downward into his chest.

"Do you have anything to drink?" he rasped.

"You are a memory, Buchanon. For one generation, maybe. The lifetime of someone who cares."

"Nobody gives a fuck."

"Then you are nothing."

The old woman was suddenly beside him, offering a cup of strong-smelling tea. The man in the straw hat held his head as the woman poured it down his throat. It tasted terrible, but he gulped it down.

"I wonder if you are worth it," Héctor said.

"I need a drink."

"If I had left you in Escuintla—"

"Where am I?"

"The mountains. A small village. This place is not on any map."

Buchanon fought down a wave of nausea.

"If I had left you in Escuintla," Héctor continued, "he would have you by now. You would be gone. You're gone now if I send you back."

"He wouldn't dare touch an American."

"But you have made too many insults, too many threats. Mago has had time to check, to see if you are important, if you will be missed. *Are you important,* Buchanon? Will your people lodge a protest when you disappear?"

"More likely they'll throw a goddamn party."

"I thought as much."

"Give me a drink, Héctor. I've got money."

"You have nothing."

"My World Series ring."

Héctor shook his head. Buchanon raised his hand. The ring was gone.

"I've decided to get you out," Héctor said, making it sound as if the decision were already regretted. "You stood up to Mago. And to his pimp, Reyes. You did it out of stupidity, but it was seen by others. It gives hope. If I let Mago have you, the people see that his power is even greater, that he can even cause the big *Norte Americano* to disappear. But if I get you out, then they see that even a *borracho,* a worthless drunkard, can insult Mago and get away with it. And perhaps, with that in mind, they will leave the fields and come into the mountains where we will train them to be freedom fighters."

"You're a goddamn rebel!" Buchanon accused.

"Buchanon, when you were just coming out of your stupor a few minutes ago, a jeep was driving by. There was a *Kaibil* in back with a bullhorn, a pinto from Mago's unit. He said, 'Beware all those who support the insurrection! We annihilate the insurrection! We annihilate the children of the insurrection!' If you feel more comfortable with them, you may wait outside. Another patrol is sure to be along any minute. There's been a full mobilization."

"Because of me?" Buchanon asked dully.

"Don't flatter yourself. A band of Quiché refugees raided the garrison at Santa Rosita in Petén. It's excuse enough."

"Héctor, just get me a drink. Get me jump-started and I'll be okay."

"I'll get you out, Buchanon. I'll save your life. That's all I can do for you."

"*Jesus!*" Buchanon turned to the old man. "*¿Gallo? ¿Indita? ¿Botran?*"

The old man shook his head to each of the requests.

"*¿Venado? ¿Monte Carlo?* C'mon, pal. *¿Chiricuta, cusha?* What do you say?"

"He doesn't have enough to feed his children dinner tonight," Héctor cut in sharply. "Don't be offended he cannot offer his guest liquor."

The boy watching at the door turned suddenly. "*¡Ya vienen!*" he said urgently.

"Just a taste," Buchanon persisted.

"Shut up!" Héctor snapped. "Be quiet and we might live."

Ten or twelve vehicles roared by at high speed. Unintelligible announcements blaring from a loudspeaker whooshed by with them. After a short pause, the throaty engine of a large troop-carrier could be heard coming up the road.

The old man released Buchanon and climbed up on a chair. He reached up into the thatched roof and pulled out an ancient bolt-action rifle which he handed to the boy at the door. Then he extricated a shotgun for himself. Héctor slid a magazine into a Beretta automatic. The old woman stationed herself by a window and pulled a carving knife from her apron. The younger woman held a corn pestle like a club. The oldest of the three children cradled a machete.

With difficulty, Buchanon pulled himself up, staggered over to the front window and looked out through a slat in the wooden shutter. There was a row of small huts on either side of a dirt road. About fifty yards away, a small clearing passed for what, with some imagination, could be considered a town square. Wilted flowers lay at the feet of a plaster statue of the Virgin nestled in a modest stone alcove. A signpost pointed the way to Uspantán and San Cristóbal Verapaz. Off to the side was a water spigot. A young boy was filling a bucket. His mother called to him frantically. He dropped the bucket and ran to her, leaving the water on. A puddle formed and rivulets snaked out.

The troop-carrier parked in front of the little shrine. Moments later, a jeep eased up beside it. A machine-gunner drew back the bolt of a 50-caliber mounted on its rear fender. His assistant deftly fed in the ammo belt. An officer stepped down from the front passenger door, crossed himself perfunctorily as he walked past the statue and bent down to shut off the water. Then he crossed over to the troop-carrier, scraped the mud off his boots on its rear bumper and made a slight waving motion that caused a sergeant to start barking orders. Soldiers carrying Galils scrambled down from the truck and marched off in pairs toward the closest of the houses.

Two of them were headed straight for Buchanon. They had that stony look about them, like umpires, that dutiful, somber, merciless air of superiority. They would have no compunction at all about pulling triggers.

The scout heard the metal-cricket sound of old guns being cocked in the room behind him. He turned and looked at them, the girl with her corn-masher, the old man with his bird gun, Héctor with the puny nine-millimeter automatic. It came over him that they were all about to die. It was a fuzzy notion, clouded by his condition and the state of the room, which, from time to time, insisted on spinning counterclockwise. It was a distant observation, a detached perspective. It was as if he had walked into the wrong theater at one of those subdivided suburban movie houses. He didn't belong. He had paid for a different show. He held onto the window sash as the room pitched leeward, rocked, and finally steadied.

Buchanon found himself staring at the youngest of the children, the little girl. She huddled with her beloved kitten in the furthest corner, petting it, whispering in its ear. Then she did an amazing thing, something which Buchanon would never be able to forget. She took the kitten, held it up, rubbed it against her cheek and then quickly snapped its neck. Without a tear she laid her dead pet at her feet, and Buchanon knew her heart was broken. She had done it to keep the soldiers from doing it. She couldn't be more than five years old, but she understood death.

It was only then that it fully struck him: *He was going to die too.*

Suddenly, he recalled Kandler telling him not to go to Guatemala: "The whole fucking place is a zero." He remembered going 0 for 9 in a doubleheader on a hot August day in Boston. He remembered not stretching for the third baseman's low throw on a play that wound up being scored the only hit of an otherwise perfect game in Cleveland. He remembered the commissioner telling him he was a disgrace, his televised apology to a goddamn umpire, the quiet, easy way his manager turned his back. He remembered Santiago Akabal and the equipment bag on a table in a purple bar in Escuintla. He remembered Mago, his silk shirt and ruby cuff links, the python smile.

He was sober. He knew what had to be done.

There was a heavy, clay-encrusted mattock leaning against the wall. He picked it up and swung it over his head, feeling its heft, its balance, letting his wrists rotate, his forearms stretch, his shoulders flex. It was the same routine he'd gone through a thousand times with a weighted Louisville Slugger in the on-deck circle. His head still throbbed. He was still shaky and weak, but if he was going to die—in a place that wasn't even on the map, with people he didn't know—then he would at least go down swinging.

"I'll take these two assholes," he whispered to Héctor, not a trace of doubt in his voice. "You and the old man go for the others."

Héctor was astounded by the transformation. Moments ago the American had been lying in the dirt begging for booze. Now he was assuming command, ready to take on two professional, heavily armed soldiers with no more than a rusty farm implement.

Buchanon set the mattock down, spit into his hands, rubbed them together, picked the mattock back up and assumed his position just inside the door. He opened up his batting stance more than usual, a concession to age, and held the handle of the adz-like blade more horizontally than was his customary style. The first guy through would catch it between the ribs. That would be easy. The tricky part would be wrenching the mattock free and swinging again before the second one had a chance to shoot.

There was a commotion outside, shouts, a confusion of orders. He heard the two soldiers, who were just outside the door, turn away and run back toward the clearing. Buchanon dashed over to the window and cracked open the shutter. A teenaged boy was staggering toward the jeep, a rum bottle in hand. The soldiers were yelling at him to keep away but he appeared to be too drunk to understand. Suddenly the boy dropped to his knees and curled over the bottle. When he rose to his feet a few seconds later, he was no longer staggering. The kerchief which had been around his neck was now wrapped around the bottle and on fire. He lobbed it into the jeep and it exploded before the machine-gunner got off the first round. The gunner and his assistant catapulted out of the vehicle in flames and rolled, screaming, in the damp earth at the base of the shrine.

The teenager started running for the tree line just beyond

the clearing. The closest soldier took aim and let loose a short, economical burst, little more than a burp from the muzzle of his Galil. The boy slammed to the ground face first, dead before he hit it, his spine shattered, most of his heart and lungs punched through his rib cage.

A woman ran out from one of the houses, screaming and crying. Buchanon could see she was the boy's mother. The woman's husband and another son raced after her, trying to stop her. One of the pintos reached her first. He leveled her with a swipe to the jaw with the butt of his Galil. Four other soldiers grabbed the husband and the boy as a dozen others charged into the house from which they had come. Moments later they reappeared, dragging three young girls and another boy out into the street. One of the girls cradled a baby in her arms. They were all thrown together into a cowering heap in the center of the road.

The pinto who had struck down the mother reached for the crucifix which hung from her neck. He ripped it from its chain and shook it in her face, as if to accuse her of some blasphemy. The oldest boy rose up from the tangle of trembling limbs and spat in the soldier's face. Without a moment's hesitation, the pinto shot the boy with a long, magazine-emptying burst that picked the boy up and danced his body out and away from the others.

Enraged, the officer, who had been inspecting the damage to the jeep, ran over. The pinto came to attention. The officer slapped him repeatedly. For the first time, Buchanon recognized the officer as Capitán Reyes, Mago's messenger. Reyes shouted an order and the pinto fixed a sixteen-inch bayonet on his weapon.

"What's going on?" Buchanon whispered to Héctor.

"Reyes is disciplining the one who shot the boy," Héctor answered.

"I don't figure him for no humanitarian."

"He's disciplining him for wasting ammunition."

One of the other soldiers wrested the squalling baby away from the clutching arms of its sisters. The whole family screamed as he threw it into the air. The infant arced over them, did a half turn and fell belly-first onto the bayonet of the "disciplined" soldier.

Buchanon lurched back from the window, driven back as if hit in the head with a Nolan Ryan fastball. "Fucking bastards!" he cursed, once more taking up the mattock and stepping toward the door.

Héctor placed himself between the door and the big American. He aimed the automatic at Buchanon's nose and shook his head.

"There's nothing you can do here," Héctor warned.

The nine-millimeter did not stop Buchanon.

The tragic, ineluctable truth of Héctor's words did.

He dropped the mattock and retreated to the window. He raised the loose slat and looked out.

The soldiers had just herded the family back into their house. Three others jumped down from the thatched roof. Buchanon saw two gasoline cans on the roof and another by the front door. Reyes took a Bic lighter from his pocket and handed it to the "disciplined" soldier. The soldier ignited the diaper on the dead infant, which was still impaled on his bayonet. When the baby was completely engulfed in flames, he flung it onto the thatched roof.

Reyes and his pintos drove away.

The house burned.

The trapped family screamed and died.

•

Matt could not get a table for lunch at the most exclusive restaurant in Beverly Hills. Plenty of tables were available, but none would be given to him. His face was known. Like Armand Soltz, Don Koslowski and others of his kind ("ilk" was actually the word used by François, the maitre d'), Matt was persona non grata.

In order to get the picture of the heavy metal rock star dining with the wife of the well-known movie producer, it was necessary to bribe André, the head busboy. André was a reliable, loyal source, if a bit expensive due to his growing dependency on cocaine. The negotiations were handled ahead of time over the phone and went smoothly enough. As usual, André insisted on taking the shot himself. It was less risky smuggling the camera in than slipping Matt past the captain in a filched uniform. Matt grudgingly agreed, knowing from past experience the photography would be serviceable.

Matt met André behind the restaurant, handed him the Nikon and tucked a folded fifty into the breast pocket of his uniform jacket. The busboy ignored the money and examined the camera.

"What, am I supposed to pay for the film out of my end?" André asked haughtily.

"What are you talking about?" Matt demanded.

"There's no film, Matthew."

"You've been sniffing too much of that white shit, André. I loaded it last night. One thousand ISO, the fastest—"

André sprang the door on the back of the camera. It was empty. Matt stared unbelievingly into the vacant chamber where the roll of film should have been.

"It was in there last night," Matt insisted.

"Last night is history, Matthew."

"I know I loaded it," Matt persisted, shaking his head in mild bewilderment.

"They're going to miss me pretty soon," André said impatiently. "Get me some film and I'll get you the shot."

"Yeah, sure," Matt mumbled. He searched his pockets and came up with a roll of 400 ISO.

"That'll work," André said. "I'll push it." He took the roll and fed it quickly into the camera. "I held off cleaning table number 10 so they'd get seated at 12. Better light, Matthew. Nicer background, good contrast. You got an eighty-A?"

"No."

"How about a B?"

"I don't have any filters with me."

"And you call yourself a professional."

"All of a sudden you're goddamn Stieglitz. Just get the shot."

"The faces will be yellow."

"Jaundice," Matt snapped. "They just got over hepatitis. Okay?"

"Some people still take pride in their work," André retorted indignantly. Then he spun on his heel and marched back into the restaurant, the Nikon tucked inside his jacket.

Matt paced behind the service door, his aggravation complete now that a junkie busboy had lectured him on the work ethic and the finer points of candid photography. Even more annoying was the stubborn conviction that he *had* loaded the camera last night. He was sure of it—almost. Just as he was almost sure he had placed the acetate with the fingerprints in the unlabeled folder and not in the one marked BACKGROUND. And how long had he wasted looking for the latest *GAN Notes* tape, which had yet to turn up?

Nothing seemed to be where it was supposed to be lately.

Himself, most of all.

It was an interesting thought, if not a particularly enlightening one: he and his possessions suffering from the same symptomatology, misplaced from their rightful locus without apparent reason, some mysterious force manipulating the coordinates, twisting the axes x through z, upsetting the inertial navigation, making things drift from their right place, taking him away from Coombe's Ditch and the film from the Nikon. It would make a nice entry on *GAN Notes #115*—if he ever found the damn cassette.

André reappeared, looked around, and, satisfied he wasn't being watched, pulled the camera out of his jacket.

"Got it," he announced nonchalantly as if it had been no trouble at all. "Just put it on the dessert cart between the Napoleons and the eclairs and snapped away."

"How'd you focus?" Matt inquired.

"Focusing goes another fifty, Matthew."

"Since when?"

"Higher overhead." André put his index finger against one nostril and sniffed through the other.

"That's your problem," Matt argued.

André tossed the Nikon to Matt. "Yours too," he replied laughing.

Matt caught the camera. It felt slimy. He wiped his fingers against his pants leg.

"Beurre blanc," André explained before slipping back inside the restaurant through the service door.

Matt marched back toward the car, kicked a Dr. Pepper can (wishing it were something able to experience pain), fumbled with the lock, dropped his keys, scooped them up, fumbled with the lock some more, wrenched the door open, threw the camera into the Adidas bag and got in, thumping his head soundly against the door frame.

The Mazda usually required three tries to start. Today it demanded seven. Matt jammed it into reverse and stomped the accelerator. At the last possible second he saw an old green Buick filling his rear-view mirror. He slammed on the brakes. His eyes closed instinctively, but did not shut out visions of smashed grill work, cervical collars and evil lawyers from Encino. He braced himself for impact and waited for the thud. The tires squealed briefly and the Mazda came peacefully to rest. Matt hesitantly opened one eye and glanced in the mirror expecting to see the irate driver of the Buick tossing him a one-fingered salute, but there was nothing behind him except some newspapers drifting gently across the parking lot like slow-motion, airborne mantas.

He made his way out of the parking lot at funereal speed and eased into the light traffic on the boulevard. It occurred to him he could now add the Buick to the list of things that had wandered from their rightful place. In some black hole in the cockeyed galaxy of his karma resided the film, the cassette and the dark green Electra.

Two blocks passed uneventfully, but then a casual glance in the mirror resurrected the Buick. It was back there, behind him about ten car-lengths, moving innocently enough with the flow of traffic. Matt accelerated slightly. The Buick seemed to keep pace. He stopped at a light. The Buick pulled over to the curb, maintaining the same interval. Matt turned and the Buick followed. He turned again, and again the big green Electra crept into the mirror.

"I *did* load it!" he said to himself, finding no comfort in the proclamation of his own sanity.

He cranked the wheel and cut a U-turn over the "double-double" solid yellow lines. In many states, the maneuver was legal. In others, it constituted a minor, often unenforced, moving offense. In California it tended to invite close encounters with surly *gendarmes* in knee boots and sunglasses. The fine was major. The obligatory attitude-readjustment session was universally dreaded.

Rational, sober individuals did not intentionally violate section 21651(a) of the California Vehicle Code. Matt crossed over the double-double at high speed in broad daylight in the middle of Beverly Hills. The Buick followed.

Matt was reasonably sure the Buick had no intention of overtaking him. It seemed content to hang back at what it probably considered an inconspicuous distance. But his growing feeling of panic was not in the least alleviated. He felt as if there were no place to run, no place his pursuer had not already visited, nothing he didn't already know.

The guy in the Buick had his missing things. He had taken them. The film, thankfully, was unexposed. The tape, however, was full—both sides. No one had ever been permitted to listen to a *GAN Note*. Once when Kelly had mistakenly slipped one into her Walkman, he had torn the earphones off her head, pulling out a handful of hair in the process and inciting one of their more memorable battles. If he had been born Catholic and found himself on his death bed looking into the eyes of an absolving priest, whatever he might say would be but a fraction of what he had confessed to those tapes. He struggled to remember just what was on *#115*.

The guy had obviously handled the acetate, as well, even though there had been only one set of fingerprints on the sheet when he handed it to Schiff.

He must have used gloves.

He broke into the apartment and used gloves. Probably photographed the acetate.

The guy was a professional.

Coombe's Ditch came to mind—the cot, the blood dripping on his shoe, the wind singing in the dead man's mouth, the eye dangling like an uprooted flower, the moon and the star shining coldly through the cleft in the rocks.

Matt floored the Mazda and swerved around the next corner on two tires. It was a one-way street and Matt was traveling in the wrong direction. An Eldorado saw him coming, tried to get out of the way and spun out. Matt saw the handset of a car phone fly out of the open window and wrap itself around the antenna of a two-tone Volvo. A UPS step van slammed on the brakes. A cascade of packages tumbled through the cab door, engulfing the driver. A Jaguar cut over, jumped the curb and wiped out a newspaper vending machine. A big black woman in a battered Chevy threw something at Matt as he sped by—a taco, he thought, seeing a yellow-red-green shrapnel spray from the corner of his eye. People on the sidewalk watched dumbfounded and slackjawed. After three blocks of such madness, Matt turned off, zigzagged at high speed through a number of formerly sedate Beverly Hills residential lanes, cut back onto the boulevard past the restaurant, shot across a shopping center parking lot, barreled down the drive-through lane of the local Bank of America branch, and came to a sudden stop in front of a Ralph's Foods.

He looked apprehensively in the rear-view mirror.

A woman pushing a cart. An old man adjusting his suspenders. Two joggers crossing by, right to left. A beer truck pulling away from the store.

No Buick.

The sign in Ralph's front window read: BANANAS—25¢/LB.

•

Rebecca attempted to remove the last ear of corn from a deep aluminum cauldron on the stove. It kept diving to the bottom of the pot, masked under a haze of steam and evading the blind forays of the tongs. The pot was far too large and heavy for her to carry to the sink where it could be dumped into a colander, and she was hesitant to ask one of the men to do it. Nor did she want to disturb Sergio and Yolanda who were bathing Sebastian in the basin. She kept poking away with the tongs until her hand came too close to the surface of the water.

"Damn!"

She was appalled to hear the mild profanity fly from her lips. It was a shock more disturbing to her than the steam burn which had scalded her hand.

The tongs dropped into the pot and clanged against the bottom. Sebastian laughed and splashed in his bath water. Sergio and Yolanda grimaced in sympathy with Rebecca's pain but made no effort to help. They wanted to—she was sure—but they just couldn't bring themselves to get involved. That was their way: the smile at ten paces, the wrinkled brow of concern at twelve.

Rebecca's hand, withered by a second wave of pain, clenched and became a tightly closed fist. She cupped it, squeezed it, pressed it to her breast, trying to ride it out.

Cristina was suddenly at her side, gaunt, white-skinned, appearing as if conjured out of the steam billowing from the top of the cauldron. The sullen woman was the last one in the group Rebecca would have expected to respond to her distress. Most of the time Cristina kept to herself, huddled catlike in a corner, watching from behind the ever-present sunglasses, listening without giving evidence she had heard, taking everything in, giving nothing back. She was a refugee at rest, if not at peace. There was a heaviness about her—more a stagnant aura of permanence than a sedentary nature—which made her seem a part of the place. She had the forbidding presence of a gargoyle—one well weathered, bleached by the sun, worn by the years and much eroded by acid rain, but still able to fend off interlopers just by being there. She took her meals after the others were done, quickly, automatically, as if it were an obligation and no more. She was always the first one up in the morning and routinely commandeered the shower well before dawn, disregarding the posted schedule. Rebecca had never heard her speak. She had seldom seen her move: Cristina was in this place or that, but never in between, never in transit; she simply materialized in the far corner of the cellar or at the table or in the shower or, in this case, right under Rebecca's nose.

Cristina stared at Rebecca's injured hand but made no further advance. Rebecca tentatively extended it, thinking to herself that God was truly wonderful in His infinite mystery, that He had caused her wound in order to ignite the dying embers of compassion in Cristina's heart. Rebecca watched as Cristina unfastened the wrist button of her own shirt and rolled up the sleeve, evidently preparing to render aid. Rebecca reached further, nodding, her eyes wide, inviting the other woman to touch, to heal, to make a bond. But Cristina drew back, making an almost imperceptible movement with her head, but one which clearly signified refusal. "It's all right," Rebecca said warmly, her most fetching smile reinforcing the words. Then, just as Rebecca felt she had finally made contact, drawn her back into the caring family of humanity, without warning, without a sound, without any telltale change of expression, not so much as a hairline crack passing through the stone mask of her face, Cristina plunged her bare arm into the hot cauldron and scooped out the ear of corn. She held it out toward Rebecca like an ingot fresh from the smelting oven, an obscene golden thing, glowing and smoking. Rebecca drew back, but the woman caught her and pressed the corn into her hand, mashing it into her palm, forcing Rebecca's fingers to close around it. She felt the kernels bursting one by one under the pressure of her fingers, popping like fat, hot bugs, each little explosion prolonging the pain. Rebecca cringed, bit her lip, somehow suppressed the urge to cry out.

Suddenly, Cristina retreated. Like a machine clicking into a different cycle, she simply stopped what she had started—without any indication the process was finished, that a purpose had been realized, that there had been any point to it. An internal switch had been tripped; it was over.

Rebecca tried to carry the hot cob to the platter, but it fell to the floor. She flexed the fingers of her twice-wounded hand and watched the corn roll slowly across the linoleum, leaving a wet trail like a giant slug, toward Cristina's favorite corner. Amazingly, the woman was already there, back at her usual spot, curled against the wall.

Angry as she had ever been, Rebecca glared at her, and then at Sergio and Yolanda who were drying Sebastian. The baby smiled, breaking a thread of drool that had connected him to Yolanda. Sergio reached into the sink, pulled out the stopper, and gave his attention to the whirlpool of dirty water being sucked down the drain. Yolanda hurriedly finished drying Sebastian's feet as Pablo approached and asked for the towel. He said something which caused Yolanda to pass the baby to Sergio. With Pablo's gentle encouragement, she then began shuttling the bowls and platters of food over to the table.

Pablo draped the towel over his arm like a waiter, took a few steps toward Rebecca, stopped, became a bullfighter, executed a stylish veronica and closed the short distance between them as a turbaned sultan. Rebecca didn't laugh. Nothing was funny. Nothing in the whole sad world. Her hand hurt. She hurt.

Undaunted, Pablo delicately cradled her hand in the towel. Trying not to irritate it further, he wiped away the mashed bits of corn which coated her fingers.

"Thank you," Rebecca said brusquely. The words were forced and cold.

"You're welcome," he returned, parroting the same formal inflection.

It did sound comical, the niceties exchanged like warning shots on the high seas. But she still couldn't laugh. Not yet.

"The Maya people believe we were made from corn," he explained. "Well, maize, actually."

"Is that why she did this?" Rebecca asked, looking back over toward Cristina. "Is that her way of teaching me your beliefs?"

"It's the way you taught us your beliefs."

"I welcomed you into my home," Rebecca replied sharply. "That's all I've done."

"True enough, Mrs. Miles. You don't look like a *conquistadora* and we are not Indians, however self-serving it might be to identify with them in our current circumstances. So, the allusion is twice flawed, isn't it?"

"Your English is excellent. Just as Father Townes said."

"You say that as if it concerns you."

"It's curious. That's all."

"I was born there. I grew up here—my father was in the coffee business. We went back there for a time. Then I came back here for college."

"Then back again?"

"Doing research for my master's thesis."

"And now here."

"Not by choice."

"I would imagine so."

"You couldn't begin to imagine. Forgive me for being blunt."

"*She* doesn't forgive, does she?" Rebecca nodded toward Cristina.

"No. I suppose not."

"I don't understand how a human being can be that way."

"Perhaps that is what she was trying to teach you."

"What?"

"Pain."

"I don't understand."

"Precisely. You do not understand pain. What it can be. What it can do to someone."

"Do you?"

"No. Not in the way they understand. You and I are different from them in that regard."

"You're one of them," she clarified.

"Yes and no."

"*¡Shó!*" Coh interrupted. He was sitting at the head of the table with old Abraham to his right and Soto to his left. Sergio and Yolanda, with Sebastian nestled on her lap, were fanned out at the other end. Coh's good eye was trained on his plate as he mopped up gravy with a chunk of sourdough bread. The glass eye was "looking" directly at Pablo. Soto snickered and mumbled, "*Cabrón.*"

Pablo stiffened, released Rebecca's hand and said, "Excuse me," before slinking off to the back room.

Rebecca did not "excuse" him. She needed his kindness, his interest, his young, clean, handsome face. He was compensation for Cristina's treachery, for Soto's foulness, for the exasperating timidity of Sergio and Yolanda, for all she feared and didn't know about screams in the middle of the night and the man butchered on a desert road and Pastor Vail dead in his church. She wandered over to the table, wanting to say, *What's going on? This is my house. I've got a right to know.* Instead, remembering her mother's favorite burn remedy, she dabbed at the butter with the towel and spread it over her scalded hand.

"*Sí ella quisiera, le echaría mante quilla,*" Soto grunted as he chewed on an ear of corn.

Coh shot him a disapproving glance. Soto ignored it, his attention fully on the corn, which he held clumsily between the palms of his thumbless hands. It slipped out of his grasp and fell loudly to his plate.

Rebecca became intrigued by Soto's attempts to pick up his food. She watched as he fumbled with the ear, trying to turn it to the uneaten side. How hard it was for him, she thought—a simple thing, a taken-for-granted thing. But for him, difficult. It required patience, deliberation, dexterity. She wondered if prosthesis was available for such a handicap. *What would artificial thumbs look like? How would they work?* She tried to imagine other everyday occurrences that would give him trouble.

"Eez hard to wipe my *culo,* too," he said, as if reading her mind. Soto abandoned the corn, slipped out of his chair, bent over and pantomimed the action he had just described.

Rebecca felt a hot flash of embarrassment reddening her face. She tried to avert her eyes, but the vulgar little man was moving in her direction. She deemed it prudent to keep him in view.

"Shovel?" Soto asked rhetorically, staring at Rebecca, the crooked smile twitching as he came closer. "Nooo," he answered, drawing the word out as if it were the ending note of a favorite song. He paused to demonstrate how ridiculous he might look trying to use one.

"*¿El azadón? ¿La pala?*" he asked, taking a step and then pausing to mimic a farmer tilling his field. The invisible hoe kept slipping out of his hands. He shook his head and moved closer.

"*¿El tenedor? ¿La cuchara?* Nooo." He scooped up a fork and a spoon, holding them as a young child might, pointing up like drumsticks from his fists. Sebastian laughed. Yolanda clamped her hand over the baby's mouth. Soto let the silverware drop to the floor.

"Punch? No, not so good." He made a fist and jabbed. His fingers flew open at the end of the blow. A hook and an uppercut fared no better.

"Steer *el carro?* Very hard. Gear shift? Pretty good. Brake?

No problema." He hopped on one foot, depressing a "brake" with the other and "steering" madly as if to avoid a crash. His hands, unable to get the proper "grip," kept sliding off the "wheel." The "collision" occurred just in front of Rebecca. Soto fell to the floor at her feet, his arms crossed protectively in front of his face.

Rebecca took a step backward. Soto jumped to his feet. His face was inches from hers. The smile was gone.

"Paint? No. Comb? No. Shoestring? *¿Escribir?* No. Flip the Bic? Open the knob? Turn the channel? Pull the zipper? I don't think so. And eempossible—*absolutamente imposible*—to hold *la pistola.* Trigger finger eez worth shit when you cannot hold gun. You keep guns. You keep bullets. You take away *los dedos gordos. No problema.*"

Soto was looking into her eyes, his own full of rage. Rebecca wished Nathan would suddenly barge in, returned from his trip into town. Or that Pablo would come back into the room, saying something to draw the man off. She looked away, her eyes escaping, searching for anything, a spot on the linoleum, a crack, a wandering bug, anything to home on to, anything to get away.

No! Wrong! Bad signal. It looks weak.

She forced herself to stare back at him, meeting his gaze head-on. She felt him entering her through her eyes, getting in where she didn't want him, peeking, poking about, testing her, becoming angry when she didn't look away.

Was it like with dogs—looking him straight in the eye? Was it a challenge?

She lowered the trajectory of her focus just a bit, down to his mouth, just enough to break the beam, the connection. She became conscious of her own hands hanging idly at her sides. They started to move, heading for the pockets in her dress—only there were no pockets in her dress. But once in motion, she had to do something with them. So, she fumbled with a button. Just a vacant, nervous little act. Just rolling the button between her thumb and index finger.

"Can't do that either, Señora," Soto said quietly. His face was a soft, crushed thing. The fury had washed out of his eyes.

Rebecca's hands fell to her sides like doves shot out of the sky. "I'm sorry," she heard herself say. It was a reflex. The words just came on their own.

"Cannot even pray *rosario*," he said plaintively, holding his hands out to her.

Coh laughed and said something to Abraham. The old man made the sign of the cross, ending it with a flourish of his hand, as if he were casting away evil spirits. Coh shook his head in disgust, angry that Abraham could not find humor in the ludicrous idea of Soto praying a rosary.

Rebecca took Soto's hands into her own. It was not an easy thing to do, but once done, it felt right. She saw the moment as a test. The choice was hers: be moved or simply move away. She held on and the pain in her own hand seemed to diminish. She asked, "How did it happen?"

"Magic," he answered. "Most terrible of magic."

"Soto!" Coh shouted, pounding the table so hard all the dishes jumped.

Sebastian began to cry. Pablo appeared in the doorway. Sergio put his arms around Yolanda and the baby. Abraham began mumbling something which might have been a prayer. Rebecca detected Cristina stirring from the corner. It was noteworthy: Cristina actually in motion.

"Magic disappeared my *dedos gordos*," Soto continued.

Rebecca heard a chair scraping against the linoleum as Coh pushed himself back from the table. He stood up and the bentwood chair flopped over onto its back. *"Cuidado con lo que dice o le corto la lengua,"* he said sharply.

"What did he say?" Rebecca asked Soto.

"He say you are a beautiful woman," Soto lied. *"Muy bonita."*

"¡Basta!" Coh shouted.

"What did he really say?" Rebecca asked.

Pablo answered from the door: "He told Soto to be quiet or he'd cut out his—"

Cristina screamed, a high-pitched screech, a sound like feedback ringing out of a PA speaker.

"The journalist," Soto said to Rebecca over the din, smiling broadly, apparently enjoying the commotion. He cocked his head toward Cristina. "Listen."

Cristina continued to scream until she ran out of breath.

"You understand, Señora?" he asked.

Rebecca shook her head.

"She say the night fill with bad magic."

"Do not listen to him," Coh ordered. "He's crazy."

"Sí. Muy loco. But not so crazy I think I am safe in this *gringo* church."

Coh grabbed Soto by the arm and shook him.

"Leave him alone!" Rebecca protested, still holding on to Soto's hands.

"Señora, this man is a criminal," Coh explained.

"With your bombs and your guns what are you so holy?" Soto retorted.

"He lies!" Coh continued, his grip tightening on Soto's arm. "He is confusing you."

"Don't hurt him," Rebecca warned.

"Oh, he no hurt me," Soto whined, obviously in pain. "Not in *santuario.* Nobody hurt me in *santuario."*

"That's right!" Rebecca agreed.

"Not the devil from hell hurt me here."

"Well . . ."

"Not God too hurt me no more here. I spit in His face. He do nothing to me now."

Soto's eyes rolled upward. He laughed—a long, shrill peal appropriate to the sacrilege. Coh choked it off, his huge hand clamping around Soto's throat.

"Leave him alone!" Pablo said from the doorway.

Coh ignored the young man, but Soto tore free, whirling around to face Pablo. "Go fuck yourself, *maricón!*" he hissed. "You say nothing to me."

Soto headed back over to the table to resume his attack on the corn. Before sitting down he snarled at Pablo, reminding Rebecca of a neighbor's dog back in Michigan—part Lab, part Shepherd, all crazy, the muzzle always sticking out under the wooden gate, always growling when anyone walked by. Coh drifted to the stove, the good eye flitting from Soto to Pablo and then to Cristina who was crouched on her haunches back in the corner. Satisfied with the modicum of peace that had clumsily settled over the room, he removed a cigarette from behind his ear and lit it off one of the burners. Pablo shook his head and retreated into the other room.

Rebecca followed, drawn through the doorway even though good sense told her to head for the stairs, to escape and lock the door behind her. She picked up a dust mop that was leaning against the wall. The mop gave her an excuse—which she really didn't need—for entering the sleeping quarters.

Nathan's plan called for subdividing the back room of the cellar into individual sleeping compartments. Partitions spaced at six-foot intervals off a central corridor would form cubicles eight feet deep. The cots were to go in lengthwise and the walls were to stop six inches from the ceiling, thereby allowing for ventilation while still providing a semblance of privacy. Curtains would afford closure along the corridor. Nathan had planned it all so meticulously, but only one of the cubicles had been completed in time. It had been promptly claimed by Cristina, who immediately turned her cot ninety degrees and stuffed blankets into the airway. The rest of the compartments were only framed in, the evenly spaced two-by-fours giving the unfortunate appearance of cell bars.

After a few meandering passes with the dust mop, Rebecca wandered over toward Pablo's area. The young man was sitting on his cot, studiously bent over a blueprint-sized paper. He seemed to be checking the minutia of detail which covered the page. His finger traced slowly down a long column of strange, hand-drawn glyphs.

"What's that?" Rebecca asked.

"A riddle."

"I'm good at riddles."

"This is a riddle within a riddle. I don't know what it means and I can't explain how it came to exist."

"It looks like hieroglyphics," she remarked, sitting down on the edge of the cot so she could get a closer look.

"It is the written language of the classic Maya," Pablo answered wearily.

"Can you read it?"

"Mostly. Yes."

"What is it?"

"It's an inscription. I copied it from a stela—a stone monument—found at a place called Nim Xol Carchah. It means the Great Abyss at Carchah. The classic period Maya erected stelas all over Guatemala, Northern Honduras, Chiapas and the Yucatán. They usually marked the date of a noteworthy event: births and deaths of kings, foundings of cities, great victories in battle, the beginning or end of an epoch of time. They stopped erecting stelas in the last part of the ninth century—about the same time they began to disappear from the lowland jungles, from the great cities of Tikal, Palenque, Copán, Seibal and others, from the places where they had erected their most impressive pyramids and temples, observatories, ball courts, causeways, palaces. They stopped putting up stelas and gradually abandoned the cities which represented the most advanced civilization in the entire hemisphere."

"Why?"

"Nobody knows for sure. There's no lack for theories—plague, invasion, famine, revolution, the principle of diminishing returns. There's an old fable that says the Maya became so self-satisfied in admiring the symbol of the water lily which they had painted on their buildings that they neglected to tend the real water lilies that fed the fish that fed their economy. Others say that they were the victims of their own calendar. Every day had its own patron gods and its own unique augury. They may have become fatalistic as a particular ill-omened period was about to commence. Or they may have looked at it as an inescapable re-peating cycle. They may have believed that history is circular."

"You don't believe that's the explanation, do you?"

"I never used to."

"And now?"

"As the lowlands decentralized and faded, the Maya popula-tion seemed to move in two directions. One was north into the Yucatán of Mexico, to cities like Chichén Itzá and Mayapán. Today, Indians from all over Guatemala are being forced from their homes and are fleeing into Mexico. There's anywhere from fifty thousand to two hundred thousand of them in refugee camps near the border, depending on whose numbers you believe. The Mexican authorities are nervous. They don't want a New World Palestine so close to their southern frontier. So they're trying to move the refugees north to Campeché—in the Yucatán peninsula, basically the same area they moved to almost a thousand years ago."

"Don't you believe in the possibility of coincidence? In a thousand years isn't there the chance for a simple coincidence?"

"It's not important what we believe. If the Maya believed it a thousand years ago, if they believe it today—that's what matters. If they believe that it's ordained, their will to resist will vanish. History *will* repeat."

"You said they moved to two areas, though. Not just the Yucatán, right?"

"They also moved south, into the highlands. The Quiché Maya who live in the highlands today may have passed through Nim Xol on their migration. The place is mentioned in the *Popol Vuh,* their sacred council book."

"How do you know all this?"

"It's my major, pre-Columbian archaeology. I was doing research for my master's thesis when I got this sudden urge to travel north."

"What happened?"

Pablo looked toward the door, into the other room. "It's better we talk about old things."

Coh was leaning against the door frame, watching intently, with the cigarette held and poised like a dart about to be thrown.

Rebecca decided not to press him. "So what's the riddle?" she asked.

"Do you see this series of glyphs?" Pablo asked, pointing to the paper. "These bars and dots?"

"Yes."

"That represents the date the stela was erected. The Maya originally measured time in something we call the long count. Just as we measure our years from a fixed point, Maya time started at a fixed point over three thousand years before the birth of Christ.

They measured time in different increments than we do. A *kin* was one day. That's this lowest figure here in the series. Twenty *kins* made a *uinal*, the next glyph up. Eighteen *uinals*—three hundred and sixty days—formed a *tun*. Every seventy-two hundred days—or twenty *tuns*—you had a *katun*. Every twenty *katuns* gave you a *baktun* of one hundred and forty-four thousand days."

"It's complicated."

"It's simple. We choose to aggregate our years in multiples of ten—decades, centuries, millennia. They collected their units of time basically in twenties."

"It's complicated," Rebecca repeated, smiling. "Take my word for it."

"Each day had a name, as well. It determined which gods held sway, what their expectations might be, what was within the realm of human possibility, what was not. The day names were determined by the intermeshing of two different cycles."

Rebecca laughed. "Simple, huh?"

"One of the cycles was the almanac of two hundred and sixty days. There were twenty day names in the almanac. Each day name had a prefix, a number from one to thirteen. After the thirteenth day, the next day name was used starting with the prefix one again.

"The other cycle was the *haab* of three hundred and sixty-five days—"

"A full year," Rebecca observed.

"There were nineteen months of twenty days each in the *haab* and a closing month, *Uayeb*, which was only five days long."

"Oh, that makes sense," Rebecca said playfully.

"As much as our repeating cycle of seven-day weeks and our twelve months of thirty or thirty-one days. And then there's always February and leap years to contend with."

"This little five-day month . . . it almost sounds like an afterthought."

"*Uayeb* was an unlucky period. Bad things happened. People stayed in their houses and didn't tempt fate."

"It's hard to imagine."

"For the Maya, each day was special and sacred. That the sun rose every day, that the seasons changed, that the stars didn't fall from the sky were acts of divine intercession. The gods watched over the coming and going of each day, carried it into the world. The Maya's chief spiritual responsibility was to keep the days of the gods, to know their names, to do what was appropriate on each day. Because of the way the almanac and the *haab* interacted, a specific day name could only repeat once every fifty-two years. Special priests kept track of the days and even today there are diviners called daykeepers."

"So when was this written?"

"On the day called 11 Ik 12 Yaxkin, on the long-count date of eleven *baktuns,* one *katun,* ten *tuns,* one *uinal* and fourteen *kins.* That's February 12, 1254 A.D."

"I thought you said they stopped putting up these . . ."

"Stelas."

"I thought they finished with them in the ninth century."

"They'd also stopped using the long-count notation by then. Sort of makes this the archaeological find of the century, doesn't it?" Pablo smiled.

"I guess so."

"And it was in a place where no other structures seem to exist. That's a riddle as well."

"What's the explanation?"

"The easiest explanation is that the stela is not authentic. That it's some incredible practical joke."

"Is that what you believe?"

"It's possible. The workmanship is crude. There's a lot of inconsistencies to earlier work. The scale is relatively small. Some of the glyphs are barely recognizable. Others I can only guess at. But if it's real, over three hundred years had passed since a stela had been made. There would be a dearth of artisans, right? Language and writing would have evolved."

"Aren't there tests?"

"Yes. Carbon-dating."

"Did you do it?"

"We didn't have the chance."

"Why?"

"One night while I was dreaming of the great honors to be bestowed upon me by the scientific community, as I was visualizing how my name would go down in history beside those of the great Mayanists of all time—Morley, Thompson, Schele, Lounsbury, Proskouriakoff—the stone was stolen."

"By whom?"

"By those who did not want it to be real. By those who tried to kill everyone who had even seen it."

"The army?"

"G-2 . . . *Kaibiles* working for the G-2 . . . what does it matter? By those with the guns and the power to use them."

"The rebels have guns," Rebecca pointed out.

"The insurgents seldom wear uniforms or hang old men or arrive in helicopters or murder little children in front of their parents or . . ."

Pablo's voice trailed off. His eyes closed as if to shut out the memory. Rebecca allowed him a few moments to compose himself. "Why?" she asked quietly.

"Because it's a prophecy," Pablo whispered, his eyes opening. "That's the second part of the riddle," he continued, his voice growing louder as he went on, the words coming faster, in excited, urgent spurts. "Prophecies were usually written in books, not on stelas, which were reserved for historical events. The most famous are in the *Books of Chilam Balam.* Very few books survived. The missionaries burned most of them in the 1500s. But then again there is a very thin line between what the Maya understood as prophecy and as history. The former is but the latter waiting for its appointed time. Whoever wrote this wanted it to endure. Three hundred years after the last stela was erected, someone foresaw a distant history, what we would understand as 'the future.' He decided his vision must last. So isn't it logical that he'd carve it in stone, using the format he'd seen at what were already then ancient sites? He wanted it to survive until the date foretold."

"When is that?" Rebecca asked, caught up in his excitement.

"That's the strangest part yet, Mrs. Miles. Do you see this glyph? It's the day of the almanac 11 Lamat. But I interpret the next glyph to read 'the Yearbringer.' That means New Year's Day, the classic Maya New Year, the first day of the *haab,* 1 Pop. So together they describe a day called 11 Lamat 1 Pop. Then it says, 'Before the last *katun.'* There's the mystery. This was written in the eleventh *baktun.* So it could mean, 'when 11 Lamat 1 Pop occurs in the *katun* prior to the last one of the eleventh *baktun.'* That would place it in our year 1566, during the tail-end of the Spanish conquest. That makes some sense, but it's also possible it means before the very last *katun* of the Great Cycle of Man. The cycle ends in the year 2012. There is only one occurrence of 11 Lamat 1 Pop in the *katun* before the very last one begins in 1993."

"It's close, isn't it?" Rebecca asked with a sense of foreboding and not really wanting to know. It was one thing to talk about the ancient customs of an ancient race, but now she felt their pagan shadow reaching out toward her. Prophecy and fortune-telling were the province of Satan. She rose from the cot.

"About two weeks from now. April 11," Pablo announced. "Isn't it amazing?"

"That's Easter Sunday," Rebecca observed dully, as she headed for the door, anxious to get away before Pablo told her any more.

"I didn't realize," Pablo admitted. "Remarkable!"

•

Kelly Wode's coworkers from the *Times* were proud of her. Congratulations were offered; toasts were proposed; tributes and homage rolled glibly from tongues used to coining just the right phrase.

The Yellow Pages had just climbed into the national best-seller lists, and the back room at Lena's, the favored watering hole, had been commandeered for a hastily organized after-work celebration. The narrow, dingy alcove was just big enough to accommodate one long table. Two dozen *Times* staffers were packed in tightly around it. Some were forced to stand. Others were sitting on laps. Everyone was talking at once, raising glasses, telling shop stories no outsider could hope to understand. One of the fluorescent lights flickered intermittently overhead, as if short-circuited by all the commotion.

Kelly sat at the place of honor, at the far end of the table, behind seven untouched Cuba Libres. She was crying—not from sadness or joy, but simply because there was far too much smoke in the room and her contact lenses were giving her fits. Her jaw throbbed from the constant strain of the mandatory smile. Wedged in tightly at the dead end of the alcove, she felt trapped, all the more so because the soles of her shoes were stuck to the floor. She worked them free and balanced them atop some fallen beer nuts. They rolled under her feet like casters, making her wish she could duck under the table and glide away, just slip off unseen on a carpet of ball-bearing goobers. Suddenly she remembered the two dozen wilted yellow roses ridiculously lying across her lap like the door prize for Miss Congeniality. The flowers were recalled at that moment because she had pricked her finger on a thorn. She blotted the drop of blood on a cocktail napkin, smearing a risqué cartoon. Suppressing a yawn, she tossed her head back and squirted some rewetting drops into her eyes.

At the other end of the table, a burly photographer from the Sports Department paid for a round of drinks. It was a rare event; no one could remember when it had last occurred: someone from Sports actually picking up a bar tab! An old-timer from the City Desk immediately began to compose a 72-point banner headline on the tablecloth to commemorate the phenomenon. A number of clever remarks were made. There was a renewed wave of laughter, loud talk and pounding on the table. Ice cubes rattled in uplifted glasses. Somebody accidentally tipped over a carafe of chablis. Kelly borrowed a Kleenex and dabbed at her eyes. "Damn contacts," she mumbled.

Mae Gower from International leaned across Gus Amenta from Metro. In her struggle to gain closer access to the guest of honor, her armpit inadvertently became positioned directly over the man's face. He didn't seem to mind: The seven glasses on the table in front of him were all empty. He sat there without protest, motionless as if asphyxiated, looking all but comatose.

"You've really got it, kiddo," Mae gushed. "The cream always rises."

"And eventually curdles," Kelly replied with a nervous little laugh.

"No chance, honey. You're on the move. You won't be in one place long enough to go bad."

"Think so?"

"I know it. You're on your way."

"Just hit it lucky, Mae," Kelly said modestly.

"Oh, that's a lot of crap. You're good and you know it. Don't trot out that Mary Jane humble-pie bullshit with me."

"I'm not comfortable with this. That's all."

"What's not to be comfortable with?"

Kelly struggled to find the right word. "Success, I guess."

"Oh, God. You're a hopeless case."

"That's probably close to the truth."

"Lighten up. Enjoy."

"I'm trying."

"Make hay while the sun shines and all those other good old clichés. Take it from me. Fame *is* fleeting."

"What about talent?" Kelly asked earnestly.

"There's no cure for that," the older woman admitted with a shrug.

Kelly respected and trusted Mae. The seasoned veteran had bagged a Pulitzer during the Days of Rage in '68. A book she had penned about the Khmer Rouge in '71 had foretold with uncanny accuracy the holocaust about to consume Cambodia. Her journalism was precise and insightful. She had never succumbed to the demand for quick, flashy news, for the fluff that foolishly tried to compete with the immediacy of the tube. Mae had bounced around from paper to paper before finding her current niche at the *Times*.

Mae slumped back into her seat, her eyes locked on Kelly's, sharing something that was both proud and sad.

Gus stirred to life and bellowed, "Another round!"

Everyone cheered. Orders for Manhattans and martinis from the old guard and wine coolers from the younger crowd poured over the harried waitress. Somebody actually asked for a Tanqueray Tall—"no ice." The burly photographer, who hailed from

Chicago, demanded an Old Style. A Baltimore-bred rewrite man countered with a request for National Premium. A heated discussion ensued with each man claiming the superiority of his favorite. The argument abated when an editor from Financial pointed out that both of the regional breweries were now owned by the same conglomerate. Another Cuba Libre was requisitioned for Kelly. Hours ago, Kelly had said, "I'll have some Coke." Across the noisy table, "some Coke" apparently sounded like "rum and Coke." The drink arrived with a wedge of lime, and from then on, every time a round was ordered, Kelly wound up with her "usual."

Matt was slumped against the bar in the other room, wedged in between an older couple out celebrating their twenty-fifth wedding anniversary and a group of commodity brokers whose discussion of platinum futures took brief, lecherous detours whenever a comely woman happened to walk by. Matt tried to listen in on the goings-on in the back room, but the excited report on granddaughter Gwen's first tooth on his left and the ardent discourse of the bulls, bears and wolves on his right drowned out all intelligible language emanating from Kelly's party. He downed his third Jack Daniels and motioned for a fourth. When he noticed the waitress emerging from the back room, he waved her over and ordered a bottle of French champagne.

"For the queen of the ball," he explained.

"Any message?" the waitress asked.

Matt shook his head, then reconsidered. "Just tell her it's from an unnamed source."

He slapped some money on the bar and stormed out before the waitress could ask for further clarification.

Matt plunged into the night, moving as fast as he could. The air was cool, with a slight promise of rain. He left his jacket open, hoping the chill might have a sobering effect. A full block elapsed before he realized he'd turned the wrong way coming out of the bar. Wheeling on his heels, he did an abrupt about-face, thinking that things had a tendency to go downhill rapidly when he was both drunk and angry.

Something changed direction with him. He caught the reflection in a shop window as a car drove by, its headlights sweeping over as he turned, illuminating the mannequins behind the glass. On the other side of the street—a shape, a shadow, *a man*, pivoting, turning with him, his image slipping between the shop dummies like a ghost among graveyard statues.

Matt heard it, too. The interruption in the soft, pulsing rasp of shoe leather on concrete, a sound he hadn't noticed until it stopped, hesitated, and then renewed, distantly, following like echoes of his own footsteps.

Before he knew it, Matt was running. He sprinted, gunning up quickly to the maximum his out-of-shape body could tolerate. No one else was on the street to slow him down, although it was unlikely anyone could have caused him to diminish his speed. A copy of *Here and There* wormed out of his back pocket and fluttered away into the darkness. He straightened his hands so that they cut through the air more efficiently. Racing technique came back to him, the high pumping action of his knees and crisp rhythmic kick of his feet, drawn instinctively from the long dormant experience of high school track days. But no memories of potbellied coaches or fourth-place finishes or dismal meets under overcast skies came to mind for reference. He was beyond all memories save the one from which he now fled, the one he had replicated a million times on the front page of a tabloid. He tore past his car even though he saw it parked at the curb, waiting to spirit him away. It was as if *it* went by him, rather than the other way around—like a train speeding off in the opposite direction on a parallel track. His panic was total, and once converted to motion, there was no way to stop or direct it.

Matt's terror drove him blindly into the courtyard of a bank building. He cut diagonally through a grid of palm trees, each one growing out of a neat, squared opening in the brick-paved plaza. He ran around a small fountain pool in the middle of the place. The pump had been turned down for the night. The water was barely flowing, just enough to recirculate. It had the friendly, burbling sound of a living room aquarium. Matt took some low, wide steps two at a time, stumbling on the last pair. He staggered up to the doors of the bank. They were locked. He pounded on them. Nobody came. He looked around and realized his fear had stampeded him into a box canyon of concrete and glass with no way out save the one by which he had entered.

Matt listened to the steady rhythm of his pursuer's approach, a disciplined trot, methodical, even and unhurried, each footfall pulsing like a stonemason's chisel cutting away at the distance between them.

The sound stopped. The man had come to the narrow mouth of the courtyard. Matt dove behind a steel abutment, hoping he hadn't been seen.

The footsteps came again, now slower, a walk, meandering, hunting, winding in and out of the trees, then up the steps and back down again to the fountain. Matt heard him spit into the pool, cough, scrape something off his shoe. There was a brief, terrifying silence. Matt's ears were filled with the sound of his own breathing. Then, the pulse started again, left, right, left, right, the even beat of a barber's straight razor on the sharpening belt, getting louder, coming closer, homing in.

There was nothing else to do.

Matt lunged out. Screaming and swinging wildly, he caught his pursuer flush in the nose. The man staggered backward and Matt swung again, intending to run off after he had the guy on his back. But his wide, roundhouse right missed altogether. The man caught Matt's arm and pulled him off balance, thwarting his escape. Together, they fell over a bench and rolled down three of the wide steps. Matt landed on top. He hammered away at the man's head with his left hand.

"Crissake!" the man gasped. "It's me . . . it's me!"

Matt stopped swinging. He grabbed the man's tie and pulled his head up off the brick step. It was Don Koslowski.

"You asshole!" Matt shouted. He released the tie. Koz's head dropped back with a thud. Matt climbed off.

"Christ! I think you broke my nose," Koz mumbled. His hands clamped over the lower part of his face. Blood dripped through his fingers and ran down his shirt.

"You're lucky I didn't kill you, you stupid bastard!" Matt kicked him in the side of his thigh.

"I'll sue," Koz threatened.

"Sue this, fuckball!"

Matt gave him another kick, this one harder and landing just under the ribs. Koz rolled down to the next step. Matt kept after him, kicking repeatedly, catching him on the legs and in the ass. Koz scrambled onto all fours and scurried down the two remaining steps. Matt forced him over the low wall of the fountain pool. Koz collapsed in the ten-inch-deep water. Totally exhausted, he reclined on his back and propped himself up on his elbows, looking like an old man soaking in a mineral bath.

"Was that you in the Buick today?" Matt demanded.

"Yeah."

"You asshole!"

"What's the big deal?" Koz asked plaintively.

"You . . . you . . . you asshole!" Matt stammered.

Matt's rage was somehow frustrated by the water. He paced around the perimeter, but didn't enter the pool. Finally, he grabbed a heavy wire-mesh trash container and hurled it at Koz. It splashed in behind the older reporter, wedging up against the base of the fountain. Koz leaned back, using it as a chaise.

"You were in my apartment, right?"

"Maybe."

"You fucked around with my film, my tapes—"

"One roll of film."

"What about the tapes?"

"A few."

"What's on them?"

Koz laughed. "You. You're on them, Teller."

"What am I saying?"

"All kinds of things."

"What kinds of things?"

"Personal shit. You should know."

"I want them back, Koz."

"No can do, Teller."

"Why not?"

"Well . . . the tapes themselves are actually back in your apartment. I put them back this afternoon after you lost me in Beverly Hills. I recorded over them. Old Lawrence Welk albums. I thought I'd get them back before you noticed them missing. Would've been a great gag, huh?"

"How'd you get in my place?"

"Your cleaning girl."

"Rosa?"

"I got some friends at INS to pick her up. I told her if she let me in I'd get her a green card. She gave me the key. I've had it a while. I never thought I'd have the balls to use it."

"Where's Rosa?"

"Shit! Mexico, I guess."

"I thought you got her a card?"

"Hell, you know I can't do that."

"I'm gonna drown you, Koz," Matt warned, his voice low and rough, still battling for air. "I'm going to enjoy it. I'm gonna watch your eyes bug out. I want to see you swallow your tongue. And when it's all over I'm gonna pull up a bench, sit down and watch you float."

"Hey Teller, I'm just getting even."

"Is that what this is all about?"

"You stole my story. Nobody does that."

"You had it fucked up anyway. You missed the whole point."

"Oh, yes. Two heads, one soul. Murder or suicide. Very deep."

"If it's any consolation, that piece landed me on the pet desk."

"No it didn't. Your girlfriend put you there. Her sweet little book hung you. That don't settle shit between us."

"You're way past the bend, Koz. You didn't break into my apartment and mess with my camera and screw up my tapes and follow me all over town just because I ripped off notes to a page six story. Even you're not that crazy."

"It's the truth. I just wanted to get even."

"I'm not buying it. You're way past even. You were even when you blocked my shot at Malibu."

"The Beldine story could've been big for me. I might've crossed over on that one."

"Bullshit!"

"Without my notes, I couldn't even get the names straight."

"You're gonna take a long drink, Koz," Matt warned, taking a step closer to the pool.

"You're not going to kill me. You don't have the nuts for it."

"You listened to my tapes. What choice do I have?"

"Okay. So I know a little bit more about you than you'd like. . . ."

Matt sat on the wall of the pool, yanked off his shoes and rolled up his pant legs.

"What's the big deal?" Koz pleaded. "I didn't make copies or anything."

Matt stepped into the fountain.

"Okay . . . shit . . . just go back out. I'll tell you the whole thing."

Matt continued toward him. Koz squirmed onto his belly and tried to regain his feet, paddling frantically like a nerve-gassed salamander. Matt grabbed him by the belt and pulled him back into a sitting position. Then he picked up the trash can, turned it upside down and dropped it over Koz's torso, caging him inside the mesh. The older man's hands pushed out against the metal, keeping it away from his face.

Matt sat back down on the edge of the fountain and said, "Talk!"

"You got a call about a two headed shar-pei, right?" Koz began.

"Yeah."

"That was me."

"What?"

"Fucked you around good. That's how I was gonna get even for the Beldine story. Send you on a wild goose chase out in the desert."

"That was you," Matt said dully, obviously confused and surprised by Koz's confession.

"In the meantime I'd be screwing around in your apartment . . . 'cept I chickened out. I didn't get up the nerve to go in your place until yesterday."

"You sent me out for the sharpie?"

Koz smiled behind the tight wire grid of the trash can.

"I'd been out there over a long weekend," he continued,

"tooling around on my dirt bike, when I ran into those three Okies—"

"You're the biker from San Diego!" Matt said in amazement. "They told me about you. You tried to boost an icemaker or something."

"Who knew anybody cared about all that old crap? Crazy bastard pulled a shotgun on me. That's when I got the idea to send you out there on a bogus hook. I knew you were on the pet desk. You wouldn't be able to resist a two-headed sharpie. Worked, didn't it?"

"It worked," Matt admitted.

"He pull the shotgun on you?"

"Yeah."

"Perfect. Just as I figured . . . except for . . ."

"Except for Coombe's Ditch."

"I still can't believe it," Koz fumed, his mood quickly going dark. "I suck you in with total horseshit, get your ass out in the middle of goddamn nowhere and you trip onto the friggin' story of your life. It's not right, Teller."

"Hardly the story of my life," Matt clarified.

"Don't give me that. I saw you in there with those *Times* assholes. You're gonna cross over on this one."

"They don't even know about it."

"Yeah. Sure. You're gonna get the fat job with the *Times* on my story. You wouldn't have even been there if it wasn't for me. I put you there."

"Jesus! This is like some crossbreed O. Henry-Stephen King mutation."

"It's my story and my job you're after!" Koz screamed. *"Mine!"*

"That's why you're following me?" Matt's voice was tired. "That's why you took my stuff?"

"It's my last chance!" Koz cried.

He was on the verge of some sort of breakdown, Matt was sure. Whatever thin glue held him together was about to decompose. Matt could picture him oozing through the sieve of the trash can in wavy Silly-Putty extrusions.

"Don't you understand?" Koz went on, almost in tears. "I can't work at the *Eye* for the rest of my life."

"And you think I'm gonna waltz into some star reporter gig for the *Times* on this one. That's what's eating your ass."

"It's my turn, Teller! I can't do this anymore!"

"You stupid asshole! You actually think I want to work for them? Turn into one of those Grade A, homogenized Velveeta idiots, for crissakes? I'm a writer, shithead! This just pays the bills."

"Oh, excuse me, Mr. Hemingway."

"I could work for them," Matt snapped. "Never wanted to."

"Yeah. Right."

"You get stuck there. You get to thinking you're something fine and wholesome. It's a dead end. You don't go any further. You think you've made it. But you're still lying everyday. By what you leave out, by what you don't cover, you're lying every day. At least we're honest about our lying. We've got no delusions of grandeur on our side of the tracks. At least I don't."

Koz rolled his eyes. "You're destined for bigger things, I suppose."

"Count on it."

"Well, I'll tell you something, big-timer. When I started at the *Eye* I had three manuscripts started. Last New Year's Day I found eight lying around the house. All started. All so promising. None of it finished. I piled them up, took them outside and burned the motherfuckers. I finally figured out what I was, Teller. I came to grips with it. You're the one with your head in the clouds. You think you're just slummin', passing through. But you're spinning your wheels in bullshit right with the rest of us, and if you can wangle a job with the *Times* you're gonna do it faster than a case of Tijuana trots."

Matt pulled his feet out of the water and swung his legs around to the pavement. He stomped lightly on the bricks, shaking off as much water as he could. He patted his feet dry with his socks, which he then balled up and stuffed in his pockets. He slipped his bare feet into his shoes, stood and turned back toward Koz.

"I never killed anyone, Koz," he said evenly, "but I could've killed you tonight."

"But you're not going to," Koz replied, pushing the trash can up over his head. It fell into the pool, splashing water on both of them.

"No."

"And just how is it that I'm worthy of such compassion?"

Matt didn't answer. He started back for his car, leaving Koz sitting in the water. He just couldn't bring himself to admit that Koz was the only person he knew who really believed someone had died at Coombe's Ditch.

6

II MEN   I3 CUMKU

AT THE COMPLETION OF
I2 BAKTUNS
I8 KATUNS
8 TUNS
I4 UINALS
I5 KINS

three days later . . .

Time was a mirror. But the mirror was cloudy and the Daykeeper could not see its reflection. What had happened in the age before man, before the Day Zero, that would shape this present *kin?* What was the symmetry? What gods were in attendance? What names needed to be recalled?

He struggled, but the augury eluded him. Everything seemed to be slipping away, fading into obscurity. "White clarity" would not come to his divination. He could not complete the *ubixic,* the reading of 11 Men 13 Cumku.

Yet he had a strong sense of converging forces, of something imminent and critical on course through space and time. . . .

A child walked by carrying a bowl carved from a calabash gourd. He called her over. "Do you know the origin of this?" he asked, taking the bowl into his hands.

"No, Mother-Father," she answered timidly.

"The Lords of the Underworld sacrificed One Hunahpu and Seven Hunahpu. They buried them at the Place of Ball Game Sacrifice, but they put the severed head of One Hunahpu in the fork of a tree. This tree had never before borne fruit, but when it did, it was difficult to tell the difference between the fruit and the head of One Hunahpu. That is the origin of the calabash tree, which still bears its fruit in the size and shape of a human head."

The girl nodded.

"In time," the Daykeeper continued, "the head of One Hunahpu became a skull. A maiden of Xibalba, a girl named Blood Woman, came to the calabash tree and looked upon it. The skull spit into her hand and she became pregnant with Hunahpu and Xbalanque, the divine twins."

In the sky over the camp, two great flocks of *zopilotes* came together into one massed, black sheet. The vultures soared en masse toward the hills south of La Salvación, banked toward the river and descended.

The Daykeeper patted the young girl on the head. "Go now, little one, and remember this story of the calabash. Remember how from death came life."

•

The news wire had looked routine when Kelly's editor had handed it to her a few hours ago. Now, Kelly wasn't so sure. She reread it:

LOS ANGELES (AP)—Raúl Armando Morán García, Los Angeles Consul General of Guatemala, expressed deepest regret at the murder earlier today of Hernando Cuellar Real, a fellow consulate officer. In a short statement which was delivered to the wire services, Mr. Morán stated that a $5,000 reward would be offered to anyone providing information leading to the arrest and conviction of Cuellar's killers. Mr. Morán praised Cuellar, calling him "a most dedicated and patriotic public servant." Cuellar had been assigned to the Los Angeles office last November.

Cuellar was found at his apartment by Los Angeles police officers responding to reports of a break-in. He had been shot once in the head and once in the throat. Apparently he surprised burglars who were in the process of looting the apartment. A television, a stereo and a number of paintings were reported missing by Cuellar's housekeeper, who was not in the apartment at the time of the murder.

Police have no suspects at the current time.

Mae Gower walked up and sat on Kelly's desk, as usual, a cigarette in one hand and a lipstick-stained coffee mug in the other. "I heard you're looking for me," she said.

"Got a name for you," Kelly replied. It sounded like a challenge.

"Shoot."

"Hernando Cuellar Real."

"The Guatemalan?" Mae asked.

"You're amazing, lady," Kelly said, thoroughly impressed.

"There's a low-level Assistant to the Assistant Adjutant Interior Minister in Uruguay named Cuellar, but I think his first name is Ricardo. . . . Or is it Antonio? . . ."

"Now you're showing off," Kelly chided.

"It's Ricardo."

"Is there anyone you haven't heard of?"

"I can only assume so," Mae answered without cracking a smile.

"It's the Guatemalan, Mae. What do you know about him?"

"Very dark character. Linked to the death squads in the late seventies. His name comes up a lot concerning the Panzós massacre."

"Some Indians were killed or something. . . ."

"At least a hundred of them. Machine-gunned in the town square by regular army and a group of landowners."

"Why?"

"Oil. It was found in the region they call 'the strip.' For thirty years the government had been moving landless campesinos into the area, which was no big deal because the land was considered worthless anyway. Then they found oil and decided the Indians had to go somewhere else."

"And they resisted?"

"Predictably."

"So they killed them."

"The official story is that the army, with the help of some patriots, put down a spontaneous, armed insurrection."

"Does it hold water?"

"There's a number of witnesses who claim that mass graves were dug by army bulldozers days *before* the massacre."

Mae pointed to a Xeroxed sign which hung over Kelly's desk. It read: PLAN YOUR WORK AND WORK YOUR PLAN.

"And this guy Cuellar is connected?"

"As best as anyone can really say for sure. It's debatable whether he actually participated in the main event, but there's good evidence he helped in the mop-up."

"Death squad stuff?"

"Tortures, mutilations, burnings. These people were very zealous in their work."

"What kind of mutilations?"

"Please, Kelly, I just had lunch."

"Really. I need to know."

"Well, as I remember the Amnesty International reports, they especially liked to cut things off: fingers, toes, noses . . . You know. . . ."

"Makes you wonder, doesn't it?"

"Makes me sick."

"Makes you wonder if evolution is some warped cosmic joke. . . . I mean, if we're capable of . . ."

"What's your interest in Cuellar? You finally decide to come over to International?"

"He's dead here in L.A."

Kelly handed Mae the wire. She read it quickly.

"Didn't know he'd been transferred up here," Mae commented.

"It was very quietly done, I'm finding out."

"Doesn't surprise me."

"So why does the Consul General make a public statement and offer a reward? They slip him in here with mirrors and smoke, and then they shoot off firecrackers when he's croaked."

"You are treading in the labyrinthine world of international diplomacy, honey. Anything is possible . . . save, of course, unadulterated simple truth."

"They had a statement to AP before Jonesey could even write up his lead . . . and he was at the goddamn scene with the coroner's wagon."

"How'd you get it, if it's Jonesey's story?"

"Ray thought there might be an angle with that immunity thing I've been working on. Rapists, murderers, drug dealers, kleptos, flashers—I got a whole file on creeps with diplomatic immunity who can't be prosecuted. With the violent death, Ray just thought it might be worth a look. The guy might be mixed up in something. Jonesey is just doing the straight police story."

"What's he say?"

"He says it's tough dying for a nineteen-inch TV and a Korean boom box."

"Karma, I guess."

"Jonesey also says no one in the building heard shots and no one fesses up to calling the cops."

"I don't think that's too unusual."

"The shots were real clean, too—voice box and the cerebellum. Can't talk, can't think, lights out."

"There's not a hell of a lot of competency left in this world. I guess you got to take it where you find it."

Mae drained the coffee, grimacing at its bitterness, and headed back to International.

Kelly opened her desk drawer and removed the article she had clipped from the front page of the latest issue of *Here and There.* She laid it next to the AP wire and contemplated her next move.

•

The Daykeeper sat on a wooden box outside his tent in the camp at La Salvación. He was dressed in the traditional way: black woolen knee pants, a matching jacket embroidered with red trim, and a sash. His head was wrapped in the crimson scarf called a *tzut.* The clothes were as out of place as he was, removed both from their time and their mountain home. The two apprentices who sat bare-chested and sweating on the ground at his feet did not understand how the Chuchkajawib could endure the warmth of the heavy garments. The Daykeeper's face had the texture of a mummy's. His skin looked as shriveled as a piece of fruit left too long in the tropical Chiapas sun. The two youths worried that the Mexican heat and the many nights of bloodletting had been too much for him.

The Chuchkajawib hadn't stirred or said a word since the sun had moved into the western sky. Now, the sun was low and red, about to fall behind the distant Quiché mountains, from which they had been exiled, to make its passage through the underworld. The Daykeeper peered unblinkingly into its waning glow, the innumerable wrinkles of his old face fanning out in tangled furrows from the corners of his squinting eyes.

"How did man come to be made?" he asked suddenly.

The two young men were only burners, *poronel,* the lowest position of the novitiate. They looked at each other in confusion. The answer was so obvious that the question itself had to be questioned. It was some sort of test, they reasoned. Manuel Xom Calel, who was the more quick-witted of the pair, thought he saw the Daykeeper's purpose.

"Mother-Father, do you mean according to the preaching of God?" Manuel asked.

"No," the Daykeeper grunted. "By the *Oher Tzih,* by the Prior Word."

Again, the two apprentices were perplexed. How man came into being according to the teachings of Christendom was quite different from the story of creation as told in the *Popol Vuh,* the Council Book, the older account of the dawn of life. Manuel had been clever to seek the clarification, but the Daykeeper's answer led them back to the seemingly apparent, to what every young Quiché child knew. They did not understand why the Chuchkajawib would ask them such a simple question.

"Mother-Father," Juan Guarcas Tol responded tentatively, "from maize were humans sown."

"That is how man was *accomplished,*" the Daykeeper said

gruffly. "But did the gods not try on three other occasions to fashion humans?"

"Yes, Mother-Father," Juan answered sheepishly, still not entirely sure what point of instruction the Daykeeper was trying to impart.

"Tell the story," the Daykeeper ordered.

"The first attempt to make humans gave us the animals of the forest," Juan recounted. "Then the gods modeled a human form from mud, but it dissolved into nothingness."

"Then?" the Daykeeper asked.

"From wood," the young man continued. "The gods carved wooden manikins. And they spoke and they walked and they multiplied—"

" 'But there was nothing in their hearts and nothing in their minds, no memory of their mason and builder,' " the Daykeeper quoted from the Council Book. " 'They did not remember the Heart of the Sky.' "

"And they became monkeys," Juan said, finishing the account.

The Daykeeper let his mind drift back to the Vision, to the Monkey Scribe he'd seen climbing up the back of the Serpent. The Monkey Scribe was, at least, a familiar sign, one with a point of reference and seen often on the old buildings—the third failed human experiment, sitting at the foot of a lord, recording his deeds. It was the Monkey Scribe's companion following him up the back of the Vision Serpent who posed the bigger riddle. The Daykeeper had never before encountered Girded Tapir. Not in stone or dream. What did it mean? Such a lumbering beast, the largest in his world, fitted with the *tzuun,* the waist yoke of *chaah,* the ancient ball game? The gods taunted, dealing out contradictions to test the limits of human comprehension. Monkeys who could write, tapirs adept at sport . . .

"So how did man come to be made?" the Daykeeper asked again, returning to the lesson at hand.

The two apprentices still lacked the answer. Their heads bowed under the shame of their ignorance.

"By trial and error, by perseverance, by experiment, by ingenuity, by invention," the Daykeeper explained. "Any of these is the right answer. These ways are the ways of gods—perseverance, experiment, ingenuity. Think of the twin gods Xbalanque and Hunahpu. They anger the lords of the underworld by playing ball at Nim Xol."

Manuel and Juan could see the celestial twins playing the ancient game in the primordial heavens over the Great Abyss, each fitted with the ball-player's yoke around his waist, striking the ball with the protruding paddles but never touching it with their hands.

"The twins are summoned before the Lords of Xibalba," the Daykeeper continued. "They are faced with insurmountable ordeals, yet they survive. By ingenuity, by perseverance they endure. They endure and the sun rises for the very first time."

The Daykeeper watched as the wave of understanding washed over the two boys. Would that he were so blessed. What he would not give to know those things which yet eluded him.

"Could it be," Manuel asked, his eyes bright with the promise of some gleaming thing just discovered, "that this is what is meant?"

The Daykeeper motioned for the youth to continue, feeling suddenly as if the roles of master and apprentice had reversed, as if by teaching he had now earned the ability to learn. All day long he had felt the subtle forces building, moving toward a moment, a convergence. He wondered if now was the time, if this was the place.

"Everyone has taken it that the return of Xbalanque and Hunahpu is told on the Stone of Nim Xol," Manuel went on.

"It reads, 'In the ways of Xbalanque, in the ways of Hunahpu,'" the Daykeeper quoted from memory. He took his eyes from the setting sun, suddenly aware that there was something else he was to see.

"Yes," the young man said, his body almost shaking with excitement, *"in their ways.* It only says, *'In the ways* of Xbalanque, *in the ways* of Hunahpu, through the deeds of two—'"

The Daykeeper finished the quote: "'Through the deeds of two comes Sky-Sword Bringer, Calabash, the True Lord of the Mat, Begetter of the New Age, Preparer of the Last Katun.'" The old man lifted himself from the stool, his bones creaking as he stood. He felt the moment coming. He readied himself.

"And this is brought about *in the ways* of the twin gods, *not* by their actual return," Manuel said with all the enthusiasm of youth. "Could it not be?"

The Daykeeper did not answer. His eyes had rooted on a giant of a man who walked a crooked, hulking path across the compound. He watched as the man staggered over to a group of small boys who were playing the modern ball game with some of the Red Cross volunteers. The big man talked with one of the volunteers, then took up a stick shaped like a long, thin club. He held it over his shoulder as another of the volunteers threw the ball at him. The big man swung the club, hitting the ball high into the sky, over the tents, far out toward the setting sun where it vanished in its red light.

Young Manuel Xom Calel, finder of the lost piece of the Stone of Nim Xol, had brought the moment. He had found an *ibal*, a seeing instrument, to overcome the gods-limited scope of human sight. He had seen something very new in the old words, and in doing so, had given them life. The signal had been given.

The Daykeeper knew the time had come. He moved toward his destiny, toward the convergence, toward the completion of the fragile harmony.

Buchanon had wandered into the camp the night before, guided past the pintos and led across the Rio Usumacinta by Héctor, who had since returned to Guatemala. He had had the extreme good fortune to be recognized by a Red Cross worker who not only was a rabid Yankee fan but who possessed the only two bottles of Scotch in that part of Chiapas. While the volunteer busied himself making arrangements for Buchanon's documentation and transportation back to the states, the scout had spent the day draining both liters of Johnny Walker Red. Somehow, while vast quantities of distilled spirits could horribly impair his powers of speech, reason, virility and general locomotion, they never affected his ability to crush the old *cow*hide. He stood in the center of the compound, swaying but upright, waiting for the swarm of kids to find the ball that had sailed at least three hundred feet into some scrub just past the last row of tents. He placed the bat behind his back, bracing it against the base of his spine, and twisted back and forth to work out the kinks in his *transversus abdominis*.

The convergence occurred at the flattened Pepsi carton which served as home plate.

The Daykeeper beheld Girded Tapir.

Buchanon saw an old man in short pants, a sash and a red turban and thought of an aged Aladdin.

The Daykeeper gave Girded Tapir the final piece of the Stone of Nim Xol, transferring its weight, its generations of age and knowledge, its warning, its promise, its pain.

Buchanon took into his hand a chipped piece of rock, looked at it, tried to read what was etched on its face, shook his head, felt its heft, considered hitting it with the bat and then just shrugged.

The Daykeeper told Girded Tapir the name of the man to whom he must deliver the stone, the name of the True Lord of the Mat, the Preparer of the Last Tun, the only one who could stop the annihilation, the exile.

Buchanon heard a language he didn't understand. One of the Red Cross workers translated: "Give it to He Who Walks in Old Words." He still didn't understand.

The Daykeeper walked back to his tent.

Buchanon passed out at home plate.

•

The Sacred Heart of Jesus occupied an incongruous place in a narrow passage high on the wall just opposite a back entrance to Saint Jerome's School in Los Angeles. Last year's parish calendar, co-sponsored by a mortician and a transmission shop, was just to the right and slightly below. A poster from the Christmas pageant of three years past was to the left, along with a plaque commemorating participation (but not victory) in an archdiocesan swim meet. There were also some charts related to the upkeep of the nearby boiler. A fire extinguisher was clamped to the wall just over the switch panel that controlled the lights. No one could remember who had hung the Sacred Heart on that cluttered wall, but for as long as anyone could recall the faded, brass-framed picture had been there, looking like a dusty relic plucked from over the bed of some old woman. It was the first thing seen by those who were allowed to enter by that particular back door: priests, nuns when there had been nuns, maintenance people, and, in recent years, the refugees who arrived in the middle of the night, making the sign of the cross as they passed, before heading down the stairs to the basement sanctuary beneath the adjacent church.

Father Calderon didn't notice that the picture was hanging crooked as he came up the stairs. He had other things on his mind. There had been an automobile accident. A man was dying, a parishioner—although he hadn't recognized the man's name when the hospital called. He had to administer Last Rites. The doctor (Father Calderon could not remember a doctor ever having called before; a nurse, an aide, but never a doctor) had said to hurry. "Mr. Usserman will be dead in fifteen minutes," the doctor had stated with total certainty, as if the event were timed to a schedule. *Doctors were getting so arrogant,* thought Father Calderon. *Almost as arrogant as bishops.*

He was reluctant to leave his sanctuary without supervision, but what else could he do? Father Zell, his assistant, was not due back from the CYO boxing tournament for at least two hours, and Frank Struthers, the one deacon in the parish, was preparing the CCD second-graders for their first Holy Communion up in a third-floor classroom. He considered interrupting Struthers, asking him to come down and watch over the refugees, but doing so would leave twenty eight-year-olds unattended. The prospect of a score of public school kids running wild through the halls of Saint Jerome's was more frightening to him than leaving eight adult illegal aliens alone in the basement.

He flicked one of the light switches and opened the back door. The parking lot was dark. He reached back and hit the switch again, but the spotlight that the switch controlled still failed to go on. He added a burned-out bulb to the ever-growing list of things to do which he kept in his head. It was something to mention to the sexton in the morning.

Father Calderon stepped out into the darkness, locked the door behind him and ran to his car. He sped off toward the hospital praying that Mr. Usserman—whoever he was—would outlast the smug doctor's timetable. He failed to notice the chocolate-brown Mercedes parked at the far edge of the lot.

Moments later, a pounding shook the back door. It shuddered a number of times, then the lock gave out and the knob fell to the tile floor, bounced and rolled away. The door blew inward, pivoting hard on its hinges, slamming into the stop and rattling the walls. The Sacred Heart slid down the wall and crashed to the floor facedown. Four men dressed in black with hoods over their faces stormed inside. They ran down the stairs toward the basement sanctuary as a fifth man trailed them into the passage. He leaned a sledgehammer against the wall. Its head came to rest on the back of the fallen icon. The fifth man was out of breath from the effort of smashing the door. He tugged at his hood, pulling it out from his face so he could breathe more easily. He remained stationed near the doorway, on lookout over the darkened parking lot.

The four others burst into the sanctuary. Five Guatemalan women gathered around a TV set screamed. Three middle-aged men seated at a table playing cards lurched up out of their chairs. They looked around in alarm, appearing for a moment as if they were about to take some defensive action. Then, just as suddenly, they sat back down. The hooded ones were not carrying weapons, but the fear they instilled was nonetheless crippling. The men stared down at their cards; the women stopped screaming and peered vacantly at the perfume commercial playing on the television.

The intruders marched over to the men, wrenched them away from the table and threw them against the wall. They did it brutally, inflicting as much pain as was possible in such a direct, quick action upon subjects who were not offering any resistance.

One of the hooded men removed a photograph from his pocket. He adjusted the eye-holes in his shroud so he could see more clearly. He held the photo next to the face of the first refugee and made a comparison. The refugee was not the man pictured in the photograph. This made the hooded one angry. He made a gesture which caused one of his accomplices to kick the refugee in the groin. The refugee made no attempt to cover up. The boot struck hard and unimpeded. The man grunted but did not cry out. His body contorted, tightened, twisted in pain, but he held his place against the wall.

The episode was repeated with each of the two remaining men with much the same results, although the last victim felt a bit less pain than his companions, having been castrated over four years ago. If those who had taken his manhood had sought to numb certain pleasures, then they had also—quite unintentionally —numbed certain pains. It was an imperfect justice, to be sure, but the man found himself smiling at his tormentors. In some small way, he had beaten them.

The hooded ones left as abruptly as they had come. They had other "visits" yet to make before sunrise. The one with the photograph slipped it back into his pocket. The picture hadn't matched any of the men in this sanctuary—nor any in the other two they had raided earlier. He didn't know it yet, but his night of frustrations would continue. He would not find the man in the photograph, for that man, the young archaeology student named Pablo Martín Méndez Córdova, was hiding beneath an old VFW hall seventy miles to the east in the desert town of Braxton Wells.

•

Matt listened to the knocking on his apartment door but made no move to open it. At the first sound, he sensed trouble. Since he'd solved the mystery of the missing film and tape there wasn't any reason for apprehension, but a feeling of dread, a clammy, ill-defined fear, nonetheless overcame him. He reasoned against it and forced himself to the door. He hesitated before grabbing the knob, hoping the caller would leave. The rapping continued, light but persistent, a familiar rhythm. He braced himself, turned the bolt and opened the door.

"Am I welcome?" Kelly asked.

"Something told me not to answer," Matt grumbled, turning and retreating into the living room.

"At least you didn't slam the door in my face," Kelly said, taking a giant step across the threshold as if she were crossing over a deep and treacherous fissure. The door swung shut behind her, fitting into the jamb with a resonant thud that sounded to Matt like the lid of a sarcophagus shutting.

"I'll regret it, I'm sure," he said. Matt sank into the old sofa, a floral eyesore he'd picked up at a garage sale. If there had been a seat belt, he would have used it. He was mad at himself for letting her in—even though he knew he was incapable of such a direct and final rejection as closing a door in her face. Their conflicts always took more circuitous routes. Doors—real and emotional— were left open a crack, at least.

Against his will, Matt was thinking how pretty she looked, remembering how good it felt to make love to her. When he'd opened the door, he'd noticed a nervous but fetching smile on her face. She was dressed simply: a thin cotton dress, gathered at her slim waist, a small ruby and gold pendant hanging bright and delicate at the base of her neck, canvas sandals and nothing more. Her dark hair was a loose tangle of short curls, a perfection of casualness which no comb or brush could improve without sacrificing her natural beauty. Matt had often seen her decked out for some special event—hair done up, makeup laid on—and although no one could say she didn't look absolutely stunning on such occasions, he preferred her au naturel, in a plain frock or a ragged pair of jeans. Her eyes were big and darker than her hair, a sable brown, a deep, warm color which looked nothing if not trustworthy. How many times had those eyes pulled him in? . . . Kelly walked slowly into the living room, studying the walls which were lined with pictures, cluttered shelves, boxes and file cabinets. She inched along, like a Sunday stroller at the Smithsonian, peering at the assortment of oddities seven years at *H&T* had collected. Occasionally, she'd pick one up and say, "I remember this" or, "I thought you were going to get rid of that." She lingered a while at a framed watercolor. "This is nice," she offered.

"The painter was born without hands," Matt explained.

"That's amazing."

"Don't you think it's a bit too yellow?"

Kelly ignored the reference to her book. "How does he do it?" she asked. "Brush in his teeth?"

"Between *her* toes."

"Didn't you have a banjo player from some backwoods nowhere who picked with his toes?"

"A guitarist. He got his hands blown off in Viet Nam."

"Let's see . . . He was from Wine City or . . . what was it?"

"Wine Island, Louisiana."

"You had a clever title for that one. Right?"

" 'Toe Jam Found in Wine.' "

"Classic! I remember the piece."

"Do you remember he hated performing for people because it made him feel like a freak? But it was the only way he could make money. Or that poor as he was, he contributed half of what he made to veterans' groups?"

"I don't remember that being your lead."

"It wasn't," he mumbled.

"Maybe it should have been."

Matt reached for the bottle of Coors that was going warm on the coffee table. He polished it off wondering why he always found himself defending his work to Kelly—and why she always seemed to get in the last shot.

"I never liked this," Kelly said. She held up a gothic-looking contraption rigged of belts and metal plates.

"I know."

"Some radio preacher was pushing these, right?"

"The answer to adultery, venereal disease and teenage pregnancy."

"Chastity belts from the Bible Belt," Kelly mused. "How's that for a lead?"

Matt didn't answer. He didn't want to admit it was a better lead than the one he'd used. Kelly set the belt back in its place, on a shelf with an "authentic" unicorn horn, an aluminum divining rod and a transistor radio through which a fourteen-year-old boy had heard broadcasts instructing him to murder his parents. She straightened one of the dozen candid, unflattering celebrity shots hanging on the wall and then studied the pattern of colored pins on a continental map which indicated UFO sightings and various other types of close encounters. In the corner, on top of a beige two-drawer file cabinet was a stack of shoe boxes all marked *GAN*. Kelly opened one, pulled out a cassette tape and read the label. "Number twenty-eight." Putting the cassette back in the box she asked, "What are you on now?"

"One-fifteen."

"And how much on paper?"

Matt didn't answer. He raised the empty beer bottle to his lips and pretended to drink.

"I remember when you started calling them *GAN* notes," Kelly continued. "I hated it. It was so self-destructive."

"Yeah. That would be infringing on your territory."

"I don't like seeing you do that to yourself."

"So much less for you to do."

"I'm sincere."

"So am I."

"Sincere bitterness sounds exactly the same as sarcasm," Kelly pointed out.

"It was just a gag, an inside joke—marking them *GAN*. It was better than just having numbers on them."

"The Great American Novel."

"It's a joke, Kelly. When I write it, it probably won't even be a novel."

"The day you labeled the tapes is the day you threw away your chance to ever write anything."

"Bullshit."

"If you reduce your dream to a joke, you've got a perfect excuse for never going after it, and that's sad." Kelly put the lid back on the shoe box. "There's more to writing a novel than talking to yourself, Matt. There's more than just standing back out of the way and making self-assuring judgments."

These were familiar waters, an oft-traveled, dark and winding river. It made for a grueling if sometimes exhilarating ride, for which he currently had neither the strength nor inclination. Without rebuttal, he got up and headed for the kitchen. Leaving the lights off, he requisitioned another Coors from the refrigerator and sat at the table. After a few minutes, Kelly followed him in. She was acquainted enough with the layout of the apartment to navigate by the weak light filtering in from the living room. She wandered over to the refrigerator.

"Mind if I have a beer?" she asked.

"I wouldn't open that."

"I can take it. I remember the bacteria cultures you used to propagate. There was a decomposing tomato once which I swear had reanimated and taken root in a bowl of—"

"Kelly, don't open the door."

"You never could throw food away. It's a noble trait. It's also disgusting."

"Kelly . . ."

As she pulled the door open, Matt saw the soft, promising

outline of her body through the cotton dress as the light from inside the refrigerator poured out into the dark kitchen. He watched her quiver, go rigid and almost lift off the floor. She pushed back from the refrigerator and slammed the door.

"*What is that?*" she gasped.

"A human hand."

"Why is it in your refrigerator?"

"It keeps better there than in the bread box." Matt was starting to enjoy himself.

"Whose hand, Matt?"

"Don't know."

"It didn't just materialize in there."

"No."

"Where'd it come from?"

"Just below the wrist, I'd say."

"It has to do with your article, doesn't it?"

"What article?" Matt asked innocently.

Kelly let it go. She glided over toward the table. "You sent the champagne the other night, didn't you?" she asked.

"I figured none of those high-rollers you hang out with would spring for bubbly."

"That was nice. . . . It was nice you stopped by."

"Well . . . I got your message on the answering machine."

"But you didn't quite make it all the way back there."

"Wouldn't think of it. A low-life like me rubbing elbows with the Brahmins of journalism. I wouldn't want to embarrass you."

"You won't believe this, but when they told me I'd made the list, you're the only one I wanted to be with. I took a chance and gave you a call. I didn't think you'd show up."

"Either did I."

They didn't say anything for a few minutes. It could have gone either way. But in the dark, Matt couldn't see her eyes. So the urge to take her back lost out to the question which had churned in his gut for months, the question he'd asked before, more than once, before sweeping it under the rug with the rest of their unresolved problems.

"Why'd you do it?"

Kelly sighed. She'd felt it too, that the night could have gone in a less painful direction. "We've been through this before."

"Again, with feeling," Matt insisted.

"I didn't betray you. I didn't spy on you. I didn't hold you up to ridicule. I didn't reveal confidences. That's the full article of indictment, isn't it?"

"One more item," Matt said softly. "All those things you didn't do, you didn't do with complete calculated premeditation."

"I wrote a book. I set things down that I knew."

"You set *me* down."

"I never identified you. Never even described a person like you."

"You set down things I told you. Things between lovers."

"Day-at-the-office stories aren't things between lovers."

"If you had cheated on me, I'd have felt less cuckolded."

"That's *your* forte."

"I never *cheated*, Kelly. I chased after a few. One-nighters. No romance. Just hormones."

"Absolution via the irresistible testosterone level."

"It was stupid, but it was never premeditated. It was never meant to hurt."

"But it did."

"We weren't married. We weren't engaged. We weren't living with each other when it happened. Hell! We weren't even going together."

"We were supposed to be in love."

"We were," Matt admitted. "It seems like it's always been past tense with us: We *were.*"

"We were past tense when I wrote *Yellow Pages,*" Kelly said quietly. "And it's over two years since I set the first word down."

"I read your book and I read stories I had told you over pizza in bed, naked, with candles burning and old 'Honeymooner' reruns going on the TV. Stories you laughed at. Stories everyone can laugh at now. It's laughable, Kelly, but you don't get quite that same laugh when the anchovies aren't falling between your thighs and Ralph isn't eating the dog food. It's a real different laugh."

"Nobody's laughing at you."

"Well they should be."

"You're never named, Matt. You're never quoted. I put a year of research into that book before I wrote the first word. There're three hundred and twenty-six pages. There can't be more than thirty that have any link to you. It's not personal."

"It's about me. It's about guys like me. *You* wrote it. *It's goddamn personal.*"

"It's not."

"It's a direct attack on me."

"It's a book on an industry."

"It's a book on my life that says you're okay and I'm a maggot."

"Why is everything I do an attack on you? It's like our own personal law of physics: things Kelly does have an equal and opposite effect on Matt. When I won the grant at school, it was your grant."

"Fuck school and fuck your grant."

"And drop out and throw three years away."

"I wasn't learning anything."

"They give me a Pulitzer I never asked for. It was like I stole it off your mantel."

"Jesus, Kelly. Are you going to run through the whole grand, glorious résumé?"

"Before that, when I got the job at the *Times*, it was your job."

"I don't give a fuck about your goddamn job at the goddamn *Times*."

"Which you prove by going to work for that . . . that . . . *pornographer* Barnie Schiff."

"It's a living."

"It's a slow death and you're satisfied with it. That's what hurts the most. You're satisfied with mediocrity. You embrace it. You've made a great craft of it. It's your reaction to my success. It's the way you cope with it, although why in God's name it's something to be coped with is beyond comprehension. Mediocrity is your security blanket. I'll never understand it."

"At last we agree."

"There was always more than one prize. It didn't have to be a competition."

"To the victor go the spoils. I bless your plunder. I bless your booty. I bless your front-page exposés and your Volvo and your brass nameplate on your office door. I begrudge nothing. I envy nothing. I compete for nothing."

"Exactly! You compete for nothing. You made our life together into a competition when it didn't have to be, and then you forfeited every contest."

"I don't want the same things you do."

"You used to . . . until I wanted them too."

"A curiosity which never ceases to amaze me."

"That your goals became my achievements? I can't explain that and I won't apologize for it either. That's the star we're under. We're drawn to the same things. We're drawn to each other."

"I'm in a different constellation now."

"You've barricaded yourself. The shades are down. You can't see the stars. You're hiding out."

"I'm out there every day. I see things you'll never even imagine."

"You're blowin' it—your work, your life. Hell, you've blown that Coombe's Ditch thing."

"*What?*"

"That's where you got your souvenir in the icebox, isn't it?"

"No . . . that's got nothing to do—"

"You had something there and you blew it for two gory snapshots on the front page and that little autopsy you wrote."

"What do you know about it?"

"I know it's news. I know we missed it and you didn't. I know there's more there. I smell it. You smell it. I know you could find it if you really wanted to."

"I'll find it."

"You better."

It was a threat. Pure and simple. If there was any doubt, Kelly erased it by quickly leaving the room, thereby suspending the statement, hanging it there in her absence so there was no chance to resolve through conversation, clarify through argument. If it hadn't been a threat, she would have remained and talked it out. Matt understood perfectly: Kelly would go after the story if he didn't. Once again they had been drawn along the same narrow path. He contemplated the sudden and unexpected turn of events. Normally, he'd be furious, but instead he could only feel satisfaction. Kelly's interest was a vindication. It was the gilt-edged, embossed and notarized stamp of approval on the authenticity of his story. Coombe's Ditch was on the map. It was real. It existed.

Matt heard the hiss of the VCR in the bedroom. "Damn!" he cursed, leaping to his feet. He bounded across the kitchen, through the living room and into the bedroom. Kelly was sitting on the edge of the bed, the remote control in her hand. Starbursts sizzled on the screen as the blank leader at the beginning of the video cassette wound its way through the playback heads, lighting the otherwise dark room like a flickering hearth. The screen resolved into an image which Kelly only saw for a brief second before Matt spun the tuner dial, scrambling the video into an indecipherable sheet of ruptured colors and rolling bars.

"What was that?" Kelly asked, fidgeting unsuccessfully with the control.

"It's private," Matt explained.

"It looked like privates."

"It's something Schiff gave me."

"Totally repulsive?"

"That's the best thing one could say about it."

"And you'd be embarrassed if I watched it?"

"I'm embarrassed that it's in the same room with you."

Kelly smiled. Their years together had had their share of good times, of caring moments, brief and blissful interludes that never lasted long enough. She took a deep breath and held it, as if it could sustain the feeling, the memory of those occasions, as if it could freeze something that seemed to be happening again, isolate it, pull it deep inside and keep it forever. But eventually she had to answer her body's demand for oxygen. She took a breath and rose from the bed. "I guess I should go," she said without conviction.

Matt didn't move out of the way. There was just enough light for him to see her eyes. He reached out slowly and put his hand lightly on the pendant at her throat. She arched her neck as he turned it gently in his fingers. But when his hand drifted down to the top button of her dress, she caught his wrist and pulled it away.

"I'll do it," she whispered.

•

It was later than usual for Rebecca to be making a visit to the sanctuary. Sergio was the first to notice her coming down the stairs. He looked toward his wife as if to say, "What's she doing down here at this time?" Rebecca nodded a "hello" which he pretended not to see. She had no intention of staying more than a few moments, just long enough to drop off the small pile of newspapers and magazines she was carrying.

"Thought you might like something to read," she announced quietly.

Pablo, who was seated at the end of the table, glanced up from the notebook he was studying. "All bearing the *nihil obstat*, I'd bet."

Ever since Pablo had found a page missing from a newspaper, he'd been accusing her of censorship. Indeed, she had been careful to remove all references to Pastor Vail's death from the scant reading materials she had supplied in prior days. Other items deemed capable of upsetting the fragile peace had been excised as well.

"Nathan does not approve of everything which the press chooses to cover," she explained, thinking that the most artful lies involved the misapplication of true statements.

"And makes that decision for us," Pablo said pointedly.

"And for me, as well."

"How fortunate we all are," Pablo quipped. He smiled to take the sting out of his words. He was not really interested in giving Rebecca a hard time.

"Nathan does not approve of the media in general, but we realize how hungry all of you must be for news of the outside world."

Having deposited her delivery on the table, she said a hasty good night and quickly ascended the stairs. She locked the door behind her and ran to the storage room, taking care not to disturb Nathan, who was contemplating Leviticus on the bed. She closed herself in without turning on the light and felt her way over to the bassinet. Trying not to make any noise, she pulled it back until the bullet of light shot up through the knothole in the floor. She knelt down, put her eye to the opening and watched.

At first, nobody approached the papers. Pablo remained at the other end of the table. Sergio and Yolanda had taken chairs nearby. Sebastian was on the table. Pablo coaxed the baby to crawl toward him. The others were not within view.

After a few minutes, Abraham wandered by. The top newspaper caught his eye and he stopped. Rebecca saw him crossing himself over and over in a fast, frantic motion that looked almost epileptic. Coh came over, evidently to determine what was wrong. The old man pointed to the two pictures of the mutilated corpse lying on the cot at Coombe's Ditch. Coh took a cautious step closer.

One by one, the others joined them, staring down at the issue of *Here and There* that Rebecca had placed on the top of the stack. At first, no one said a word. But then they began speaking rapidly in Spanish. Rebecca could barely hear and what little she could hear, she could not understand. An argument quickly developed between Soto and Pablo. Sebastian crawled onto the pile, looked up and giggled. Rebecca flinched, thinking for one irrational moment he'd seen her. Yolanda took the child into her arms as Cristina set a small metal bucket on the table. Everyone quieted. Coh rolled up the copy of *Here and There* and lit it with a wooden match he ignited with his fingernail. As it began to burn, he fanned out the pages and let them fall one by one into the bucket.

"*¡Indios locos!*" Rebecca heard Soto say.

Nathan called from the other room. "Rebecca . . . Rebecca . . . Do you smell something burning?"

7

2 CAUAC   17 CUMKU

AT   THE   COMPLETION   OF
12 BAKTUNS
18 KATUNS
8 TUNS
14 UINALS
19 KINS

four days later . . .

Matt felt a ponderous presence hovering behind his desk. It was either the Goodyear Blimp or Izzy Greene. While the former was slightly larger, the latter arguably contained more hot air.

"What d'you want, Iz?" he growled without turning from his work.

"Something I can print," the big man huffed.

"I'm working on it, Iz."

"You were working on it yesterday."

"And I'm working on it, today."

"You're still chasing that desert stiff, Teller. I know where your time's been going."

"That's my job. I'm supposed to bring in the story. Right?"

"The *assigned* story," Izzy stipulated, clearing phlegm from his throat which he then swallowed with a loud gulp.

"Would you like to finish it, Iz? An in-depth look at the twelve foods most likely to cause gas is something you could probably knock off standing on your head." The thought of Izzy Greene balanced on his dome tried the outer limits of Matt's imagination. It could only be reckoned by drawing heavily on recollections of old Fellini movies. For a brief—and ever so ugly— moment, there was Izzy, inverted, teetering on his baldness, naked, rolls of saturated fat pleating down over his chin, ten pudgy toes wiggling high in the air, ecstatic, liberated from elephantine mass.

"I don't understand how a dozen fart foods can take you so long." The editor inched closer to Matt's desk.

"After the first six it gets tough, Iz. I've got a researcher at Stanford who absolutely insists on including popcorn, but I can't get confirmation from the nutritionist at Mayo. She's lobbying for brussels sprouts. I'm in a quandary and I just can't seem to get agreement on the last two slots. I think we should let our readers decide. Let 'em vote on it. What d'you think?" Matt chuckled at the idea of *H&T*'s readers dutifully filling out flatulence questionnaires.

"I like it," Izzy said, the words once again moist with phlegm.

Matt spun around on his swivel chair. He glanced up at Izzy to see if he was kidding. It was a waste of effort. The man was without humor.

"Write it up," the editor continued, lumbering back toward his office, "I'll get a PO box set up for the ballots."

Matt formed his hand into a pistol, shot himself in the right temple and let his head fall to the desk top. He remained bent over in his chair, his forehead pressed against the laminated desk, until he heard a voice. "You are Mr. Teller, yes?"

Wearily, Matt assumed a more conventional posture and took in the man standing at his side. He was tall and thin, intelligently featured, nicely tanned and impeccably over-dressed in a tailored double-breasted suit. A canary power tie with red lozenges was handsomely knotted over a white-on-white shirt. The matching handkerchief bloomed at his lapel pocket. His left arm was smartly crooked over a calf-skin portfolio and his right hand was extended in greeting. A heavy gold name chain was wrapped around his wrist. Something said *latin*—a trace of accent, a subtlety in mannerism, the sum total of the silk, the tan, the chain—something.

"Yeah," Matt acknowledged. He shook the hand expecting it to be warm. It wasn't.

"I am Vincenzo Côrtes. A brother journalist. Could we have a word?" He pulled up a chair from the adjacent desk and sat down before Matt could answer. Carefully, he cleared a spot for his portfolio on the corner of Matt's desk.

"Who you with?" Matt asked suspiciously.

"*Ultima.*"

"Is that the Spanish-language paper out in Pomona?"

"No, no, no, Mr. Teller." The man smiled, self-amused. "It is a Portuguese-language paper in São Paulo."

"Where's that?" Matt asked, mentally reviewing a set of possibilities that slowly expanded to just beyond the limits of Los Angeles County.

"Brazil, of course."

"South America?" Matt asked dully.

"Yes, yes, yes." The smile widened. The teeth were white but slightly crooked. One of the upper incisors was badly chipped.

"You're a long way from home," Matt observed.

"And I have come to see you."

Côrtes sat back in his chair and waited for the impact of his statement to register. He produced a pack of Hollywoods from an inside pocket and offered one to Matt. The reporter crossed his arms defensively. His eyebrows knitted in defiance. Côrtes lit up and waved the smoke away.

"What's the problem?" Matt asked tersely. He was used to assaults from legal types representing personages he'd offended in the pages of *Here and There*. But he could not remember one ever having come so far. Nor could he recall having written about anyone of Brazilian extraction.

"Excuse?"

"You a lawyer?"

"No, no, no." The smile, briefly interrupted, returned. "A brother journalist, as I said. I am working on a story."

"I'm your story?" Matt evinced appropriate incredulity.

"Oh no, no, no. Certainly no. Not you. But I think you can help me . . . as a brother journalist, I mean."

"I'm not in the brother business." Matt swiveled back to his work, effecting a dismissal.

"It concerns your recent article about a NOSAL murder," Côrtes continued, ignoring Matt's rebuff.

"A what?"

"A NOSAL ritual murder . . . This article here." Côrtes fumbled in his portfolio for a copy of "Death in the Desert." It was on a long piece of shiny stock which Matt recognized as facsimile paper.

"Oh yeah," said Matt, trying to hide his galloping interest. "I remember that one."

"A phenomenal piece of work. I must commend you."

"Thanks."

"You know, no other paper carried this. I have researched quite thoroughly. This is quite astounding to us. The first recorded NOSAL killing in North America and not one word other than your article. It's quite a coup for you, I believe. Congratulations!"

"Yeah . . . thanks." Matt opened his top drawer and foraged for something which evidently was not to be found. Before withdrawing his hand, he deftly triggered the RECORD button on the Sony. He left the drawer slightly open, reasonably certain Côrtes hadn't detected his maneuver.

"Here I've been following the NOSAL story for three years now, and I almost miss this. If it wasn't for one of our correspondents spotting your article and faxing it to our office, I might have."

"Three years, huh?"

"And more miles than I care to remember. Israel twice, Germany three times—both sides, East and West. Switzerland, Poland, Paraguay, Chile, Peru. And how many times into Amazonia —I tell you, sir, I am no . . . no pioneer when it comes to snakes and insects and malaria. The river is always the hardest part for me."

"You must have one hell of a budget."

"Which I am always exceeding. But when the publisher is also your father-in-law . . . well, what can he say?"

" 'You're fired?' " Matt offered.

Côrtes laughed. "Oh no, no, no. Never."

"So you're really deep into this NOSAL thing, huh?"

Côrtes's head cocked back as if recoiling from a minor insult. His jaw went rigid. After a few moments of staring through fluttering eyelids, he seemed to be satisfied that Matt had not meant any offense.

"That is American understatement, yes?" he asked.

"Okay." Matt shrugged.

Côrtes reached into the portfolio and pulled out a handful of photographs, notes, documents and foreign newspaper clippings. He fanned them out on the desk. Matt saw pictures of other mutilated bodies exactly like the one he had found at Coombe's Ditch, headlines prominent with the word NOSAL and copies of old European travel papers. Matt gripped the arms of his chair, trying desperately to rein in his excitement.

"I dare say I am the leading authority in the world," Côrtes continued. "Of course, the Israelis always presume to be the ultimate experts in these affairs. But I tell you these Jews know nothing more than their arrogance allows them to know." He stopped suddenly. His face tightened. "Excuse. You are not Jewish, are you?" he asked tentatively.

"No."

The Brazilian sighed. "The Jews cannot be trusted. Everything is a state secret with them. I find the Germans to be much more helpful. For me, guilt has proved a much better partner than vengeance."

"I can see that," said Matt, who saw very little beyond the bonanza that had spilled over his desk.

"The path of Stephen Patricius Valdrick has been a long one but—what is the expression?—getting there is half the fun. Yes?"

"At least." Matt committed the name to memory, just in case the Sony hadn't.

"As a brother journalist, you share the same appreciation as I."

"Absolutely."

"When I saw my first NOSAL corpse, I knew I could not

rest until I had identified the man who had perpetrated such an atrocity. That it should be a war criminal never occurred to me at the time. It must have been six, seven months before I began to suspect it. And how much longer before the big breakthrough?" Côrtes's eyes went hazy. He seemed to be peering back through the years.

"A long time?" Matt prodded, trying to get Côrtes's mouth back into motion.

"A year at least."

"But worth the wait."

"Oh yes, yes, yes! To find a victim still alive, a MOSAD agent of all things—it is more than I could have hoped. And then this poor dying man, with his last breath, confirms to the doctor that *it is* Valdrick—well, the joy I felt could only be truly understood by a—"

"A brother journalist."

"Yes, yes, yes!"

"I've always been a tad fuzzy on how you put that all together," Matt ventured.

"Oh it's just a matter of following one's nose. One thing leads to another."

"You're too modest."

"Hardly."

"Oh I think so," Matt insisted. "I mean to connect Valder—"

"Valdrick."

"I'm so bad with pronunciations," Matt apologized. "Connecting Valdrick was quite a jump."

"How's that?" Côrtes asked, polishing off the Hollywood.

"How's what?" Matt stammered.

"You are joking me again, I think. I must remember about this American humor." Côrtes laughed and waved his finger good-

naturedly at Matt. "Yes. I suppose it is obvious now, those mutilations just the same as the murders in Częstochowa and Lubliniec
way back in '39. But remember, my brother, that is well before I
am born. And more before you are born. A horrible thing, but
obscure in history full of horrible things. True, we are profession-
als and we are responsible to keep track of such, shall I say, open
issues of human depravity. But still do not be too harsh on me for
taking so long to spot the similarities."

"I don't think—"

"Yes, yes, yes, it's true that as a Brazilian, as a South American even, one could argue that the connection should have been
more rapidly put together. All this talk you hear of Nazis hiding in
Brazil, Argentina, Paraguay. And no doubt much of it true. But
this is talk you perhaps hear more than me. It is, of course, a
matter of slight embarrassment to us and something that is not
the forefront of our conversation, our thinking, certainly not our
news. So, yes indeed, it took almost seven months from my first
ghastly sight of a mutilated timber worker—half-eaten by caimans
—until I theorized it was the long-lost SS colonel who was behind
these terrible killings."

"Well seven months really isn't that long. And all that
travel—"

"The real travel had not yet started. I had not left Brazil yet.
Yes, yes, yes, many many times I had to go far up the river, deep
into Amazonia, but what journalist of any repute didn't in those
days? With so many from the cities heading west, into the forest,
taking the timber jobs, and drilling for oil and searching for gold,
over a million new pioneers, such a time of excitement, and then
these evil stories begin. The Indians near Faro had told for years
and years of disappearances, of horrible, tortured corpses, of this
strange word, NOSAL, written in blood on the foreheads, but, sad
to say, no one listened. No one cared. But when the man from the

city goes into the jungle looking for his fortune and turns up in such a condition, people take note."

"Go figure people," said Matt philosophically, shaking his head in feigned shock.

"Indeed, my brother. Figure the worst and you will not be disappointed."

"Words of true wisdom."

"I am more cynical now than I was at the time."

"Aren't we all?"

"In three years I have aged ten times the pace of the calendar. Look at this gray." Côrtes pointed to the streaks of gray which showed as thin cracks in the glossy ebony sheen of his hair.

"It's nothing," Matt observed. "It looks good on you. It makes you look distinguished."

"Do you really think so?" Côrtes inquired with more than casual interest.

"Without a doubt."

"You are so kind."

"If the truth is kind, so be it."

"But it is often not kind, Mr. Teller," Côrtes continued. "It can be merciless. That we let such an animal into our country, his entry arranged with Nazi gold . . . what a crime. But one at least which could have ended the misery. I'm sure Valdrick just wanted to disappear, live out his years quietly with his wife and little boy. They say even the worst criminal, taken out of his element, given peace, given a chance to start anew, will choose more positive ways. He will become a citizen. He will become what he was not in his black past. But that could not be because these Jews will not forget anything. They will not rest until the so-called six million holocaust victims are brought back to life in the center of Tel Aviv. They tracked Valdrick down, their MOSAD agents. They hounded him but he was always one step ahead of them. No doubt, the officials in my country prospered from both sides, trading in information, keeping Valdrick just out of MOSAD's reach. How hideous is the bureaucratic soul! But at last Valdrick had enough. These self-righteous Jews pushed him back to his past: He sends his wife and small child to America and flees into the rain forest."

"What year was that, again?" Matt asked casually, as if to reinforce a hazy recollection.

"Nineteen fifty-two."

"That's right." Matt nodded in agreement.

"The boy is ten years old. The wife he will never see again. The man turns back into an animal. I make no excuse for him, but is it not understandable? He flees into the most inhospitable, dark and wild place on this entire planet and quite literally becomes an animal."

"And turns back to old habits."

"Yes, yes, yes! But to what purpose? There is no war. There are no Jews in the jungle. Why is the cult of NOSAL formed? What does it mean? Why must he continue to butcher? Why do the bodies now start turning up in Peru, in Chile, in Paraguay—*and now in California?* What has Stephan Patricius Valdrick started under the cover of the rain forest and why is it now reaching out to the South, to the West, to the North? Why do stories persist of a lost river tribe, a people unequaled in barbarity? Are the legends true? Are they the disciples and soldiers of Valdrick? If it takes another three years—or thirty—I swear I will know the answers."

"You *will* know?"

"I am not being coy, Mr. Teller. The mysteries remain. I hide nothing. I am no longer just satisfied with identifying this animal—which many will tell you I have yet to do. There are those who say it is not Valdrick, that I have created this story quite out of thin air. There are those who say Valdrick himself never existed, that he is a Zionist fantasy. As you must know, there is no end to professional jealousy. But I tell you, that MOSAD agent told the doctor with his last breath nothing but the truth. He was a hard man, a soldier, a spy, an assassin. He was a veteran of two wars with the Egyptians. He had tracked Valdrick for five years and for the last year he had lived on the river. He survived long enough to tell the doctor all he knew. It *was* Valdrick who had tortured him! It was the man MOSAD had been tracking for over thirty years. And the doctor—why would I doubt his word? A selfless man who has dedicated his entire life to helping the people of the river. He runs a small clinic deep in the forest. He has no interest in money, in fame, in power, in prestige. He is one of those rare individuals who only exists to serve others. Why would he lie to me? I am sure he did not even know the significance of the information."

"That's the best kind," Matt asserted.

"Excuse."

"The best source is the one who doesn't even know he's a source."

"Precisely."

"So now you're out to nail this guy. You want to finish the story good and proper."

"Yes. And I was following a new lead when your article came to my attention."

"What new lead is that?"

"Oh now, Mr. Teller, here's where it gets a bit complicated. So far we've only spoken of what we both already know."

"True," Matt agreed with the straightest of straight faces.

"But now we leave the printed record and enter a treacherous area. Yes?"

"Only treacherous if we make it treacherous."

"Yes, yes, yes, I concur. Simply said, there is my new lead which is of interest to you, I presume."

"A safe presumption."

"And there is your remarkable story of the first NOSAL killing in North America about which I am very interested."

"But you've already seen my article."

"Come, come Mr. Teller. You *are* making things treacherous. Your article starts in the *middle*. I am interested in the beginning. I am interested in how you found the body, the nature and details of your investigation. I had no idea NOSAL had spread to the United States. I must—how do you say?—pick your brains."

"How I found the body?"

"My proposal is that you tell me this information and I tell you about my new lead. We will rely on our integrity as brother journalists. It is a pact of honor."

"Only if you go first—brother."

"That is not right," Côrtes protested. "I have three years of my life in this."

"You came to me. You're the one doing the proposing. You're first. You show me yours, I'll show you mine."

"And you will tell me what I want to know?"

"Yep."

"How you came to find the body?"

"The whole truth and nothing but." Matt raised his right hand.

Côrtes extracted another Hollywood. He lit it, inhaled, leaned back in his chair, let the smoke out slowly and considered Matt's sincerity through the dissolving cloud. "I will trust you," he said solemnly. Matt winked his approval.

"As I told you," the Brazilian began, "the colonel had a young son, Patricius Maximillian Valdrick, who was raised by his mother in America. The son grows up, and in middle age, goes back to Brazil, to Amazonia, where he spends many years in virtual obscurity. Then he returns to America and the trail ends. It is not hard to conceive why he would choose to spend so much time on the river. If the son can be found—"

"What do you know about him?"

"Not much."

"But something."

"Yes, yes, yes." Côrtes hesitated, deliberating further revelations. With a sigh, he continued: "He is a clergyman—this I just learned. A missionary. At least that was his pretense for entering Brazil."

"Anything else?" Matt pressed.

"That is enough."

"You haven't left anything out?"

Côrtes flashed an expression of indignation. "We swore an oath of honor."

"As brother journalists." Matt wasn't completely able to conceal a smile.

"And it is your turn now, I believe." Côrtes's manner had turned coldly formal, but he was on the edge of his seat, nonetheless. For the first time, Matt noticed beads of perspiration collecting on his brow.

"I found the body as I was driving down the road at Coombe's Ditch," Matt stated simply.

"Continue," Côrtes demanded.

"That's about the whole of it. It was dusk, I was driving back after an assignment and there it was in the middle of the road. I wasn't looking for it. It was plain and simple dumb luck."

"No!"

"Yes."

"I do not believe you."

"It's the truth. Look, I don't want to pimp you, but that's all there is."

"There is more to it," Côrtes insisted.

"There ain't."

"How long have you been on the NOSAL story?"

"Since I saw the cot on County Double-G."

"But there was something else, maybe. Something which led you to the body. It often works this way."

"It often does. But not this time. I was in the area for unrelated reasons. I drove into it."

"An unreasonable coincidence."

"Exactly."

"You are driving and this is waiting for you on the road."

"You got it."

Côrtes's face went gray. He slowly rebuttoned his jacket, doing it so methodically it resembled some rite of ceremonial vesting.

"What have you learned since finding the body?" the Brazilian asked.

"That's not part of our deal."

"You refuse this? After all I have told you?" Côrtes made a grand motion over the papers on Matt's desk.

"That's all a matter of record," Matt pointed out.

Côrtes slapped the desk. He pried the portfolio open and shoveled the papers inside. Matt winced as he saw the motherlode of information disappearing into the leather jaws. He tried to think of a way to get his hands on the documents, but none came to mind other than blatant theft. He was not opposed to the idea, but he couldn't figure how to pull it off without mugging the Brazilian outright. Reluctantly, he resolved to be satisfied with the audio record being made by the Sony in his desk drawer. His concern changed focus: Were the batteries fresh? Was the drawer open enough? Was the built-in mike picking everything up? . . .

Côrtes stood, straightened his tie and glared down at Matt. "You are not a man of integrity, Mr. Teller."

"You set the terms of the deal and I gave you the information I agreed to give. That's how it was. If that's a disappointment for you . . . well, it's beyond my control."

The Brazilian mumbled something foreign—undoubtedly profane—and stomped out of the office. Matt reached into the drawer for the Sony. It seemed to take forever for the cassette to rewind. Finally, it clicked to a stop at the beginning of the tape. Matt hit the PLAY button, said a little prayer to the patron saint of Silicon Valley—or its Japanese equivalent—and listened. The voice of Vincenzo Côrtes was faint, but understandable.

•

Buchanon's trip home was an ordeal. He puddle-jumped his way across southern Mexico to the capital, where he connected on a United one-stopper to LAX via Phoenix. The Yankees had wired enough money—barely—to purchase more direct transport, but the scout instead bought the cheapest—and most circuitous—routing. Thus, he was able to skim almost a hundred dollars for use on other necessities. As the 747 made its final descent into Los Angeles, Buchanon had already come to doubt the wisdom of his chicanery. The extra money had begotten a much-needed change of clothes, a flight bag, a pair of cheap sunglasses and a rechargeable Norelco, with enough left over to keep the flight attendants busy delivering a steady supply of tequila miniatures, but the long, long day of stomach-churning takeoffs and bumpy landings was making him wonder if he should have traveled dirty, unshaven and—God forbid—sober.

The FASTEN SEAT BELT sign dinged on while Buchanon was in the john trying to get the Norelco to work. He ignored it and continued tinkering with the shaver, a task that was made more difficult by the unsteady rocking motion of the plane. Something clicked and the day's accumulation of whiskers poured out onto his palm. He fidgeted with it some more only to have it slip from his hand and splash into the commode. Buchanon slammed his fist against the door. He grappled with the latch and barged out into the cabin.

"Please retake your seat, sir," said a stern flight attendant.

"A tequila double-rocks," Buchanon requested.

"I'm sorry, sir. We can't serve liquor during our final descent."

"But I asked for it before!" Buchanon protested. He had, too. She kept "forgetting" to bring it on her many passes up and down the aisle.

"You'll have to retake your seat now, sir." The saccharine voice clashed with the officious demeanor.

The plane lurched through an air pocket. Buchanon headed back to his seat and white-knuckled the rest of the landing with his eyes glued to the window.

The passage through Immigration and Customs was not an easy one. He had no identification except for the exit permit negotiated by the Red Cross volunteer in Chiapas. It had required the judicious greasing of a number of Mexican palms, and evidently its tainted origin was apparent to the young Immigration agent, who was reluctant to let the big man enter the country. By this time, Buchanon was copiously perspiring into the cotton mesh of his new polo shirt. Conscious of his appearance, Buchanon explained his condition as a case of Montezuma's revenge. The suspicious agent was not satisfied. A superior was called over.

"I was robbed," Buchanon pleaded. "They took everything —my passport, my wallet, credit cards, clothes. They cleaned me out."

"I see," said the senior agent, sounding professionally non-committal. "So you have no luggage, either?"

"Just this." Buchanon handed over the tiny flight bag.

The senior agent unzipped the bag and found a folded cablegram, the empty box to a Norelco shaver and a small heart-shaped stone etched with strange markings. It was the stone that garnered his attention. He held it up to the light as his assistant unfolded the cablegram.

"Mr. Buchanon, I'm sure you know that the importation of pre-Columbian artifacts is prohibited by law—ours and theirs. This wouldn't be a pre-Columbian artifact, would it?"

"How the hell would I know? I wouldn't know a pre-Columbian artifact if I was sitting on one."

"What is it?"

"It's a rock. A crazy old Indian gave it to me. If you want it, keep it. I don't give a shit."

The junior man seemed to have found something of interest in the cablegram. He handed it to his superior.

"You're *that* Bill Buchanon?" the older agent asked, his eyes aglow with what Buchanon recognized as the eerie light of a true fan. "The Buster?"

"That's me," the scout answered.

"Jeez! Old Number 12!" The senior agent dropped the stone into the bag and handed it back to Buchanon. "I was thinking *maybe* . . . then I see this wire from the Yanks. Incredible. I saw you get thrown out of a game the year before I was transferred out here. You started tossing bats and gloves and helmets onto the field. And then—I'll never forget—you tried to pull the water fountain off the dugout wall. Four guys had to hold you back. I tell you it was something. . . ."

Buchanon knew he was in. It was just a matter of how many recollections he would have to endure and how many autographs he would have to sign for how many sons, daughters, nephews, nieces and next-door neighbors. The entire ritual blessedly took but five minutes and Buchanon was racing across the terminal to the nearest cocktail lounge.

It took four quick Bloody Mary's to renew his equilibrium. He was in the process of deciding whether to taxi back to his apartment in Santa Monica or take a bus, thereby preserving more of his meager funds, when he noticed what the redhead at the end of the bar was reading. She had just turned the page on the latest issue of *Here and There*. Buchanon pushed his empty drink aside, teetered off his stool, and lumbered over, toppling a bar stool in his path. Without a word, he pulled the paper out of her hands, tore off the back page and deposited the rest in her lap. Her jaw quivered and her mouth gaped open in shock. Words of indignation caught in her throat and never quite made it out. Mortified, she scurried out of the lounge, pulling her castered suitcase behind her.

Buchanon laid the page out on the bar and stared down at the picture of three unnamed men with their hands cuffed in front of them. The headline over the picture read GORED WITH GINSU: COP ATTACKED WITH TV STEAK KNIFE. He read the article. It didn't make any sense. It didn't tell him what he wanted to know. He staggered out into the terminal, taking the page into the brighter light.

It was *him*. Buchanon was sure. There on the page. The man in the middle. Standing there with *both* hands cuffed in front of him.

It was Santiago Akabal.
It was his arm!

•

From the instant Matt burst into Schiff's office yelling, "Nazis! We got Nazis," he had the publisher's total and undivided attention. Of the sure-shot triad—Nazis, aliens and sex—good, fresh Nazi stories were the hardest to come by. Matt gave his boss a quick run-through of his encounter with Côrtes and then began playing the tape. After a few minutes, Schiff excitedly summoned Izzy Greene and had Matt rewind the cassette so it could be played from the beginning. They had to wait for the portly editor, who was on the phone. Schiff anxiously paced back and forth across the office as he rambled nonstop, already making plans for the front page, figuring angles, coverage, sidebars, talking through layout ideas, calculating the press run and advertising rates. Matt wasn't listening. He could only think of Kelly, how impressed she'd be. He couldn't wait to see the look on her face when she saw the story—which, of course, would not be one second before the issue hit the streets.

Finally, Izzy sidled through the door and deposited his mass, as best he could, into a chair beside Matt's. It creaked under the torturous assault. "Listen to this," coaxed the grinning publisher. Schiff took his place behind the desk and activated the recorder. The three men listened closely to the faint but audible voice rasping from the Sony's tiny speaker. When Grace Collero stuck her head in the office, Schiff threw a stapler in the general direction of the door, thereby indicating, without missing one precious word, that he wasn't to be disturbed. However, when Marlene slipped in with some copy for his review, Schiff just put a finger to his lips and motioned for her to put it in his in-basket. Matt figured the double standard had much to do with the skirt Marlene was wearing. It was brief even by her standards. Matt saw Schiff's face go rapturous as he listened to the tale of a Nazi death cult and watched Marlene's tightly packed derriere exit the room. Schiff's idea of heaven, thought Matt. His boss lit up a Camel and drifted even further into the ethereal realms.

"Remember Patrick Vail?" Matt asked after the cassette clicked off.

"I know that name, don't I?" Schiff exclaimed, his eyes darting back and forth between Izzy and Matt as if he held them responsible for his memory lapse.

"The church that got torched in Cob City," Matt prompted.

"That's right," the publisher proclaimed.

"I saw it on the news," Izzy put in. "Two guys burned to death."

"One of them was Patrick Vail—or Patricius Maximillian Valdrick." Matt embellished the latter name with his version of a German accent. "The son!"

"How do you get there, Matthew?" Schiff asked. His tone was one of a proud papa asking a precocious son to expound for a parlorful of envious relatives. Izzy grimaced his skepticism despite his boss's enthusiasm.

"Look at the names," Matt urged.

"More," Izzy demanded. It was odd for him, thought Matt, to be so forthright in Schiff's presence.

"The names are similar and the ages match right on the button."

"And Côrtes said the son was a clergyman," Schiff recalled, rapping out a triumphant paradiddle on the desk top with two pencils.

"Vail went to Brazil as a missionary," Matt continued.

"It fits!" Schiff was smiling.

"Except for one thing," grumbled Izzy. "This Côrtes has been all over the world putting this story together. You say he's got pictures, interviews, visas, birth certificates, war records, the whole nine yards. Is that right?"

"Yeah," Matt answered tentatively, trying to sense where Izzy was headed.

"This Côrtes is one heck of a reporter, right?"

"I guess."

"He connects mutilated corpses in the Amazon jungle to some Nazi colonel who's been missing for forty years. I'd say he's one heck of a reporter to put this together."

"What?" Schiff cut in impatiently. "You want to hire him? You want to marry him? What's the problem, Iz?"

"I want to know why Côrtes can turn up all this obscure minutia and then he can't connect Valdrick's son to Vail. I mean, if Teller can put that together—"

"Fuck you, you fat asshole!" Matt's past confrontations with Izzy had been limited to the flanking harassment of sarcasm. This was the first time he'd ever opted for the direct full-frontal assault. Having said it, he immediately had regrets. Izzy, whatever else could be said about him, had Schiff's trust. It was not prudent to insult one so securely—if mysteriously—in Schiff's favor.

"Take it easy," Schiff cautioned.

"This Cob City thing was on television news, Barnie." Izzy's hands lifted off his belly and there was a tremor in the upper reaches of his torso which might have been his shoulders shrugging.

"I know," Schiff agreed. He was rolling the Camel between his thumb and index finger at the corner of his mouth. It was what he did when he was confused.

"Look," Matt argued, glaring at Izzy, "down in Brazil this NOSAL thing is big news, and we didn't know shit about it up here. A church burns down in some piss-ant town out near the Salton Sea and you're having kittens because Côrtes didn't hear about it in São fucking Paulo."

Schiff nodded. Matt had scored a point.

"Or maybe the whole thing's a red herring," Izzy speculated.

"How's that, Iz?" The Camel was now held six inches away

from Schiff's face. The distance was a barometer of the degree of
his confusion. Matt watched with a sinking feeling as the cigarette
drifted further from the publisher's lips.

"This guy gave us a lot of information. It don't make sense,"
the editor answered. "I smell a rat."

"Try taking a shower," Matt huffed.

"Easy, Matthew, Izzy's got a point. This guy pulls a major
core dump right at your desk—why?"

"He didn't think he was giving me anything," Matt explained. "He figured I knew all this stuff."

"But he did try to make you for info on Coombe's Ditch,"
Schiff pointed out.

"Which proves it's legit. That's his angle. That's what he
needed. If he just dumps, yeah, you've got to think fix. But this
guy needed something. You heard how pissed he was when I told
him I just fell into this thing. He thought he was gonna get a big
fat juicy file on NOSAL northern branch—"

A guttural sound rumbled out of Izzy. The porcine face was
inscrutable, but Matt knew the timing of the belch—if that's
what it was—was a matter of some premeditation. Izzy's reputation for unintentioned bodily emanations allowed him the latitude
of an occasional burp or cough of more devious purpose. This one
was meant to act as punctuation, to place a question mark over
what Matt had said. It challenged the very concept of Côrtes
expecting the "fat juicy file" Matt had described. Izzy did not
believe Matt was capable of producing an extensive dossier on any
subject. The supposition was, therefore, questionable in the big
man's eyes.

"Anyway, if it was a setup," Matt continued, turning toward
Schiff as the true and final arbiter of the story's worth, "he would
have left his file behind. That would be the real hook. We get our

mitts on the file, print some bogus pictures. That would be the way to fuck us over."

Schiff nodded, but Matt could see he still had his doubts.

"We've got a lot of checking to do on this one," Izzy observed glumly. "No way do we make deadline."

"Great! Fine!" Matt threw his hands up in complete exasperation. "We're four days away from the next edition as it is. We go another seven days—or fourteen—while you're dotting the i's and crossing the t's, and Côrtes *will* make Vail as his boy. Côrtes *is* good. It's not going to take him more than a few days to figure this out."

"If he's for real," Izzy hazarded.

"If he ain't, what's his angle? We've been up against the dirty tricks squad from the *Eye* and the rest of them. They've been up against us. No one's ever gone this far on a scam. There was stuff in four or five languages on my desk. Pictures that I know weren't doctored. The competition ain't got the smarts for it."

"I agree," Schiff grunted.

"The question is, who does," Izzy added.

"No one," Matt responded. "No one is that interested in making us look bad."

"Someone is." Izzy sounded resolute.

Matt suddenly realized Izzy knew more than he had divulged thus far. His resistance to the story was otherwise not justifiable simply in terms of his dislike for Matt. Schiff's initial enthusiasm for the story would have normally been enough to quell any objections Izzy may have harbored. Instead, the big man had quite uncharacteristically taken a position opposed to his boss's. He had slowly pecked away at Côrtes's credibility, and now, Matt feared, he was about to spring a trapdoor much closer to home.

"Go on," Schiff urged. The Camel, Matt was sorry to see, was suspended out at arm's length.

The chair groaned as Izzy shifted his weight. Matt recognized the subtle alteration in the distribution of poundage as an expression of the editor's attitude. Although the fleshy face remained locked in its perpetual dour mask, the body was struggling to erect itself. Izzy Greene was excited; Matt feared the worst.

"I really didn't want to bring this up," said Izzy.

Matt translated silently: The next words out of Izzy's mouth would be *exactly* what he wanted to bring up; they would be what he had been leading up to throughout the entire meeting.

"Just before you called me in, Barnie, I got a phone call from our boy in the police department. He wanted you, but you were already behind closed doors here with Teller. He finally got a make on those prints Teller brought in, the ones from this corpse of his. . . ." Izzy hesitated, as if he were reluctant to continue, which he certainly was not.

"Yeah! So?" Schiff, too, now sensed the ax about to fall. He was already glaring at Matt.

"Well, they belong to a guy we know. What we didn't know is this guy got busted for kiting checks a few years back. So, his prints are on file with the police."

"Who the hell is it?" Schiff growled.

"Don Koslowski. He's a reporter over at the *Eye.* Teller and him don't exactly exchange Christmas cards."

"Son-of-a-bitch!" Schiff threw the Sony against the wall. It ricocheted onto the floor and cycled into fast rewind. Côrtes's testimony poured out backwards and accelerated, a high-pitched, mocking chatter. Matt played the hapless Donald Duck to the Sony's taunting Chip and Dale as he scrambled over to pick it up and turn it off.

"He broke into my apartment," Matt tried to explain. "He

took some film, some tapes. He must have taken the original acetate and substituted one with his own prints for a stunt."

"Some son-of-a-bitch over at the *Eye* is laughing at me!" Schiff raved. The Camel tumbled out of his hand and onto the desk where it began to burn a hole in the paper blotter.

"Nobody's laughing at you, Barnie. We haven't printed anything yet."

"We printed this!" the publisher fumed, snatching the appropriate issue of *H&T* from a pile beside his desk. "Death in the fucking desert! We printed this!"

Schiff hurled the paper at Matt. It came apart in midair, the tabloid pages flapping and gliding in the draft from the ventilating system. Izzy lazily swatted one away from his face. "The whole goddamn thing was a setup from the start. This guy gets some stiff out of the morgue, carves it up and along comes Moby Dick here to take the bait. *And I fucking put it on the front page! Damn!*" Schiff pounded the desk with both hands, unintentionally extinguishing the smoldering Camel. *"Marlene!"* he bellowed.

"Barnie, Coombe's Ditch is real."

"Shut up."

"Even Kelly thinks it's real."

"Son-of-a-bitch!" Schiff cleared his desk with one ferocious swipe of his right arm. Paperweights, the phone, the loaded in-basket, the coffee decanter, the platinum pen-and-pencil set, the nautical clock, the still-smoking blotter, everything sailed onto the floor. Schiff sprang out of his chair and kicked the trash can into his credenza. He yanked down a potted fern suspended from the ceiling in a macramé sling. "You talked to that cunt? That *Times* bitch is laughing at me again?"

"She came to me."

Marlene entered the room, a look of absolute terror on her

otherwise perfect face. She wondered what she had done to make Schiff so angry.

"The baton is passed, Marlene," Schiff announced. "Mr. Teller has expressed an irrepressible desire to return to the Goat Patrol. The pet desk is his."

"I'm sorry, Mr. Schiff," she stammered.

"For what?"

"I don't know—I'm just sorry."

"Get the hell out of here!" Schiff screamed.

The eviction notice was meant for all of them, but, of course, Marlene thought it was directed solely at her. She went skittering off to her desk dabbing at the mascara that was already beginning to drain down her cheeks. Izzy made it through the door with comparative ease, the turn of events seemingly having lightened his load as well as his step.

Matt followed meekly, without further protest. He knew better than to press his luck when Schiff was in his "everybody's laughing at me" mood. He also knew that Murphy's Law was the single incontrovertible, guiding principle of the universe, and when under its omnipotent jurisdiction there was little to be done save tuck one's tail between one's legs and run for cover. As he slowly made his way across editorial, he tried to analyze the disaster that had just occurred. He tried to establish a precise point in time when the momentum had been reversed, when the stars had realigned. He tried to come to grips with what he really knew, separating it from what he merely *thought* he knew. The exercise only led him further into the overwhelming vastness of *what he did not know*, the fuzzy realm where apparent fact did not necessarily correlate to the truth—a concept, itself, which seemed to be drifting farther and farther from the center of his comprehension. His cognizance of his own knowledge—its quantity, quality, categorical delineation, the whole of the relational database that was both his memory and his awareness—had overheated and shut down. He was able to discern nothing; confusion was the only reality.

A woman was waiting for Matt at his desk. She was young and pretty, with blue eyes and blond hair. She was slender, and plainly dressed in a way that suggested the pristine neatness of corn fields and the matrix simplicity of small towns. She looked nervous, maybe even afraid. If Matt hadn't been so preoccupied with his own misery he might have felt some empathy for the young woman, attempted to ease her obvious apprehension, but as it was, all he could say—and say rather brusquely—was, "Who are you?"

"I can't tell you," she answered. Her voice was timid, but the words sounded determined, as if they had been rehearsed.

"Wonderful!" Matt fell into his chair and sized up his visitor. The linear images of corn rows and town squares gave way to verdant, rounded thoughts of rolling hills and gentle valleys. She actually blushed as he looked her over. It was a reaction he found intriguing—maybe even potentially exciting, if his current funk hadn't prohibited such notions. "I'll call you Madam X," he said altogether sarcastically, his eyes lingering at the disguised outline of her breasts beneath a dress that was—perhaps even intentionally—unflattering.

"Did you write that?" The woman pointed to a clipping of "Death in the Desert" stapled to a folder on his desk.

"Yeah."

"I need to know more about it," she said.

"Jesus," Matt laughed, "we're gonna have to start handing out numbers pretty soon."

"It's very important that I find out as much as I can." She seemed to feel that her tone of extreme urgency substituted for further explanation.

"Why?"

"I can't tell you."

"Then I can't tell you," Matt teased. He winked coyly.

"You don't understand."

"Amen."

"Please," she pleaded.

"Who are you? Why do you want to know?" Matt sing-songed the questions, sounding a bit like a school kid doing his four-thousandth recitation of the Pledge of Allegiance.

The woman seemed genuinely uncomfortable with her own reticence. She hesitated, looked around, saw Marlene unabashedly adjusting her stocking, Izzy openly reaming his left nostril and Larry Cruthers rearranging the layout of centerfolds pinned to the cork board over his desk. Her eyes could not come to rest on anything familiar, reassuring. They flitted back to Matt and grounded. He guessed that he alone appeared to her as someone "normal." In whatever context the woman viewed H&T, Matt knew he was somewhat of an exception. It was a thought that gave him some small comfort.

"It's dangerous for me to tell you," she answered at last, with renewed determination. "It's really best for everyone if you don't know."

"Everyone who?"

"It's just best for all concerned."

"It's not best for me."

Matt heard his own words as if they had been played over a loudspeaker, and they rang true. Suddenly he was very tired, and the blonde wasn't so interestingly vulnerable as she was suspiciously inquisitive. He could feel the bitterness rising; it had a pulse, a taste.

"You've got to work on this," he said smugly. "I like the

farmer's daughter bit and the mysterious stranger thing, but it's just missing—"

"People's lives are in danger, Mr. Teller."

"That's good. That usually works."

"Maybe you could help me save them."

"If you're going to stay in character, then you've got to expect me to stay in character."

"In the name of God . . ."

"Koslowski didn't tell you to say that," Matt snapped. "He'd know better."

"We can't keep them for much longer. . . ."

"Where'd Koz find you? You're good."

"I just want to know about the man on the road, Mr. Teller."

"Well, I'll just have to tell you."

Matt reached out and grabbed her arm. He saw the fear in her eyes—and a trace, a sliver, of something else unexpected that was even more enjoyable to him.

"First off, the man on the road is definitely not your average man on the street," he said loud enough for everyone in the room to hear. He was aware they were all watching, that others were filtering in, pulled by their sense of something going on.

"Just tell me where he's from," she pleaded.

"Oh, he's definitely an alien."

"From where?" she asked anxiously.

"From a distant, strange and incomprehensible place."

Matt glanced around, making sure his audience was appropriately attentive. "Neptune," he continued with a stage-right wink. "He came on a rocket-sled. His mattress burned up during the descent and the reaction to our atmosphere caused various parts of his anatomy to decompose."

As the others burst into laughter, Matt released the young woman. Tears had formed, giving a sheen to the blueness of her eyes. She looked around, lingering for a moment on each of those who were laughing at her. Then she glanced down at Matt, straightened her dress and walked quickly out of the office.

Matt had been laughing, too—up until the moment she looked at him. In her eyes, where there should have been nothing but humiliation and anger, there was, instead, a great and pained look of disappointment.

And there was something else, something which he had trouble identifying, so foreign was it to his experience: In her blue eyes there had been forgiveness.

•

Rebecca Miles was stuck in a traffic jam on the Hollywood Freeway. She was tired and hungry, and for a moment she considered opening the box of dried fruit she'd bought on her way into the city. But it was a gift, a little surprise for Nathan. She decided she could go hungry for another two hours. Others had certainly gone much hungrier for much longer.

Yawning, she looked down from the Ford pickup at an old Plymouth that was the source of music so loud it drowned out the collective idling of the eastbound traffic. Rebecca peered out through the greasy windshield over the formation of bumper-to-bumper cars crawling through the heat waves and the smog. She had only a vague idea of where she was going, but having somehow navigated her way from Braxton Wells to the offices of *Here and There,* she was reasonably certain she could find her way back. Somewhere up ahead was the Interstate 10 interchange, the entrance to the highway that would carry her home.

Rebecca had never felt comfortable in the big city—any big city. Los Angeles seemed especially inhospitable. She had been there only once before, shortly after the move from Michigan. At the time, she had commented to Nathan that she would not be disappointed if the experience was never repeated, although now it didn't seem all that bad. There was a feeling of adventure in being on her own in the middle of its gridlocked hustle and bustle. It was still an intimidating place, but even that now held a certain charm, as if all the veiled dangers she'd imagined in the past lent it some character, some quality of being worth the effort. But it's most endearing property was simply that it was not Braxton Wells.

Nathan had been surprised when she volunteered to pick up the new hot-water heater from a plumbing supply house in downtown L.A., the only one within a hundred and fifty miles to have in stock the precise size and type that they required. Reluctantly, he had let her go—but only after a long session of cautions and route reviews that would have put the average combat mission briefing to shame. Nathan, of course, was spared the knowledge of her other objective—as he was yet spared the knowledge of the *H&T* article and the fears it spawned. That the supply house was located only a few blocks from the office of *Here and There* was a fortuitous circumstance which Rebecca attributed to a benevolent Providence. It was just another indication that she was doing the right thing.

But things had not gone as planned. Her adventure was ending in failure. She knew not one iota more than when she had embarked on her odyssey. She had been unable to confirm her suspicions. She had placed her hopes on the reporter, on his willingness to share what he knew: Matt Teller would know something, something beyond what was in his article, something that would help her plan the next move.

But Matt Teller had told her nothing. He had ridiculed her. He had been rude. He had looked at her in a disturbing way. . . .

So why was she considering going back to him?

For the refugees, of course. To make one last appeal for help. Or was it something else?

•

Nadine Sills pulled Matt from his desk.

"He's asking *for you*, Matt," she said as she tugged on his sleeve.

"Of course he's asking for me," Matt growled. "The whole goddamn world is asking for me today."

"Well, see what he wants and send him on his way."

"I told Andra to get rid of him. I told her not to send anyone back here ever again."

"You have that girl totally intimidated. You can't expect a poor little receptionist to know how to handle these people. She didn't know what to do. She called back to Mr. Schiff's office. Lucky I took the call. Do you want Mr. Schiff dealing with this today?"

"Fine, fine, I'll talk to the guy."

"She says he's making quite a scene. She thinks he's drunk."

"Great!"

Nadine pushed Matt through the lobby doors and disappeared. Andra, the tiny, eighteen-year-old receptionist, was cringing behind her telephone console at the front desk, a look of sheer terror on her mousy face. A very large, very intense-looking man loomed over her. He had the rosy glow of a serious drunk. His eyes were bloodshot and glazed. His center of gravity had slipped a bit off its axis. The man seemed to have his inebriation under control, however. He wasn't of the falling-down, slobbering variety, Matt noted with a degree of appreciation.

Upon seeing Matt, Andra pointed at the reporter, nodded excitedly and blurted, "That's him"—all of which was meant to mobilize the troublesome visitor away from her desk. Responding appropriately, the man strode—a bit crookedly—toward Matt. "Mr. Buchanon has been asking for you," Andra added, sounding ever so relieved.

Matt offered his hand tentatively. A folded page from *H&T* was jammed into it. "You write that?" Buchanon asked gruffly.

It was the Ginsu article from the most recent issue. "Yeah, but you sure you've got the right story?" the reporter asked sarcastically; the question had become familiar enough, but curiously, the object of inquiry had changed.

"You take the picture?" the scout asked, ignoring him.

"Sure." Matt yawned. The routine was getting tedious.

"C'mon! I've got something for you." Buchanon started for the door. Matt didn't follow. "It's in the car. C'mon," the scout urged.

"Bring it in. I'll wait."

"It's too big. You gotta come out."

"What is it?"

"You'll see."

"I don't think so."

"What are you afraid of?"

"Nothing—in here."

"Why would I hurt you?"

"It's my day." Matt shrugged. He couldn't think of any other logical reason.

"Honey," the scout called over to Andra, "if this guy isn't back in here in five minutes, you call the cops. Okay?"

Andra looked plaintively at Matt. "It's all right," he assured her. There really wasn't any reason—other than the current, undeniably foul temperament of destiny—not to go with the man. Matt was not one to tempt fate, but neither was he one to think the forces governing such matters had but one directional inclination. Reasoning that he was already far, far out in the terra incognita of ill-fortune, it was somewhat logical to believe a change for the better was overdue. The question currently troubling his mind involved whether or not Murphy's Law was itself subject to the

Law of Averages. Matt's Unified Theory of Dumb Luck held that while things left to chance tended to go wrong, "wrongness"— like "oddness"—was relative. The difference between being on a roll and crapping out was slight indeed, a matter of polarity, a question of whether you were the shooter or the house.

Matt decided to go with the large man. With a farewell wave to Andra, he headed through the door. In deference to Buchanon's size, he was careful to maintain a safe distance. He reassured himself that should things go sour, he could easily outrun the larger, drunken man. Buchanon's car, a middle-aged, faded, dented Cadillac Seville, was in the last row of the lot. It was parked half a car-width away from a VW van and nosed up tightly to a high cyclone fence that rimmed the property.

"It's in the trunk," Buchanon announced.

"Open it," Matt suggested logically enough. He positioned himself beside the fender, in the opening between the van and the Caddy.

Buchanon had trouble locating his keys. He finally found them in a pocket he'd already searched twice. "You're not a baseball fan, are you?" he asked dully.

"Not so much anymore," Matt responded.

"I didn't think so."

After a number of tries, Buchanon was able to get the key into the slot. The trunk sprang open. Matt peered inside. It seemed to be empty except for a spare tire, a pair of cleated shoes and a Louisville Slugger. "What am I supposed to see?" the reporter asked.

Suddenly, Buchanon grabbed the bat and waved it threateningly at Matt. "We're gonna talk," he said menacingly.

The reporter broke toward the *H&T* building. Buchanon was faster than he looked. Drunk as he was, he was still able to run Matt down and force him back toward the parked cars. The big man had an enormous wingspan, lengthened on one side by the added reach of the bat. Every time Matt juked or dodged, Buchanon was able to pen him in. Matt came to a stop and put his hands up as if he were under the barrel of a highwayman's pistol.

"We're gonna talk," the scout repeated.

Matt backpedaled, retreating slowly along the last line of parked cars. Buchanon kept pace, smashing each set of taillights he passed. Matt understood the destruction as an indication of what the Louisville Slugger could do to his head, a demonstration of the comparative hardness of kiln-dried ash versus other lesser materials. Eventually he was forced into the gap between Buchanon's Caddy and the van. Matt thought to scramble over the Seville's hood. He started for it, but at his first move Buchanon unleashed with the bat, swinging it viciously into his own car. The sheet metal crunched and buckled.

"What do you want?" Matt asked, his eyes riveted to the dented car hood.

"Where's my arm?" Buchanon demanded.

The question was incomprehensible, yet Matt was convinced the preservation of his cranium relied solely on his ability to deliver the correct answer. But it wasn't to be found in the panicked, short-circuited data bank of his memory. "Which one?" he asked timidly, hoping to the narrow the possibilities.

Buchanon swung the Louisville Slugger into the fence, sending a sine wave ripple down the full length of the chain link. "Where's Akabal?"

"I don't know what you're talking about—I swear." Matt fell back against the fence and covered up.

"The one in the middle!" the big man shouted.

Buchanon pulled the folded Ginsu article from his pocket and flicked it toward Matt. It fell to the pavement at Matt's feet. The reporter crouched down, keeping a wary eye on Buchanon, and glanced quickly at the picture he had taken in the Brawley Sheriff's Office. "Where is he?" the scout demanded again, swinging the bat so that it hit the fence just inches over Matt's head. The reporter scrunched down further and huddled against the base of the link mesh.

"I don't know where they are!" he screamed.

"Where's Akabal?"

The bat struck again, even closer to Matt's head.

"Is that his name?"

"My arm!"

The bat whistled by, rippling Matt's hair as it passed.

"Leave me alone!" Matt pleaded.

Buchanon cocked the Louisville Slugger. It was poised on a plane level with Matt's ear. The reporter saw Buchanon's knuckles whiten as they tightened on the bat handle. He focused on the burnished, oval Hillerich and Bradsby label. The heavy ash drew back, preparing for the stroke.

"*Mago!*" the big man screamed.

Matt heard the screech of brakes. The gap between the Caddy and the van filled with a rush of blue. He heard a car door open and close, footsteps.

Buchanon didn't swing. The woman was standing in the way, protecting Matt. The same blue-eyed, blond-haired woman he'd ridiculed to tears a short hour earlier—she was there, silently offering herself to take the blow.

The bat dropped to the pavement and rolled under the car. Buchanon couldn't strike a woman. It was not in him. "I don't understand!" he cried, slumping against the Seville. "It don't make sense. . . . My arm's in Escuintla."

"Escuintla in Guatemala?" Rebecca asked.

"Fucking Guatemala's a zero. . . . They don't play ball."

Buchanon rolled over onto his side and passed out.

•

Matt led the way in his Mazda and Rebecca followed in the pickup, with Buchanon lying next to the hot-water heater in the cargo bed. By the time they reached Matt's apartment, the fresh air had invigorated Buchanon to a dim level of consciousness where he was, although still not coherent, at least passably ambulatory. Mumbling, stumbling, and with his beefy arms draped over his companions, the scout allowed himself to be guided to Matt's front door. With the first step inside, they encountered the stagnant mustiness which Matt was accustomed to, but which smelled like the inside of a vacuum cleaner bag to anyone else. Buchanon fled from his brief rendezvous with awareness. He sagged at the threshold and sprawled over the floor. Matt struggled to drag the big man over to the sofa. Rebecca lingered at the door, holding Buchanon's bat and tapping nervously with it against the threshold.

"I could use a hand," Matt said, groaning under Buchanon's dead weight.

Rebecca looked around sheepishly but didn't enter.

"What's wrong?" Matt asked.

"I don't think I should come in," Rebecca replied quietly and without noticeable conviction.

"Why not? It's not that bad, is it?"

"No, it's not that. . . . It's just . . ." Rebecca wavered, appearing for a moment as if she would enter. She leaned inside, tempted by her growing curiosity. She slipped the bat into an umbrella stand next to the door, but then rocked back on her heels and crossed her arms, surrendering to her apprehensions.

With one last mighty heave Matt deposited Buchanon on the sofa. The scout rolled onto his back and began to snore. "I've been at heavy metal concerts that were quieter," Matt complained. He yanked one of the cushions out from under Buchanon's legs and placed it over his face. It had the desired muffling effect.

"C'mon in." Matt turned his attention back to the woman at his door. "It's okay. The pit bull is in the shop."

"I'd better go," Rebecca wavered, still without transforming word to action.

Matt approached slowly, sensing she'd bolt like a frightened fawn if he made any sudden move. "What's your hurry?"

"I've got a two-hour drive."

"Relax. It's rush hour. Give it a chance to die down. You'll still get to wherever you're headed just as soon."

"No. I can't come in. . . ."

"You throw yourself in front of slugger over here and then you're afraid to come into my apartment."

"I'm *not afraid.*" She said it with just enough emphasis to convince Matt she *was* afraid.

"I know I acted like an asshole before," he admitted, "but I'm just having one of those days you wouldn't believe."

"Did your day become more believable after you made fun of me?"

Matt felt like a little boy caught red-handed at some dirty deed. It was a feeling he hadn't experienced since the day he was apprehended playing doctor with Charlene Johansen at age five. It was humiliating to the point of being painful. But the woman at his door did not look as if chastisement had been her intent or that she took any delight in his embarrassment. The question had been asked with grace, in a level tone, with an inflection of concern. She fidgeted and gazed toward an unfocused point somewhere over Matt's left shoulder, waiting for the answer that would not come.

"You're not the mystery you think you are," Matt said coyly.

Still hung up at the threshold, she was obviously wrestling

with the decision of whether to come or go. Matt was amazed at how easily the woman could be read. Her face was a marquee. It was simple enough to look at her and know what was "now playing."

"I know quite a bit about you, actually," he said, his tone slyly confident. It almost sounded like a threat.

With that, Rebecca allowed Matt to usher her in and seat her at a small, cluttered table in front of a curtained window. He brought her a cold drink she hadn't asked for and then took the seat opposite her, sipping one of his own.

"What do you know about me?" she asked nervously.

"You're *Mrs.* somebody, for starters."

Rebecca placed her hands under the table, hiding her wedding ring.

"You can't hide everything from me," Matt warned. "Although that dress does a pretty good job."

Rebecca felt him looking her over again. She took refuge in the cold drink, which she emptied quickly.

"Of course, you could be divorced," Matt continued. "But I don't think so."

"I'm not divorced."

"But you're not happy-ever-after married either."

Rebecca wanted to protest, but by the time she'd analyzed what the reporter had said and wondered how he had been led to such a deduction, he was speaking again.

"You're a WASP. That's easy enough to see. The only thing in doubt was the P, and the 'Jesus Is The Answer' sticker on the bumper of your pickup gave that away. I don't think Jesus would be the answer if you were a Jew—although I'm not real sure just what the question is. And Catholics don't go in for that kind of thing—statues on the dash, but not stickers on the bumper. I've ruled out Hindu, Moslem, Buddhist, Shinto, Hare Krishna, Bahai,

Rosicrucian and various other off-line theologies—so what's left? Got to be Protestant—just which denomination, I can't say yet."

"Salvation is the question."

"What?"

"You said you weren't sure what the question was. Jesus is the answer. Salvation is the question."

"A question nobody is asking these days."

"That's not entirely true."

"But on balance, it's true enough."

"Which doesn't diminish the validity of the answer," Rebecca argued quietly.

"If that's what you believe."

"What do you believe?"

It was a question Matt was not prepared to answer. Had she asked what he didn't believe, he could have talked for hours, he could have given her the quintessential monologue of cynicism. Something witty came to mind, something meant to deflate the inquiry, but he chose not to say it. He dipped his index finger into his drink and stirred the ice cubes. "My expertise is more in the area of skepticism and doubt," he replied.

"But your writing sounds so self-assured, even when you're describing fantastic things."

"A trick of the trade."

"Is that satisfying?"

"No."

"That's sad."

Matt tried to detect sarcasm in her voice but there was none to be found. There was nothing quite so unsettling to him as stark honesty—especially when it was sympathetic. He found it hard to trust someone who was not versed in the easy lie, the polite omission, the courteous misstatement. Foregoing a segue, he returned to the observations that had lured the woman into his home:

"On the front seat of your truck is a gift box from the Pit Family Date Market. Every time I head out toward Palm Springs on Interstate 10, I stop at Pit's for a date malt. It takes me about two hours to get that far, depending on traffic. You told me you have a two-hour trip in front of you. You're very tan, so that clicks too. You're from somewhere around Palm Springs, Banning, Beaumont, Cathedral City, Palm Desert, Indio—somewhere out that way along 10."

"The box is a gift," said Rebecca. The tan which had drawn Matt's comment was quickly reddening to umber. "Somebody gave it to me . . . a long, long time ago."

Matt felt relieved: The woman was lying; there were grounds for discourse. "Did you ever see what happens to a box of dates left out in a hot car for 'a long, long time'?"

"No."

"It's not a pretty sight." Matt's tone exaggerated the seriousness.

"I'm not a good liar," Rebecca confessed.

"It takes practice." Matt's remark had the ring of experience, and so it too stood as a confession, of sorts. It coaxed him to smile —lest the admission color him darker than he already felt.

"I'm sorry." Rebecca smiled back tentatively. She was happy to be released from the lie.

"You should smile more." Matt reflected that he sounded like someone trying to sound charming, which had not been his intention.

"I'd like to, but there hasn't been much cause lately."

"Something about people in danger? . . ." Matt was careful not to press too hard. He took the glasses and retreated to the kitchen where he refilled them. Given the space, he thought she might open up. He had never met a woman who could keep a secret—except, of course, for Kelly, who was the Fort Knox of secrets.

"People *are* in danger," she called from the other room. "The less you know, the better—for them, for my husband and myself, for you."

"For me?" Matt returned with the drinks. "You're concerned about my safety?"

"Yes."

"I guess I shouldn't be surprised after your interdiction strike with the mighty Casey over there."

"You'd do the same for me."

Matt saw no point in contradicting her: Sometimes the most effective lie was the one that wasn't. "Look. If your problem has anything to do with Coombe's Ditch, then chances are I'm in danger already. The simple honest-to-God truth is that I don't know jack about Coombe's Ditch. I was driving along and there was this body. I've tried to find out more, but I've come up dry at every turn. If you know something, I sure wish you'd share it with me. If I'm in some kind of danger . . ."

Matt saw instantly, in the pained expression which crossed her face, just how effective this tack had been. She had already thrown herself in front of a madman with a baseball bat. If she perceived he was in some kind of danger, then she was obligated to help him however she could. If she had information about Coombe's Ditch, she had to tell him.

"I won't tell you my name or where I live," she said resolutely. Matt could see she was working through the dilemma step by step, approaching the decision-points, making choices. "And I'll trust that what I do tell you won't be misused."

Matt nodded. He tried his best to assume a Lincolnian countenance.

"My husband and I have a sanctuary. Do you know what that is?"

"It's a hideout for wet— For illegal aliens."

"It's a safe house for refugees fleeing from death squads, from torture, from persecution, from human rights violations beyond imagination."

"Right."

"We have a number of Central Americans staying in our cellar."

"Guatemalans?"

"How do you know that?" she asked, alarm flashing in her blue eyes.

"Slugger over there said something back at the lot and you said—"

"I remember. He mentioned a town: Escuintla."

"You ask a thousand people where Escuintla is and nine hundred and ninety-nine ain't gonna come up with Guatemala. You did."

"By your reasoning, my refugees might be from any country whose geography I'm familiar with."

"Okay," Matt conceded. Her eyes had given it away; there was no need to belabor the point.

"On the night before our refugees were delivered to us, you found the man at Coombe's Ditch. His wounds are very similar to descriptions of tortures and mutilations we've heard about, terrible things that happen routinely in—in their homeland. My refugees are very nervous, very afraid. They've turned on each other more than once since we've had them. I believe that their previous sanctuary was raided and they fear ours will be, too. I believe the man you found at Coombe's Ditch was kidnapped, tortured and killed, and then left out there. You were unfortunate enough to find him."

Rebecca rose and turned to go. Matt reached out and took her hand. "Thank you," he said softly. "Thank you for telling me." She didn't seem to know how to extricate herself—or want to. Matt decided to find out which. He stood, gently took her other hands, as well, and said, "I think you should stay here until we get this sorted out. It's safer."

"My husband would worry."

Matt gave her a grateful, big-brotherish hug, making sure only the top half of their bodies came in contact. At first, she stiffened, then, seemingly convinced it was a platonic gesture, she clumsily attempted to reciprocate. He felt her hands light gently on his back. He squeezed just a hair tighter and her body shifted, softened, warmed. It happened so quickly, it caught him by surprise—the wave of feeling, of fear, the mixture so strong and volatile, so maddeningly seductive. She was terrified of him, of what could happen, and that in itself was enough to drive him over the edge. His hands moved far too fast, one drifting down her back, the other rising up her side. A wonderful, agonized sound came from her, softly, muffled, not meant to have been uttered. He tried to kiss her, but before their lips touched, she said, "Thanks for the cold drink." It was such an incongruous thing for her to have said that Matt lost the moment: A second of his time just vanished, taken away by his having to come to grips with such an unforeseen turn of events. When the clock restarted, she was out of his arms and vanishing through the door. The cushion tumbled from Buchanon's face and his snoring echoed through the apartment, the foghorn calling out through the mist as the steamer sailed away.

She was gone.

Matt went for the Sony:

"They say when you sneeze your heart stops. You lose a heartbeat. I don't think those lost heartbeats can ever be found, but if they could, wouldn't it be something? Collect all those lost seconds. Spread them out on the coffee table like old Polaroids. Look at what you missed while you were sneezing."

Matt sniffed his hand, hoping there would be a lingering trace of her smell. The recorder was still running.

"I've got her license plate number. Unfortunately it's a Michigan tag, which could complicate things, but I'll have her name in twenty-four hours. If DMV fails, I've got Smathers Plumbing Supply on Santa Monica Boulevard. Their label was on the hot-water heater in the back of her truck. They'll know who she is. I will find her and settle our unfinished business."

The reporter wandered over toward Buchanon.

"The snoring is compliments of a Mr. Buchanon. He is stone-cold drunk, polluted-passed-out on my living room couch. Earlier today he tried to kill me with a Louisville Slugger. It should have occurred to me at the time, his swing being so level, the top hand being just so, that I was being assaulted by a professional. However, it was only after I peeked at the name tag in his jacket and saw the stitched sobriquet, Buster, that I realized I was in the presence of a celebrity. Thus, if I should be found with my skull crushed by some passing citizen who shall then have the bad manners to eavesdrop on this tape, at least know that the Buster here is not strictly partial to pummeling umpires. I would suggest looking for him in the nearest gin mill. As to why he has been dragged into the bosom of my very domicile—well, let it be said he has aroused my curiosity, which having gotten the cat, should be sated enough to allow me a pass."

Matt replaced the cushion and clicked off the Sony. There was one more item on his agenda that needed to be addressed. He grabbed the phone, consulted his pocket directory and pounded out the number next to the entry, EYE. Somewhere in the quagmire of his day were the murky footprints of Don Koslowski, sloshing through and mixing with those of Côrtes, the woman and the Buster. Somehow. Koz could not be allowed to end his day without knowing that vengeance, diabolical and unavoidable, was being plotted.

A woman answered the phone. Matt asked to speak to Koz. The woman hesitated, stammered, then, after putting him on hold, transferred him to a voice that obviously did not belong to Don Koslowski.

"Are you a member of the immediate family?" the voice wanted to know.

It was an unusual question. "Yes," Matt lied. "I'm his cousin."

There was a pause. Matt sensed that a hand was over the mouthpiece at the other end. The voice was consulting with somebody. "I'm sorry to be the one to tell you this," the voice resumed haltingly, "but your cousin is dead."

It was now Matt's turn to pause, to be confused, to wonder, to fear, to feel more heartbeats being stolen. When time restarted, he heard the voice saying, "Hello. Hello. Are you there?"

"When?" Matt asked dully.

"Last night."

"Heart attack?" Matt was hopeful.

"Ah . . . no . . . Perhaps you should call Louise."

"We don't get along."

"Well . . . I suppose you'll find out sooner or later. . . . It looks like a suicide. . . . Used a shotgun . . . just like Hemingway."

3 AHUA   18 CUMKU

AT   THE   COMPLETION   OF
12 BAKTUNS
18 KATUNS
8 TUNS
15 UINALS
0 KINS

the next day . . .

Buchanon's snoring terminated abruptly at eight-thirty in the morning. He sat up in one quick rigid motion, bending forward from the waist like a B-movie Dracula rising from his coffin (although Bela Lugosi never had to catch his head with both hands to prevent its pickled contents from sloshing out through his eyeballs). Matt was curled in the chair next to the table, the Louisville Slugger cradled in his arms. His eyes were bloodshot from the long, sleepless vigil and his mind was weary from countless meandering passes through the twisted labyrinth that started at

Coombe's Ditch and wound through a burnt-out church in Cob City, a Nazi enclave in the Amazon, a cellar sanctuary somewhere out near Palm Springs and a morgue down in San Diego that contained the remains of Don Koslowski.

As much as he despised the man, Koz's death had shaken him. After all, they were, as Côrtes would say, "brother journalists." Matt's murderous feelings toward Koz when he was alive had been transformed easily into guilt now that he was dead. It wasn't as hard to deny notions of complicity as it was to understand their murky origins. That Koz had been through his things, heard his tapes, prowled his apartment, also troubled him: It seemed reason enough for his ghost to return to the scene of the crime; or if not his ghost, then the demons who had pushed him to suicide.

Strangely enough, it was Buchanon's presence that had carried him, however shakily, through the night. Matt was vaguely familiar with the Buster's tempestuous career. A number of phone calls had filled in the gaps. He couldn't help but be intrigued by the big man. He admired his "get-out-of-my-way" attitude, his willingness to convert emotion to action, no matter what the consequence. Buchanon was everything he was not: He was straight-ahead muscle, brawny and direct; he was someone who had made it in his chosen field; he was also a drunk. Matt could look up to the All-Star—or down at the lush. All in all, the scout made him feel safe—the brute who had tried to crush his skull, the snoring drunk; it made about as much sense as anything else did.

"There's nine cans of Coors hidden around the apartment," Matt announced in hoarse, morning voice. He cleared his throat and yawned. "Coors niner—answer some questions and they're yours."

Buchanon looked around, scanning for brew-sign. The apartment was so cluttered, there was hardly a place which could not have sufficed as a stash. Buchanon groaned at the prospect of searching through it all. He reached under the cushions but nothing was there. "I wasn't really going to hurt you," he said plaintively, as if to imply that Coors concealment was infinitely more sadistic than mere assault with a 36-ounce baseball bat.

"Under the couch," Matt yawned. Benevolence was the handmaiden of fatigue, he thought.

Buchanon pounced on the solitary can. "It's warm," he complained. Then he popped it open, chugged it down and belched.

"Salud," Matt replied.

"I scouted this kid in Guatemala," Buchanon said matter-of-factly, in payment for the beer. "Santiago Akabal was his name. Best arm I've ever seen. You took his picture the day after some asshole army jagoff cut it off. In the picture, he's got both arms."

Matt assessed the information. He was intrigued by the recurring connection to Guatemala, but he was at a loss to understand the link between a missing baseball prospect and Coombe's Ditch. Once more, the pieces failed to mesh. He had dragged a homicidal drunk into his house in hopes of getting closer to the truth, only to wind up with more riddles still.

"That's worth eight more or I'm gonna take that bat, stick it up your sorry ass and turn you into a scumsicle," Buchanon threatened.

The ultimatum didn't sound all that serious. Still, Matt took heed. He did not for one instant believe his current possession of the bat gave him any physical advantage. In fact, it almost seemed provocative, like the Saturday-night special in the dresser drawer whose very existence demands attention and eventual use. "I have no great yearning for slivers in my rectum," he said dryly as he pointed with the bat to eight different caches within the room. Buchanon scurried, as best he could, from one buried treasure to the next, appearing to Matt like an addled grizzly bounding after salmon stranded in a tidal pool.

"Did you actually see this guy get his arm hacked off?" Matt asked.

"No," Buchanon snapped.

Matt shrugged. He realized too late that the gesture challenged Buchanon's credibility and was therefore potentially inflammatory.

"A piss-poor Indian kid doesn't get out of Guatemala and all the way up to California in less than twenty-four hours," Buchanon said gruffly. The beer can crumpled in his hand.

"Not without help."

"Who's gonna help?"

"Ever hear of the sanctuary movement?"

Buchanon shook his head.

"Bunch of do-gooders hiding illegals in church basements," Matt explained. "They've got a whole network. It's a regular underground railroad. I bet they've got the juice to get your boy out."

Buchanon was off the sofa in a flash. He hovered over Matt, who cringed behind the bat. "How do I get in touch with them?" the scout demanded.

"They're not exactly in the phone book."

Buchanon stuffed a beer can into each of his pockets and turned for the door.

"Where are you going?" Matt asked.

"Get my car."

"It's been towed. My publisher has a service come in every night and clean out the lot. It'll cost you a hundred and fifty bucks to get your Caddy out of hock."

Matt had been through Buchanon's pockets and knew them to contain eighty-seven cents, his keys, a matchbook from the

Mexico City Holiday Inn with exactly one match left in it and a tin of Red Man. Predictably, the scout veered course and headed back to the sofa. He sat there, staring blankly at the floor and squeezing the beer can in his left hand, a slow, steady, contemplative pulse of restrained contractions. The aluminum creaked like a rusty gate hinge.

"There was a girl," said Buchanon. The comment was not conversational. It was, more or less, a dispatch to a memory in need of reinforcement.

"She's gone."

"Pretty," the scout whispered. "True-blue eyes," he added.

"She's hooked up in this sanctuary thing," Matt volunteered.

Matt reflected on his use of the word "hooked." Was that what he was trying to do? Set the bait? Draw Buchanon in? As what—A bodyguard, a sidekick, drunk in residence? How difficult it was to follow the workings of a tired mind, Matt thought— especially his own.

Buchanon set the can down. There was a deliberateness in the way he rotated it. Matt's remark had swept away the last of the cobwebs. "I want to talk to her," he announced; it was an imperative.

"So do I. Trouble is, I don't know her name. I took her license plate number but it's a Michigan tag. I've been on the phone all morning and all I can find out is that the truck is registered to a church in Flint. I call the church and I get an answering machine saying everyone's off at some prayerathon or something. No one's due back till tonight. I left a message."

"So what do we do?" Buchanon asked.

"We?"

"Yeah. We both want to talk to her."

"From what little I know about you, you don't exactly play and get along well with others."

"Don't believe everything you read."

"No argument there, but—"

"But nothin'! Can you find her or not?"

"I've got some leads."

"You think she could be hiding my arm?"

"Extremely doubtful," Matt replied. It was an honest, if incomplete, answer. He decided not to tell Buchanon that the three men in his photo had been turned over to the INS and that by now, almost certainly, they had been deported.

●

"Yeah, I remember her," said the clerk at Smather's Plumbing Supply, gruffly, his attention divided unequally between the two men standing on the other side of the "will call" counter and the baconburger lying on it. He meticulously arranged an onion slice concentric to the patty and added a squirt of ketchup from a small foil envelope. With fingers blackened by the various sediments of the plumbing trade, he pruned away the shredded lettuce and whisked the greens into a paper bag. He had not yet looked at the man who'd made the inquiry, nor at his companion. He was not in the habit of being civil to customers who called during lunch, and it had not been established that the two men standing on the other side of his counter were even that.

"Would you have her name?" Matt asked.

The clerk focused on Matt and Buchanon, his eyes narrowing over a fistful of greasy bun. Suspicion reinforced his contempt.

"We're supposed to do the installation on the hot-water heater," Matt explained. "My secretary lost the paperwork and for the life of me I can't remember the lady's name and address. All I can remember is that she said she bought the unit here."

"So you guys are plumbers," the clerk stated incredulously. He put the sandwich down and picked at a sesame seed lodged between his two front teeth. When it proved resistant to his efforts, he removed a small, plastic-handled screwdriver from his breast pocket and used it to pry the obstruction loose.

"We don't do the work ourselves anymore. My brother and I"—Matt nodded toward Buchanon—"are general contractors."

"What's the name of your firm?"

"Yellow Brothers," Matt ad-libbed hurriedly. It was much to his dismay that this was the first thing to come to mind.

"Never heard of you."

"Well, we're out in Riverside. Don't do much work in L.A."

"Yellow Brothers, huh?"

"Yallow. It's Finnish. Yeah, we've been in business for twenty-seven years. First it was Dad. Now it's just Harry and me."

"Out in Riverside, is it?"

"The PO box is in Riverside but the office is actually in Colton." Matt glanced over at Buchanon. He was proud of this last embellishment and wondered if the scout had noticed. But Buchanon gave no indication of having appreciated the subtlety and depth of Matt's improvisational flair. The scout was glaring back over the counter at the clerk, a snarling, bulldog grimace on his face.

"You boys must have bid on the new IBM building out in Redlands," the clerk ventured.

"Little too big for us," Matt replied, effecting a self-effacing modesty.

"You got the request for quote though, didn't you? I heard they sent it to anyone who had a pulse and pipe wrench."

"Oh sure, we just didn't—"

"There *ain't* no new IBM building in Redlands," the clerk snapped. A clever grin, moist with the residue of secret sauce, indicated a superiority unchallengeable in the realm of copper, cast iron and PVC, of galvanized nipples and chrome-plated shutoffs, of valves and ball cocks and things that went flush in the night.

"Okay . . . right," Matt stammered. "You're too sharp for us. I could see it the minute we walked in. I knew this plumbing thing wouldn't work. It's just that it's so embarrassing for us. Until it happens to you, you just don't think it's possible."

The clerk didn't bite—at least not at Matt's bait. He did, however, give the baconburger a number of large chomps which reduced it to less than half its original size.

"She went and joined one of those damn cults—our baby sister." Matt took out his handkerchief and blew his nose. He sighed, hesitated as if gathering strength, and dabbed at a tear that wasn't there. "God only knows what they're up to out there. They're fanatics, this bunch. We've heard they use the young women for . . . for breeder stock . . . to start their own blood-line. How sick can you get? Can you imagine?"

"No," the clerk answered smugly. He gulped down the last of his sandwich, balled up the wrapper and hooked it into an open drum about fifteen feet away. "Two points," he said to himself. Then, as if no one else were in the room, he scooped up a clip-board and began ticking off entries on an inventory log with a felt-tipped pen.

"You see, she's not using her own name," Matt continued. "Someone spotted her leaving here. If you can just give us a name, maybe we can track her down before it's too late."

The clerk shook his head, leaned back on his stool and once more tended to the deseeding of his incisors with the small screw-driver. Matt dug into his pocket and produced a ten-dollar bill. The clerk grimaced as if he had just sucked on a lemon. Matt replaced the first bill and liberated a twenty, which he folded lengthwise and set on the counter. The clerk slid off his stool and approached the money, his head cocked to the side, his squinting eyes trained disdainfully on Matt. With the back of his hand, as if to keep from dirtying further what was already filthy, he pushed it back toward the reporter. "Don't let the door hit you in the ass on the way out," he hissed.

"Maybe there's someone else we could talk to," Matt tried.

"They're all out to lunch."

"Give us a break. How 'bout it?"

The clerk made a gesture—an indication it was time to go—a fist with the thumb pointed out, quickly arcing away and aimed at the door. It was precisely the same motion numerous umpires had used to eject Buchanon from numerous baseball games. Before the thumb had completed its full trajectory, Buchanon lunged over the counter and grabbed the clerk by his shirt. Matt watched in stupefied silence as the now bug-eyed clerk went airborne, sailing past him, ricocheting off the plywood endcap of a pallet rack and falling into a bin of assorted three-quarter-inch galvanized fittings.

"The name!" Buchanon demanded.

"Screw you!" the belligerent clerk replied, righting himself as best he could in the bin. He fished a union out of the pile of fittings and hurled it at Buchanon's head. The scout caught it nonchalantly and set it on the counter. Enraged, the clerk similarly fired a tee and an elbow in rapid succession. Buchanon plucked them both out of the air without any apparent problem. He placed the elbow on the counter next to the union, but retained the tee, turning it in his right palm a number of times, curling his fingers around it thus and so, experimenting with different grips. The clerk realized, in horror, that the big man was preparing to return the heavy fitting to its place of origin, presumably as a high-speed projectile. He dove out of the bin and scrambled down the aisle, a split-second ahead of the arrival of the tee, which embedded itself in the plywood endcap.

"Cut him off!" Buchanon yelled as he took off down a parallel aisle.

Matt was too stunned to move. He stood there at the opening of the main aisle, shaking his head, wondering why he'd hitched his wagon to such an unstable character as Buchanon and listening to the frenzy of running feet upon the concrete floor. Before long, the clerk reappeared in his aisle. On seeing Matt he reversed direction, but Buchanon had already turned the corner behind him. The clerk was trapped between the two men and hemmed in on both sides by long racks of copper pipe. Matt detected panic in the man's eyes, but then saw it replaced by the flash of an idea. The clerk reached into his pocket for the small screwdriver. Smiling slyly, he took a step toward a supporting I-beam. Matt noticed a shiny length of electrical conduit running down the column. "Screw you both," said the clerk as he inserted the screwdriver blade into one of the four outlets at the end of the conduit. There was a pop, a shower of orange sparks, a few seconds of sputtering strobe, a puff of smoke, and then the warehouse went dark—a complete, utter, back-side-of-the-moon absence of light.

Matt heard the clerk laughing at them: "Now what are you two tough guys gonna do?"

It did seem to be the appropriate question, Matt thought. Despite the current predicament, he rather enjoyed being called a "tough guy."

"Don't let him past you." It was Buchanon's voice.

Matt reached out, flailing his arms in the darkness. His knuckles painfully struck one of the racks. "Ouch!" he whimpered, sounding not at all like a tough guy.

"I'll get past you all right!" the clerk called out. "I know this place like the back of my hand! I'm gonna get out, lock you in and call the cops!"

"He sounds like he's still between us!" Matt yelled to Buchanon.

The clerk's hyena laugh rang out, echoing shrilly through the lengths of pipe and sounding all the more demented in the darkness.

"Stay where you are," Buchanon ordered.

It was an unnecessary command: Matt had no intention of moving. From Buchanon's end of the aisle he heard a wrenching sound like nails being pried from wood. Before he could ask, the clerk called out in a troubled voice: "What are you doing?" In answer came the sound of countless lengths of copper pipe pinging onto the concrete floor and rolling across the aisle.

"Now what?" Matt asked.

"Shut up and listen!" Buchanon barked.

Eventually, the pipes blanketed the floor and came to rest. There was a brief interlude of silence, then Matt heard them rolling again, the sound coming from the last place he'd seen the clerk. From farther down the aisle, Matt heard a second disturbance. He pictured Buchanon moving, probably on hands and knees, toward the source of the first sound. Then the warehouse went quiet again. The sequence was repeated twice more: the clerk trying to get away; the pipes spinning underfoot, betraying his position; Buchanon clambering toward him, moving, as it were, by ear. Then, Matt heard the distinct thud of knuckles impeding upon flesh, the grunts of a struggle, the crash of bodies falling on metal. There was a soft ratchet sound—like a socket wrench clicking backward—which caused the clerk to cry out: "My God! What are you doing?" The ratchet came again, and again the clerk screamed: "No more! Stop it, Jesus, stop it!"

It wasn't long before they were able to feel their way to the outside door. Matt opened it and looked back as Buchanon and the clerk came into the shaft of sunlight. Buchanon had fastened a chain wrench around the clerk's head and had tightened it down as if the man's skull were no more than an old drainpipe ready to be twisted off. Matt was so shocked by what he saw that he closed the door lest somebody else witness the brutality.

"Take it off," Matt said, his tone more pleading than commanding.

"The name of the girl!" Buchanon demanded.

"Rebecca," the clerk blurted. "I remember she called in and said to hold the hot-water heater for her. . . . No last name, no address, nothing . . . Honest."

The chain tightened around his forehead with two clicks of the ratchet.

"That's all, I swear. Just hold for pick-up . . . No . . . Hold for 'just Rebecca.' . . . 'Like Rebecca of Sunnybrook Farm,' I said to her on the phone. She said, 'No. Not like her at all. It's just Rebecca.' So that's what I wrote on the ticket—'just Rebecca.' "

•

Matt and Buchanon did not have any better luck at the Pit Family Date Market. Nobody could remember the woman in question among the throngs of tourists and locals who had visited the store the previous day in quest of dates, figs, prunes, nuts, preserves, dried apricots, jellies, taffy confections, fudge, marmalades and the other various featured specialties. That the trip not prove a total failure, Matt joined the lengthy queue of thirsty pilgrims waiting to order date malts. But the sight of Buchanon glaring ominously at a young man in a Mets cap convinced him to forego the tasty treat and depart the premises as soon as possible.

Throughout the early afternoon, they investigated a number of churches in the sun-bleached little towns along Interstate 10—including the Kundalini Institute of Elevated Consciousness which they came across on a Banning street corner in what once had been a Philips 66 gas station—but found neither Rebecca nor anything resembling a cellar. From time to time Matt checked with his answering machine to see if the church in Flint had returned his call, but the only messages were from Nadine Sills, who was doing her best to hide Matt's absence from Schiff. As the day wore on and the sun burned hotter, Buchanon's temper shortened. At one point, Matt offered to stop for "a bite and some beers." Surprisingly, Buchanon refused, punching the dashboard and shouting, "Don't you ever say that to me again!" Matt took it to mean the big man was bent on fighting the good fight of abstinence—at least until he'd found "his arm." But by late afternoon, after the engine temperature warning light had caused Matt to shut down the Mazda's air conditioner, it began to appear as if the scout's resolve was melting away. His hands shook and his eyes lingered on each tavern and liquor store they passed. Finally, as they approached a sign which read LAST BEER FOR 23 MILES, Buchanon reached over and grabbed the steering wheel.

The Mazda skidded sidelong, and momentarily out of control, onto a gravel-covered parking lot. Buchanon bolted the car while it was still churning through the stones, and disappeared into the cloud of grit it raised. When the dust had settled—mostly on seven nasty-looking Harleys parked nearby—Matt beheld the seediest bar he'd ever seen. It was the kind of place fathers warned their sons about and mothers never even mentioned to their daughters. Not one window was clean enough to see through and at least two were punctured by bullet holes. The door knob seemed capable of transmitting unspeakable diseases. If the place had ever been painted it didn't show, except as a scaly cast which looked more like pork gone bad than pigment on wood. A faded confederate flag hung down from an awning and the placard over the entrance read ABANDON ALL HOPE.

Matt—always the champion of discretion—decided to wait

in the car, but when a number of burly, long-haired, bearded, tattooed, greasy men, all wearing one-percenter patches on their sleeveless denim shirts, exited the building and found their motorcycles thoroughly coated with limestone powder, he quickly reconsidered. It was obvious the bikers were not pleased to find their vehicles so defiled, as it was obvious, from the gentle, rolling puffs of dust still billowing from the Mazda's wheel wells, just who had perpetrated the outrage. There was the strong impulse to abandon Buchanon and make a run for it, but it was countermanded by Matt's complete faith in the accelerative superiority of American hogs over what he had increasingly begun to refer to as his "Japanese pig": The old Mazda just didn't stand a chance on the open road against the gimmicked Harleys. There was little else to do—save calling in an air strike—but retreat *into* the bar and find Buchanon, who now, at last, seemed to have a purpose.

Inside, a gaunt, stoop-shouldered bartender with muttonchop sideburns lazily guided a push broom between the tables with little noticeable effect. Two sleepy patrons watched a soap opera on a TV mounted high in the corner. A gray cat strolled leisurely down the bar, its tail passing lightly over a bowl of pretzels, its slit-green eyes trained maliciously on Matt, whose own eyes were having trouble making the transition from the desert glare outside to the cave-like dimness inside. Next to the bar was a small alcove which served as a package goods store. A chesty woman in jeans and a pink halter top was leaning against the cash register, looking bored and waiting for Buchanon to come up with the money for a six-pack. The scout rummaged through his empty pockets repeatedly, as if the process itself might alter the outcome. Matt charged over to the counter and paid for the beer, "I've got that," he announced. Buchanon grunted his appreciation. "Time to go," Matt said nervously.

The bikers came through the door just as they turned to

leave. "Hey, Milo, told you there was two of 'em," said one to another. The man addressed as Milo stepped forward, moving with the sure, steady bearing of leadership. "You ain't goin' nowhere," he announced.

"Excuse me," answered Buchanon, in entirely too docile a tone, thought Matt.

"No!" Milo snarled. "You fucked up our bikes! I don't excuse that at all, man!"

Buchanon was perplexed. He turned to Matt, a bewildered, inquisitive look on his face. It was not a reassuring expression; it was not the chiseled, rock-hard, sneering, confident and invulnerable expression Matt was hoping for.

"We sorta raised some dust when we pulled in," Matt explained quietly, trying at all costs not to make eye contact with any of the bikers.

As Buchanon turned back to where the door should have been, he seemed mystified by its absence now that it had been eclipsed by the tightly packed group of angry young men.

"What you gonna do about it, man?" Milo demanded. He positioned himself nose to nose with Buchanon. He was slightly bigger, Matt was sad to see.

"About what?" Buchanon asked dully.

"About our dirty bikes, man. What the fuck you gonna do about it?"

Matt thought it a reasonable question; Buchanon, evidently, did not. Suddenly, the scout's arm shot up, the six-pack bristling from his fist like so many mallet heads. Just as suddenly, the fist crashed down, smashing pile-driver fashion into Milo's skull. It happened so fast and the cans struck with such force that they crumpled on impact, exploding and drenching the other bikers in a mist of Budweiser. Milo silently buckled at the knees, wobbled like a cartoon character and sagged to the floor, a wilted, dirty heap of unconscious denim and leather.

Matt was in awe: He was eight years old and the playground bully had just been vanquished by the big brother he didn't have; the confrontation had been settled—swiftly, violently, decisively, without lies and words and deceptions and charms; the world was somehow different, simpler, a place less gray and with sharper lines between things. But then, quite in a fog, he heard something menacing chipping away at the borders of this wonderful new world—a click, a soft, understated and therefore all the more ominous metallic click, followed rapidly by five others. The deadly sounds, he knew without even looking, of switchblades opening in the hands of the six bikers who were yet standing and conscious.

The bikers advanced, murder in their eyes, the blades gleaming, cutting slow, threatening swaths through the air. Buchanon fended them off as best he could with a chair held lion tamer-fashion, forcing some distance between them as he and Matt retreated toward the back of the room. Matt could only see the blades, the points, the razored edges, closing in, flanking, cutting off escape routes. Suddenly, the woman in the pink halter top yanked open a thick metal door. "Over here!" she called urgently. They broke for it, Matt whispering a frantic "thank you" to the woman as he barreled through ahead of Buchanon.

Something was wrong: The bikers were laughing; the woman was smiling. The door closed behind them.

They had managed to "escape" into the beer cooler. There was no way out other than the door through which they had blundered in. Matt pushed against it, but it had been barred from the outside.

"They're going to kill us," Matt predicted. His teeth were already chattering—as much from fear as from the chill.

Buchanon did not seem worried. The sight of so much cold

beer all around compensated for what might otherwise have been an unpleasant situation. He dropped the chair and went from one stack of cartons to another, sampling brand after brand and remarking on their various merits and shortcomings. When he found a box of beef sticks, he set them on a half-barrel of draft beer and pulled the chair over. He settled in behind the keg, put his feet up and said, "Want some?"

"I don't want to interrupt your picnic," Matt replied, his voice tremulous in the frosty air, "but don't you think our pal Milo is going to be a bit cranky when he wakes up?"

"Who's Milo?" Buchanon asked between gulps of a Lowenbrau held in his right hand and a Dos Equis held in his left.

"The lad you just crowned with the Budweisers."

Buchanon considered the information as he polished off the two bottles. "The king of beers," he replied with a shrug.

"I'm not saying it wasn't appropriate. . . ."

"He's an asshole."

"But one with a knife and a headache and six ugly friends who want to play vegamatic with us."

"Don't worry about it." Buchanon dismissed Matt's concern with a wave of his meaty hand.

"Why not?" Matt asked in exasperation.

"It don't help."

"What would?"

"A gun."

"Sorry, I left my Uzi in my other suit."

"Then there's only one thing left to do."

"What's that?"

"Bust out of here and run like hell."

Matt sighed. "Your understanding of the apparent is only outweighed by your grasp of the obvious."

"That's me."

Matt hugged himself in an attempt to keep warm. "Doesn't the cold bother you?"

Buchanon ignored the question. Matt blew a column of steamy breath in his direction.

"My luck has taken an evil turn since I've met you." Matt pounded on the door. "And it was none too good before I met you."

"That's not altogether surprising," Buchanon replied, a beef stick protruding cigar-like from the corner of his mouth.

"You're not exactly Sally Sunshine, are you?"

"Not hardly."

Matt started working his way around the room, checking behind cartons, climbing up on crates to inspect the ceiling, banging on the walls with an adjustable wrench he found lying on the floor—all of which only emphasized the hopelessness of their situation. "What are we going to do?" he asked.

"You're going to figure a way out of here."

"And you?"

"I'm going to eat lunch."

"You are what you eat, after all."

"I got us out of the dark, didn't I?" Buchanon asked rhetorically. "I can't do everything."

"You got us *into* the dark," Matt snapped. "You didn't have to get macho with the plumber. I would have conned him out of the information—what little he had."

"I didn't like his attitude."

"Obviously."

"I figured a way out. Now it's your turn."

"You don't think I can do it."

Buchanon shook his head. "I don't think you could find your ass with both hands."

"I'll get us out!" Matt retorted angrily. "Just do what I say."

"Gladly, chief." Buchanon chugged another beer.

Matt inspected the wall through which the beer lines ran. A tangled mess of rubber hoses ran from tall orange cylinders to aluminum half-barrels of various brands and then through wall openings stuffed tight with insulating material.

"This must be behind the bar," he deduced.

"Brilliant, Sherlock."

Matt grabbed one of the hoses. A portion of the wall shook. With the wrench, he pried off a piece of the light-gauge sheet metal which lined the room. While the rest of the walls seemed to be solid underneath, the section through which the beer lines ran appeared to be nothing more than a plywood partition.

"Think you could kick this out?" Matt asked.

Buchanon walked over and gave it a look. "Sure. We'll just pop on through, jump on the bar and dance the cancan for our buddies out there."

Matt shook his head. "They're gonna be dancin' the cancan in here."

Buchanon's face contorted with appropriate incredulity.

"You see these?" Matt asked, pointing to the orange cylinders.

"They look like scuba tanks," Buchanon observed.

"Just about. They're compressed CO_2. These air tanks push the draft beer through these lines. Without these, the suds don't flow when the guy on the other side pulls the tap."

Buchanon was suspicious. "How do you know all this?" he demanded.

"A story I covered. This bartender in Salinas was hooking one of these up. It tipped over and the regulator snapped off. The goddamn tank took off like a torpedo. It bounced off the wall, ricocheted back and broke the guy's legs. He fell. The thing went spinning around the room, shot back over and smacked him in the head. The guy died."

"How much pressure is in those?" Buchanon asked with newfound respect.

"I don't know. The gauge here goes all the way up to five hundred PSI. But the regulator is set down at twenty-five." Matt tapped the wrench against the side of the tank. "They must use this wrench to connect all this shit."

The scout shrugged. "Let's give it a shot."

Buchanon assembled a rampart of beer cartons and kegs. Then he stripped the rest of the metal sheeting from the partition. Matt carefully positioned two of the five-foot-high air cylinders. He placed them so that when pushed over, the regulators would snap off on a cast-iron drain pipe that ran horizontally along the back wall.

When all was ready, Matt said, "Get 'em in here."

Buchanon ripped the beer lines out from the wall. He started kicking the partition. "What's wrong, you faggot assholes?" he shouted. "Ain't you got no balls?"

"That should do it," Matt ventured.

Within seconds the door burst open and the knife-wielding one-percenters rushed into the room, cursing and otherwise threatening various forms of mayhem and bodily harm. Matt leapt up, grabbing hold of a support I-beam. He swung his legs and kicked over both of the tanks. The first one bounced harmlessly off the pipe and rolled out of the way. The regulator on the second one caught on the drain pipe and tore off as intended. The tank went crazy. It spun across the floor like a runaway lawn mower blade, cutting the legs out from under the stunned bikers. Those closest to the door tried to escape the tornadic dervish, but Buchanon quickly toppled a stack of cartons to fall as a barricade. As the tank bounced off the cartons, beer from the broken bottles seeped onto the floor. Matt made his way along the I-beam as the canister shot madly back and forth across the floor beneath his feet. He jumped onto the rampart and helped Buchanon kick out the partition.

Before slipping through to freedom, they took a quick look back. Both of the tanks were now in motion, the first one evidently having been activated by a collision with the second. They skimmed across the floor, sloshing through the slow-rising pool of pilsner, lager and bock, spinning like angry tops, churning the brew into frothy whirlpools and eddies. The panicked bikers hopped and danced out of the way as best they could, splashing through the beer and over each other in a mad, tangled effort to avoid impact. One of them tried to follow Matt and Buchanon onto the safety of the stacked cartons, but the pounding of the tanks had undermined the rampart. It collapsed and he fell screaming onto his back into the middle of the chaos.

Buchanon laughed. It was the funniest sight he'd seen since an umpire split his pants bending over to dust off home plate.

•

Matt was thinking of truffles, of fat french sows rooting for buried mushrooms. Odd thoughts on an odd day, but not incongruous ones now that the "Japanese pig" had begun to oink. That something made of iron, rubber, plastic and glass could make such an organic sound struck him as truly remarkable—and worrisome. Breaking down on a seldom-traveled road in the arid barrenness of the high desert was not an encouraging prospect.

Matt and Buchanon hadn't said much to each other since escaping from the beer locker. Their subsequent passage through the towns around Palm Springs had not been productive: No one knew of a pretty young blonde named Rebecca; nobody remembered seeing a blue Ford pickup with Michigan plates; few of the churches they encountered had cellars. However, a white-haired minister at a Baptist church did speculate that there was a sanctuary in the area. "That one in Cob City," he'd said with no attempt to conceal his contempt for such enterprises. "They smuggle in criminals, communists, perverts with AIDS, and then they wonder why the whole place goes up in hell fire."

At about four o'clock, Matt turned south, heading into the desolation of the San Jacinto foothills. The journey seemed aimless at that point, but they were compelled to continue. There seemed to be scant choice in the matter, given what little each of them had to go back to. Although it remained unmentioned, both of them felt the desert had taken over. The further they traveled away from the towns and into the emptiness, the less they were in control. The isolation pinpointed them for the inexorable forces of destiny—what Matt was inclined to call "dumb luck" and Buchanon often cursed as "voodoo-black-fucking-magic."

As the Mazda chugged around a stand of orange rock, the oink turned into a squeal. Matt cut the engine and coasted, as if by the hand of fate, to an unmarked turnoff which they otherwise would have bypassed without notice. Two barely visible parallel wheel tracks wound through rocks and greasewood to a group of wooden structures behind an abutment.

"Maybe they got a phone," Buchanon speculated.

"There's no wires," Matt observed glumly.

"Maybe they got beer." Buchanon got out and headed up one of the tracks.

"Well then, by all means," Matt grumbled, trotting to catch up on the parallel trail.

It was that time of late afternoon when the shadows were just beginning to lengthen, rippling out crinkle-cut in the shimmering heat waves, stretching like something not quite awake. The sun's peak was past; the heat now came from the earth, from the rocks that seemed to glow with the day's absorption of radiation. The air was still, and each step upon the gravel rasped intrusively against the hush. It was the time of day when daydreams came easily and when twenty strides up a forgotten trail might just as easily have been twenty leagues into the sea or twenty light years into the astral void.

Entranced, the two men's eyes were drawn to the dark amorphous shapes moving along the crest of a cliff. There appeared to be a canyon just behind the buildings. The cliff face on the far side was somewhat higher and cast its shadow across the opening. The motion was there, and then it was not, flickering like old movies, ghostly, appearing and disappearing so quickly it was impossible to determine just what was folding in and out of the landscape with such chameleon ease. It occurred to each of them it might be a mirage.

"Horses," guessed Buchanon, after they'd come closer and the vision failed to evaporate. He was more fascinated than concerned.

"Deer maybe," Matt offered.

One of the shadows growled. The two men slowed their pace, but then the activity stilled.

"Probably dogs," Buchanon said tentatively.

A deep threatening roar echoed up from the rocks behind them.

"Big dogs!" Matt gasped, wheeling to see what had circled in behind them.

Three mountain lions bounded out of the rocks. They were on them quickly, approaching along intersecting paths, blunt, yellow, sinewy forms rolling forward like panzers. The two men stood rooted in place, barely even breathing as the pumas converged, circling around, now maneuvering with the slow deliberation of feline inscrutability, each movement a studied, exaggerated, leonine *asana*. Their huge heads were poised low to the ground.

Their combined growl rumbled like a subterranean engine at idle. Matt noticed each of the lions was disfigured: One had but half a length of tail; another's right rear leg was shriveled; the third one looked as if it had been scalded on one side of its face. The largest of the cats showed its teeth, huge white daggers sprouting from tar-black gums. It was just a peek, a brief glimpse, given seemingly for effect. The others stalked in closer.

"I keep thinking we've reached the low point . . ." Matt whispered.

"Shut up!" Buchanon hissed.

". . . but you have unlimited capability for attracting fresh disasters, don't you?"

"You're kind of a shit-magnet yourself, you know."

"I admit it. I'm not having a good year."

"Me neither."

"Well, together, I think we've just synergized ourselves into the blue-plate special."

"You think they're hungry?"

"Four hundred pounds of Tender Vittles on the hoof just wandered in. Yeah, I think they're hungry."

Buchanon extracted a handful of beef sticks from his pocket. Gently, he tossed one onto the ground. The motion excited the collective growl to its next level of menace. The closest cat snarled angrily and pawed the air as the others came over to investigate. Matt and Buchanon began slowly backpedaling toward the buildings. The pumas briefly disputed claim to the tiny snack, settling only when the largest animal cuffed the other two and gulped it down in one bite, wrapper and all.

"Give them another one!" Matt said, his hushed voice crackling with urgency.

Buchanon tossed a second beef stick onto the path. It fell in front of the midmost puma, who gobbled it down without breaking stride. The flanking lions roared their disapproval.

"We're not gonna make it!" Matt groaned. He ground to a stop, his legs rigid with fear.

Buchanon hurled the rest of the beef sticks as far as he could. They scattered in the air and fell like tiny javelins behind the cats. When the pumas turned to pounce on the beefy manna, Buchanon took off for the nearest building, a lean-to, barnlike structure braced against the abutment.

"Dig, Matt, dig!" Buchanon urged as he flew past.

"They're coming!" Matt cried.

"So's Christmas!" Buchanon yelled over his shoulder. "Pick 'em up and put 'em down, goddammit!"

It was precisely what Matt had in mind to do, but his legs would not cooperate. His joints fused, his bones petrified. Jolts of adrenaline short-circuited, bottling up and back-flushing into his legs like molten slag. That he might die as a dinner entrée was an enervating realization wholly canceling all exigent tendencies. In the blink of an eye he underwent a humbling reevaluation of his place within the cosmos; it caught him like the high-speed shutter of a psychic camera, the wide-angle lens taking in much more than he'd ever seen before, reducing him to a mere speck in a cluttered panorama. Never before had he considered himself as something to be digested. Every previous moment of his life suddenly seemed false, irrelevant. If there was a connection, it was one of burlesque, his life as a long, drawn-out setup for this incredibly sick and final punch line.

Buchanon was already at the barn, pulling on the sliding door, leaving it open just enough for Matt to pass through. "Move it!" he shouted. "I'll kick your pussy ass!"

It was a doubly ridiculous thing for Buchanon to say. To threaten him just then was ludicrous enough, but to impugn his masculinity as the cats were bearing down was an absurdity raised to the umpteenth power, an inane logarithm with trailing decimals in baggy pants. Matt had always considered humanity's capacity for humor to be one of the unique qualities which set man apart from—although not necessarily above—the animal kingdom. That he could now laugh at Buchanon's remark, actually laugh out loud as the cats were loping in behind him, grunting with each stride, closing for the kill, seemed to be the ultimate proof of the hypothesis. It struck him almost simultaneously that Schiff had just demoted him back to the pet desk, and thus, his impending demise might be viewed as one incurred in the line of duty. He could picture the funeral, *H&T*'s version of a state service, Schiff delivering a tearful four-letter eulogy, Marlene looking more vampish than mournful in her clingy black sheath, Izzy grazing on the carnations. . . .

Life flowed out of the laughter and back into his legs. He began to run, not yet with any sustained speed or direction, but at least he was moving. His arms flapped wildly, his feet caught on every rock and crag. The faster he ran, the louder he laughed. The sum total effect was to confuse the cats, who slowed their pursuit and gathered in the shade of an old red truck as if to discuss the questionable sanity of their quarry.

"Hustle, goddammit!" Buchanon screamed.

Their consultation over, the cats charged from the truck with renewed determination. Matt stumbled through the barn door. Buchanon slid it shut just in time, almost pinching the first puma's nose.

"What are you laughing at?" Buchanon demanded.

"Myself," Matt answered. "Who else?"

A fluttering of hidden wings echoed down from the rafters, a sound like scattered applause drifting down from a second balcony.

"What's that?" Buchanon asked.

"Evil spirits," Matt cackled. "Look no further!" he called up to rough-hewn beams which crossed over their heads. "We're still here! We haven't run out on you!"

"Shut up!" Buchanon commanded. His eyes were trained on the high sloping ceiling, where dark shapes flitted about.

"Buchanon, what is it?"

A shot rang out, the sharp, crackling blast of a rifle fired from within the barn. The air was instantly filled with the frenzied, screeching madness of bats flushed from their roost. Matt and Buchanon dropped down and covered their heads as wave after wave descended from the rafters. Matt crawled along the ground. The scout wriggled after him. The bats kept coming, endlessly, darting down from the joists, sometimes brushing a wing against them, but never actually landing or biting. The two men scrambled into a length of corrugated metal culvert lying next to a dismantled pump. At either opening, a black, diaphanous, windswept curtain of bats shut them in.

Matt heard the door grate open. Sunlight penetrated the barn in a widening shaft of fiery orangeness. A short, leathery old man with white, blotchy whiskers marched into view, centering himself in the stream of light. The three pumas lazily rubbed up against his legs, purring like milk-fed kittens as the hurricane of bats blew past and out the open door. The man had long gray hair, which hung down in a ponytail behind his back. A lizard-skin headband circled his head. He was wearing a light deer-hide vest and faded jeans. A revolver was strapped to his leg. He aimed an octagonal-barreled Winchester toward the opening of the pipe.

"Get outta there," the old man ordered.

Matt and Buchanon crawled out of the pipe as the last of the bats flew out the barn.

"You boys are trepassin'. I could shoot ya legal."

"We meant no harm," blurted Matt. "My car broke down and—"

"This ain't no fill-'em-up."

"True, but the car did shut down right at—"

"What kinda car?"

"It's a Mazda."

"A who?"

"A Mazda. It's one of the original Wankel jobs. It seemed like a good idea at the—"

"That's a Jap car, ain't it?"

"Well . . . yeah . . . but I think the technology actually is—"

"Best little fighters I ever come against. Only reason we won is we had better and more of everything—guns, people, boats, planes, bombs, bullets. Only reason we ever win is we got better and more. 'Cept now they got better and more, huh?"

"The car's a loaner, you see. My Chevy is in the shop—not that there's anything wrong. Just a little preventative Mr. Good-wrench."

"That's bullshit," Buchanon cut in. "Don't lie to the man. We're on his land. He's got the rifle. Tell him straight. The car is yours. There ain't no Chevy in no shop."

"Who might you be?" the old man asked.

"My name is Bill Buchanon."

"You *that* one?"

Buchanon glanced back up toward the ceiling, which was now blessedly still. He pretended as if he'd not heard the question.

"You the one?" the old man persisted.

"Which one?" Buchanon mumbled.

"The one who popped the umpire."

"That's what they say," Buchanon answered softly.

"Hmmph!" the old man grunted. He shouldered the rifle. "Don't know much 'bout what's goin' on back in the hive. Don't care. Do have my battery radio, though. Good old Emerson job. Listen to a lot of baseball. Only game without a goddamn clock, you know. Follow baseball quite a bit. Followed you special." The old man turned and walked toward the door. The cats accompanied him, two walking beside him, the third trailing with his head cocked back to watch the two trespassers. "You ever swim with catfish?" the old man asked.

Matt and Buchanon looked at each other inquisitively.

"C'mon!" the old man commanded from the doorway.

Matt and Buchanon followed at a distance, making their way down a path that wound through a cluster of odd-shaped outbuildings. Each of the structures had been fashioned from available materials and seemed designed to fulfill some unique, arcane purpose. Each bend in the path brought them further into what appeared to be an oasis. Barrel cactus gave way to scraggly pines and finally to century plants and palms of all kinds. The path ended abruptly at an impenetrable-looking stand of trees and thick scrub. But there was a narrow, concealed trail, and the old man led them through and down some wooden steps into a small terraced canyon hidden below the cliff.

The canyon floor was naturally terraced into three levels. On the topmost level had been erected an apparatus that appeared to be some sort of windmill. A telephone pole jutted up out of the rock. Two vertically mounted cylindrical devices rotated atop a crossbeam, evidently churned by the wind that whistled through a notch in the rock wall but did not penetrate down to the lowest level where they now stood. A large contraption of intermeshing gears and reciprocating pistons operated effortlessly at the base of the pole, where a network of pipes sprouted out toward various parts of the canyon. Some of the pipes were as large as the culvert they had hidden in back in the barn. Others were as tiny as the copper tubing back at Smather's Plumbing Supply. On the middle level was a fantastic, sprawling house with a veranda and a parapet that might have been an observatory. The lowest level had a small lagoon fed by a sluice. Frequently, fish broke the surface, causing a roil of bubbles. At the furthest reach of the pipes was a garden. Matt spotted corn, beans, onions, tomatoes and zucchini. Behind the garden was parked a backhoe, a tractor and a gigantic road-grader. For the life of him, Matt could not determine how the machinery had made it into the canyon.

One of the pumas thrust its nose into Matt's crotch, sniffing curiously. He stiffened as she rubbed her huge head along the inside of his leg.

"That's Belinda," said the old man. "She likes you."

"Likewise, I'm sure," Matt replied nervously.

"Pulled her out of a trap up on Pinyon Flat. Ain't s'posed ta be any big cats left 'round here. Poachers know there's still a few left. Make a coat, I suspect, for some blue-skin dame back in the hive. Thought she'd lose the leg, but she's a gamer."

"What about that one?" Buchanon asked, pointing to the lion with the scarred face.

"Chemicals. Goddamn factories dumpin' over in the Soboba. Haulin' the shit in. Guess old Jessica must've stuck her nose in somethin' nasty. Don't know how Carlotta lost her tail."

Matt extended his hand timidly down toward Belinda's head, meaning to place it between her and his privates. The cat licked it. "So they're your pets, sort of," he speculated.

"You don't see no leash, do you?" the old man snapped. "They live here with me. I take care of them. They look after me. We share everything. They can come and go as they please."

"But they're tame. I mean . . . they wouldn't have actually eaten us, right?"

"Hell, no. They'd a gnawed on ya a while, but I doubt they'd eaten ya up. Don't like the taste much, far as I can tell."

Belinda rubbed her ear up against Matt's crotch. He winced and tried to gently push her head away. "You wouldn't have a phone, would you?" he asked.

"No phone. No electricity. No gas. No city plumbin'." The old man pointed toward the windmill. "Just the eggbeater. That does it all. Pumps the spring water up into the cistern on that ledge. Runs down the pipes through the roof of the house. Keeps it nice and cool. Then it drains into the catfish tank." He nodded at the lagoon. "Catfish eat our garbage and we eat the catfish when the game is scarce. But mostly, we just go in for a dip, the girls and me. That's the thing."

"How long you been out here?" Buchanon asked.

"Since after the war. Seemed like the place to be after they wouldn't let me do what I wanted to do back in the hive."

"What was that?"

"Play second base."

"You played, huh?" Buchanon nodded as if it should have been obvious.

"Cubs organization. Thirty-five to forty-one."

"Ever make it up?"

"Far as I got was an invitation to spring training. Catalina Island in them days. Then the Japs bombed Pearl."

"Tough break."

"They weren't gonna let me up anyway. Too damn short. That's all they saw: What I didn't have. Hell, that's what they called me. Edgar Short. My given name is Edgar Schantz, but since '38 they been callin' me Edgar Short."

"Lots of little guys playing now," Buchanon said sympathetically.

Edgar Short laughed. "Lots of monsters, too."

The two former ballplayers chuckled. Matt continued to fend off Belinda's advances.

"You wouldn't have a beer, would you, Edgar?" Buchanon asked.

"No. Ain't temperance or any such. Just don't need it no more. But feel free to have at the tank. Cool you down just the same. Better, I'd wager."

"No thanks."

"Go on," Edgar urged. "You'll forget about the beer. You'll come out of there a new man. Nothin' in the world like swimmin' with catfish."

Buchanon slipped off his watch and placed it along with his wallet on a flat-topped boulder. Reluctantly he removed his shoes, socks and shirt. "Oh, what the hell," he said as he dropped his slacks and his shorts. He charged into the tank, bare-assed and screaming "Geronimo!" A tremendous belly flop sent waves lapping at the far banks, beaching a spiny-finned catfish as the water quickly receded. It gulped for air, flapping and wriggling, trying to make it back to the water. Belinda abandoned Matt and pounced on it.

Matt watched as Buchanon backfloated contentedly in the center of the pond. His eyes drifted lazily past the tank, over the garden to the collection of construction vehicles. "Where'd all that come from?" he asked.

Edgar winked slyly. "You'd be surprised what you find lyin' on the road."

Matt could have told him that he of all people would not be surprised at all by what could be found lying on the road. But he didn't. He just nodded understandingly.

"Damn fools leave it," Edgar explained. "I take it and put it to good use. All they'd do is build more damn roads so more damn nobodies can get nowhere faster."

Matt pointed to the windmill, Edgar's "eggbeater," and the pump at its base. "You're pretty handy, it looks."

"Got to be. Ain't no Sears and Roebuck up the bool-ee-vard."

"Think you could get my car going again?"

"I better. You might stay if I don't."

Buchanon called from the far end of the tank. "C'mon in, Matt. Edgar's right."

"Why not?" Matt sighed.

Edgar nodded his approval. Matt stripped and walked in, preferring a less dramatic entrance than his partner. The water was surprisingly cool, and tingly with a natural effervescence. The bottom dropped off sharply and soon he was in over his head. Dog-paddling, he headed toward Buchanon. Matt felt something on his back, something like a kiss. He lurched away. Then he felt it again, this time on his ass. He submerged with his eyes open and peered out into the clear spring water. It was the catfish. They were all around, their whiskered faces looking at him inquisitively. One swam up and nuzzled his chest. Matt was not sure what it was doing. Tasting him, perhaps. Checking to see if this floating thing was edible, if it was garbage? Others were doing it too. It wasn't a totally unpleasant sensation, but it was strange. When he resurfaced, Buchanon was beside him, a big grin on his face. "It's something, ain't it?" the big man said. "Yeah, but what?" Matt answered. Buchanon laughed and paddled off back toward the deeper water. Matt noticed Edgar making his way back up the wooden steps. The cats were lying regally in the shade of a live oak, the lazy whisking of the two good tails being the only indication they weren't sleeping.

Time passed easily. The sun was entirely behind the cliff and the whole canyon was now blanketed in shade. Matt and Buchanon swam and floated and splashed and dunked each other like a couple of country kids at the local water hole. For a while there was no corpse at Coombe's Ditch and no arm in a zippered bag. There was no sanctuary that needed to be found other than the one they *had* found.

One of the lions yawned. Matt and Buchanon looked toward the bank. Edgar was back. The old man brought the Winchester to his shoulder and took aim. The gun was pointed toward them.

Edgar fired. Matt imagined he could see the bullet coming at him, a shiny thing, spiraling like a football but flattening as it approached. He wondered who would fall dead first, himself or the scout.

A plume of water kicked up between them. Then something jerked violently just below the surface, working up a froth of bubbles and cutting a twisting wake. A puddle of dark blood pooled like an oil slick where the bullet had struck. As the water calmed, the two men saw the headless body of a six-foot rattler float by. In seconds, the catfish had it, pulling it below the surface.

"Holy shit!" Matt gasped.

The two men moved quickly out of the tank.

"That's the only problem," Edgar said philosophically. "Goddamn snakes like to swim with the catfish too."

"Hell of a shot, Edgar," said Buchanon.

"Wasn't nothin'."

"That's an old one," the scout said, referring to the rifle.

"It's an original 1892. Takes a forty-four caliber, forty-grain cartridge. You seen what it done to that snake's head. Do the same to a man's. Belonged to my daddy. He was a marshal up in Sweetwater County, Wyoming. Truest I've ever shot. Got a big varmint scope on it. Let's you see at night. Fog-proof too. Once you got that double-X lined up, you can't hardly miss."

Buchanon, still naked and dripping wet, walked over to look

at the Winchester. Edgar placed it in his hands. The scout aimed at a tree limb up on the highest ledge of the canyon floor.

"How far would you say?" he asked.

"Good hundred and fifty yards. You got a little right windage up there."

Buchanon pulled the trigger. The limb snapped off cleanly.

"You've handled a Winchester before, ain't ya?" said Edgar, an approving, yellow-toothed smile on his face.

"Did some hunting when I was down on the farms. Instructional League, Double-A."

"You got a touch for it." Edgar turned to Matt, unholstering his revolver. "Try this, sonny."

"No. That's all right."

"Go on," Edgar insisted, offering the gun, butt first.

"No, no. Forgot to pay my NRA dues. Wouldn't want any trouble with the Grand Kleegal or anything."

"Don't be an asshole," Buchanon growled.

"It ain't gonna bite you," Edgar coaxed.

Matt sighed and took the gun, feeling a bit ridiculous standing there in the nude with a six-shooter in his hand.

"That's an authentic Colt .45," Edgar explained. "That's the piece that won the West, boy."

"It's heavier than I thought."

"A gun's a heavy thing, boy. A gun that ain't heavy is lyin' to ya."

Matt took careful two-handed aim at a post about fifty feet away. He pulled the trigger. A cup-sized divot plowed up ten feet short of the target.

"You're a real wormkiller, ain't ya?" Edgar chuckled.

"Reminds me of when I was trying to be a pitcher," Buchanon chimed in. "Had a hell of a fifty-nine-footer."

Both of them laughed as Matt rubbed his right shoulder.

The recoil had caught him by surprise. The Colt was down near his hip, about where it would be if he were wearing a holster. A crazy notion came to mind. He drew the .45 up quickly and fanned off three quick shots from the waist. Fist-sized chips of wood exploded from the post.

"It's the tank!" Edgar said gleefully.

Matt stared unbelievingly at the post. He felt Edgar gently taking the Colt out of his hand.

"You don't go swimmin' with catfish, you don't make that shot," the old man continued. "You're a new man, boy. I take a dip every day. I'm a new man every day. Every single blessed day. The hive's gettin' older. I'm gettin' younger."

Edgar reclaimed the Winchester and walked off in the direction of the house. "C'mon, girls," he called to the pumas. They rose slowly, stretching, yawning, then followed him up to the second ledge. As he stepped onto the veranda, he turned back toward the two naked men below. "Fixed your car. Pretty slick little machine, that Mayz-da. You gotta take better care of it is all."

Then, Edgar Short disappeared into his house and closed the door.

•

Matt drove up Indian Avenue through Palm Springs on his way back to the interstate, past the famous hotels, the spas, the chic boutiques, past the boulevards named after the stars of stage and screen, past the air-conditioned malls, the Rolls-Royce dealership and the exclusive country clubs. None of it seemed real. It was all just something painted on the other side of the car's windows. Swimming with catfish had been real, the snake shot out of the water, the cats ready or not to eat them. The eggbeater had been real. Edgar Short had been real.

The sun was about down as they reentered the desert on the

northern outskirts of the city. The sky had gone deep violet, with thin furrows of mauve cirrus. Matt pulled into a filling station just before the interstate turnoff.

"I'm going to try the answering machine again," he told Buchanon.

"Imagine what Edgar could do with those," the scout replied obliquely, his eyes peering across Matt and out the side window.

Off beyond the west side of the road, stretching out for over seventy square miles, was the San Gorgonio wind corridor. In the desolate pass between the San Jacinto mountains to the south and the San Bernardino range to the north, where the hot air rising in the Coachella Valley drew the cool marine air from the west through a natural funnel, a windfarm had been erected. Turbines of various designs churned atop metal towers ranging in height from forty to over eighty feet. As the prevailing winds gusted over the mammoth rotors of wood, fiberglass and aluminum, wheeling the blades like so many gigantic airplane propellers, electric power was produced and sent downline to nearby Palm Springs, where it was gobbled up as fast as nature and machine could produce it.

The two men got out of the car. They sat on the hood and watched the last minutes of the sunset beyond the battery of windmills.

"Old Edgar don't need all those," Matt observed. "Just give him one and he'll work miracles."

"It's kind of spooky, ain't it? The wind blows, those things spin, and a toaster oven lights up in Rancho Mirage."

"It does look like someone went a little crazy with the erector set out in the sandbox."

"Look at that big one out there," said Buchanon.

A colossal Scottish-made Howden stood quite by itself, towering over rows of Danish Micons and American Enertechs. Its hub stood eighty-two feet off the desert floor atop a massive tubular steel column. Its three wood/epoxy blades had a diameter of eighty-five feet, giving it an overall height of over one hundred and twenty feet. It was capable of operation at any windspeed between thirteen and sixty-one miles per hour and could deliver up to three hundred and thirty kilowatts of power, but now the rotors were still. As the smaller machines hummed in unison, their yaws adjusting to every slight deviation in the direction of the wind, the blades of the big, solitary Howden stood motionless against the darkening sky.

"That's Edgar," Matt pronounced.

"He's tall now," Buchanon added. "Head and shoulders above the rest."

"Edgar Tall, the steady, the rock, while all around, the real shorties, the shrimps and the half-pints, go with the wind."

"To Edgar Tall," Buchanon said wistfully, tipping a cap he wasn't wearing.

"I'll drink to that," Matt replied eagerly. "I think they sell beer here."

"No thanks," Buchanon answered, his eyes focused on "Edgar Tall." "I've been swimming with the catfish," he explained.

"So you have," Matt agreed, smiling as he slid off the fender. "I guess I'll just call the answering machine then."

Matt started for the pay phone.

"I might have some problems . . . over the next day or so," Buchanon reflected.

Matt paused.

"It could . . . get a little strange," the scout continued haltingly.

"You mean stranger than being shut in the dark in a pipe warehouse and being chased with switchblades and locked in a beer cooler and almost eaten by lions and attacked by bats?"

"I've never been this far gone before."

"Strange is my business, Buchanon. I'm good at strange. Don't worry about a thing."

Matt went to the pay phone and dialed his answering machine. He triggered the message playback and listened to the Reverend Ernest Middenhaugh of Flint, Michigan, tell him the exact address of Nathan and Rebecca Miles's Church of the Word in nearby Braxton Wells.

•

Finally knowing where they were headed, it was inevitable Matt and Buchanon would get lost on the way. The church at the top of the hill, so easily found by those on their way elsewhere, hid from them. After a number of wrong turns, a doubling-back over the brushy slopes of the moonlit chaparral and a meandering detour through the Morongo Indian reservation, they finally came upon it. The blue Ford pickup was parked in the drive. Next to it was a tan Ciera with a Hertz license plate frame.

"Who the hell is that?" Buchanon asked.

Matt didn't respond, but he, too, was troubled by the added presence. They got out of the Mazda and headed to the church.

The side door was open and the two men made their way inside. They moved cautiously, slipping through the shadows like Indians on the hunt. Buchanon parted the silver curtain just far enough to allow them to peek into the other half of the room.

"I haven't been in a church for a while," Matt whispered, "but this isn't the way I remember it."

"Me neither," Buchanon agreed, taking in the bed and the odd collection of furniture.

"I hear voices," Matt said, motioning for Buchanon to be quiet.

The two men strained to hear the muffled sounds that seemed to be coming from below. Buchanon pointed to the door leading off the vestibule. They approached it stealthily. Matt tried the knob.

"It's locked," he whispered.

"No problem," the scout replied.

Before Matt could stop him, Buchanon threw his bulk against the door, caving it in. His momentum carried him forward, through the splintered door frame and unexpectedly onto the stairway. He went tumbling down on the seat of his pants, with one leg bent and trapped beneath him. Matt tried to grab his collar, but he pitched forward and missed the first step. He wound up on Buchanon's back, thumping clamorously down the stairs with his head banging against the scout's. Buchanon reached for the doweled railing only to have a two-foot chunk break off in his hand. As they came to rest on the basement floor, Yolanda screamed and little Sebastian instantly went to bawling. Coh grabbed a chair, snapped off one of the legs and took a position of defense between the clumsy intruders and the residents of the sanctuary. Buchanon rose to his feet and faced off with the one-eyed giant.

"Who are you?" Nathan Miles demanded, sounding indignant but afraid.

Matt's eyes drifted to the speaker. Next to him was the woman they'd been searching for.

"I've been looking for you, Rebecca," he said shakily, pulling himself up off the floor.

"Matt! . . . Ah . . ." Rebecca was surprised to hear herself call him by his Christian name. Yesterday she'd addressed him as "Mr. Teller." But now, in the shock of his sudden arrival, she'd gone so quickly—and embarrassingly—to the familiar.

"Do you know this man?" Nathan asked, thoroughly confounded.

"We've met," she answered nervously, trying desperately not

to blush. She felt the warmth rising, glowing on her neck and spreading to her cheeks, betraying her to Nathan before she could explain. She turned to her husband and saw his confusion transform into hurt. She felt as if someone were spying down at her now, peeking through the knothole in the storeroom floor but seeing only what was wrong.

"Well that's a twist I didn't expect." The voice—impossibly familiar—came from somewhere behind the young couple with the squalling infant and the old man who kept looking up to the ceiling as if he expected it to come crashing down at any moment; from behind the thumbless, birdlike man who sulked off to the far side of the room, where a death-faced woman wearing sunglasses sat motionless in the corner; from behind the young, good-looking man who then took the older one by the arm and led him away. The couple followed with their baby. "I suppose I shouldn't be surprised though," Kelly added.

Matt couldn't believe it. He rubbed his eyes but Kelly failed to vanish from her place at the head of the long table. A portable recorder and a note pad lay on the table next to her open briefcase. Empty coffee cups, dirty plates and butt-filled ashtrays were all around. It looked as if she'd been there for some time.

It was beyond bad luck and Murphy's Law. It was a curse. Had to be.

"How?" was all he could say, a quaking, pathetic utterance of confusion, humiliation and defeat. He stepped toward the table, his hands outstretched, his eyes wide open and begging for an explanation. Coh motioned him back with the chair leg. Buchanon countered with a wave of the handrail.

"It's all right," Kelly interceded. "Mr. Teller and I are old friends."

Coh let Matt pass. He lowered the chair leg to a less provocative position. Buchanon held his ground but shouldered the hunk of thick oak dowel.

"How'd you get here?" Matt pleaded. "Did she come to you, too?" He pointed at Rebecca.

Nathan's jaw clenched. His lips disappeared. His arms crossed over his chest and his eyes fell to the linoleum. He knew Rebecca had kept things from him. He closed himself off, afraid to learn how much.

Rebecca turned to her husband, wanting to explain, expecting him to understand, but he would not look up at her.

"I got here by being a reporter," Kelly replied acidly. "You should try it some time."

"I almost got killed today trying to find this place—more than once. Don't tell me about being a reporter."

"Well, you *did* find it," Kelly admitted. "It was a grand entrance, too. I just knocked."

"I worked hard on this one, Kelly. If I'm going to get stuck with the crumbs, at least let me know what I missed."

"No harm. I'm breaking this tomorrow. You'll have to wait until next week."

"Looks like you've done it again, doesn't it?"

"But not to you. It's got nothing to do with me and you. I even warned you on this one. You had it first, all alone. You had every chance."

"Just tell me," Matt said quietly as he dropped into a chair across the table from Kelly.

"It starts with Hernando Cuellar Real. Do you know who he is?"

"No."

"Then you didn't work so hard, Matt."

"Who the fuck is he?" Matt demanded. His disappointment was starting to resolve into anger. Kelly was acting too smug. It wasn't her style. Normally she was gracious even in victory—which was exasperating in itself. Something else had turned her to bitterness. Matt recalled her opening comment. Some things just never changed: She thought he was involved with Rebecca. He decided not to clear up the misunderstanding. If he was going to lose, at least he'd have some small satisfaction.

"He was a junior envoy type for the Guatemalan consulate office in L.A.," Kelly continued. "He was murdered in his apartment six days ago. Before entering the refined field of diplomacy, Mr. Cuellar ran death squads in Guatemala. Supposedly, he was the victim of an armed burglary, but it looked more like an assassination to me. I checked the police report and the autopsy. Turned out he had traces of magnetic iron oxide on him, under his nails mostly."

"So."

"It's a chemical used in incendiary explosives. Along with aluminum powder it makes for a nasty little concoction known as thermite. This stuff burns at over thirty-six-hundred degrees. Guess where else it turned up?"

"Cob City Lutheran Church," Matt answered without hesitation.

"Good. Maybe you *have* worked a bit on this. The church in Cob City was definitely an arson. It's also pretty obvious that the good Pastor Vail was using the building as a sanctuary. It's just as obvious that whoever he was sheltering was gone before the fire started. Connecting Guatemalan envoy Cuellar to Cob City via the thermite suggests they were Guatemalans."

"And here they be," Matt concluded.

"You're way ahead of it, Matt. It builds one brick at a time. Do you want the whole thing, or not?"

"Yeah," he grunted.

"I got to wondering about the John Doe they found in the

church with Vail. He wasn't a member of the congregation because no one in the area was reported missing. He could be a
refugee. He could be someone who just wandered in on the wrong
night. Or he could be someone from the sanctuary network. I
asked around and one name kept coming up, Father Gregory
Townes. He's the top man in this area for bringing in
Guatemalans. And no one knows where he's at. He just disappeared. Now this guy is involved with things clandestine and it's
not totally unheard of for him to drop out of sight for short
periods of time. So nobody's too concerned. But it did strike me as
a bit coincidental that the last time he was seen was a few days
before the fire in Cob City."

"Is Townes the John Doe?"

"I managed to get a copy of Townes's dental records and
slipped them to a contact with the Imperial County Coroner's
Office."

"Minus the good father's name."

"Of course."

"And they matched?"

"As far as anyone can say."

"You're withholding evidence in a murder investigation,"
Matt observed caustically. "They put you in jail for that," he
added.

"These farmers are nowhere on this case. They'll take all the
help they can get. The deal is they get the name the morning we
break the story. They make a quick announcement and look
smart. We look fast."

Matt shook his head. He understood out-and-out chicanery;
he didn't understand the winked-eye ways and means of "deals,"
the hocus-pocus of mutual consent, and that mysterious alchemy
which rendered crooked things straight.

"How'd you get from Townes to here?" he asked.

"I got lucky. I went to Townes's place in San Diego. He lives in an apartment near La Jolla. The mailbox was full. Envelopes were sticking out. Some were lying on the floor. One of them was his American Express bill. He rented a U-Haul truck in Indio the day before the fire. Returned it the same day. I headed out to Indio and took a look at the rental contract. He put a hundred and sixty-four miles on the truck. Figuring he went from Indio to the church in Cob City, then directly to his destination and back to Indio, would have given me a rough idea of how far he could have gone in any direction."

"That's still a lot of real estate. We had it narrowed down that much."

"The truck hadn't been out since Townes rented it. Looks like he stopped for oil in Braxton Wells. A cash receipt was in the glove box. And this is the only church in Braxton Wells."

If Matt's luck had turned to shit, then Kelly's had turned pure gold. She'd been smart all right, he reflected, but it was luck that got her there first, a conclusion that made the situation no less intolerable. "They told you about NOSAL?" he asked, hoping they hadn't.

"They told me everything."

"Why?"

"Because I've promised to get them safely up to Canada."

"All these folks in one rented Ciera?"

"I'll make better arrangements, but for now we'll just have to squeeze everybody in, at least as far as L.A."

"So Cuellar was part of the NOSAL cult, is that it?"

"What cult?" Kelly asked, an inflection of sad amusement coloring the last word.

"Looks like *you* didn't work so hard on this, Kelly."

"There's no cult," she stated firmly. "I don't know what you're talking about."

"I'm talking about NOSAL. It's the juicy part of this business, believe me."

Kelly rolled her eyes. "No sale, Matt."

"I don't care if you buy it or not." Matt grinned. It was his turn to be smug. "I'm not gonna tell you about it."

"It's *no sale*. The writing on your corpse's forehead. *No sale*. Evidently the *e* was torn away when they scalped him."

"What?" The word limped out, a crippled thing.

"There was a raid on Vail's sanctuary," Kelly explained. "Probably men working for Cuellar. They took one of the refugees. You saw what they did to him."

"Why would they write 'no sale' on his forehead? It doesn't make sense," Matt protested.

Kelly hesitated. "I don't know if I want to go through this part again."

"Jesus!"

Kelly shook her head and closed the note pad. "I've told you enough." She placed the pad and the recorder in her briefcase.

"I don't believe it," Matt fumed. *"No sale, my ass."*

"It is true," Coh broke in. "When people disappear in my country sometimes they are taken to the PX. It is a name the pintos call the place. A big metal place and they have put many cells and cages in it. Some say it is where there used to be a secret American army base. Nobody knows, but there are many things there still. Like a store. Shelfs and counters like a store—only empty now. There is an old cash register. It does not work so good. If you press one button for three, you know, maybe a five or a two will pop up in the little window. When the guards are bored they will bring this thing into your cage and they will gamble with it. They will bet on what number will come up. And they make you bet, too. But since you have no money, you must bet your fingers or your toes, an ear, a nose, something. . . ."

Coh paused to light a cigarette, catching a flame from the stove burner as was his habit. The length of dowel slipped from Buchanon's hand and rolled under the stairs. The scout sat on the first step, his head cupped in his hands, thinking of the long zippered bag on the cantina table in Escuintla.

"Cristina and I have been to the PX," Coh continued. "She lose her tongue. I lose my eye. If you refuse to play their game, they make the bet for you. If it come up 'No Sale,' you lose and they kill you. It is a big joke for them. That is why they write this on our *compañero.*"

Matt started to push his chair back from the table. He wanted a closer look at Coh's face. He wanted to peer into the one good eye and see what was there. But the man's statement had stunned the room to a silence so overwhelming it felt like a weight upon him. The scratching of the chair on the linoleum was an irritation drawing its focus, its force, to smother the sound, suffocate the noise, keep him stationary. He waited for someone else to break the hush.

"I'm looking at it as a signature murder," Kelly said at last, her soft voice slipping through a crack in the stillness and prying it open. "It's a message which can only be understood by those who are meant to understand, those who've escaped like Coh and Cristina. It's a very private, select act of terrorism. It says, 'We'll find you; you can't get away from us.' It tells the people in sanctuary—this one, in all of them—that there is no safe ground, that there's no hope, that they won—and sanctuary lost."

"So I was supposed to find the body," Matt concluded, following her logic.

"*Someone* was supposed to. Anyone," Kelly clarified. "They wanted publicity. That's my guess, anyway."

"So why didn't they just leave the body at Coombe's Ditch?" Matt asked. "Everyone would have had the story then."

Kelly shrugged. "Who knows? Plans change. Priorities shift. Maybe they got the wrong guy and that's why they went back two days later to waste the whole church."

"Except nobody was home but Vail and Townes," Matt put in, finishing the thought.

"Maybe it was a renegade operation to begin with," Kelly speculated. "Maybe Cuellar was on his own and when the bosses found out they whacked him. There was a coup d'etat back home about a week and a half ago, nothing too serious, just a bunch of generals playing musical chairs. Maybe Cuellar hitched his wagon to the wrong despot. There's a lot of possibilities." Kelly shut her briefcase and rose from her chair.

Matt stood, as well. "Who was he? The guy at Coombe's Ditch."

"We only know him as Felix," Coh said quickly, almost before Matt had completed his question.

Matt waited, but there was nothing more. He felt like saying, "No. That can't be all. It can't end this way." But it was Kelly who once more broke the lull. "We should really be on our way," she said, directing the comment to Nathan.

Nathan was about to answer her when Buchanon suddenly cut in. "Not yet!" he snapped, lurching up from the step. He approached the group by the table. "Where's Akabal?" he asked. "Was he with your group?"

"Who?" Kelly asked.

"He's no here!" Soto shouted from the corner.

"We don't know this person," Coh clarified, flashing a silencing glance toward Soto.

Buchanon took the picture out of his pocket. He showed it to Coh who shook his head. The scout tried Sergio and Yolanda. "Did you ever see these men? The one in the middle?" They looked away without answering. "What about you?" he asked, turning to Abraham. The old man grabbed the clipping, his bony hands clutching it like claws and holding it just inches from his eyes. *"Nuestros compañeros indios,"* he said brightly. *"Estan vivos."*

Coh snatched the picture away. "His thinking not so good," Coh explained. "He is very confused."

"He didn't sound so confused to me," Buchanon countered belligerently. "What did he say?"

"He say they remind him of his grandsons," Soto declared.

"No," Rebecca objected. "He said something about Indians." She turned to Pablo. "Didn't he?" she asked.

"Ah . . . I wasn't listening," Pablo stammered as Coh approached with the chair leg in hand.

"Yes," Rebecca persisted. "He said something about Indians, just like Soto the other night when I let them see Mr. Teller's article."

"Es una bruja," Soto protested, remembering Rebecca had not been present in the room when he made the remark.

"Shut up!" Coh commanded.

"Let me see that," Rebecca asked, motioning for Coh to give her the clipping.

Reluctantly, Coh handed the picture to her.

"Do you know this boy?" Buchanon asked, pointing to Akabal.

"No . . . But it's strange. . . ."

"What?" Matt asked.

"Well . . . I thought maybe there'd be four men in the picture, but there's only three."

"Why is that strange?" Matt pressed.

"We were expecting twelve people," Rebecca explained. "That's what Father Townes had told us to expect. Then he arrived with just eight. But I'm still one short, if these three are the missing men."

"No you're not," said Kelly. Her eyes locked with Matt's. They'd seen it simultaneously.

Rebecca shook her head in confusion. "These eight and the three in the picture are only eleven."

"Plus the dead man at Coombe's Ditch makes twelve," Matt explained.

"What do you say, Coh?" Kelly inquired. "Are you holding out on me?"

"Maybe these three come from another church," Coh replied. "I don't know."

"These pilgrims were out in the sand. Way out," Matt argued. "There ain't no churches out there. There ain't no sanctuaries out there. There's just fuckin' nothin' out there. Vail's church is the only one close enough."

"I don't know," Coh insisted.

"Bullshit!" Matt snapped.

"Are you protecting them, Coh?" Rebecca asked. "Did these three go after the men who took Felix?"

"I'll get them out, too," Kelly promised. "Just tell us the truth."

"You have what I say," the big man replied.

"Jesus! I just want to make this guy rich!" Buchanon ranted. He snatched the picture away from Rebecca.

Pablo laughed. "So you are going to make Akabal rich. What a noble thing. You think you are gods."

"*¡Basta!*" Coh shouted angrily. "*¡Shó!*"

"How much longer?" Pablo asked him angrily. "When does it end?"

"What do you want to say, Pablo?" Kelly coaxed.

"He has nothing to say!" Coh snarled, clamping his left hand on Pablo's shoulder.

Buchanon pushed Coh away. "I want to hear this," he shouted.

Coh swung the chair leg, inadvertently shattering one of the ceiling fixtures. Bits of glass and fluorescent particles rained down. Buchanon evaded the blow, grabbing onto Coh's wrist and preventing him from striking again. The two men locked up, spun around and slammed into the table.

"Stop!" Nathan shouted. "This is *my* house!"

Pablo laughed again. "This is craziness. It's all craziness."

"*¡Quieto, traidor!*" Coh shouted as he grappled with Buchanon.

"Yes, these three were with us," Pablo went on, ignoring Coh's warning. "Is that what you *periodistas* want to hear?"

A high-pitched scream shrieked from Cristina's tongueless mouth, jolting Coh and Buchanon from their struggle. They broke off and, like the others, wheeled toward the sound. Cristina lunged across the table and drove a knife into Pablo's shoulder.

The young man didn't make a sound. He stared in disbelief at the blood running down his shirt, then looked around the room as if for an explanation. All he saw was his own shock reflected in the faces of the others. He teetered and slumped into a chair.

Cristina was still screaming. She scrambled off the table and raised the knife for a second thrust. Matt saw it in slow motion, only a few feet away, yet he was unable to intervene.

Nathan was yelling: "This is *my* house! This is *my* house!"

The blade started down, headed for Pablo's heart. Matt heard another scream, layered over Cristina's, lower-pitched, not oscillating as much. Kelly's scream. Kelly, who never did.

A large form was rushing up on the woman, frantic motion detected at the extreme periphery of Matt's vision. Buchanon.

Throwing himself at her, but from too far away. Not too little, but definitely too late.

Matt felt himself moving. Not away as would be logical, but toward the threat, toward the blade. He reached out.

Suddenly Cristina was careening away from him, tumbling back toward her corner. The knife was sliding across the linoleum, spinning, flashing light with every turn, finally disappearing under the refrigerator. The sunglasses skidded off in another direction. The scream ended.

Matt felt wetness on his hand. His own blood. A thin line of it running from a superficial slit across his palm. "Fucking catfish," he mumbled under his breath.

Buchanon heard the comment, nodded understandingly and handed Matt a napkin to wrap around his hand.

Rebecca rushed over to Pablo and examined the stab wound. "It's deep," she announced.

"We'd better call the paramedics," Kelly advised, trying to catch her breath.

"No," Pablo groaned.

"The authorities would get involved," Rebecca explained. "He'd be deported sooner or later."

"We can't just let him bleed to death," Kelly replied.

"I've had some medical training. Nathan and I were volunteers at a clinic a few summers back. I think I can stop the bleeding."

Kelly remained skeptical. "What about infection, nerve damage? . . ."

"What about the PX?" Pablo asked, wincing in pain. "You heard about the surgery they perform there."

"Take the others," Rebecca told Kelly. "We'll take care of Pablo."

"I can't stay here," Pablo protested. "If *they* can find us"—
he pointed to Kelly and Matt—"then Mago can find us too."

At the mention of Mago's name, Buchanon, who'd been
keeping a wary eye on Cristina and Coh, came over to Pablo.
"What about Mago?" he demanded.

"He is out of his head," Coh cut in.

"Who's Mago?" Kelly asked.

"He lose too much blood," Coh went on.

Pablo's eyes were glazed and dilated. "You're going to make
the Indian rich. . . ." He smiled at Buchanon and passed out.

"Damn!" Buchanon cursed. "Wake him up."

Rebecca and Matt lifted Pablo onto the table.

"Okay . . . I guess I'll have to leave him," Kelly said. She
picked up her briefcase, took a few steps, set it down again. "But
I'm not taking her." She pointed to Cristina.

"She goes," Coh insisted.

"She just tried to kill someone. She's crazy."

"She is like you," Coh explained. "A *periodista.* Only on the
radio. A *locutora.* She say things that you are not supposed to talk
about. So they cut out her tongue. Maybe you go crazy a little bit
too if this happen to you."

Kelly watched as Cristina crawled across the floor to retrieve
her sunglasses. She shook her head. "No . . . I can't."

"I'll watch her," Nathan volunteered. "Rebecca and I will
follow in the truck. We'll take responsibility."

"I have to take care of Pablo," Rebecca pointed out. "But
you can go with Miss Wode."

"I can't just leave you here," Nathan protested. "Pablo is
right. If these people can find this place, then others can."

"I know a place where nobody could find us," Matt offered.

"And Mrs. Miles goes with you?" Kelly's voice was tight and
chilly.

Matt nodded toward Nathan. "And he goes with you."

"Is that what we should do, Rebecca?" Nathan asked his wife. His voice sounded detached.

"It seems to be the only way," she answered without looking up from Pablo's wound.

Momentarily the room quieted, the space filling with all that was felt but left unsaid between husband and wife, pushing the others into silence.

Kelly gravitated over toward Matt. "Looks like you got more than the crumbs," she hissed.

Matt didn't know if Kelly was referring to Rebecca or to Pablo, but her comment was true either way: The woman was a prize because Kelly had seen her that way, as a rival, as someone he'd picked over her; the young man had value because it now appeared he knew more about what had happened.

"You promised these folks Canada," Matt replied. It came out sounding petty and smug. Not what he'd intended, but he was in no mood for backtracking. "Best be going," he added.

"I'll deliver my promise," Kelly snapped as she gathered up her things.

"I never doubted it."

There was a flurry of silent activity as everyone prepared to leave.

Nathan counted heads. "Where's Soto?" he asked.

•

Soto stood at the intersection of two narrow, unmarked roads and tried to determine which way was North. He looked to the stars and the moon but they were just uncaring lights in the sky. They told him nothing, much as he expected. As usual, he was on his own.

He yanked out a hunk of sage, threw it into the air and watched to see which way the wind would take it. The wind would be coming from the West. It always came from the West. He was sure of it—almost.

He watched the sage drift away and then he started down what he now determined to be the North road.

Alone, in a strange place, at night. He didn't really know where he was headed. There was no evidence of humanity anywhere. No houses, no cars, no electric lights, no music coming from radios, no motors humming, no smells from factories or cook stoves. Just sand and rocks and grass and scrub. Sometimes a gust of wind. Occasionally the rustle of an animal moving in the brush.

He was afraid. But not nearly as afraid as he had been in that crazy *santuario*. Mago would have found him there for sure. The lady reporter had found him, hadn't she? And the other two gringos. They'd found him. Hell, anyone could find him if those two could. He'd take his chances in the desert with the snakes and the scorpions. It was much safer.

Soto heard something. A car engine. Could it be? On this forsaken road?

Headlights punched up over a hill. A car *was* coming. His luck was changing. All he had to do was step over to the edge of the road and stick out his—

¡Madre de Dios!

How could he hitchhike without a thumb? He tried, but it looked ridiculous. Like he was sticking his fist out over the road.

The car zoomed by.

"¡Mago!" he screamed. *"¡Hasta infierno será muy bueno para usted!"*

Time went by slowly. Each step brought him further into the nothingness. He started to sense that perhaps he'd taken the wrong road.

Then he heard the sound again. Another car.

This time he was ready. He wrapped his fingers around a

short, thick branch and let just enough of it protrude to look like a thumb. In the darkness no one would know the difference.

The car approached. It was traveling much slower than the previous one. When the headlights picked him up, it slowed even more. Finally it stopped, only about thirty feet away.

Soto smiled. Not only was his luck changing, it was changing in style. The car was a Mercedes.

•

Given their fixation with the broken and dispossessed things of others, Matt was surprised to see just how much Dale and his brothers had left behind at the shack. The full inventory of gutted appliances outside and most of the swap-shop furnishings inside were still there—not that any of it was worth dragging a thousand miles cross-country to Oklahoma. Just as astonishing was that the electricity and the propane were still connected. All and all, the place looked like it would make a tolerable hideout.

Buchanon was having a rough time. He'd begun to shake uncontrollably. Wracking fits of dry heaves came and went. His clothes were drenched in sweat. Matt wrapped him in a blanket and sat him in a dilapidated naugahyde recliner positioned opposite a television table. The TV was gone. Somewhere in Oklahoma, Matt thought, it was tuned to a rerun of "Gilligan's Island."

Pablo was semiconscious. With Rebecca's help, Matt laid him on an orange-and-white-striped sofa. Rebecca swabbed the wound with a disinfectant she'd brought along with some other supplies. She worked silently, not paying Matt any mind. Her preoccupation was complete, but Matt sensed it had more to do with her sudden estrangement from her husband than anything else. She handed Matt two large needles and a length of nylon thread. "Boil these," she said quite brusquely.

Matt had trouble getting the pump to work, but finally it

kicked in and he was able to draw a pot of water from the kitchen tap. He fired up the propane stove and sterilized the needles and thread. Returning to the front room, he glanced at Pablo's wound and decided he really didn't want to watch Rebecca's stitchery. "I'll move the car and the truck behind the house," he volunteered. She handed over the keys to the pickup. "No one can see them from the road that way," he explained.

Getting the truck had been the cause of a last-minute argument back at the church. Kelly had the more obvious need for it, with seven adults and a baby to transport, but Matt had insisted that his remote hideout, the exact location of which he stubbornly kept to himself, required the extra vehicle. It would be needed, he argued, for acquiring provisions and in the not unlikely event the Mazda gave up the ghost. Kelly saw through it. "Bullshit" she'd said. "You'll ditch them as soon as you get what you want. You'll leave them the truck and take off." It had been an ugly scene, Kelly only giving in because time was against her. As it was, she had little chance of making deadline for the morning edition. Nathan and Rebecca had remained strangely quiet, even though it was their vehicle that was being discussed.

As Matt moved the two vehicles, he could hear Pablo groaning as Rebecca sutured his shoulder. He grabbed the Adidas bag and waited for the moans to subside. When he reentered the house, he found the young man weak but alert, jolted to wakefulness by the agony he'd endured. Rebecca asked for her keys back: It was a mechanical reflex, a psychic grappling line thrown out by auto-sensor, something other than blood to connect her to present time and circumstances. Buchanon, still wrapped in the blanket and looking like a cigar-store Indian, was standing over Pablo.

"You said Akabal was with you," the scout said hoarsely.

"Yes . . . he was there," Pablo murmured, grimacing as Rebecca dressed the wound.

"Please don't bother him," Rebecca urged. "He needs rest."

Buchanon was undeterred. "I just want to know about my arm, lady. I got my own problems."

"*Your* arm!" Pablo laughed through the pain.

Buchanon doubled over. His faced convulsed, looking as if it might explode. Just as suddenly, the spasm passed. "I want to know about *Santiago Akabal*," he said through gritted teeth.

"Then I can't help you," Pablo replied.

"You said he was there," Buchanon persisted.

"*Carlos* Akabal was with us. Santiago's twin."

"Twin," Buchanon repeated in disbelief.

"Please leave him be," Rebecca pleaded.

"That explains it," Matt cut in. "The picture ain't your arm. It's this . . . Carlos." Matt unzipped the bag and turned on the Sony, hoping it still worked after its recent collision with Schiff's office wall. He set the bag down near the sofa. Pablo didn't seem to notice.

Pablo pulled himself upright. Rebecca tried to make him lie back down, but he refused. "It's all right, Mrs. Miles. I want to talk about it. I've been quiet too long. It takes my mind off the pain."

Reluctantly, Rebecca gave in. "I'll unpack your things," she offered.

"That shouldn't take long," he quipped.

Unpacking Pablo's bag was another link for Rebecca, another way to connect her to the new now that she was disconnecting from the old. Events seemed to have her in tow—ever since the trip to L.A. How easily, how quickly had she been pulled from Nathan, she thought. Just one little lie, an omission, a fact left out —the detour to *Here and There*. Then the encounter with Matt, going back a second time, being in his apartment. Just one little lie, and now it had roots and limbs and great curled branches reaching out in every direction. It had Nathan thinking the worst. That was the way of lies, she reminded herself, to get people thinking falsely.

"The picture is brother Carlos," Matt explained to Buchanon, "and your arm must still be back in—"

"I know where it is," Buchanon interrupted. The life was gone from his voice. He walked slowly back to the recliner, shuffling woodenly like an old man. He sat down and drew the blanket tightly up to his chin.

Matt turned his attention back to Pablo. "Who are the two others with Carlos in the picture?" he asked.

"They're Quiché Indians, like Carlos. They were helping me on an archaeological dig near Nim Xol. Santiago, too. We found a stela, a carved stone. It was unique. A Maya prophecy preserved in stone. I've told Mrs. Miles about it. Nothing else like it has ever been found before."

Rebecca remembered the conversation, how intrigued she'd been, how frightened. Prophecy was the devil's work. She considered leaving the room, but it seemed such a cowardly thing to do. If she ran, she gave it credence; if she stayed, it was just superstitious writing on an old stone. She knew what Nathan would have said, but Nathan wasn't there. She stayed.

"What's the prophecy?" Matt asked.

Rebecca listened closely as she began unpacking the laundry sack which contained the sum total of Pablo's earthly possessions.

"It's not easy to say," Pablo replied. "To translate the glyphs is one thing, but to understand the translation is something else again. That's why I had the Quiché with me. It's a theory I've been working on. I thought if I could involve the indigenous peoples, tap their cultural memory, they'd have insights no one else could hope to have."

Rebecca came upon the folded, blueprint-sized paper she'd

first seen on Pablo's bunk back at the sanctuary. She spread it out on the couch so Pablo could refer to it. If it was a night for running *away*, she reflected, then it was also a night for running *to.*

Pablo winced as he twisted around to glance at the paper. "I was only allowed to teach one of them how to read the glyphs."

"Allowed by who?" Matt asked.

"By the Quiché themselves. By their council. This is very special knowledge. Only the oldest and wisest of their holy men was allowed to learn. A full Mother-Father. A daykeeper."

"This guy is the big-time holy Moses and he don't know how to read this thing?" Matt asked incredulously.

"The stone is over seven hundred years old. The glyphs on it represent a language that flourished centuries before that. When the Spanish came in the sixteenth century, they destroyed all the Maya books, everything. The missionaries executed most of the literate population. All knowledge of the written language was obliterated. We've only discovered how to translate the glyphs very recently. I taught the Daykeeper last year. That was the first phase of my project."

"And then he helped you dig up this stone."

"I had funding for fifteen assistants. Besides the Daykeeper and his novices, there were others from his village, among them the twins."

"After we found the stone, the rebels hit a convoy in Huehuetenango and a bridge on Route 1. There were other incidents, too. Very brazen and very successful. Their triumphs were coming one after another. The authorities had heard about our find. They got it in their heads that the insurgents had been encouraged by the prophecy. Inspired even. Our stela was blamed for the whole offensive. The pintos hit our camp at night. Some of us got away—some didn't."

"Did they kill the ones who didn't?" Rebecca asked timidly.

"Very slowly."

"Why? What's the prophecy?" Matt pressed.

"The stone seems to foretell the coming of a savior-king. One who comes in the time of destruction and killing, when usurpers rule. But he must be brought forth by the day Eleven Lamat, the Maya New Year, which happens to fall on Easter Sunday."

"That's a week from tomorrow."

" 'Eleven Lamat, the Yearbringer, Before the Last Katun'—it will be over three hundred and fifty years before that day occurs again. To the Quiché, to the twenty or so other Maya lineages, it means that many more years of misery."

"Unless this king shows up," Matt clarified.

"Do you prefer happy endings, Mr. Teller?"

"They're nice, when you can get them."

"I'm afraid you're out of luck this time."

"Don't you believe your rock?"

"I believe Galil rifles will prevail over hoes and axes. I believe napalm will consume straw and flesh. I believe the three percent of the people who own over sixty-five percent of the land will do what they must to to keep it. I believe I will never see my home again. That is what I believe."

"But you don't believe this king is going to happen?"

"Even if I was to believe in such things, it is far too complicated and there is too little time. The stone says that he must be brought forth through the deeds of two others who come before him, two others who work in the ways of Xbalanque and Hunahpu."

"Who?"

"Two gods. Twins who played *chaah,* the ancient ball game in the heavens over Nim Xol. I'm afraid this is the part which

doomed the Akabal twins. They were both excellent baseball players, Carlos and Santiago. They were both at Nim Xol when the
stone was found. The coincidences were too great to ignore.
There was much excitement, many rumors. The talk came to the
attention of a powerful man, a man who is responsible for much
of the killing, the torture, the disappearances. Your friend, I think,
knows this man." Pablo nodded toward Buchanon. "He is called
Mago."

"Someday I'll kill him," Buchanon grunted. "Carve that in
stone."

"They say Mago truly admires the old things," Pablo went
on, "that his house is full of artifacts from Kaminaljuyú, Tikal,
Uaxactún. They say he tells his troops to be as fierce and brutal as
Kaibil, the Maya chief who fought against the Spanish. If Mago
fears anything, it is that the four million Indians of Guatemala
will rediscover their warrior heritage, that they will become the
new *Kaibiles*. Mago believes this prophecy. He is afraid of it. He
will not let it come to pass. He will not allow anyone to so much
as think it will come to pass. It was not enough that he took the
stone. He decided the Akabals must disappear. But they escaped
the night of the raid. Carlos and two of the novices came with
me. The Daykeeper fled to a refugee camp in Chiapas. Santiago
Akabal could not be persuaded to leave." Pablo paused and turned
once more toward Buchanon. "He had dreams of becoming an
American ballplayer. Santiago did not want to miss his tryout."

"Jesus Christ," Buchanon groaned.

"So with the twins out of the way," Matt ventured, "there's
no chance for the king to come along. Is that it?"

"That's what Mago would think, but I'm not so sure. It was
easy for the Quiché to see Carlos and Santiago as Xbalanque and
Hunahpu, but something else might be meant by the prophecy. I
had a lot of time to think about it. Perhaps the Quiché have

realized this as well by now. You see, the stone doesn't really say that Xbalanque and Hunahpu must reappear. It only says that two others must bring about the coming of the king *in the ways* of Xbalanque and Hunahpu."

"What ways are those?"

"Well, there is a story in the *Popol Vuh* which tells how Xbalanque and Hunahpu underwent a number of trials. They seem to always get through it more by cleverness than anything else. First there was Dark House, a place of total darkness."

"I've been there," Matt joked, remembering the episode at Smather's Supply.

"Then there was Razor House, the place of daggers."

"Hey, sounds like Milo and the gang," Matt laughed, winking at Buchanon. The scout's face remained grim.

"Next was Cold House."

"What?"

"Then Jaguar House and Bat House, all of which they survived. When they finally do perish, they are reborn as catfish."

Buchanon sat up in the recliner. He stared at Matt, the light of revelation burning in his bloodshot eyes.

Matt turned away, shaking his head. "No. Don't even think it," he said.

"How would these two guys know who the king was?" Buchanon asked. "Does he have a name?"

"I don't know. The piece of the stone which held the name glyph was chipped away. A piece about this big." Pablo indicated the size with outstretched fingers.

Buchanon's hand happened to be in his pocket. His own fingers were wrapped around the carved stone given to him by the old man in Chiapas. It was the same size. He struggled to remember what the old man had said.

He was to give the stone to somebody . . . to somebody walking? . . .

He couldn't remember. His head was all cobwebs and fog.

"What's this?" Rebecca asked. At the bottom of Pablo's sack she'd found a small glazed tile on which some glyphs had been inscribed.

"It's a present. It was made by the Daykeeper after I taught him how to read the glyphs. He was grateful, I suppose. It's the name he gave me. It means He Who Walks in Old Words."

Buchanon lurched out of the chair. The blanket dropped to his feet. He stumbled over to Pablo and placed the last missing piece of the Stone of Nim Xol on the tile.

"I think this is yours," he said.

9

4 IMIX   19 CUMKU

AT THE COMPLETION OF
12 BAKTUNS
18 KATUNS
8 TUNS
15 UINALS
1 KIN

the next day . . .

Just before dawn, Matt made his move. With his equipment bag in hand, he slipped out of the back bedroom, through the kitchen and out the rear door. The sun wasn't quite up yet, but there was enough light to see his way to the Mazda. He got in, making as little noise as possible, and turned the key.

Nothing happened.

He tried it again.

Not a whimper. Not a sputter. Not so much as a click.

"You need this," Buchanon called.

Matt hadn't seen him on his way out. The scout was huddled against the back wall of the house, sitting cross-legged on a pink washing machine next to a shuttered window. He held something up. At first Matt thought it might be a snake. He got out of the car and came closer.

"Your battery cable," Buchanon explained.

"Why isn't it on my battery?" Matt tried for an inflection of mild indignation. His voice cracked and it came out sounding like he felt, like the kid caught with his hand in the cookie jar.

Buchanon glared at him from under a cowl of blanket. "Then your car would start," he growled.

"That's the idea, isn't it?"

Matt moved a few steps closer. He smiled and shrugged.

Buchanon coughed. He cleared his throat and spit out a gob of phlegm which splattered near Matt's feet. "Out for the morning Danish?" he asked sarcastically.

"Something like that. I figured everyone would be hungry."

"Do you always take your camera and your recorder when you go out for breakfast?"

"I take my camera and my recorder when I go out anywhere."

"I don't recall you had them at the pipe store or at that bar yesterday."

"That was not a typical day, Buchanon."

"Or when we went swimming with catfish."

"Give me a break."

"I am. I'm keeping you here."

"Listen Buchanon, this is a hell of a story. I've got to file. I'm back off the pet desk with this."

"And the hell with us!" Buchanon snapped, his voice rising. "Maybe you'll find *us* carved up out on the road next time. What a story that would be."

"Nobody's going to find you out here."

"What's the rush? Your lady friend is going to beat you to the punch anyway."

"Don't you understand? She doesn't have it all. She's missing the best part. She doesn't know about the stone, the whole king business. I got it all. I got the story. I got the king."

Pablo and Rebecca were listening in the doorway, drawn by the commotion. Pablo charged toward Matt.

"Oh yes, here I am!" Pablo trumpeted. "Sky Sword Bringer, Calabash, Preparer in the Last Katun, Begetter of the New Age! Do I not look the part? Am I not the regal one?"

Pablo pulled himself onto one of the dryers that were lined up in a loose, crooked row with other appliances. With one arm bandaged to his side, it was a difficult maneuver to negotiate. Rebecca started after him, afraid he would fall, but he waved her off. He stood on top of the dryer, assuming a lordly pose.

"The royal vanguard, the two who come before!" he said, addressing Matt and Buchanon. "The Forerunners! The Bringers! Celestial Midwives! Princes of the New Citadel! . . ." He laughed and turned his attention to Rebecca. "My Guardian! Nurse and Seamstress to the Majestic Shoulder! You're not mentioned on the stone, you know. Undoubtedly an act of sexism. But we will make amends."

Pablo ran along the tops of the washers and dryers, jumping from one to another. He scampered up onto the top of a refrigerator and gazed down from the higher vantage point. Matt and Rebecca traded looks of concern. Buchanon stared dully out into the seeping grayness of the predawn sky.

"What an impressive company!" Pablo continued. "The last hope of a civilization!" He sighed. "The eyes of the Quiché are upon us! The Ixil, the Mam, the Pokomam, the Cakchiquel, the Chuh, Chorti, Kekchi, Pokonchi, Tzutuhil, all of them!"

He placed his hand over his heart. His eyes glimmered with the unmistakable sheen of madness. It was not his madness—he'd never felt saner, more able to discern the true nature of things— but the madness of what was happening.

"Behold the savior! So it has been ordained! A mere student yesterday, with life so simple, just an interest in old things. Not in politics, not in dangerous affairs, unpleasant realities. No. Just the old. The safe. The sheltered."

He paused, took a deep, steadying breath.

"What a dream. What a child's dream."

Pablo hopped down from the refrigerator. He slowly retraced his steps across the other appliances.

"He Who Walks in Old Words did so very quietly, not ruffling feathers, his eyes cast down to the ground, to the dig, turned away from the ugliness. Out of harm's way, he thought. A concern for buried things—that's all. What harm? What threat?" He laughed, a cynical, self-deprecating snicker. "But even old words cry out. The finger is pointed. The old words cry out and he is marked for death. He is exiled. He is hunted. *He is king!*"

Pablo crouched down and motioned for the others to come closer, as if he were about to impart some great revelation. No one moved an inch.

"Contemplate the birth of zero," he began, his voice suddenly going theatrical. "Deep in the jungle night. On the temple steps. Copal burning in the fire. Who thought of it? The astronomer? Or the executioner? Did he hold the moon stick or the sacrificial dagger? Was it science or blood? Do we possess the legacy or the curse? Contemplate this, each time another disappears, each time we have another *desaparecido*. Each time another zero is born, think of this."

He stood back up.

"I am a zero. Pablo Martín Méndez Córdova is no more.

There is just the savior-king, the savior of nothing, the king of zeros."

Pablo leapt onto the hood of Matt's car.

"And you are so anxious to write my story, to write what you don't understand for those who don't give a damn anyway. Just like Miss Wode. So sure of herself. So positive. And so wrong."

"What do you mean?" Matt asked, his voice quivering with excitement.

"She will write what she wanted to hear, what she was told. She will write lies."

Pablo slid off the car and stood face to face with Matt.

"What you are afraid of, you are capable of. You become what you fear. That is what fear can do. That is the way of it, the fruit, the germination. The good people of sanctuary knew such fear."

Pablo drifted away from the Mazda. The others followed after, catching up to him at a pyramid of washing machine parts.

"There was no raid on the sanctuary in Cob City," he began, talking softly, slowly. "Well, at least not the way Coh told it.

"There were eleven of us at Pastor Vail's church: Sergio, Yolanda and the baby, old Abraham, Cristina, Coh, Soto, Carlos Akabal, the two other Quiché and myself. That last night there . . . it never cooled down. It was sweltering. The men had their shirts off. We were sweating. And the wind . . . It was an angry wind . . . hissing. There was a smell in the air. . . . Some plant, I suppose. A sweet smell, musky, almost like the scent of a woman. I remember Soto found a scorpion under the sink. A big one. He put it in a coffee can and burned it. The Quiché got very upset. There was a big argument. Soto opened the bathroom door. He was going to flush it down the toilet. All this steam poured out. And then we saw Yolanda. She had just stepped out of the shower. She was naked. We all stood there staring at her and her at us. It seemed like such a long time before she wrapped the towel around herself. It was a strange night. You just had the feeling something was going to happen.

"Later—maybe an hour or two—Father Townes brought in a new man. He introduced him as Felix. I didn't pay much attention. I knew we were being moved the next day. I was thinking mostly about that. Coh was sleeping at the time. Townes and Vail left us in the dormitory and we prepared for bed. We all fell asleep. Hot as it was, we fell asleep."

Pablo bent down to pick up one of the parts, a mixing valve with a length of black hose attached. He looked at it closely and blew the sand out of the mechanism. "I wonder what this does," he said wistfully, sounding like he really wanted to know. The thing had such a solid feel to it, a practical feel. He wished he could understand it, fit it into something and make that thing work. But mechanical devices were a mystery to him. He could divine the use and meaning of the arcane, of that which had been buried for a millennium, but he could not operate, let alone fix, the simplest of machines.

"Coh awoke. Who knows why," he continued after a few moments. "He found the new man standing over Akabal's cot, smothering the boy with a pillow. Coh pulled him off. There was a terrible fight. The rest of us awoke. The new man was smaller than Coh, but I've never seen anyone fight so viciously. He held his own. Finally, the three Quiché helped out. Me too. We subdued this Felix.

"Coh told us what had happened—and something more. Coh recognized this man as Ramon Vega Mejía, a major in the G-2. We had all heard of him. Next to Mago himself, there was no one more feared. Mayor Vega was in charge of the PX when Coh lost his eye. His atrocities were legend. It was said that he lived by the pain of others. It was his food, his sustenance. . . ."

Pablo tossed the valve back onto the pile. "You don't suppose all of those are broken, do you?" he asked.

"Depends on if this is the good pile or the bad pile, I guess," Matt answered.

"It could be neither," Pablo observed. "It could be the one that hasn't been sorted yet, couldn't it?"

"Yeah." Matt looked around, trying to ascertain if there was any such logic to the brothers' operation, but there didn't appear to be any perceptible order to anything on their property.

Pablo started walking again, slowly meandering through the junk, stopping occasionally to open a freezer door or fiddle with a lint-catcher. "At first Vega denied everything," he went on, "but we knew he was lying. Finally he admitted it. He bragged about the things he had done, the women he had raped, the unborn babies he'd kicked from the bellies of their mothers, the men he'd castrated, the teeth he'd ripped with pliers from the mouths of young boys. He told us these were the hard things that had to be done to protect the country, the faith, the family, the hemisphere. These were the things that had to be done to preserve a way of life. Honor and decency depended on it. Nothing would he take back. Given the chance, he would do it all over again. That's what he said. He would eliminate the insurrection once and for all, the mothers and fathers of insurrection, the children, the seed, the womb of it, its godless breath, its obscene voice, the very memory of Communist subversion.

"He was not afraid of us, and as I looked around, I saw that we were very much afraid of him. He was one. We were many. He was grinning. We were trembling.

"Then it began. I don't remember how or exactly who made the first move, but suddenly, without a word, we grabbed him, stripped him naked and tied him to one of the cot frames. We had amazing strength. I remember feeling like I was still asleep, dreaming one of those dreams where you know it's a dream but you go along anyway waiting to see what happens next. One of those dreams where you let yourself be seduced by the feeling of it, the movement, the wave of it like surf. You go for the ride.

"We forced the door open and carried him out into the desert. It was like some pagan caravan, walking out further and further under the moon, into desolation. . . . Moloch looking on. . . . Baal, Marduk, Isis, Nebo, Dagon . . . And all of us with no homes, no one to answer to, no god of our own really, not anymore. All of us with some blood debt. All of us afraid.

"When it seemed like we'd gone far enough, we set the cot down on this narrow ridge. I remember there were fine threads of blowing sand, twisting, rising up into the night. And there was this twisted plant, a horrible thing. It looked like it had been forged in flame. The wind was whistling through its gnarled branches, rustling them, talking to me, whispering. I listened . . . and then I heard the scream.

"Coh was holding Vega's head and Cristina was forcing a knife, a steak knife from the sanctuary, into Vega's mouth. There was blood running all over his lips and his gums, but he kept his teeth clamped together. One of the Quiché did something to force his mouth open. Cristina stabbed down, cut, hacked—all the time she was screaming. Finally, when she was done, she tore out this mangled, shredded thing that was Vega's tongue. Only then did Cristina stop screaming. She knelt down, dug a little hole and buried it."

Pablo hesitated. He looked at the others, his eyes lingering a moment on each of them. "I could have left Vega there. I admit it," he said. "I could have left him there for the desert and the sun to do our dirty work. But this I couldn't do. I didn't have the taste for it. It sickened me. I swear it did. I tried to wrestle the knife away from Cristina, but the rest of them overpowered me.

They held me back. They called me a coward and a traitor. They made me watch.

"The knife was passed to Soto. He sawed off Vega's thumbs, slowly, deliberately. I remember the horrible sound as the blade grated against the bone. And the gurgling, blood-choked, wordless screams. Soto took one of the bloody thumbs and wrote NO SALE on Vega's forehead.

"Then one of the Quiché took the knife and sliced off one of Vega's toes, just as one of his had been hacked off by a pinto corporal.

"The other Quiché pushed the tip of the knife into Vega's right ear, just enough to puncture the ear drum. It was for all the nights he had lain awake listening to sobbing mothers and children, for all those terrible sounds in the night that had kept him from dreams.

"Old Abraham was weeping, crying for his grandson who had been dragged off by his hair through the streets of his village, never to be seen again. He took the knife and peeled away Vega's scalp.

"Sergio took it next, and for his wife who had been raped for months by soldiers in a basement room of a local barracks, he castrated Vega.

"Yolanda had a lighter, one of those inexpensive ones you can buy in a grocery store. She held the flame under Vega's right ear until there was nothing left. All the while she kept repeating the name of her husband who had burned to death in a union hall bombing.

"Coh was next. He worked like a surgeon, so delicate, so precise, as he cut around Vega's eye. A little at a time, through each layer of skin, of muscle and sinew, cut away individually until finally the man's eye just fell loose, hanging there on the stalk of nerves and the blood vessels.

"The knife was passed to Carlos. Since Vega had tried to kill him, it was left for him to finish him off. He said he would cut Vega's heart out, while it was still beating, just as his ancestors had done a thousand years ago. For all the Quiché people he would do this thing. He would stand under the moon and raise this enemy's heart up to the heavens.

"But the other Quiché protested. They were novices of the Daykeeper. They had had some instruction in the performance of ceremonial rites, although nothing they had learned could possibly have prepared them for this. Still, they insisted the place was wrong for such solemn sacrifice. It was not aligned properly. Nor was the sacrifice something to be done in front of others. It was the ancient way of the Quiché and those who came before the Quiché. Only they could take part.

"It was finally decided that we would return to the church and leave Vega with the three Indians. After they had finished with him and disposed of the body, they would return to the church as well.

"I was given one last chance. 'Just cut off his nose,' they said. 'Join us. Take a finger. They made you run, so at least open the soles of his feet. It's only justice,' they said. I refused. I don't know if it was because I was right or because I was weak, but I refused. I thought they might kill me. With me it would have been unanimous. When there is unity in madness, it is no longer madness. There would have been no doubts. They cursed me and spit at me, but they didn't harm me. There had been enough blood. It hadn't solved anything. It hadn't brought back what they had lost. More blood wasn't going to make it any better.

"We headed back to the church. The three Quiché carried Vega further into the desert. We never saw them again."

They'd wandered over to the green Kelvinator lying on its back with its door hanging open. Matt stared inside at the crust of black crud which was the blood of Major Vega. He wondered what had possessed the three Indians to dump the body there. Had they panicked? Were they lost by then? Was it the place itself, all those strange contraptions lying around? What could it have looked like to them? Matt lifted the door and dropped it into place.

"When I found Vega at Coombe's Ditch," said Matt, "the cot was lined up with this rock formation. The moon and a bright star were between the two towers of rock."

Pablo nodded. "Probably Venus. That would be a good place to do it."

"They had sliced him from one armpit to the other," Matt recalled.

"That's how it's done."

"But his chest wasn't open."

"They'd probably just started when you pulled up. You scared them off."

"I guess they finished when I left," Matt speculated.

"Not if Vega was dead. There'd be no point if he was dead."

"He was dead all right."

"Then he died between the time you scared them off and the time you actually examined the body."

"Couldn't have been more than a minute. What timing!"

Pablo shook his head. "Bad timing. You cheated the gods. Another minute and they would have had Vega's heart."

•

Just after dawn, the young pilot clumsily guided his AH-64A Apache helicopter into a low hover behind a shielding ridge of the Cuchumantane mountains in western Guatemala. He repeatedly overcompensated with the collective torque adjustment, bobbing the attack ship up and down a number of times before his VSI gauge leveled out. When he was excited, as he was now, he tended to be a bit heavyhanded with the controls. He took three deep breaths to calm himself. Then, with the help of his gunner, he checked his stores: The short hop from the base at Sololá had not used up much fuel. There were still over two hundred and seventy-five gallons left, more than enough to complete the mission.

The flare and chaff launchers were empty. With no reason to fear infrared or radar-guided anti-aircraft weapons, they had decided not to carry any decoy devices. The chance of encountering opposition was almost nonexistent, and if subversives did happen to be in the area, the Apache was more than adequately armored against their small-caliber rifles and machine guns.

For similar reasons, no Hellfire or Sidewinder missiles had been loaded. The Hellfires were primarily designed for use against tanks. The Sidewinders were good only against other aircraft. The insurgents had neither.

They *had* loaded four pods of FFAR's, unguided 2.75" folding-fin aerial rockets. The two outside pods were each carrying nineteen high-explosive warheads while the two inside ones were equipped with the same number of white phosphorous incendiaries.

The only other weapon was the nose-mounted 30-millimeter chain gun. Computer-controlled and capable of firing over sixty rounds per second, it was their deadliest and most versatile armament for "soft targets": people and structures.

Satisfied with his inventory and systems check, the pilot radioed the "ready" code back to Sololá: *"Rabia."* In seconds, the radio crackled with the "go" command: *"Suero."*

The gunship ascended as the pilot added collective torque to the main rotor. The Apache lifted over the top of the ridge and their target came into view, the tiny Quiché village of Rax Uleu.

Crooked tails of smoke were curling out of thatched roofs,

trailing up from the cook stoves where *nixtamal,* maize boiled in lime water, was being prepared; chickens and goats milled lazily in pens; a few campesinos were walking down the road toward the *milpas,* their mattocks braced on their shoulders like rifles; a dog scampered out of one of the small *ranchos* and began barking. The farmers stopped and looked up.

The dog could bark all he wanted, thought the pilot. It was already too late for them. They were already dead.

The Apache shot up over the crest of the ridge. The pilot needed added elevation for what he had in mind. At three hundred feet of clearance he pushed the joystick down, sending the ship into a high-speed power dive. Within seconds he reached an attack speed of over one hundred knots as he swooped down toward the target. The campesinos were running back toward their houses. They tried to round up the children who had wandered out, drawn, no doubt, by the barking dog. They, too, looked up to the sky.

At one kilometer, the gunner triggered the two full pods of high-explosive FFAR's. He didn't bother to aim with any degree of precision. The concussive force alone of the thirty-eight missiles would be enough to incapacitate the entire populace. A direct hit just wasn't necessary. Those who were not actually torn apart by blast fragmentation would be slammed to the ground so violently most would lose consciousness. The earth itself would rumble as if shaken by an earthquake. Those at the far periphery of the village would likely only suffer disorientation, but it would be enough to delay and thus doom their escape.

The pilot pulled back on the joystick. The Apache zoomed up and banked away as the double-pod volley of FFAR's detonated. The shock wave sent a shudder through the aircraft, banging it sidewards. The pilot easily regained control and completed a tight loop which brought him over the center of Rax Uleu. He looked down and saw to his satisfaction that the FFAR's had wiped out at least ten houses on the north end of the village. Unfortunately, however, the structures to the far south had suffered little damage.

He slowly headed south—there was no reason to hurry—keeping about thirty feet over the roof tops. At about seven-tenths of a kilometer from the furthest undamaged rancho, he eased the Apache into a hover. The gunner armed only two of the incendiary FFAR's, one from each of the inner pods. He fired and the rancho exploded in flames. Patiently, the pilot rotated the craft so it was lined up with the next furthest dwelling. Again the gunner fired and again the target disintegrated in a raging fireball. Methodically, they continued to rotate, target and fire, until all nineteen pairs of the incendiary rockets had been launched. When they were finished, the village was encircled by a raging fire-wall of chemical flame.

The gunner armed the chain gun and adjusted the targeting monocle of his computerized helmet. As he turned his head to seek out survivors, infrared sensors in the cockpit tracked his every move. TADS, the Target Acquisition and Designation System, aimed the chain gun congruent with his line of sight. When a family fleeing from one of the burning houses came into view, stumbling into the reticle cross hairs of the gunner's sighting monocle, TADS saw them too and the chain gun automatically locked on target. A one-second burst cut them to shreds.

The pilot detected a man galloping away on horseback. He gave chase, closing in seconds. Foolishly, the gunner let loose with a three-second volley, over one hundred and eighty high-velocity shells. The recoil jolted the Apache backward. When the dust had settled down below, there was only a bloody mound of smoking flesh. From the air, it was impossible to determine what had been equine and what human.

Circling back toward the village, the pilot waited for other survivors to come crawling out of the inferno. As they did, the gunner looked at them through the monocle, smiled and pressed a button. TADS and the chain gun did the rest. For the next thirty minutes they "cleaned up," making passes up and down the road and out over the trees until they were sure no one had gotten away, that everyone was dead.

The last pass over the village was strictly for fun. There were still over four hundred rounds left in the chain gun and they'd been uncharacteristically authorized to deplete all stores. Yelling like an American cowboy, the pilot motioned his gunner to fire until he was out of ammunition. The Apache jerked convulsively from the tremendous recoil. The pilot held onto the joystick like it was the saddlehorn of a bucking bronco. Down below, a stucco retaining wall was reduced to dust.

The gunship steadied and the two-man crew looked down on their morning's work:

Rax Uleu was no more. No longer would the communist insurgents find food and shelter there. No longer would they recruit young Indian boys of the village into their ranks. Soon the army bulldozers would arrive and the miserable place would be scraped off the map once and for all.

Something was moving in one of the animal pens. The pilot dipped down for a better look. It was a young man. A red kerchief was around his neck. The rest of his clothes were in tatters. One leg was all but blown away. Blood was pouring from two dark holes in his belly. Yet the man continued to move, crawling, getting to his feet, staggering forward, falling and starting all over again. He seemed to be headed toward a small two-wheeled cart at the far end of the pen. The pilot eased in closer, fascinated by the man's stamina.

Eventually, the wounded man made it to the cart. With

great effort he removed a canvas cover and struggled to lift something up onto his shoulder. The two-man crew of the Apache looked on with bemused interest.

Down in the pen, with the last ounce of his strength, Héctor lifted a twenty-pound SA-7 "Grail" SAM-launcher onto his shoulder. He aimed and pulled the trigger. The 70-millimeter fragmentation warhead rocketed into the Apache at Mach 1.5. In the split-second before the helicopter disintegrated, Héctor saw the expression on the pilot's face change from smug curiosity to sheer, bug-eyed, helpless terror.

The blast threw Héctor back across the pen. He landed on a pile of dead chickens, raising a blizzard of white feathers. He watched as they drifted back down like flower petals. Gently, they floated onto him and turned red in his blood.

I am Quetzalcoatl, The Plumed Serpent, he thought. *And they have felt my sting.*

Then he died.

•

Buchanon sprawled out on a faded old red bean bag chair. As his bulk settled in, four stitches in a weak seam gave way. A thin flux of ersatz legumes trickled out, flowing with hourglass consistency onto the ground. He'd spent the better part of the day moving the chair into and out of the shade according to his varying tolerance for the heat. Alternately, he'd suffered sweats and chills. All in all, his twenty-four hours "on the wagon" hadn't been as bad as he feared—not that he looked forward to ever repeating the experience, or that he thought he was even close to being out of the woods yet. It was just that as the day wore on and the sun did its late-afternoon worst—easily topping one hundred degrees—he'd begun to feel he was going to make it. Despite the three blankets he'd soaked through with 80-proof perspiration, the awful Brillo pad taste in his mouth, despite the cramps, the headache, the occasional double vision and the relentless craving for a tall cool one, he really felt he could pull himself through.

Pablo was fiddling with an Amana side-by-side. For hours he'd been trying—for no apparent reason other than to pass the time—to fasten the grid-like condenser to the back of the cabinet. Buchanon watched him with growing impatience. Without tools or the use of his right arm (not to mention any perceivable mechanical aptitude), Pablo did not seem to be making any progress.

"Give it up," Buchanon urged.

Pablo looked at him as if in a daze. He dropped the bulky condenser and peered out over the rest of the marooned appliances.

"A thousand years from now," Pablo replied, "some poor soul will find this place, and the world will be forced to make the effort to integrate this into their understanding of what life was like in the twentieth century."

"No one's gonna find this," Buchanon countered.

"Everything gets found, sooner or later. Everything but the explanation. That we simply invent."

"It'll all be blown up by then."

"No doubt. But they'll start over. Someone will think he can get it right the next time."

"There's always one, I guess," Buchanon conceded.

"So what will they think this was, this place?" Pablo asked. "They'll dig away the sand and rope it off. Everything they find will be numbered and scrupulously examined. They'll check all the available literature but they won't find the answer. They'll ponder the geometric significance of the placement of each and every item here. They'll find relationships, something complex and mathematical which will describe in precise detail the orientation of dryers to refrigerators to washers to the moons of Jupiter and the menstrual cycle of wombats in Australia. Order will come out of chaos. It will take a thousand years, but a history will be written for this place. And it will make sense, much more sense than what our journalist friend tells us about the brothers who lived here before us." Pablo sighed. "Truth can be so puny."

"It can be a son-of-a-bitch when it wants to be," Buchanon added.

Pablo nodded, then, to Buchanon's dismay, he began tinkering again with the Amana.

Inside the house, Matt bent over the kitchen sink and doused his head with the vegetable sprayer. Over the whoosh of the running water, he heard the pickup truck pulling up outside. A moment later, Rebecca walked in with two bags of groceries. Matt turned the faucet off.

"The shower doesn't work," he explained.

"I know," Rebecca answered tersely.

"I had to cool off."

Rebecca nodded and began unbagging the groceries. She opened the refrigerator. The light did not go on. She felt inside with her hand. The walls were warm.

Matt laughed. "That's just about perfect."

"Maybe it's not plugged in," Rebecca speculated hopefully. She traced the cord to a wall socket.

"Try the knob inside," Matt suggested.

She turned the dial to MAX COOL but nothing happened. Rebecca closed the refrigerator door and dejectedly slumped against it.

"Where'd you go?" Matt asked.

"Cob City. It's the closest town."

"Did you go past Vail's church?"

"There's nothing left," she answered solemnly. "It's all been bulldozed." She sighed and blotted the sweat on her forehead with a paper napkin.

"You look fried," Matt said.

"I'm not really a sun person."

"You're more of a night crawler then," Matt said playfully.

"I'm cut out for a more temperate climate, I guess."

"So what brought you to the desert?"

"It was my husband's idea."

"And you just went along."

"Yes. What else would I do?"

"Your place is with your husband," Matt droned as if reciting some graven dictum.

"Of course."

"Except now."

"There were reasons for separating."

"You make it sound permanent," Matt pointed out, catching something in her tone.

"No. I'm just hot and tired."

"Your husband thought you and I were an item." Matt smiled devilishly.

Rebecca tensed. "Nathan expects total honesty," she explained. "He was surprised I'd been to see you without telling him. That's all."

"From the look on his face, I'd say that wasn't all."

"You're mistaken," she insisted.

"Kelly jumped to the same conclusion," Matt recalled. "What do you make of that?"

Rebecca fidgeted and looked away. "I don't know."

"Strong vibes, I'd say."

Rebecca once more gave her attention to the groceries. "How am I going to keep the milk from spoiling?" She scanned the kitchen for a suitable storage compartment.

"C'mon," Matt pressed. "Your husband and my old girl friend both get it in their heads that we're—"

"You don't know that."

"I wouldn't bet against it."

"I've never given Nathan any reason to believe—"

"But he does anyway. That's the pisser."

"He's got no reason—"

"What about that little squeeze in my apartment?"

Rebecca hesitated. "What do you mean?" she asked quietly.

"Rebecca." Matt wasn't going to let her off the hook.

"You took advantage, Mr. Teller."

"We're back to last names," Matt observed wryly. "Isn't that overdoing it?"

"I think it's best."

"I'll tell you what I think," Matt replied. "I think Kelly and old Nathan figured we were making it, because that's exactly what was supposed to happen. You've been thinking about it and I've been thinking about it. It was supposed to happen in my apartment, but you ran off. We both wanted it. No wonder we looked guilty as hell. They could see it. Sometimes events present themselves and people just don't act upon them, but they're there just the same. The dirty deed was there, Rebecca, whether we did it or not."

"That's ridiculous," Rebecca said without conviction.

"Sometimes it works out that way."

"You can't believe that."

"And you can't believe we didn't feel something for each other."

"Whatever I felt, if it was wrong, I'm glad I had the strength to walk away."

"You can't walk away from what you feel, Rebecca."

She struggled to answer, to deny. "You don't know what I feel," was all she could truthfully say.

"I know what *I* feel," Matt replied. He turned the water

back on. "Believe me, cold showers are everything they're cracked up to be." He leaned over the sink and sprayed himself, letting the cool well water flow over his head, down his back, not minding if it ran onto the floor.

He felt the warmth of her body, the closeness of her heat. She was at the sink, standing next to him. "Me too," she said softly, her eyes downcast. It was a confession, the two little words carrying a complicated load of sadness, courage and desire.

Matt backed away and Rebecca bent over the sink, taking his place. He ran the nozzle over her head, thoroughly soaking her fine blond hair. She straightened up and faced him, her eyes wide now and looking right at him, frightened, wondering, expectant. Matt reduced the water pressure and gently placed the nozzle at the base of her neck. She stiffened as the cold water trickled onto her skin. Goose bumps rose on her flesh. The water dripped down, slow, crooked fingers slipping under her dress. Matt watched as the thin fabric soaked up the wetness and drew tight across her body. He saw her chest heave and the outline of her nipples push out against the wet cloth. He took her trembling hand and led her into the back bedroom.

10

5 IK   THE SEATING OF UAYEB

AT THE COMPLETION OF
12 BAKTUNS
18 KATUNS
8 TUNS
15 UINALS
2 KINS

the next day . . .

Rebecca awoke suddenly. She sat up in the strange bed wondering where she was. The air smelled of human exertion. The sheets were damp with sweat. Sunlight shone in through a dirty window in two dusty, warm beams which splayed out over the bed. The cover slipped down and she realized she was naked. Her arms crossed instinctively over her breasts. They were slightly sore. After a few disoriented moments she placed herself. She was in the back bedroom of the little desert shack, in the narrow, dingy room where she had made love with a man she barely knew, made love for an entire afternoon and most of the night, done things she'd never done before, or even thought to do before—not with Nathan. It had been wonderful: the touching, the kissing, the patient way he'd led her from one new sensation to the next, the momentum she'd felt after getting over the initial awkwardness, the tingle, the excitement, the bliss, the giving, the trusting, the opening up, the dozing off in warm embrace, the waking again to more, always more, until she drifted off once and for all, fell into blessed sleep, forgetting everything and feeling beyond satisfied.

But it was morning now, afterward, the time she feared, the time of inevitable complications and looking back and second thoughts. How turned around things were: Night used to be the doubt-bringer.

Still drowsy, she closed her eyes and yawned. She denied the sun. All night long she'd dreaded its coming. Whatever bitter wisdom the morning carried, it could wait. She was not yet ready to accept delivery. The night was still with her, still a dark and delicious thing in which she was alive and lost.

There was a commotion outside, a slamming door, Buchanon's voice. Was that what had awakened her?

The second wave of wakefulness washed over her.

Something was wrong. Something was missing.

Buchanon burst into the room. "Where is he?" he shouted, echoing her own thoughts.

"I . . . I don't know," she answered dully, still not ready to believe Matt wasn't there cuddled up beside her.

"Did you give him your keys?" Buchanon demanded.

Suddenly, her heart was beating furiously. A trapdoor sprang open. She felt something dropping away deep inside.

Rebecca scanned the room for her dress. The keys were in the dress.

Oh my God!

Her panties were draped over a lamp shade. Her bra, torn apart at the front seam, was dangling from the handle on a dresser drawer. Sordid reminders mocking her in silence, telling her she'd gotten what she deserved.

Buchanon bulled his way across the room and picked up something that was balled up in the far corner. Her dress. He searched the pockets then examined the floor.

"Damn!" he fumed.

Breathing was difficult. Tears stung her eyes.

"He's off in your truck!" Buchanon snapped. "My bet is we're all gonna be on tomorrow's front page. We've got to get out of here." He headed for the door. "Get dressed." He threw her the dress and stormed out.

The adventure was over. It had taken Rebecca away from Braxton Wells and from Nathan only to leave her stranded in shame, agonizing over her weakness. Still she didn't feel like running back. Things could never be as they were before. She was sure of this. Boundaries had been crossed; waypoints had been passed. The logistics of return were full of flaws; the objectives were no longer trustworthy. Loneliness overcame the guilt and humiliation, a great, sad emptiness which grew within her.

Rebecca was hollow.

The night had slipped away.

Morning had come—with a vengeance.

•

A number of concerns preoccupied Matt as he drove the last few miles to *H&T.* First and foremost among them was the calendar. Because he'd spent the entire night with Rebecca, it was now limbo day, that useless period sandwiched between deadline and publication. He did not understand why he'd remained with her so long. That had not been the plan. With Buchanon's vigilance on the wane, the idea was to have Rebecca asleep by nightfall and to be on his way shortly thereafter. That would have given him half a chance of reaching Schiff in time to get the story in. It would have meant changing the press run again, but it could have been done. Instead, he'd stayed with her until dawn. He could have slipped away earlier, but he hadn't—and he couldn't fathom why. He'd been a prisoner in that bed. He'd seduced her, but once it had begun, he had been as powerless to resist as she was. It was only as the sun came up that he'd found the strength to break away.

Strength?

No, it didn't feel like strength. It felt like something he did because he'd done it before. It just felt like an old habit.

And now he felt bad about leaving her. That hadn't been in the plan either.

Matt was also troubled about Kelly's story—or more precisely, the lack of it. He'd stopped on the way and picked up both yesterday's and today's *Times.* The story wasn't in either edition. At first he'd been heartened by the development, but now he was beginning to have doubts. It was entirely possible she'd missed yesterday's deadline altogether, but she had had plenty of time to get the story into today's issue. There could be only one explanation: She'd discovered the flaws in her story. He would be denied the pleasure of discrediting her.

Then again, what did it matter if Kelly printed errors or not? A lie in the *Times* became the truth; the truth in *Here and There* would always be a lie. That was simply the way things were.

As he approached the office there seemed to be less and less reason for getting the story out. He'd even begun worrying about Pablo. The story could endanger him, after all. Certainly it would have some effect on his ability to fulfill the prophecy—

What prophecy?

It was just a bunch of superstitious foolishness. It was just a story.

So why did he drive right past *H&T*'s front door?

"Damn catfish!" he cursed, pounding on the steering wheel.

He thought of Earl and Elmo Beldine, the two-headed man, how Elmo had grabbed a revolver, put it to Earl's head and pulled the trigger on their mutual existence. That's where it all started, when he filched Koslowski's notes. That's what got him, albeit ever so circuitously, to Coombe's Ditch.

He drove around aimlessly, totally confused, feeling like *he* had two heads, an old one that was going dormant and a new one that was just waking up. Eventually he found himself driving toward his apartment. It seemed a suitable destination, a place to regroup, think things out, figure the next move.

Coming through the front door, he immediately sensed something was wrong. He looked around, but everything seemed to be as he'd left it. Then he heard it, the sound, the moaning from the bedroom.

Impossible.

Even if he'd left the VCR on, Schiff's tape couldn't still be playing after two days. He tried to remember if the damn video machine had some sort of auto-replay function.

He threw the bedroom door open and barged in.

The tape *was* on.

And Kelly was there—on the bed, spread-eagle, her wrists and ankles tied tightly to the bedposts. Her head was propped up so she could see the television. Her eyes, wide with terror, fled to Matt, then quickly to the screen and to the three men who were positioned around the bed. Vincenzo Côrtes, the Brazilian journalist, was seated beside her, his hand idly stroking her thigh as he watched the video. A chinless, yellow-toothed, skull-faced man hurriedly zipped up his pants. The third man was sitting at the desk, his back to the door. He swiveled around in the chair and smiled, gazing up at Matt over half-eye reading glasses perched on the end of his nose.

"Ah, Mr. Teller, you've arrived," the third man said. Then he nodded to a fourth man whom Matt had not seen hiding behind the door.

A hand clamped over Matt's face. There was a terrible smell. Chloroform, he suspected. Maybe ether. He struggled. A fist exploded into his left kidney. His knees buckled.

The room went in and out of focus, divided, reformed, layered over itself like something seen in opposing mirrors. Then everything began to vibrate, each and every presence in the room resonating like a tuning fork, giving off its own peculiar frequency. Matt's head filled with the confluence of sound, the gnawing buzz of the television, the squeaks of his bed, the endless clatter of his typewriter, the smooth words of Vincenzo Côrtes, the skeletal rattle of the chinless intruder, the smiling hiss of the man in the half-eye glasses.

But over it all was the moaning of the woman on the screen—

Or was it Kelly? . . .

•

"Mr. Teller, are you with us?"

Matt could barely hear through the cacophonous bedlam which filled his head. He struggled to open his eyes, but blinding fists of light pounded them shut again. His sense of equilibrium capsized in the cranial turmoil. Churning corkscrews twisted up out of his gut. He threw up. He felt the muck running down his chin, backing up in his throat, burning his esophagus. He gagged and passed back into unconsciousness. . . .

"Mr. Teller, we are waiting."

When he awoke the second time, he found the chinless,

skull-faced bastard standing next to him, attentively holding a bucket. He tried to use it, but he just couldn't get his head to move. Despite intense effort, the nerves and muscles and bones weren't quite ready to collaborate. Finally he decided he didn't feel like puking after all—which was good because the chinless bastard wasn't there anymore and neither was the bucket. . . .

"I must apologize, Mr. Teller."

It was the man with the half-eye reading glasses. He sounded friendly—thank God. Matt struggled to focus, but it was impossible to keep his eyes open. The lights were still too tough.

"The fool gave you too much ether. No wonder they seldom use it anymore in your country. Such unpleasant side effects. And so unpredictable. You awoke and started to sing just as we were carrying you from your apartment. We looked suspicious enough dragging you and Miss Wode to the car, and then you go to singing. I thought for sure we'd be detected. But thankfully we seemed to benefit from that legendary Anglo indifference we hear so much about. If anyone saw us, I'm sure they just took us for a bunch of drunks. That's so much easier than getting involved. Nonetheless we felt it necessary to give you a second dose. You have been unconscious far longer than we planned. The day is almost gone and our timetable is all the more pressed."

Matt closed his eyes. None of it was real. It wasn't happening —not really, not to him, not now. But then the man with the glasses pried his right eye open and the other one jammed a bottle of smelling salts under his nose.

It was real all right.

"You are confused," the man continued. "Let's see, how can I help? Well, place is always good to start with. You are in Orange County, Mr. Teller. So you shouldn't feel too disoriented. You are relatively close to home. This place here"—the man looked around and shrugged—"it's a warehouse, I suppose. Maybe it could accommodate a small machine shop. That kind of place. Very thick concrete walls and no windows . . ."

The man paused as if his last statement had some special significance. Matt struggled to understand, but his head was still spinning.

"And I am Coronel Efraín César Alvarado Guzman. You have heard of me, perhaps? . . . No? . . . Well, then perhaps you are familiar with the name my enemies have given me."

Matt tried to respond, to form the word he knew but feared. Distantly, he heard a voice say "Mago"—his voice, sounding feeble and scared.

"Good. Then we spare much of the introduction. If you know me by that name, then you know me well enough for our purpose here. But, be that as it may, I must insist that you call me Coronel Alvarado—for the sake of propriety. I'm sure you understand, Mr. Teller."

Matt understood nothing. Not a goddamn thing—except that increasing wakefulness did not necessarily bring increasing comprehension. He tried to put it together, to make some sense of it, but then Vincenzo Côrtes appeared at Mago's side, materializing out of the bank of lights that continued to restrict his vision.

Mago nodded and smiled. "More confusion, I see. Understandable. We so enjoyed listening to your recording of your meeting with Vinicio here." Mago held up the Adidas bag. The "Brazilian" pulled a GAN tape from his pocket. Matt's camera was in his other hand. "What a performance. Extremely convincing, I thought." Mago patted his confederate on the back. The "Brazilian" beamed with pride. "We were so disappointed when you didn't publish Vinicio's little melodrama. We put so much effort into it. It would have been so much better for you, too. You would have suffered some embarrassment after the story was found to be a hoax. But this happens all the time in your profession, I would suppose."

"A red herring," Matt grumbled.

"Excuse."

"It was supposed to lead me off the trail."

"Of course," Mago agreed brightly. Then his face clouded over. "Pity it didn't."

Matt's equilibrium had settled enough for him to determine he was lying down. He strained forward, but a strap was cinched tightly across his chest, restricting his movement.

"Oh, I am sorry," Mago apologized. "I should have told you about that. These facilities are so crude. We have so little to work with here."

Mago snapped his fingers. Vinicio loosened the strap one notch.

"You must relax," Mago cautioned.

Matt tried to move his hands. They were also restrained. So were his ankles. And his back hurt like hell. It felt quilted, a crisscross grid of pain—

Jesus!

He was on a cot. He was lying on the bare wire frame of a goddamn cot.

Just like the guy at Coombe's Ditch.

"What do you want?" Matt gushed. His trembling caused the cot to rattle beneath him. "I'll tell you anything. I swear."

"Don't tell him shit!"

It was Kelly's voice—hoarse and thick and tired, but sounding as strong and determined as ever.

Matt called her name and twisted his head toward the sound. He peered out into the lights. His eyes stung and burned, but he kept them open. Eventually the lights surrendered; his vision cut through.

Kelly was on the other side of the room, bound to a chair. Her face was swollen and she looked twenty years older than when he'd last seen her. There was a crust of blood caked under one nostril. Her hair was matted down with sweat. She was wearing a man's shirt. It had been buttoned hastily and the collar was crooked.

"I didn't tell him a goddamn fucking thing!" she shouted, her voice cracking on the last word.

Matt experienced one of those incongruous, lucid moments that occur without warning in the midst of insanity. He thought how odd it was to hear Kelly use profanity. As he considered it the thought imploded, and he was left to ponder how it was that at a time like this, his brain had chosen to register the harshness of her vocabulary and the crookedness of her collar. He wondered if perhaps it was some built-in defense mechanism which concentrated on the mundane in order to blot out what was intolerably painful.

"Again, I apologize for the facilities," Mago cut in. "You really do deserve private accommodations, but we are short on space and we must make do with what we have."

As Matt's sight strengthened, something else came into view at the far end of the room. In the opposite corner from Kelly, a man was hanging upside-down from an overhead pipe. His arms were twisted behind him and his wrists had been tied to his ankles. It was Soto.

Mago saw the horror register on Matt's face as the reporter tried to fathom how the human body could withstand such contortion.

"It's called the parrot," Mago explained. "It's very effective and not too messy. And it doesn't really require any special equipment other than a sturdy horizontal support—although normally I do prefer the *capucha.*"

Mago walked over and lifted Soto's head, tugging it by the hair. "This one's gone. But I don't think he knew more than he told us. He gave us Miss Wode here and the church in Braxton Wells. It's too late for that to be of any use, I fear."

"I got them out!" Kelly cried. "I did it, Matt! They're on their way! He's too goddamn late!"

"Capitán Reyes," Mago called, a note of minor annoyance in his voice.

The chinless bastard marched over to Kelly and struck her over the tops of her bare thighs with a cane.

"Fuck you!" Kelly shouted.

"Leave her alone!" Matt cried.

Mago nodded and the man struck Kelly again. The colonel watched Matt, intently studying his reaction.

Reyes continued to strike Kelly until her curses were no more than pained, defiant whispers.

"This isn't happening!" Matt screamed, his eyes filling with tears.

"Unfortunately it is, Mr. Teller," Mago replied, his tone sympathetic.

"Make it stop!" Matt pleaded.

Mago laughed. "It hasn't even started."

"Please!" he begged.

"You know I must thank you for having that video program available. I am not given to such distractions, but my men did find it inspiring. I trust Miss Wode found the morning to be entertaining."

"Sonovabitch!"

"Yes . . . well . . . Now on to business." Mago motioned to Vinicio. The "Brazilian" approached the cot with a spool of lamp wire, letting it trail out behind him. Reyes followed him carrying a levered device which reminded Matt of a model train transformer.

Matt could not disguise the fear in his voice. "What are they doing?"

"Their job, Mr. Teller. You don't realize what soldiers like us must do so that you can have your silly little newspaper and your filthy video programs."

"What the fuck are they doing?" Matt screamed. He strained to see what Reyes and Vinicio were up to at the foot of the cot.

"Now Miss Wode insists that Pablo Méndez is with the others," Mago explained. "She tells us that they are all under the protection of her publisher, and if that is so, there is nothing we can do. But I am inclined to believe only half of her story. She has been so strong and brave, one wonders why she has told me this and nothing else. So, I've chosen to believe that the others are out of my reach. That part of it agrees with what your friend over there told us." He pointed toward Soto. "But I cannot accept that the young archaeology student is with them. You see, Mr. Teller, the tape in your recorder seems to be of this Pablo Méndez, and from the context I can only deduce it was made after the others had already left with Miss Wode."

"I'll tell you where he is," Matt interrupted, sensing that Vinicio and Reyes were about done with their preparations.

"Of course you will," Mago smiled.

"Don't tell him anything!" Kelly screamed.

Matt gazed up at Mago, at the dark, unreadable eyes, at the tight, controlled, lying smile. He felt entirely helpless. "I'll tell you everything," he promised.

"We do not have time for 'everything.' Everything is confusion. I require clarity."

"Jesus. I'll cooperate!"

"I have not asked for cooperation. Cooperation implies complicity. Collaboration between you and me is impossible. I am just here to listen and you are just here to tell the truth."

"I didn't tell him shit!" Kelly screamed. She tried to wriggle out of her bonds. The chair hopped forward, screeching as the metal feet skidded against the concrete floor. "Be strong for once!"

"This is easy for her to say," Mago whispered to Matt. He winked conspiratorially. "She's comfortable. She's been fucking my men all day. She's not suffering."

"Oh God . . ." Matt was sobbing. "Please, please . . . I'll tell you."

Mago held up his hand. "One moment."

Matt heard a low hum. His legs began to tingle and shake. All in all, it didn't feel too bad.

"What a shame," Mago commiserated. "You really don't belong here." Then he nodded toward Reyes and Vinicio.

A flash of blue-white light exploded behind Matt's eyes. His body jolted off the cot frame, convulsing violently against the restraints. A tooth went through the tip of his tongue and blood sprayed from his mouth. He was filled with the acrid smell of burning hair. There was a feeling of wetness in his ears.

Mercifully, it stopped.

"It's amazing, isn't it?" Mago adopted a clinical tone. "You feel it can't go on. You feel you will burst, that your eyes will pop out of their sockets, that your bones will crumble. You feel you will die. You *want* to die. But you don't. You could go on like this for days. And relatively undamaged, if we control the voltage properly. With luck, we won't leave a mark on you."

Mago nodded and once more the current surged, hotter, stronger, longer. Matt's body quaked and wrenched. He was in the grip of something frenzied and mindless. There was no reasoning with it, no way to understand it or cope with it. There was just pain: total, complete, seemingly without end.

But again, it stopped.

"You would think that a numbness would set in. But it just seems to get worse, doesn't it? And that was only a few seconds, by the way. Imagine what a minute of this would feel like. We're just using radio batteries, by the way. If you're curious, that little box which Capitán Reyes is cranking is called 'the little pepper.' "

Matt's bladder gave way. He wet himself. Steam rose from the floor. "I'll tell you," he gasped.

"Yes, and now I won't have to wonder what is fiction and what is truth. With someone such as yourself—excuse me for saying so—that could be so time-consuming."

Mago glanced toward Vinicio and Reyes, as if he were about to order another surge.

"No!" Matt screamed. "My God . . . I'll tell you."

Mago pulled up a chair and sat next to Matt. Reyes produced a bucket of water and a sponge. Delicately, Mago began washing off the blood which had sprayed from Matt's tongue.

"Where is Pablo Martín Méndez Córdova? Where is He Who Walks in Old Words?" The voice oozed seductively, flowing with the water squeezed from the sponge.

"He's at a place out on—"

"Don't you understand!" Kelly shouted. "We're dead! You tell him and more die!"

Mago leaned in closer, positioning himself like a priest ready to take a death-bed confession.

"He'll let us go," Matt said hopefully.

"Don't blow it again!" Kelly shouted just before Côrtes kicked her chair over onto its back.

"Where is he?" Mago whispered urgently.

Matt hesitated. His body stiffened. He gritted his teeth,

closed his eyes, formed his hands into fists. Mago knew he had made a crucial mistake.

The colonel sighed, pushed the chair back and stood up. He assessed the situation: The woman was strong. That had been obvious from the very beginning. It wasn't surprising. In his experience he'd usually found women to be stronger than men. Sensing she could withstand any physical pain he inflicted, he'd turned his efforts toward humiliation. But even that seemed to backfire. She'd become more belligerent as the day wore on. So he had pinned his hopes on the reporter.

He wasn't sure of the reporter's feelings for the woman, so he'd been careful to dress her for the initial confrontation. In that regard he'd also made sure that his men hadn't seriously disfigured her. He had more options that way, more to deface, more to strip away in front of him. But now it didn't look as if the questioning would head in that direction. There was something between them, all right, but it didn't appear to be romantic. It was more of a contest, a race. Her last remark had challenged the reporter. It had been boastful, full of pride. It had given strength to the weakling. Now the reporter would endure the pain just to prove he was better than she.

"Capitán Reyes," he called. "Our guests have something to prove to us—or to each other. I'm sure you can accommodate them."

II

6 AKBAL   I UAYEB

AT THE COMPLETION OF

12 BAKTUNS

18 KATUNS

8 TUNS

15 UINALS

3 KINS

the next day . . .

The Jardinita Motor Lodge off Highway 86 in Indio catered mostly to transient workers who labored "in season" as busboys and dishwashers in the hotels and restaurants of nearby Palm Springs. It was a one-story sprawling eyesore of faded turquoise stucco and dirty jalousies. The pool out front hadn't been filled since 1967 and now contained an overturned old VW bug, a curiosity which the tenants seemed to accept. The framework of a swing set and the fulcrum of a teeter-totter stood defiantly in a small playground area otherwise claimed by weeds and discarded

car parts. The "Free Ice" machine next to the office was perpetu-
ally out of order. The Coke machine, which required "proper
change only," always worked, and its bright red-and-white illumi-
nated panel glowed vigil-like through night and day.

When Buchanon had checked in the day before, the clerk in
the office had been honest enough to say, "Anglos don't normally
stay here." Buchanon just grunted, paid the $27.77 room rental
and signed the register "The Smith Family." The clerk smiled at
that, handed over a room key and said, "Have fun."

The mantle of leadership had descended—quite uncontested
—onto Buchanon's broad shoulders. Without being asked, he'd
taken charge. Pablo and Rebecca were so preoccupied with their
own personal dilemmas that it was relatively easy for them to
acquiesce to the scout's wishes—even though Buchanon's own
battle with alcohol withdrawal made him less than reasonable at
times.

Just after sunrise, Buchanon announced he was going into
town "to check things out." Pablo and Rebecca were to stay put.
Rebecca passed the time by skimming through the Gideon. Pablo
was content to gaze out the window, watching the activity in the
parking lot. The night shift of unskilled labor was filtering in from
Palm Springs. After a while, he asked Rebecca to change the
dressing on his wound.

"It doesn't look bad," she commented as she removed the
bandage. "There's no sign of infection."

"Thanks to you," Pablo returned graciously.

"At least I've done something right."

"You're being hard on yourself."

Rebecca shook her head philosophically. "What you must
think of me . . ."

"I think of you as someone who opened her home to strangers."

"I mean now," she interrupted.

Pablo hesitated. "Do you really want to know?" he asked.

"Very much."

"I think of you as someone who is even more lost than I am," he said. "I do not have a home, but I have been handed my identity, whether I want it or not. You have a home, but you do not know who you are. You're a stranger in your own house. You're a stranger to yourself, I think."

Rebecca nodded. "For my entire life I've been doing the will of others. Parents, teachers, Nathan—God, I thought. I never got to know my own will. I never got to know myself."

"It's not too late." Pablo smiled encouragingly.

Rebecca sighed. "I must appear so foolish to you."

"Because the reporter ran away?"

"Because I ran to him."

"I don't think that's foolish," Pablo ventured. "In fact, I think he will come back to you."

"He's charmed you too, I see."

"People are what they are. He is a reporter. We gave him the story. He had to run."

"You're generous, Pablo."

"He's not so bad. He left us the keys to his car, didn't he? Buchanon didn't have to hot-wire it. That shows some concern."

"It's a blessing to be able to see the good in people."

"It's a blessing to have something to see."

The door burst open. It was Buchanon. Cradled in his arms was a pile of newspapers. He tossed the new *Here and There* on the bed.

"There's nothing in there," he said, shrugging and shaking his head. "I've been through it front to back."

"They have deadlines, don't they?" Rebecca asked.

"I guess," said Buchanon, stroking his three-day-old beard.

"Maybe he changed his mind," Pablo suggested.

"Then that woman reporter changed hers, too. There's nothing in the *Times* either." Buchanon threw the remaining stack of newspapers on the bed. "I had a hell of a time getting yesterday's and the day before's. There ain't a word in any of them. It don't make sense. They were both so hot to trot."

"Maybe they're waiting," Rebecca speculated.

"I called Matt's apartment from a pay phone," Buchanon recounted. "I got the answering machine. I just hung up."

"He's probably at work," Pablo offered.

"I called there, too. They're pissed. They haven't heard from him in days."

"He could be anywhere," Rebecca observed.

"I called the *Times*," Buchanon continued. "Kelly Wode didn't show up for work either—yesterday *or* today."

"They're together," said Rebecca, a little too quickly and with a bit too much bitterness in her voice. "Don't you think?" she asked, hoping to draw them to the conclusion and render it less personal.

Buchanon nodded. "Yeah," he grunted.

Pablo sat on the edge of the bed and stared at the pile of newspapers. "They are together all right," he said gravely. "They are together and Mago has them."

Rebecca's hand went to her mouth. "Oh my God!"

"He has all of them," Pablo continued. His voice was level, solemn and sure.

"We don't know that," Rebecca argued.

Buchanon paced across the room, deep in thought and still rubbing the coarse stubble on his chin. He paused at the door to check the deadbolt and chain lock.

Pablo leafed through one of the papers. "One of them would

have published. One of them would have shown up for work. You saw how anxious they were."

"Nathan!" Rebecca gasped. "I've got to get back to the church."

"That's the last place we're gonna go," Buchanon retorted.

"Buchanon's right," Pablo agreed. "It's not safe."

"I don't care," Rebecca insisted.

"No!" Buchanon snapped.

"What did they say at the *Times* when you asked for Miss Wode?" Pablo inquired.

"It was weird," Buchanon recalled. "They wanted to know who I was, where I was calling from, why I was calling. It was a real goddamn third degree."

"What did you tell them?"

"Just some bullshit. I think they knew it was bullshit."

"They don't know where she is," Pablo concluded. "She's disappeared and they are rightfully suspicious of your phone call."

Buchanon punched the door. The entire wall shook. "I think you're right."

"Mago has them," Pablo repeated. "I know it."

"What do we do?" Rebecca asked, her voice thin and tremulous.

Buchanon stopped pacing. "We get them back," he answered without a moment's hesitation.

•

At eight-thirty in the morning, the telephone rang at the Guatemalan Consulate in Los Angeles. The caller demanded to speak to the Consul General. His personal secretary explained politely that the Consul General was unavailable. When the caller persisted, the secretary threatened to hang up. Then the caller angrily told her to deliver a message to "that fucking son-of-a-bitch Mago." She took out her pen and a sheet of consulate letterhead. As instructed, she carefully wrote down exactly what the man said:

> *"This is Buchanon.*
> *I've got Pablo Méndez.*
> *I'll trade him for Matt Teller, Kelly Wode, Nathan*
>   *Miles and the refugees.*
> *Get them all to Edgar Tall.*
> *Be there at exactly hidden Coors P.M.*
> *Matt Teller will know what I mean.*
> *If you're there at the right place, at exactly the*
>   *right time, we'll trade.*
> *If not, the king goes home."*

The secretary's first inclination was to pitch the message into the closest trash can. But then she began to reflect that the cryptic note might represent something more than a crank call. The consulate had seen more than its share of unusual activity since the murder of Hernando Cuellar. So many strange faces coming and going—police, reporters, people from the American Justice Department. Even just before the murder, there had been a number of strange occurrences. She had been asked to expedite diplomatic visas for two G-2 officials, a Special Forces officer and four *Kaibiles.* And then there had been the vouchers for cash and the payments for cars and rented space out in Orange County—all of which she had done without so much as a raised eyebrow.

How could she question anything? Her husband had just been awarded a lucrative contract to broker cardamom to the Arabs. Her children were living in America and going to American schools. Her salary in one year alone was more than her father had made in an entire lifetime. What was there to question?

She really didn't want to break in on the Consul General

during his trade meeting with the American fruit company executives, but finally she decided she had no choice. When she saw the expression on his face as he read the message, she knew she had chosen correctly.

•

Kelly and Matt slept fitfully on the concrete floor beside the cot that had been the instrument of their torment throughout the night. Alternately, one of them had been strapped to the cot and shocked to the limit of endurance while the other was made to watch. Mago and Vinicio had not participated. Capitán Reyes, assisted by two burly guards, had supervised the procedure with meticulous precision. Reyes was an accomplished master of pain. He knew exactly how hard to crank the "little pepper," just when to reverse its direction, how long to let the current flow, just where to attach the electrodes. His skull of a face never changed expression. He never asked even one question. He just went about his work: dedicated, relentless, professional.

At an arbitrary point, Reyes and his two assistants had departed, locking the door behind them. Matt and Kelly were amazed that neither of them showed any sign of the anguish they'd just endured. Just as Mago had predicted, there wasn't a mark on them. Not a bruise, not a scratch or a burn—at least not from the electric shocks. Only the cot had left its brand on them, the checkerboard of abrasions from the wires on their backs.

"We seem to be none the worse for wear," Matt had said, trying to sound encouraging.

"That's why they quit," Kelly had solemnly observed. "So we'd realize how much more of this they can do to us before we—"

They had left the rest unsaid, distracting themselves by inspecting the room, looking for a means of escape. Eventually they gravitated to the spot beside the cot, where they huddled on the cold floor, trying to keep each other warm. Just as they were about to fall asleep, Reyes and the two assistants stormed back in. Matt was strapped to the cot while Reyes held Kelly. One of the others readied the "little pepper," but then a command from Reyes caused him to disconnect it and rig a different apparatus to the AC line at a junction box. The first guard turned a rheostat. There was a loud hum; the lights dimmed. As the other guard approached with the two electrodes, Matt's body began to convulse long before they were even close to his flesh. Reyes nodded and the apparatus was shut down. As abruptly as they had entered, the *capitán* and his two assistants once more departed.

Matt and Kelly clung to each other on the floor, finally understanding the true nature of the damage that had been done to them. Now they knew that fear alone could cause pain. It was as if all those electrons were now stored deep within them, lying dormant in the marrow of their bones, waiting to recharge, waiting for a catalyst, some unexpected circumstance, a sudden trigger from a mind in panic, the flashpoint at the end of a jangled nerve. Then the electrons would surge and shake them apart from the inside out. That was Mago's plan, that they realize the palpability of fear, its ability to torture them from within. From time to time a sound would come from the other side of the door and they would quiver. They'd squeeze each other tightly, hoping to calm the treacherous forces within them.

Hours later, after they had cried, after they had cursed and threatened, after they had thought of all that was now lost, after they had given involuntary audience to the endless parade of regrets, after they had suffered the vision of all that could have been different between them, after they had talked in sputtering, irrelevant fragments which rattled about in the silence but never connected in dialogue—then, in the absolute fatigue of hopelessness, had they fallen asleep.

The bolt in the door pinged open, the sound jolting them awake. The door opened slowly, silently, admitting a dull, hazy wall of light. Reyes stepped through. For the first time, the skull-like face spoke to them: "Good morning."

•

The Consul General had decided not to trust the telephone. There hadn't been time to set up a "secure" line to the facility in Orange County. He had ordered his secretary to type Buchanon's message onto plain white bond. Then the original had been shredded, and the typewriter element and ribbon had been destroyed. Roberto Foppa, a consulate clerk who had exhibited prudently limited curiosity in past undertakings, was given the copy sealed in an unaddressed generic envelope and told to deliver it to a location in Buena Park.

Foppa had done his best to fight through the late rush-hour traffic on the Artesia Freeway. He sensed that he was engaged in some critical affair of state and that his expeditious performance would affect his future in the diplomatic branch. As he approached his turnoff, he nervously considered the consequences of screwing up. He was comfortable in his job. He enjoyed living in L.A.: the exciting nightlife, hanging out in the joints along Sunset, passing himself off as a coffee baron to the eager, and wonderfully easy, American girls. He dreaded being reassigned to Guatemala City—or even worse, being posted to the Mideast. He was preoccupied with dismal thoughts of untouchable, veiled Arab women as he approached the on-ramp to the Santa Ana Freeway. Disneyland was just up the road. Orange County was not an area he was comfortably familiar with, but he remembered that Beach Boulevard, his turnoff, was also the turnoff for the Magic Kingdom.

He realized his mistake too late. Harbor Boulevard, not Beach, was the turnoff for Disneyland. Beach Boulevard, which he had overshot by at least five miles, was the way to another theme park, Knott's Berry Farm. He cursed his ignorance as he made his way back onto the Santa Ana and headed north toward the Artesia. Just past the interchange and less than a mile from Beach Boulevard, he found himself at a standstill. He pounded on the horn, drawing a casually flicked middle finger from the truck driver in front of him.

Impervious to his horn, the traffic remained gridlocked. Roberto Foppa groaned and thought of long, lonely, celibate nights in Dubai.

•

Matt and Kelly watched with building apprehension as the two guards set up a small table. They unfolded the legs, causing the pivots to screech like scalded parrots. Three chairs were pushed into place and the top of the table was covered with white linen. Soon china, silverware and crystal were brought in. Three place settings were arranged. A bud vase with one long-stemmed rose graced the center of the table.

At length, after the preparations were complete, Reyes led Matt and Kelly to their places on opposite sides of the table. Just behind them, Soto's dead body still hung from the waterpipe.

Mago entered and took the third chair, sitting between the two of them. He was as fresh as they were worn, as clean as they were filthy. He smiled and draped a napkin across his lap.

"I trust you are rested," he said pleasantly.

Mago nodded and one of the guards poured coffee for them. The other one used tongs to place a croissant and a pat of butter on each of their side plates. The first guard returned with a pitcher of juice. He filled their glasses.

"It is a new day." Mago sipped his coffee. "We will try a new approach."

Matt picked at the croissant. He was famished, but he was also distrustful of Mago's sudden largess.

"Mr. Teller finds our poor Mayor Vega in the middle of the desert and winds up here. What a bad piece of luck."

Mago tore his croissant in half, buttered it and wolfed it down. He motioned to the guards and they brought fresh fruit, which they spooned out of a large bowl.

"Miss Wode shows up at Mr. Teller's apartment while we are waiting for him and now she is here as well. Another bad piece of luck. And what a wealth of information you both brought with you, tapes and notes and pictures. We had no idea you were so interested in Hernando Cuellar's murder, Miss Wode."

"You killed him," said Kelly, her voice soft and emotionless.

"It is better that Mr. Cuellar has gone to his peace. I'm afraid he was a complication for all of us." Mago removed his glasses, for a brief moment chewing contemplatively on one of the templates. "I suppose there's no harm in telling you." He slipped the glasses back on. "When Cuellar saw the picture of his dear friend Vega on the front page of Mr. Teller's paper, he swore vengeance. He was familiar with Vega's assignment and, quite without any authority from us, he took matters into his own hands. So like Cuellar, so headstrong. The destruction of the church in Cob City was a stupid act. What could it hope to accomplish besides drawing attention? Especially the use of military explosives. Incredibly stupid." Mago paused to eat a strawberry. "I wish I could trade Cuellar for Vail or Townes," he added wistfully. "They would have led us easily enough to Pablo Méndez."

"Vega wasn't after Pablo," Matt remarked. He speared a strawberry with his fork. He took a small nibble. It was tasteless.

"I sent Vega. His mission was to infiltrate Townes's sanctuary network and eliminate the Akabal twin. It was a mistake. I misunderstood the prophecy. I thought the twins were the key. I didn't know about this Pablo Méndez yet. I would not know even now if the insurgents themselves hadn't told me. They made a petty little raid on one of our border garrisons. They actually painted this title, this 'Walks in Old Words,' on the walls. It was fairly easy after that to find out just who this person was. And now I must kill him."

"Why?" Matt asked.

"Because, Mr. Teller, half of the eight million people of my country are Indians."

"And if they had even one shred of hope," Matt replied, "they just might kick your sorry ass."

"What a tragedy that would be. We fall, then Mexico, then Texas."

"The domino theory is out of vogue," Kelly remarked.

"There are no dominoes, Miss Wode. We are an extension of you. We are the fence, the buffer. We are the part that stays awake while you sleep. We are the part that does the dirty work in the night. We branch from the same stem."

"I'm not going to tell you where Pablo is," Matt said resolutely. "He's going to go back there. Before the New Year. And four million pissed-off Maya are gonna take their country back."

"It's a shame we weren't as efficient at genocide as your forefathers were. Then *we* would have the luxury of such righteousness."

"People will come after us," Kelly warned.

"Oh yes. We are going to help them. Within the hour, the police will get a call. A neighbor will complain anonymously that there are suspicious noises coming from Mr. Teller's apartment. The police will search. They will find evidence of a struggle— pieces of your clothing, Miss Wode. They will find this interesting video program playing. They will find traces of your blood on the bed and indications of restraint, abuse, depravity. They will even find a dismembered hand in Mr. Teller's refrigerator, strangely enough, and some tapes on which Mr. Teller recorded interesting observations about a book that you wrote. All in all, I'm afraid it looks quite incriminating. They will conclude, of course, that Mr. Teller has abducted you. They will search for the two of you. Eventually they will determine that you are dead, the victim of foul play, and that Mr. Teller has made good his escape."

"But you still don't know where Pablo is," Matt said triumphantly.

"True. You have resisted admirably. But, you see, I did not know what your relationship was. I was counting on you being the weak one, Mr. Teller. I was going to probe, see how Miss Wode reacted to your pain, you to hers. But then the unexpected happened yesterday. Miss Wode said something and suddenly the weakling became strong. That is odd. I haven't seen that before. I was confused. I didn't know how to proceed. I turned you over to Reyes. I knew he wouldn't be successful, but it was necessary that you understand certain things. While you were engaged with the good *capitán*, I slept. One should never rush a critical decision. When I awoke I knew the answer. You are competing with each other. You are trying to see who is the best. If you do indeed have a relationship, that is it. It is a rivalry, a race. That is what this stubbornness is all about, this pain you are causing one another. But the solution is simple. . . ."

Mago paused. He motioned toward the untouched bowls of fruit in front of them. "Aren't you hungry?" he asked.

Neither of them answered.

"The strawberries are especially good," he said.

Matt pushed his bowl away. The vase tipped over and water spilled out on the tablecloth. Mago picked up the rose and handed it to Kelly. Reluctantly, she took it. She held it under her nose, but she could not smell the fragrance.

"The two of you are having a contest," Mago continued. "This is interesting, but I'm afraid I must put this contest to an end. Since there is no winner, I have chosen a loser."

Matt and Kelly looked down at the fruit, staring blankly into its colorful, mocking ripeness and waiting for Mago to pronounce sentence.

•

After exiting the freeway, Roberto Foppa ran two red lights and made an illegal left turn in his frenzy to deliver the envelope. He shot into the industrial park which contained the building he was looking for and sped to the end of the road where the last complex was situated. He scanned the row of doors for the right number and screeched into the closest parking space. He ran from the car and knocked frantically on the front door, but nobody came. He thought to inquire of one of the adjacent tenants, but decided it was not wise to draw any undue attention.

Frustrated, he looked around. There was a sign at the mouth of the parking lot: PICK-UPS & DELIVERIES IN REAR. He raced head-long toward the back of the building.

•

Mago leaned back in his chair, content to let the painful moment linger. Reyes tended to the wiring, grounding the cot to an exposed water pipe and stripping twelve inches of insulation from the wires that dangled from the control box. The two guards took up positions behind Matt and Kelly. Vinicio sidled up beside Reyes and lit a cigarette.

"You see, I really have no choice," Mago said, his voice hissing over the table. "It's a question of who is more valuable."

Matt glanced up. He wanted to see Kelly for one last time. If it was a question of value, the choice was clear. Kelly had always been better. At everything. In every way. He had let it doom their relationship. Now it had doomed him.

"Goodbye, Miss Wode," Mago said.

"No!" Matt shouted. He lurched from his chair, but the guard pinned him down.

The other guard yanked Kelly from her seat. He dragged her over to Reyes, who wrapped the exposed copper wire around each wrist. Vinicio doused her with a bucket of water.

"Don't do it!" Matt screamed, straining to free himself. Matt pushed off with his feet, propelling himself backward. Suddenly faced with no counterforce to his grip, the guard found himself off balance as Matt toppled backward. The chair tipped over. Matt's feet kicked out, upending the table. Everything spilled onto Mago.

Enraged, the colonel leapt to his feet and screamed, "Kill her!"

Matt twisted free. He gained his feet but was quickly tackled by the guard. No match for the trained *Kaibil,* he was easily restrained.

The other guard lifted Kelly over his head. "Be strong!" she cried.

At a nod from his *capitán,* the guard threw her onto the cot. While she was still in the air, Reyes twisted the rheostat. A loud hum instantly filled the room.

"Kelly!" Matt screamed.

Kelly fell onto the metal frame. Her hands closed involuntarily on the wire trusses. Her body popped off the cot in a shower of sparks and smoke, but her hands could not let go. The deadly, gripping reaction to AC current forced her fingers to clench the wire. Again and again, she arced up, shook and convulsed. The hum became a loud buzz. The lights dimmed and flickered.

Suddenly, a bell began to ring in loud, insistent blasts of

random lengths. Reyes and Vinicio turned quickly toward Mago, looks of deep concern on their faces. Mago waved and Reyes dialed the rheostat down, cutting the current. Kelly's body continued to quiver for a few seconds before finally coming to rest. Mago barked an order in Spanish, dispatching Vinicio and Reyes to see who was ringing the shipping dock doorbell. In moments they returned, presenting the plain white envelope to Mago. He ripped it open and read the message hurriedly. Then he whispered something to Reyes and Vinicio which caused them to run over to the cot, disconnect the wires and lift Kelly off the frame. They laid her on the floor. Vinicio felt for a pulse, first at the wrist and then at the neck. He put his ear to her mouth and listened. After a few moments, he shook his head.

"She can't be gone!" Matt cried. He struggled, but he was helplessly in the grasp of the guard.

At a prompt from Mago, Reyes began administering CPR.

"Not him!" Matt protested. It was inconceivable that the skull-faced bastard could possibly breathe life back into Kelly. "Let me do it!" Matt screamed. Even though he didn't know the rudiments of CPR, he felt he would do better than Reyes.

"Capitán Reyes is well versed in this technique, Mr. Teller. It is often necessary for us to reclaim, however indefinitely, that which death has prematurely taken," Mago explained in his usual imperturbable manner. He walked over to Kelly and looked down on Reyes's efforts. "But this time I believe the good *capitán* will fail. What a shame." Mago gestured with the message. "But for another minute . . ."

●

Buchanon drove slowly up the rocky twin ribbons toward the shadowy cliffs. The three pumas ran alongside the car, snarling and pawing at the tires. When he'd gone as far as he could, he beeped the horn until Edgar Short showed himself. The old man recognized the Mazda and walked down to the car. Predictably, the Winchester was cradled in his arms; the .45 was strapped to his leg.

"That Mayz-da ain't made for off the highway," he said gruffly.

"I've got some trouble," said Buchanon. "I need to borrow the forty-four-forty and the Colt."

The old man bent down and squinted into the car. "Where's your friend?" he asked.

"We don't know, Edgar. But we sure as hell are gonna find out."

"Who're they?" Edgar inquired suspiciously, nodding toward Rebecca and Pablo.

"Friends. They're gonna help."

"They don't look up to it," the old man observed caustically.

"They will be—once we teach them how to shoot."

"Hell, *I'll* help ya," offered the old man. "*I* already know how to shoot."

"No, Edgar. You stay here. You got to look after the girls."

Carlotta put her paws up on the door and poked her head in the window. Rebecca and Pablo nervously slid over in their seats. Edgar took one more dubious look into the car, shook his head in disgust and said, "C'mon."

They made their way along the trail, through the cluster of outbuildings and onto the terraced plateau beneath the cliff. Rebecca and Pablo maintained a cautious distance from the cats and were relieved when they loped off to their resting place beneath the big live oak. Edgar went up to the house, returning after a few minutes with two large boxes of cartridges. At Buchanon's direction, Edgar handed Pablo the Colt.

"Have you ever fired a handgun?" asked the scout.

"Never," Pablo answered.

"Just wonderful." Buchanon expelled a generous stream of Red Man "tea."

"I'll learn," Pablo promised. "I'll do what I have to."

"Edgar, can you show him?" Buchanon asked. "He's gonna have to be accurate at about forty feet."

"Showin' is easy," Edgar groused. "Doin' be the hard part."

He tossed Buchanon the Winchester and led Pablo up toward the high plateau. Buchanon loaded the rifle and presented it to Rebecca. She refused to take it.

"I can't shoot a man," she announced resolutely.

"You've got to," Buchanon retorted.

"I won't," she persisted. "I had no idea this is what you had in mind."

"You're not going to be shooting a man. You're going to be shooting a monster, an animal."

"That's not my judgment to make."

"What's wrong with you?" Buchanon barked. "Don't you want to get them back? You know what he's going to do to them."

Rebecca wavered. "Yes," she answered tentatively.

"Then you've got to kill the son-of-a-bitch. It's that simple."

"I've made enough mistakes lately," she confessed. "I'm not going to add murder to the list."

"Jesus Christ! It ain't murder when you shoot a mad dog. It ain't murder when you kill a snake in the grass. This bastard might have your husband for all we know. I'll lay odds he's got your lover."

Rebecca turned away, crossing her arms and biting her lip.

"I'm sorry," Buchanon apologized. "But there's no other way."

"You do it then."

"I'd love to, but I can't. I won't have the chance. It's got to be you."

"I won't kill another human being. If I do, I'm worse than him. I know better."

"Shit!" Buchanon cocked the rifle and fired into a post on the far side of the plateau. The single, echoing boom of the Winchester was answered by six sharp reports from the Colt up on the higher level. A wispy curl of bluish smoke trailed out of the octagonal barrel.

"Do you think you could just shoot at the ground?" he asked in total exasperation. "If I taught you, could you just pepper the ground in front of the bastard?"

Rebecca considered the proposal. She felt she had to do something. She'd always been the advocate of action, oftentimes quarreling with Nathan over his sedentary reliance on prayer. "If I was sure I wouldn't hit him," she answered.

"Then you've got to learn quick. Right now. You've got to listen to everything I'm going to tell you, and you've got to believe you can do it."

"I can do it," she said decisively.

Buchanon handed her the Winchester. At first she handled it clumsily, as if it were something alive and treacherous. But after Buchanon explained the basics, showed her the safety, how to load, cock, aim through the scope and fire, she began to relax. Her first twenty rounds didn't hit anything. Then, a splinter chipped off the side of the target post.

"Good," Buchanon said. "You've got to be able to do that every time."

It wasn't until about an hour later that she began to have any consistency. After nine hits in a row, Buchanon let her rest. He took the rifle and inserted a full load of thirteen cartridges into the magazine.

"Okay. The post is Mago. You won't shoot him, so I want

you to aim at the ground, right in front of the post. About twenty feet. Can you do that?"

Rebecca took the Winchester, sighted the cross hairs well off the post and fired. A divot plowed up thirty feet short and far to the right.

"No," Buchanon snapped. "In front of it. Right in front of it."

"I don't see any reason why it has to be directly in front," Rebecca argued.

"The reason is he's going to be holding a gun on me. The ground has got to kick up right in front of him if I'm going to have half a chance. Off to the side and he's not going to rattle. If you don't put the shot right on the dime, I'm a dead man."

Rebecca sighed. She lifted the rifle to her shoulder and fired. A cloud of sand kicked up about fifteen feet in front of the target.

"Beautiful!"

She emptied the magazine. All the shots hit in a tight ring in front of the post.

"Is that good enough?" she asked.

Buchanon smiled. "You're a natural."

Edgar approached with Pablo. "He ain't no Wild Bill, but at forty feet I'll bet he'll hit anything bigger than a dog and slower than frozen snot."

"Good enough."

"I doubt it."

"You two go back to the car," Buchanon commanded.

Rebecca and Pablo did as they were told. Once they were out of sight, Buchanon fiddled with the elevation adjustment on the scope, turning it through a number of half-minute clicks. He aimed and fired. The bullet sailed high, pinging off the rock wall of the far cliff. He made another adjustment and tried again. Splinters kicked up at the base of the post.

"What the hell are you doin'?" Edgar asked.

Buchanon gave the knob one last turn. He fired and hit the post dead-center. He handed the rifle to Edgar. "Aim twenty feet in front of the post," he told him.

The old desert rat shouldered the gun and fired. The bullet struck about three feet up on the post.

"How come?" Edgar asked, staring inquisitively at the scout, one eye still shut from aiming the gun.

"She's got scruples."

"Shit!"

Buchanon shrugged. "It don't matter. We're probably all gonna get killed anyway."

•

Matt was handcuffed to a pipe and left to watch as Reyes, Vinicio and the two guards eliminated all evidence of what had transpired. The electrical apparatus was packed away. The cot was dismantled. The table and chairs were removed. Cleaning solution was poured liberally on the floor and then hosed off into a drain. Finally, the two corpses were loaded into oil drums and wheeled off on a pallet jack by the guards.

Matt watched in silence. He was beyond grief. Mago had robbed him of that, too. Something fundamentally human had been ripped away, the wound cauterized by millions of searing electrons. He could only feel anger, an animal rage no less relentless than the current which had torn through his body.

Mago approached carrying Matt's bag. He set it at the reporter's feet. "You'll find your camera and recorder intact."

"Well that puts everything right with the world," Matt shot back, glaring at the colonel and pulling with all his strength against the manacle.

Mago stared at Matt and marveled at the remarkable transformation. "We've made something of you, haven't we?"

"Nothing you want to bump into in a dark alley."

"You'll get over it, Mr. Teller. The human being has infinite capacity to accept loss."

"Human beings do."

"I see."

Mago sighed and looked at Buchanon's message, which was still in his hand:

Get them all to Edgar Tall.
Be there at exactly hidden Coors P.M.

He deliberated the many problems posed by Buchanon's offer:

Only Teller could lead him to this "Edgar Tall" where the trade was to occur; only he would know how to decipher the appointed time. But Matt Teller would never allow himself to be exchanged for Pablo Méndez. After all he had gone through to protect the student, there was no reason for him to suddenly cooperate. Not now. Not after the death of the woman. Mago knew from experience that a man is most intractable when he has weathered a loved one's death and has accepted the inevitability of his own.

And even if he could trick the reporter into divulging the whereabouts of "Edgar Tall," he did not have the full ransom which Buchanon had demanded—a less significant dilemma since he did not for one instant consider actually making the trade. Once at the site, once Pablo Méndez was in view, he planned on killing them all anyway—Méndez, the reporter, Buchanon and anyone else foolish enough to be involved.

"Your luck has turned," Mago began. "Mr. Buchanon, whom I had the pleasure of meeting not long ago, is evidently a friend of yours. He has kidnaped our Consul General and is offering to trade him for you. I've appealed to my superiors and strongly suggested that the loss of one petty bureaucrat is of no concern, but alas I am overruled. First and foremost I am a soldier, and a soldier must follow orders. It appears as if you and the archaeology student will live to see another day."

"Go to hell!"

"It's the truth. Your Mr. Buchanon has turned the tables."

Matt was suspicious. "You're lying. I know too much. You can't let me go."

"I agree, Mr. Teller. But Guatemala City does not. They feel your journalistic reputation will effectively cast into doubt any outrageous allegations you might make."

"The boy who cried wolf," said Matt, his voice weary with the irony.

"Yes. And then there is this business with the police which we have engineered. That too will tend to undermine your credibility."

"I'll get the story out." Matt threatened. "No matter what, I'll get it out."

Mago was unruffled. "As I said, it is not my decision. I would much prefer to continue our interrogation until its inevitable outcome."

"No doubt."

"There is always tomorrow." Mago gave him the smile, the one that had reminded Buchanon of the python at the Bronx Zoo. "We may meet again."

"There's no tomorrow for you. Maybe there's no tomorrow for me. Tomorrow is for Pablo Méndez."

"Perhaps, but now we must be concerned with getting to Edgar Tall."

"What?"

"Yes. This baseball player is more clever than I would have

imagined. He has given the location and the time only by references you know—no doubt to negate any countermeasures we might plan. We are to be at this 'Edgar Tall' by 'hidden Coors P.M.' That could be anytime between noon and midnight. It's almost noon now. Do we have time to get there?"

"Maybe."

"I think we have plenty of time. If I was Buchanon I would set the rendezvous for after sunset. That is the smart thing to do."

"Who said he's smart?"

"You fear we might have time for another party with Capitán Reyes."

The two men glared at each other. Matt shuddered as he felt the electricity awakening deep in his bones. He gritted his teeth and steadied himself.

"No, I can't risk that," Mago continued. "There's always the chance of heart failure, brain hemorrhage, a fatal seizure. You must be our guide. There's no other way. We're done here. I'll leave you my watch. When it's time to go, you'll tell us."

Mago slipped the Rolex onto Matt's free wrist. The colonel patted the back of Matt's hand and smiled. Matt clamped onto his forearm. Reyes and Vinicio started over, but Mago waved them off. He pulled back on Matt's thumb, easily breaking the grip. The colonel shook his head as if disappointed over the behavior of a belligerent child. Then he glanced down at the message. "Buchanon is also demanding Miss Wode, Nathan Miles and the rest of that rabble they were hiding. Once we are there you must convince him that we do not have these others."

"You *had* Kelly," Matt hissed, his eyes flashing hatred.

"Most unfortunate as it turns out. Think of it as bad timing, Mr. Teller."

"I'll think of it all right," Matt promised. "I'll never forget."

Mago folded the note and slipped it into his pocket. "So. Can you determine the time and place?"

"Yeah," Matt answered.

"And you will show us the way?"

Matt did his best to imitate Mago's smile. "Straight to hell."

Mago left the room and made final arrangements for their departure. He felt very confidant that even without foreknowledge of the location, he would be able to kill all of them. He Who Walks in Old Words would soon walk with the dead.

Still, he wanted an edge. Something unexpected that would rattle the already unstable baseball scout. As luck would have it, he had just the thing.

●

The Daykeeper looked out over the arid plains of his Mexican exile and saw nothing that gave him hope. The tent rows of La Salvación stretched out far beyond where the fences had once stood. The camp had grown past all expectations. But then again, the violence on the other side of the border had grown beyond expectations, too. It now seemed to be feeding on itself, whatever purpose it originally possessed lost to the blood and flames. With all his wisdom, the Daykeeper could not fathom it.

He knew what a rebel was. He knew the rebels had promised them land, the land stolen five hundred years ago by the Spanish. He knew that at times his people had given the starving bands of ragtag young men some food, what little they could spare, being hungry themselves. But he did not know what a Communist was, or why the pintos had such fear of them. He could not imagine that the Communists—however terrible they must be—could be worse than the raids in the middle of the night, the mutilated bodies found in shadowy ravines, the firebombs thrown into the houses of women and children. Whatever these Communists were, they seemed to possess a powerful magic: Fear of them, alone, had destroyed his country.

What did it matter? It was the first day of Uayeb. All the portents were dark. The New Year was but five days away. He Who Walks in Old Words now had to overcome the most ill-omened days of the calendar. It was too much to expect.

There was a disturbance at the main gate. A long caravan of heavy trucks was arriving. A brown cloud of dust trailed behind them. They were the trucks that would take them even farther away from their homes. Within a week they would be leaving for the Yucatán.

Uayeb had come.

The trucks had come.

He Who Walks in Old Words had not.

•

Matt recalled Buchanon fumbling through his apartment to get at the nine hidden cans of Coors. He was seated between Mago and Reyes on the engine housing of a nondescript Dodge van. A solid partition behind the driver's compartment separated them from the rest of the vehicle. At precisely 9 P.M., after hours of directing them back and forth over the western half of Riverside County, he instructed Capitán Reyes to turn off Indian Avenue into the San Gorgonio windpark.

Matt pointed the way, guiding them along the bumpy service roads that cut between the rows of lesser windmills and toward the big Howden he and Buchanon had christened "Edgar Tall." Just as on the night they'd first seen it, the mammoth stood immobile, its three rotor arms stationary, etched white slashes against the indigo sky, resisting the steady winds which easily drove the other machines. They turned down a narrow lane which rose at a mild incline toward the Howden. It was bordered on either side by smaller, lattice-towered mills. Moonlight glinted off the metal framework in angled silver strands, pointing the way to their summits, to the nacelles which housed the transmissions and generators that converted the rotary motion of the hubs into electric power. At intervals of every twelve turbines, small, flat-roofed blockhouses stood atop elevated platforms about ten feet above ground level. The blockhouses served as control stations to regulate the operation of the bank of turbines to which it was connected. A large, drum-shaped transformer was attached to an exterior wall of each of the structures. Beyond the towers and running parallel to them were steep embankments leading down to dry, rock-bedded dikes which had been excavated to help replenish the area's aquifer.

As they approached Edgar Tall, Buchanon stepped out from behind the far blockhouse. He stood at the crest of the lane. Moonlight rode easily on his shoulders. He looked bigger than ever. Waving a baseball bat, he motioned them to stop.

Mago climbed down from the van. "So good to see you again, Mr. Buchanon!" he called out over the hiss of the wind and the Om-like drone of the turbines.

"Cut the headlights," Buchanon ordered.

"How will we see?" Mago asked.

"By the moon."

"My eyes are not that good," the colonel protested.

"Mine are," Buchanon snapped. "Cut the fucking lights."

Mago gestured to Reyes and the headlights went out. "What do we do now?" he asked.

"We just stand here a while." Buchanon peered out through the forest of steel towers toward Indian Avenue. "We make sure you weren't followed."

"I assure you, Mr. Buchanon, we were not."

Buchanon waited until he was certain. "Did you bring what I asked for?"

"I brought what I had. You'll have to trust me."

"Let me see."

Reyes dragged Matt out the driver's door. He held a nine-millimeter Uzi machine-pistol to his cheek.

"This is all I can offer!" shouted Mago.

"Where's the rest of them?" the scout demanded.

Matt answered: "Kelly's dead. So is Soto. The rest of them got away."

Buchanon hesitated. "How do I know?" he asked.

"It's the truth," Matt called hoarsely. "It's up to you. A few hours ago I was dead anyway."

Buchanon believed him. Never before had he heard the reporter sound so forthright, so honest. He wondered what they had done to him.

Mago took a few steps toward Buchanon. "It's my turn to ask, Mr. Buchanon. Where is your part of the bargain?"

The scout waved him back with the bat. "Hold on!" he shouted. Momentarily he disappeared behind the blockhouse. Then he dragged Pablo into view. The young man appeared to be bound at the wrists. He collapsed at Buchanon's feet.

"No!" Matt screamed. He struggled to break free from Reyes. "Kelly died for him! I died for him!"

Reyes struck Matt with the Uzi. The reporter dropped to his knees, stunned and groggy.

Pablo lurched away from Buchanon. The big man caught him and threw him back to the ground. The student crawled toward the blockhouse. Buchanon went after him with the bat.

Mago watched in bemusement as the scout pummeled away in the shadows. Again and again the bat came crashing down until there was no resistance and Buchanon was able to drag the limp body out onto the road. The scout raised his Louisville Slugger for a final swing.

"Save your strength!" Mago shouted. His eyes twinkled. He smiled broadly, looking as if he was trying not to laugh at some hilarious inside joke.

"I thought you liked this kind of thing," Buchanon replied sarcastically.

"I did enjoy it, but I am afraid it is wasted effort. You are all going to die anyway."

Vinicio advanced from the back of the van carrying an M79 grenade-launcher. He slipped a high-explosive 40-millimeter cartridge into the open breech. Snapping the barrel closed, he took a position behind Mago and pointed the weapon toward Buchanon and Pablo.

"Goodbye, Number 12," Mago called.

Buchanon kicked the prostrate body at his feet. Its head rolled down the road toward Mago. Crumpled pages of *Here and There* and the *Times* burst out of the torso and fluttered away in the wind.

Mago held up his hand, indicating for Vinicio to hold his fire. The casaba melon came to rest at the colonel's feet. A moronic smiling face drawn with a marker grinned up at him. The colonel kicked it toward the embankment.

"Way to go!" Matt yelled. He snickered as he watched the casaba roll over the crest of the embankment and down into the dike.

"Very clever," said Mago, sounding somewhat humbled. "You are full of surprises."

Buchanon opened a fresh tin of Red Man. He popped a generous wad into his mouth. His right cheek bulged. He sneered at the man standing at the other end of the road and spit. "I got more, asshole."

Mago was not unnerved. "So do I."

Reyes marched to the back of the van. Moments later he

reappeared, herding before him two bare-chested men manacled to each other at the wrists. They were positioned one behind the other, and although they were faced the same way, it was difficult for them to coordinate their movement. They stumbled and fell. Reyes prodded them with the Uzi until they regained their footing and staggered out in front of the van.

Buchanon's jaw dropped. His whole body sagged and the moonlight slid off his shoulders.

It was the Akabal twins.

"The arm we gave you in Escuintla was from a worthless campesino," Mago explained. "I had a feeling this one might yet have value. I have learned to trust my instincts."

Buchanon faltered. The head of the Louisville Slugger dropped to the ground. The nub dangled loosely from his fingers.

"I had intended to arrange for these two to be arrested for the murder of Hernando Cuellar," Mago continued smugly. "We were going to let them be found in one of these laughable sanctuaries. The authorities would find the murder weapon and some of the items stolen from Cuellar's house. I really liked this plan, but I have also learned to be flexible."

"*Mago!*" Buchanon screamed.

"I present your future, Mr. Buchanon. *Double!* I suggest you revert to form. Swing from the heels." Mago removed his glasses. His eyes went deadly cold. "Give me this Pablo Méndez piece of shit!"

Buchanon started for Mago. The plan was forgotten, replaced by rage—the old, familiar, insatiable rage, all the more virulent now without the dilution of booze, all the more blinding now that the stakes were so high. He marched down the road with the bat held up menacingly over his shoulder.

Vinicio readied the M79. Mago slipped a short-barreled .38 from a shoulder holster and pointed it at Buchanon.

"Need I remind you, Buchanon? The sacrifice is still the worst play in the book. Words to live by, I'd say. *Your words.*"

Buchanon continued relentlessly down the road. Mago nodded to Reyes. The captain turned the Akabal twins so that their right arms, their throwing arms, were visible to Buchanon. A figure-eight of piano wire was twisted around a small wooden handle at their shoulders. Reyes gave it a turn. The wire bit into their flesh. They grimaced, but they didn't cry out. Blood drained down their arms.

It was supposed to slow Buchanon down, but it didn't. It just made him madder. "You're gonna die!" he screamed.

Rebecca didn't know what to do. This was not in the plan they had discussed. By now Pablo was to have opened fire from the right flank, but from her position on the roof of the blockhouse, she had seen Pablo lose his footing on the steep embankment. He'd slid all the way down to the bottom of the dike and was having trouble climbing back into position. Mago was going to kill Buchanon. She didn't understand how shooting the ground in front of him was going to prevent that from happening.

Buchanon was closing.

Mago cocked his weapon.

"God forgive me," Rebecca whispered. She raised her aim and centered the cross hairs over Mago's heart. She squeezed the trigger.

The .44 slug whistled over Mago's head and struck Vinicio in the throat. Before he fell dead to the ground, the M79 discharged. High above them, an explosion rocked the nacelle of the giant Howden. Bursts of flame and sparks flowered from the hub. A gush of embers showered down. The monstrous rotor broke apart and the three blades rocketed up into the night sky. The first two plummeted down, silent and unseen, one crashing through the roof of the van, the other bouncing high off the rocks and smashing like a battering ram through the door of the blockhouse. The third blade was still ascending. Finally, it reached its zenith, coming to rest for one heavy second before plunging down. Spinning, it showed itself in the flashing light of the disintegrating nacelle. Careening downward it sliced through the night like a reaper's blade, a colossal scythe sweeping round, roaring closer, fast and massive, slashing, unstoppable under the stars, lit by the moon, called to the earth. It struck with a ground-shaking thud at the top of the embankment.

None of it slowed Buchanon. He kept on coming through the rain of flaming debris sprinkling down from the shattered turbine. As everyone else ducked for cover, he continued on down the road. Bits of glowing metal peppered the ground all around him. A persistent ember smoldered on his sleeve. In the flashing light, his glaring eyes shone like ingots, burning through the chaos, locked on Mago and bearing down. His tobacco-laden cheek gave him a deformed, lopsided aspect—like something pulled from taffy or a waxen visage beginning to melt. The Louisville Slugger led the way, now held straight up and in front of him like a standard to be followed by ten thousand maniacal crusaders, by the host of zeros Pablo had told him about, by the avenging angels of all *los desaparecidos.*

Mago steadied his aim. At point-blank range, he fired.

The bullet struck the bat and slammed it into the scout. The impact knocked him flat on his back. He lay there, dazed and barely conscious. Mago walked over so that he could look into the Buster's glazed eyes as he delivered the fatal shot.

Matt scrambled to his feet and charged. From the corner of his eye he saw Reyes cock the Uzi. As he ran toward Mago he wondered which would happen first, the nine-millimeter burst from Reyes into his back or the single blast from Mago into Buchanon's skull.

The Uzi went off first—a long, staccato fusillade. Mago hesitated, turned toward the sound. Matt kept coming; he wasn't hit.

Matt crashed into Mago at full speed, his shoulder low like a middle linebacker's and catching the colonel squarely in the solar plexus. Mago recoiled from the collision and tumbled onto the roadbed. The .38 skittered away along the stones. Mago made a dive for it. Matt got there an instant ahead of him and kicked the revolver over the embankment. Mago looked back for help from Reyes, but the captain had been pinioned between the two manacled forearms of the twins. Their hands were locked and their arms were clamped against Reyes's throat like scissors blades. The chinless, marzipan face had gone blue. The Uzi, which had voided itself harmlessly into the desert sky, dropped from his hand. A spasm rattled his limbs as his lungs were once and for all weaned from oxygen.

Mago ran off toward the blockhouse. Matt chased after him. He was still weak from his ordeal and his last effort had thoroughly exhausted him. Mago quickly outdistanced him.

The colonel scurried up the short ladder to the blockhouse catwalk, arriving just as Rebecca climbed down from the roof. She began to cock the Winchester. He grabbed the forestock with both hands and wrenched it away from her. The open finger-lever struck the side of the blockhouse, crimping the pin which connected to the cartridge carrier. Mago tried to force the lever closed, but the breech mechanism was hopelessly jammed. He threw the useless rifle over the side of the catwalk and seized Rebecca. He dragged her into the blockhouse, pulling her over the rotor blade that had wedged in the doorway.

When Matt stepped through the shattered door he found Mago holding Rebecca by the hair. Her face was just inches from one of three fist-sized terminals. The tip of the rotor blade was jammed into the corner over his head. Mago was standing on a

large metal door which the blade had ripped off the massive control panel and which now lay bent and dented on the floor. A
steady trickle of orange sparks flowed down from a cable where
the blade had cut the insulation. The step-up transformer on the
other side of the wall could be heard buzzing with the aggregate
output of the twelve wind machines to which it was connected.

Mago shook Rebecca's head, forcing it closer to the terminal.
"Shall we see what happens if we touch her nose to this?"

Matt threw up his hands, signaling surrender. "Leave her
alone," he said.

"And you will leave me alone," Mago replied. "You will walk
out that door and back to your friends. When you are far enough
away, I will release her."

Buchanon staggered through the doorway, climbing over the
blade. "He's not going to get away," he threatened.

"No!" Matt cried in alarm, grabbing the big man. "You
don't understand."

"I understand just fine," the scout replied. "Listen."

The wind had died down, dropping below the cut-in speed.
One by one, the turbines were shutting down. Before Mago realized what was happening, the trigger board in the control panel
opened the contacters along the thyristor bank, disconnecting the
load side of the panel from the circuit.

Mago pushed Rebecca into the contacter, releasing her as he
did so. The side of her head bumped against one of the terminals.
Her hand came to rest on another. But there was no surge, no
shock. There was no power coming from the turbines to cause her
any harm.

Buchanon brought the Louisville Slugger to his shoulder.
"Time to die, asshole."

"Time to pay for Kelly," Matt added.

Rebecca stumbled away from the panel, rubbing the side of her head. "You see! I have not harmed her!" Mago gushed.

Rebecca joined Matt and Buchanon at the door. "Make your peace, Colonel Alvarado," she said quietly. "Hell is forever."

The fine mustache glistened with sweat. The dark eyes, normally so steady and focused, twitched and darted, searching desperately for a way out. "I can make you all very rich," Mago pleaded. "I can give you whatever you want."

"Give me Kelly," Matt hissed.

"I can give you women. All the women you could ever—"

"Give me Kelly," Matt repeated.

"Anything . . . anything at all."

Matt and Buchanon stepped toward him. Buchanon slapped the bullet-pocked bat against his open palm. Trembling, Mago backed away, brushing up against the rotor blade. It slid down from the corner, pushing against the colonel and forcing him against the panel.

The gust of wind came from the south, a hot blast which raked over the top of San Jacinto and into the pass. The vanes on the turbines noted the change of direction. Relays tripped, activating the active yaw mechanisms. The nacelles slowly rotated toward the wind flow. Machine number 12 was the first to reach the cut-in speed.

"Please," Mago begged.

In quick succession, the dozen turbines in the bank reached cut-in, took the energy from the hot south wind and sent it to the blockhouse.

The trigger board sent an impulse which caused the contacters to close. They activated with twelve loud metallic cracks, like so many gunshots fired in the room. Three live terminals locked into Mago's back like the talons of a monstrous bird of prey. His eyes bulged with horror. Outside, the transformer buzzed louder, making a crackling, angry sound as it pulled the current through the added resistance of Mago's body.

He began to shake, to vibrate so fast and so violently it was as if his spinal column no longer existed, as if there was nothing at all rigid left in him, nothing that could resist the current. Blood ran from his ears and his nostrils. His clothes began to smolder.

Mago was still alive when his left eye exploded. He was still alive when he bit off his own tongue and when the uncontrollable spasms of his right arm against the sharp metal edge of the control panel shredded the flesh from his hand. He was still alive when his hair exploded into flames. And he was still alive when Matt, Buchanon and Rebecca turned their backs on him and walked out.

The wind from the south blew stronger. The blades caught it all. Whatever force it had, the rotors gathered and sent on into the blockhouse, into Mago.

The twins were at the top of the embankment, staring down at the third rotor arm of the Howden. It protruded from the rocky slope like a giant sword. Buchanon loosened the wire around their shoulders, while Rebecca unlocked the manacles with a key she'd rummaged from Reyes's pocket. Matt retrieved his bag from the van.

It was only after Rebecca and Buchanon had finished extricating the twins from their restraints that they realized what was wrong. It was only then that they looked down toward the colossal blade and saw the decapitated body lying beside it.

"They won." Buchanon's voice was full of bitterness and defeat.

How simply he said it, Rebecca thought. How simply had the whole of the tragedy been summed up—all that had happened, all that was yet to perish, expressed in the blunt logos of the athlete: The other guys had won; the contest was over. But simplicity was not always completeness. There was another side to the equation, the second line to the couplet. "Sanctuary lost," she whispered.

There was a flash of light down in the gully at the bottom of the dike.

"Where's Matt?" Rebecca asked, suddenly concerned.

Two more flashes lit up the embankment.

"I thought he'd changed," Buchanon said softly.

Matt shot again. The flash unit of the Nikon pulsed. Even from up above, Buchanon and Rebecca could now see, in the split-second of its fleeting light, down below in the dike, caught in the tangled branches of a creosote bush, the severed head of Pablo Martín Méndez Córdova, Sky-Sword Bringer, Calabash, True Lord of the Mat, Begetter of the New Age, Preparer in the Last Katun, He Who Walks in Old Words.

12

II LAMAT   I POP

AT THE COMPLETION OF
12 BAKTUNS
18 KATUNS
8 TUNS
15 UINALS
8 KINS

five days later . . .

The gray dawn of the New Year came reluctantly to La Salvación. The blunt light barely penetrated the rippling shroud of diesel fumes layered over the camp. Trucks were loading near the main gate. The low, rumbling growl of engines abraded the morning calm. An announcement in Spanish rasped over a loudspeaker. The Indians didn't understand the words, but instinctively they started for the trucks, silently, slowly, carrying what little they possessed as if it weighed much more than it did, their eyes downcast, their feet barely stirring the hard earth of their Mexican exile.

The Daykeeper allowed himself to be led to one of the waiting flatbed trailers. In his head he was calculating the next occurrence of a Yearbringer named 11 Lamat 1 Pop before a last *katun.* Such a day would not come to pass for twenty generations. It was not so much a date in the future as one fixed by the past, a reflection of an event on the other side of the Day Zero, a symmetry to take form in the shape of history. The anonymous carver of the Stone of Nim Xol had looked back as much as he had looked forward. All that was to be was determined by what already was. But the ancestors could still see. They yet possessed the knowledge which the Daykeeper, for all his lifetime of study and dedication, could only touch, could only blindly feel about a frayed and timeworn edge. From afar he had looked, and he had decided this was the day, *the* Yearbringer, the time of He Who Walks in Old Words.

But he had been wrong.

The destruction of the land and the annihilation of the people would continue.

It was inevitable, unalterable, unavoidable.

•

An hour later, dawn came to Braxton Wells, bringing the first light of Easter Sunday. Rebecca sat in the back of the pickup and watched the gradual brightening of the chaparral. A hawk glided high overhead, soaring and banking effortlessly in the thermal drafts. Nathan finished loading a rented U-Haul parked near the side door of the church. He carried the bassinet out into the parking lot.

"What should I do with this?" he asked.

"Why don't you just leave it in there?" Rebecca suggested. "Maybe whoever buys the building will want it."

He set it down, looking at it as if it were the repository of all his hopes. "Do you mind if I keep it?"

"You think I'll change my mind."

"Everything changes—sooner or later. When I got those people to Canada, when they felt safe, really safe, not just hidden away, they changed. They were alive again. They *were* reborn."

"That must have been truly wonderful to see."

"It was. That's when I decided to take over Father Townes's network. Whatever I can do, I will."

"You'll be good at it, Nathan."

"I'd be better with you at my side."

Rebecca looked away. This was the hard part; if she looked at him, she might falter. "I won't be there," she said firmly. She'd said it before, when they'd first talked after his return, when she'd told him everything, but only now did it seem final.

Nathan walked over to the pickup. "I don't care what you did with that other man."

Rebecca knew he was sincere. It made it all the more painful. "I know."

"It doesn't matter," he said fervently.

"It does," she insisted.

"Do you love him?"

"I've told you I don't."

"But you've stopped loving me."

Rebecca looked into his eyes. She had to. There was no running from the truth—and he deserved the truth. "If I truly loved you, then I could never forgive myself for what I did."

Nathan hesitated. Never before had he been forced to say something so painful, so absolutely true and hurtful. "You must forgive yourself."

"I have," she answered, nodding, knowing the anguish she was causing. "That's the problem."

Nathan took a deep breath. He hurt. Every way possible he ached. "I haven't stopped loving you, Rebecca."

Rebecca came to the back of the pickup and knelt beside the tailgate. "I have to find out what it is that you love," she said, her voice pleading to be understood. She took his hands into her own. "I have to meet that person, Nathan. I have to get to know her."

It took a while, a long time of staring into her eyes, but finally Nathan said, "I understand."

She kissed him, a light peck on his cheek. "Most wouldn't," she said.

Nathan took the bassinet and put it in the U-Haul. He drove away, past the FOR SALE sign at the top of the hill.

Rebecca hopped down from the cargo bed, closed the tailgate and circled around to the cab. She glanced back at the church, which more than ever looked like what it had always been, and climbed in behind the wheel. There was a letter from Matt in her breast pocket. She'd read it a dozen times: He was sorry; he was there if she needed him; he wanted very much to see her again. She took it out, unfolded it and spread it on the dash. It sat there in the glare of sunlight streaming in the windshield, a possibility, one of countless many, and like the bassinet she'd entrusted to Nathan, one that rendered the great, looming mystery of the future a shade more comfortable.

13

7 AKBAL   16 UO

AT THE COMPLETION OF
12 BAKTUNS
18 KATUNS
8 TUNS
17 UINALS
3 KINS

five weeks later . . .

Vancouver, British Columbia

The priest's voice rang out: "The peace of the Lord be with you always."

"And also with you," answered the sparse congregation, not quite in unison, but with a feeling of practiced certainty.

"Let us offer each other the sign of peace," intoned the priest, his voice trumpet-like in the marbled resonance of the large church.

The worshipers extended their hands to each other. The priest came down from the altar and approached the group seated together in the front pew. He took Sergio's hand and said, "Peace be with you." Sergio tentatively answered, "Peace." Similarly, the priest welcomed Yolanda, Abraham and Coh. "Peace," they each answered, the word crossing their lips clumsily, foreign as it was both in language and in substance. The priest lifted Sebastian into his arms and kissed him on the forehead. The baby screamed and wriggled, struggling to be reunited with Yolanda. Smiling, the priest handed him back. Then he addressed Cristina: "May peace be with you." She formed the response, stiffly signing it to him with her hands.

The memorial mass continued. The Eucharist was shared. The blessing was dispensed. When it was over, they filed out of the first pew and lit candles for Kelly Wode and for Soto. They even lit one for Pablo. They had forgiven him. They had forgiven themselves.

Then they left.

Outside, others were waiting for them, others like them, exiles all. They belonged to a community again. They were part of a family. They were safe and they were free.

Coh lingered behind. He was an atheist. He hadn't been in a church since he was a child. He wasn't sure what it meant, but he lit each and every one of the remaining vigil candles.

Still there weren't enough. Not nearly enough.

Nashville, Tennessee

The catcher for the Sounds put down one finger and tapped it against the inside of his left thigh. Santiago Akabal nodded, went into his windup and hurled a ninety-three-mile-per-hour strike over the inside corner of the plate. The batter swung lamely, well after the ball was already in the catcher's mitt.

The crowd cheered wildly and gave their new hero a standing ovation. His teammates on the Double-A team rushed onto the field and congratulated him, shaking his hand and patting his back. The radio announcer launched into a delirium of superlatives.

No one could remember the last time two rookies had pitched back-to-back shutouts in a doubleheader. If it had ever been done before, it certainly hadn't been done by twins.

Nobody doubted it: Santiago and Carlos Akabal were going to be stars.

The Yucatán

Buchanon had all the budget he wanted. He could go wherever he chose. If he requisitioned tickets for Bora Bora, they would be supplied, promptly, happily and without question. He no longer reported to Kandler. He had a direct link to the G.M. Promises had been made about a coaching job for next season.

There'd been no trouble in securing an advance for a foray into the Yucatán. New York hadn't even balked at the extra ticket he'd demanded for a "travel consultant." Anyone who could deliver the two best pitching prospects to come along in twenty years deserved to be indulged.

Matt had accepted Buchanon's sponsorship, and together they'd searched for the Daykeeper, scouring the dismal little resettlement villages scattered throughout the province of Campeche. They were thoroughly discouraged as they drove in a rented jeep down the miserable road between Hecelchakán and Dzitbalché. They'd begun to think they'd never find him or that perhaps he was dead. They hadn't spoken to each other in hours, when suddenly Matt said, "I know what the problem is."

"What's that?" Buchanon asked as he downshifted to navigate a steep hill.

"We've all got two heads and just one soul."

Buchanon was used to these cryptic pronouncements. They'd been coming with increasing frequency over the last week as Matt drifted further and further into long, depressed bouts of introspection. "That's the problem all right," the scout replied tolerantly.

Unexpectedly, they encountered a cluster of tents situated in a hollow off the road. They left the jeep and approached a makeshift canvas pavilion where food was being distributed to a long line of patient, waiting refugees.

"*¿Tienen hambre, caballeros?*" asked a crusty old missionary woman who was presiding over the soup kettle.

"Do you speak English?" Buchanon replied.

"I do," she answered.

"We're looking for a little old man. He's a Quiché daykeeper. They call him coo-ka-ja. . . ."

"Chuchkajawib. 'Mother-Father.' I speak Quiché too."

"Can you help us?" Matt asked.

"Depends," she answered suspiciously.

"I've got something that belongs to him," Buchanon explained. He took the stone glyph from his pocket.

An excited murmur rippled through the soup line. Heads turned, eyes opened wider, necks craned. From far back in line the Daykeeper stepped out and approached. Manuel Xom Calel and Juan Guarcas Tol accompanied him.

"That's him," Buchanon announced.

The scout returned the last piece of the Stone of Nim Xol to the Daykeeper. "I tried," he said. The missionary translated.

The Daykeeper took the carved glyph and dropped it unceremoniously into his *morral*, the small agave bag which hung from his shoulder. He nodded sadly and turned to retake his place in the line.

"Just a minute," Matt called. From his back pocket he pulled out a copy of *Here and There*, the last edition to carry one of his stories before he quit. He opened it up and handed it to the old man.

The Daykeeper saw the picture of Pablo's decapitated body beside the giant rotor blade and another showing his severed head in the creosote bush.

Sky-Sword Bringer! Calabash!

The missionary translated the text. Excitedly, the Daykeeper converted the Gregorian date to his own calendar:

The event had occurred before 11 Lamat, the Yearbringer!

Suddenly everyone was talking, pushing closer, trying to get a glimpse of the four-week-old paper. Matt got other copies from the jeep and passed them out. Little children snatched them out of his hand and ran back with them to their parents. Someone started singing and then others joined in. Four old men began to dance.

"He really does walk in old words," the reporter mused.

Buchanon nodded, watching in wonder as the celebration grew.

Somehow, within an hour, without any abatement in the festivity, the entire camp was packed and ready for travel. Matt and Buchanon were never aware such preparations had been in progress. The dancing and singing had drawn them in, and they just hadn't noticed. But suddenly everyone was on the road, walking south, heading home, leaving the two of them behind and abandoning the stupefied missionary to peer blankly into her cauldron.

Matt watched in awe as they disappeared down the road, looking more like a joyful army than a ragtag group of vagabond refugees. He could envision other camps joining their ranks, swelling their numbers, making them strong.

"We did it!" Buchanon shouted. He picked Matt up off his feet and spun him around.

Once he was returned to solid ground, Matt pushed himself away. "Give me a minute, okay?" he mumbled.

Buchanon understood. He nodded, backed off and slipped a Maconudo Prince Philip from his pocket. He lit it with the last match in the book from the Mexico City Holiday Inn.

Matt got his bag out of the jeep and climbed to the top of a hill overlooking a deep ravine. He took out the Sony and loaded a fresh *GAN* tape. He pressed the RECORD button and then stood there mutely as the tape wound past the recording head. He looked at the Sony as if it was responsible for his sudden loss of words. After a few moments, he ejected the cassette and threw it into the *barranco*. He rummaged through his bag and turned up four more *GAN* tapes. He pitched them all into the gorge. Then he hurled the Sony as far as he could. It struck a boulder and shattered into countless pieces.

Kelly was right. It wasn't about talking to yourself.

The only paper in the bag was a small pocket notebook. He found a blunt, stubby pencil, sat down on a lightning-struck log and began to write:

I'm here about the two-headed shar-pei.

Author's Note

In keeping with generally accepted convention, the Maya day names and "long count periods" at the head of each chapter and elsewhere are expressed in Yucatec. Although it can be reasonably argued that I should have opted for the Quichéan equivalents, I felt it best to utilize the most widely known representations.

The calendar notations were computed based on the algorithm presented in *The Ancient Maya* (4th Revised Edition) by Morley, Brainerd, and Sharer. I used the revised GMT (Goodman-Martínez-Thompson) correlation constant of 584,283 to do the conversions.

References to the Maya New Year are based on the "classic period" concept of that date. By the time of the conquest, the "yearbearers" had shifted forward by one day (according to Morley). The contemporary Quiché observe New Year's on a different day altogether. However, since the relevance of the New Year is tied to the (fictitious) prophecy of the Stone of Nim Xol, and since the carver of the stone would have observed classic-period dating techniques, I believe my New Year's day of 11 Lamat 1 Pop to be the best choice out of the available alternatives.

For those interested, the date indicated at the beginning of the first chapter equates to March 21, 1982.